ON A CLEAR DAY

ON A CLEAR DAY

Anne Doughty

This first world edition published in Great Britain 2001 by
SEVERN HOUSE PUBLISHERS LTD of
9–15 High Street, Sutton, Surrey SM1 1DF.
This first world edition published in the USA 2001 by
SEVERN HOUSE PUBLISHERS INC of
595 Madison Avenue, New York, N.Y. 10022.

British Library Cataloguing in Publication Data

Doughty, Anne, 1939–
    On a clear day
    1. Orphans - Ireland - Fiction
    2. Grandparent and child - Ireland - Fiction
    I.   Title
    823.9'14 [F]

    ISBN 0-7278-5750-9

Except where actual historical events and characters are being
described for the storyline of this novel, all situations in this
publication are fictitious and any resemblance to living persons
is purely coincidental.

Typeset by Hewer Text Ltd.,
Edinburgh, Scotland.
Printed and bound in Great Britain by
MPG Books Ltd., Bodmin, Cornwall.

For Margaret, my sister

Acknowledgements

T he Ulster into which Clare Hamilton was born in October 1936 is now as remote as if she had been born in some much earlier century. Clare's story is her own, but I have tried to be accurate about the details of everyday life in that very different world, a world where telephones were rare and the pony and trap was more common than the motor car. I am grateful to all those who gave their time to help me, particularly the staff at Armagh Museum, Armagh Ancestry and the Irish Studies Centre in Armagh, who were all not only helpful but welcoming. I hope they will think their efforts were worthwhile. My greatest debt, however, is to my cousin John Ross, who lent me the newspaper and magazine articles written by my uncle, William John Ross of Salter's Grange. Writing on many topics for Ulster publications he catches the mood and the preoccupations of the time, even down to the post war beauty hints which he wrote under the name of Doris Gibb!

Anne Doughty
Belfast, June 2001

Prologue

To the west, Armagh was outlined against the brilliant blue of the sky, the twin spires of the new cathedral so sharp they seemed to have been etched in with the aid of a ruler. On the hill opposite, less dramatic, more earth-bound, the square tower of the old cathedral rose out of its enfolding trees, its heavy stonework dark with age. Around both great buildings, like currents of water eddying where they will, the small stone houses and later brick terraces curved and wove as they followed the contours and the slopes of the hills on which they stood . . .

She wished she could climb higher, for somewhere over there, below Cannon Hill, lay the farm at Liskeyborough, only a mile or two away for the jackdaws who played around the church tower. Her grandmother would be feeding the hens or the new calves, or peering at the old wooden barrel in which she'd planted daffodils to have them near her front door.

If she could have seen Liskeyborough, the whole of her world would have been spread out before her, from her own front door to the furthest points of her travels. And on a clear day, too. A day for making up your mind, Granny Hamilton would say.

1

June 1946

Beyond the tall, dusty windows of the schoolroom the
afternoon sun beat down with unaccustomed fierceness.
Dark shadows lay in pools beneath the spread of the full-leafed
chestnuts that bordered the playground. From its worn tarmac
surface, polished smooth by the daily abrasion of running feet,
the light dazzled and reflected, picking out the architectural
details of the sharp-edged brick building that in 1931 had won
the admiration of all. The Lord Lieutenant with his sword and
plumes, the local dignitaries in their Sunday best, the men in flat
caps and the women in cloche hats, platform party, teachers
and maintenance staff had all without exception said the same
thing. In the single, familiar and often-used Ulster phrase, they
expressed their unanimous approval. 'The new school was "the
last word".'

Though the windows stood open as wide as the unpractised
metal hinges would tolerate, the classroom where Clare
Hamilton sat was thick with heat and heavy with the mixed
odours of chalk and dusty floorboards and perspiring bodies.
From greasy, screwed-up paper bags piled in the large waste-
paper basket, placed precisely below the wall-mounted pencil
sharpener, came the lingering remembrances of lunch, an event
now receding as the oppressive afternoon moved on towards
that longed for moment when the hands of the clock would
stand at half past three.

Attracted by the faint aroma of country butter, home-made
jam or the shop-bought pastes that had provided lunch more

than an hour previously, a large bluebottle fly hovered over the wicker basket. At once, its presence was observed. The teacher spoke. A large, heavy-breasted girl put down her work, received the rolled-up newspaper held out towards her and launched herself at the offending insect. She knocked over the wicker basket and bent the newspaper against the wall while the bluebottle buzzed into the open space between the line of girls waiting by the teacher's desk and the immaculately clean blackboard beyond.

It soared vertically, as high as the Union Jack pinned on the bare wall over the blackboard itself, then, sensing some change in the chalk laden air, it swerved violently to the left, sailed out through the window, rose high into the blue dome of the sky, a tiny, ever-diminishing speck soon lost even to the sharp eyes of the dark-haired, nine-year-old in the front desk who had watched every movement of the unfolding drama without appearing to raise her eyes from the fragment of red-checked gingham on which she was working so meticulously.

In the hubbub that followed the bluebottle's departure, as the teacher retrieved her bent newspaper and the girl her 'garment', Clare looked up at the clock and sighed. It was not even three yet. The bell that would release them into the sunshine still rested on the Principal's desk, the senior boy who would agitate it through all the empty, echoing corridors was still at work in the flowerbeds below the open windows, hoeing the minute weeds in the dry soil between the flourishing annuals. There was still more than half an hour to go.

Usually Clare enjoyed handwork classes on a Wednesday afternoon. Miss Slater, who normally presided, was also her class teacher and one of the younger members of staff. She wore make-up and pretty blouses and when she leaned over to look at your work she smelt of perfume and exactly the same Creme Puff powder that her mother wore if she was going out. She smiled often and always told Clare that her hemming stitches were the smallest she'd ever seen. Besides, Miss Slater read them stories while they worked. Sometimes they were Bible stories

4

with battles and chariots and walls falling down. Often there were descriptions of palaces and gardens with kings coming and going, having banquets and dreaming dreams, calling their servants to do their bidding, or waving their hands in farewell to princesses who were going to the river with their ladies to bathe and find babies hidden in the bulrushes.

She liked the way Miss Slater told stories 'with expression', tossing her coppery curls and raising her finely-pencilled eyebrows and changing her voice to suit the different characters.

Sometimes there were stories about a little coloured boy called Epamanondas who had a knack of getting himself into difficulties in the forest. But what forest it was, Clare had never managed to find out. At the end of every adventure Epamanondas somehow managed to find his way back to his grandfather who lived beside the great, grey, slow-moving river that flowed through the forest.

'Please, miss, what was the name of the river?' she asked one afternoon as Miss Slater closed the book.

Miss Slater seemed surprised.

'Why do you want to know, Clare?' she asked brightly.

She waited with the closed book in her hands while Clare shook her head and said that she'd just wondered.

'In a story it doesn't matter about names and places, Clare, it's just the story that matters,' she explained patiently.

Clare smiled and nodded. She didn't agree at all, but Miss Slater was her very favourite teacher.

But there was no Miss Slater today. The white-haired woman who sat peering at the finer details of the senior garments was Miss McMurray. Miss Slater was away ill and her class, itself reduced by absence had been summoned to the senior corridor. The dozen or so nine-year-olds now sat uneasily in the too-large front desks of her room, overawed by the presence of so many big girls while Miss McMurray pinned and tucked and twitched the knickers and blouses that had to be finished by the end of the month.

In a few weeks' time the girls lined up at Miss McMurray's

5

desk would be leaving school. A few of them would be going to the Technical School up in Marketplace to learn shorthand and typing. Some of the others would look for a place in Armagh and serve their time to a grocer, or a draper, or a dressmaker, but most of them would be going into service in the big houses and large farms that lay along curving avenues or down long lanes, invisible to the passers-by who walked the country roads on Sunday afternoons.

'That's the Richardson's place,' her father would say as they headed out the Loughgall Road on the way to visit her Scott grandparents at Salter's Grange. He would point to an enormous pair of gateposts or a broad five-barred gate, but as often as not Clare could see no dwelling at all. But she tried to memorise the names just the same and loved making Daddy laugh by saying them before he did.

'That's the house where the general lived who helped to win the war,' she announced proudly as they passed one of the few visible residences, a handsome building completely enveloped in Virginia creeper on the much longer walk along the Portadown Road to visit the Hamilton grandparents at Liskeyborough.

How strange it would be to leave school and ride your bicycle to work and not have Miss Slater to look at your writing and help with your sums and read stories while you worked your samples. Clare was very glad she wasn't grown up and leaving like the big girls in front of her for she liked school and all the different things they did there. And she loved Miss Slater.

When she'd told her mother this one Saturday night while she was sitting in the tin bath in front of the kitchen stove, her mother said that she was glad to hear it. School days were the happiest days of your life, she added a bit later, as she put a penny in the window frame to stop the wind from making it rattle and tucked the blankets in all around her. In fact, after that night, her mother had repeated the saying regularly each day until one morning, as she was being washed at the kitchen sink, Clare asked her why she kept on saying it.

6

Her mother laughed and shook her head.

'Ach, childdear, sure mothers are always saying things like that. You'll notice yourself when you're older that people say things out of a kind of habit.'

Clare could see her mother was smiling to herself as she brushed her hair and retied her school shoes more firmly. She was still smiling as she straightened up and leaned back against the sink. 'And maybe sometimes there's a bit of magic too in what you say every day,' she went on, thoughtfully. 'Maybe there's something of a wish, or even of a blessing. If I say that every day maybe it'll come true. Indeed, I hope it will. Now, away on or you'll be keeping Auntie Marjorie waiting. I don't know where you get all the questions from or what puts some of the notions into your head. I do not,' she said, shaking her head again as she kissed her quickly and hung her schoolbag over her shoulder.

Although Miss McMurray was old and known as 'a bit of a tartar' Clare knew that she did permit conversation while you were working, provided it was quiet and sensible and directed only to your immediate neighbour. She looked wistfully at the seat beside her. The seat was empty – her 'immediate neighbour' was far away. Margaret Beggs, her best friend, who lived three doors away in the red-brick terrace overlooking the Shambles was at this moment enjoying the Methodist excursion to Bangor. Her mother, Auntie Marjorie, who walked them both down College Hill each morning before going back up to the sweetie shop in English Street where she worked, had offered to take Clare on the excursion as well. But her mother had said no. Children went free on their own excursion but had to be paid for if they went on someone else's. She was sorry. It was very nice of Auntie Marjorie to offer but seven and sixpence was a lot of money and her own excursion was only a few weeks away. If Daddy could get the day off they could all go together this year, for wee William was that bit bigger and able to walk further.

Clare thought longingly of the train rattling out of Armagh

station and into the countryside. Last year, she had sat by the window with her mother and they'd looked out at all the places they walked past on Sundays. But this year her father would be there too and she was sure they would start to talk about the places they were passing, about parties and picnics and hops they'd been to before they were married.

At the level crossing they would wave to children who had run across the fields to see the train steam past. Beyond that point the countryside was completely new to her, unexplored territory with houses and farms she had never even walked past. But her father and mother knew everybody.

'Do you remember old Danny McMaster, Ellie?'

'Och, will I ever forget him?'

Clare loved the story of Danny McMaster. He was an old farmer with plenty of money and he had a notion of Mummy. He used to come to the forge where Granda Scott worked with some excuse or other or some piece of machinery for him to mend. It was all so he could see Mummy and maybe get talking to her. But Mummy was going out with Daddy and that was that. Granda said he made a fortune out of old McMaster, for the things he brought him to mend were only five minute jobs. Sometimes there was nothing wrong with them at all except the want of a bit of oil.

Whenever her parents talked about the days before they were married Clare would remember the photographs in the album her mother kept in the sitting room cupboard. She knew the pictures by heart and who all the people were though most of them she had never met. There were crowds of men in open-necked shirts, their arms around girls in long skirts with funny-patterned shoes, some of them laughing so much that their bit of the picture was blurred because they had moved. There were tennis parties and boating parties and in one photograph there was a huge bus with all the people they knew lined up in front. There, beside her father, her mother sat holding a tiny white bundle. She had been the only baby in the whole party, her mother said, and she had been as good as gold.

That excursion had been to Bundoran. She didn't know where that was either. When she asked her father he said it was in the South, but her mother said it was on the west coast, on the Atlantic. Wherever it was, there was no doubt everyone was enjoying themselves. It must have been a very good excursion.

By now, Margaret would have eaten the contents of her lunch bag at the church hall. Corned beef sandwiches and baker's buns. Last year they each had a wafer biscuit done up in silver paper which she had unwrapped carefully and smoothed out. There were so many things you could make if you had silver paper but apart from some of the large sweets in the bag her father brought home on Saturday nights there wasn't much to be had. Sometimes if you weren't very careful when you smoothed it out it would tear and that was so disappointing.

Last year's excursion certainly hadn't been disappointing. Mummy had bought her lemonade to drink with her lunch and later when they walked down to the front she'd had a large ice-cream cone. She won a prize when the Sunday School super-visor organised races on the beach and she'd played in the water for ages, watching the tiny wavelets breaking against her ankles while Mummy sat in a deckchair knitting and talking to the other mothers.

Margaret would be down on the front by now, walking round to Pickie Pool for a swim or paddling from the beach. Clare stared at the strong grain lines in the wood of her desk and saw them change into long lines of waves, rippling in, peacefully, one behind the other, cool and fresh, all the way from the far horizon. But as she lifted her eyes to the far horizon the waves disappeared, she found she was staring at the battered, ink-stained ledge with a groove for pencils and a round hole into which the monitor would drop the pale, crazed disc of the inkpot.

She looked up again at the clock. The large black hand appeared not to have moved at all. Miss McMurray caught her eye. She said nothing, but a look was enough. Clare lowered her eyes to her work and wondered how she could tell if the clock had stopped.

Whenever the clock on the mantelpiece at home stopped, Daddy would spread a newspaper on the kitchen table and take it to pieces so that he could clean it. He kept a supply of feathers for the job in a jampot on the kitchen window sill and whenever they went to visit his parents at the farm he would send Clare and her brother down to Granny's hen run to see what they could find.

William never wanted to go down to the hen run. He always said he wanted to stay with Mummy, but Mummy told him he had to go and help Clare. The problem was that William was frightened of the cockerel and he would burst into tears if he crowed at him. Clare did her best to explain that the cockerel was just showing off, that if you shooed him away he'd run flapping to his wives and start crowing at them instead. But William wouldn't chase the rooster for himself. He'd just stand scuffling his shoes in the dust until Clare had sent him squawking and had started to gather up the sorts of feathers she knew her father liked.

Once the clock was in pieces you had to clean all the bits with methylated spirits. It was purple stuff with a funny smell that came in a big bottle with ribs in the clear glass.

'You only need a wee drop,' Daddy explained, as he poured it into an old saucer, 'but you need to get it into all the moving parts,' he went on as he poked the feather into the bits of the workings that he couldn't take apart.

Sometimes Clare wondered how he would ever get all the small pieces together again, especially with his large square fingers, but he always did. He said it was just a matter of taking your time. It was amazing what you could do if you took your time. Just look at the lovely embroidery and crochet work that Mummy did. She'd learnt a bit at school and then she'd taught herself out of a book from the library. And didn't she win a prize last year at the Armagh show.

'That tablecloth, Clare, the one with all those wee flowers took such a long time to do. I'm sure she was at it a year or more. But not as long as the sweater with the cherries on it,' he ended with a twinkle in his eye.

Clare smiled to herself. That was another story she loved and her father loved telling it. When Clare was still quite small Mummy had gone to visit one of her girl friends and left Daddy to look after her. She'd seen a pattern for a sweater in a women's magazine her friend had and she came home full of it. She was so taken with the picture of it that she went out the very next day and bought enough wool to make a start. It looked so lovely with its sprays of cherries across the yoke and little bunches on the sleeves. But, sadly, either the pattern was more difficult than she'd thought or there was a misprint somewhere in the working, for the cherries didn't come out right at all. She'd unravelled the patterned bits and redone them several times but the cherries still looked like lumpy plums. She'd tried and tried until the sight of them so upset her that she unravelled the whole thing and used the ripped-out wool to make a batch of crocheted teacosies for the sale of work at the church.

'I think it's about the only time I've ever seen your Mummy really cross,' he said, as he wrapped up the dirty feather in the damp newspaper. 'But the best of it was that those cosies sold like hot cakes. Everyone thought they'd been made specially with ripped-out wool and they wanted her to make more of them. So in the end she had to laugh.'

He'd gone out to the dustbin in the backyard and come back into the kitchen still smiling.

'Sometimes Clare, when all else fails you have to laugh.'

The large black hand of the clock had moved at last. It hadn't stopped after all. But it was still only five past three. Clare finished the final hem on her piece of gingham, anchored the thread with a double stitch and bit off the piece left over with her small, even teeth. She spread the rectangle on the desk and looked at it, pleased that it wasn't dirty or crumpled after her

11

efforts as some of the other girls' work was. Then she caught a glance from Miss McMurray and immediately picked up the two pieces of blue check that she was to join together with a 'run and fell' seam.

She knew perfectly well what she had to do but she wondered about the name. She thought of running and falling, which she and William often did when they raced each other in the big field in Cathedral Road, just round the corner from where they lived. William always cried when he fell. Even if his knees were only rubbed green from the grass he'd lie there bawling and crying for Mummy.

'If you want Mummy, we'll have to go home,' she'd told him time and time again. 'Come on then.'

But William would neither pick himself up nor let her take him home. He'd just sit up and start snivelling even though he had a clean handkerchief in his pocket. Sometimes Clare got cross with him and pretended to walk away but it was only pretend, for her mother had said she was never to leave him alone. He was too small to come back by himself even though there was no road to cross between the field and the adjoining row of red-brick houses.

William was at school now and would soon be six but it didn't seem to make much difference to the way he behaved. He would still sit wherever he had fallen and cry till his teacher came to pick him up. Then when they came home from school he'd go straight to Mummy and cry all over again as he showed her the graze on his knee or the sticking plaster the teacher had put on.

'Oh dear a dear, poor old William,' she'd say, giving him a hug. 'Sure you're here to tell the tale, it can't be that bad, now can it?'

Often her mother would nod to Clare over William's dark head for she had once told Clare that sometimes boys were far harder to deal with than girls, though most people seemed to think it was the other way round. She said that her own mother, Granny Scott, had always said it was the boys that had her heart broke with their complaints and worries while the girls just seemed to make the best of things.

'Not all wee boys are like William, Clare, just some of them. Your Daddy would never have been like that, but your Granny Hamilton said that your Uncle Jack was never away from her skirt tail till he got his first job in the fruit factory. And look at the age he'd have been by then.'

There was no doubt, Clare agreed, boys were funny. Funny peculiar, not funny ha-ha, as her father would say. You could never tell what they were going to do next. Whatever it was, it was usually a nuisance. But, as her mother always said, what you can't change you must thole.

The last of the line of big girls had reached Miss McMurray's desk. She stood awkwardly as she presented her work. The 'garment' represented the culmination of years of sewing samples and the previous year's effort of making an apron with two pockets outlined with bias binding in which to place dusters.

Mary Bratten's garment was large and shapeless and although Clare knew that it was either a blouse or a pair of knickers it was quite impossible to tell which. Of course, if it were knickers the elastic would go in last. But, even allowing for that, the voluminous spread of green gingham looked more like a laundry bag than either of the possible garments it was supposed to be.

Clare knew exactly what her mother would say if she saw it: 'It would fit Finn McCool and leave room for Mary as well.'

Miss McMurray spread the fabric out, surveyed it wearily and reached for a box of pins. Mary shifted uncomfortably from one foot to the other and tried to avoid the glances of her friends sitting in the back row. She looked all around the room as if desperate to escape the sight of the green shape that twitched and writhed below Miss McMurray's pins.

Clare felt sorry for Mary. It was all very well if you liked sewing or were good at it, but it wasn't very nice for you if you didn't. And it was clear that Mary didn't like sewing and was no good at it at all.

13

The clock clicked audibly in the quiet of the room where even the senior girls had fallen silent, their gossip expended or their observation of Miss McMurray judging it expedient.

From the corridor, footsteps sounded, firm and measured. As Clare glanced towards the window on that side of the room, she caught sight of a blue figure. The dungarees were a blur behind the moulded glass of the lower panes, but where the panes reverted to plain glass above the level at which pupils could be distracted from their work, the head and shoulders of Mr Stinson, the school caretaker, were clearly visible as he moved steadily past.

Clare didn't know Mr Stinson very well because his store-room was on the Senior corridor and he was seldom to be seen in her part of the school. Occasionally he would appear with a bucket and mop when some child had been sick in the class-room and every few weeks he would arrive with a huge bottle of ink to refill the inkpots. She always liked seeing him because he wore exactly the same blue overalls her father wore for work, and like her father's they nearly always had marks of grease or oil from some job they had been doing.

'I'm sorry, Ellie, they're a bad job this week,' her father would say when he came downstairs on Saturday afternoon, wearing his old trousers for the allotment and carrying the blue overalls on his arm. 'Ye may put in a drop of that stuff I got from Willie Coulter down at the Depot.'

'Never worry, Sam, there's no work without mess. I'll soak them in the children's bathwater tonight and they'll have all Sunday to loosen up. Sure the better the day, the better the deed. Your other pair came up a treat last week even after you working on Jack's car. That car grease is far worse than bicycle stuff.'

'That's true, Ellie. It's far heavier, it has to be, for the moving parts are so much bigger. But it's hard on you, love, that has to wash them.'

'Never worry yourself. Sure when you get the shop won't I send it all to the laundry and act the lady?' she'd say, laughing at him.

Clare loved to hear them talking about the shop. It would be a bicycle shop because that was what Uncle Harry had and he was going to retire one day and Daddy was going to buy it and it would have Samuel Hamilton over the door instead of Harold Mitchell. Her father had all sorts of plans for when he took over. Most of all he wanted to branch out into the sale and repair of motorbikes. He loved motorbikes and in the photograph album there were pictures of him in the Isle of Man at something called the T.T., which was a race. He said he never won but that wasn't the point, it was experience. You learnt more about a bike by riding it than by stripping it down and putting it together again.

He had sold his motorbike when they got married. Her mother didn't want him to but they needed the money to buy furniture and besides, in Edward Street, there was nowhere to keep it. But one day when they had a house with a garden and a workshop, he would have his own motorbike again and she and William would go for rides on the pillion. That was what you called the seat for the passenger and when you rode there, you would have to put your arms round his waist and hold on tight.

There was a knock at the classroom door. Surprised, Clare looked up and saw that Mr Stinson had come in. He didn't have an inkbottle or a window pole in his hand but when Miss McMurray handed Mary Bratten back her work and looked up at him he took a piece of paper from his top pocket and said something to her in a low voice with his head turned away towards the blackboard.

Miss McMurray stared at him and shook her head.

'Alison Hamilton,' she said aloud, as she turned back to scan the front desks and the unfamiliar faces of the juniors who sat there.

No one moved and although Clare was quite sure the message was for her, for a moment, she was too surprised to put her hand up.

'Please miss, I'm Alison *Clare* Hamilton.'

15

'Have you a wee brother called William in the infants?' asked Mr Stinson quietly.

She nodded and watched as the two adults exchanged glances.

'Clare, the Principal wants to see you in his office,' began Miss McMurray. 'Leave your work here and take your schoolbag with you. Mr Stinson will go with you.'

There was complete silence in the classroom as Clare put down the joined fragments of blue fabric, run but not felled, and fastened the buckles on her schoolbag. She stood up and found her legs were shaking. Something was wrong. Something had happened to William. He'd fallen down and broken his leg and he wouldn't stop crying or he'd forgotten where he lived. This was what happened in books. They always sent someone to fetch the hero, or heroine, like in *David Copperfield*. But that was his mother.

An awful thought hit her. Maybe it was her mother who was ill. She'd not been well this morning. She'd had an awful headache and in the middle of washing William she'd had to run outside to the lavatory. When she came back she was pale and her forehead was damp but she'd said she was fine.

'Women sometimes feel bad at certain times, Clare. You'll understand when you're older. I'll away and lie down when you go off to school. I'll be as right as rain by the time you come home.'

The Principal's desk was empty when Mr Stinson knocked and opened the door but the school secretary was at her typewriter under the window and sitting on one of the hard upright chairs by the door was William. He appeared to be completely absorbed in studying a marble he had taken from his pocket.

'There ye are,' said Mr Stinson quietly. 'I'll leave you with Mrs Graham and your wee brother.'

'Sit down, dearie, the Principal'll not be a minute,' Mrs Graham called over her shoulder as Clare sat down beside William.

16

Clare heard a car stop outside the main entrance and the heavy tread of the Principal as he came up the steps. He looked hot and uncomfortable as he stepped back into his office. His large, bald head was sweating as profusely as his forehead and the remains of his hair were damp.

'Ah, there you are, Clare and William,' he said jovially. He put out his hand to pat their heads, a habit he had when he spoke to children. He paused, withdrew his hand abruptly and stepped backwards.

'Now I want you two good children to come for a little drive with me. I'm afraid Mummy hasn't been too well today and she's been taken to hospital just so that she'll be more comfortable. I'm sure it's this heat has made her feel so unwell. Now you're not to worry at all. I'm going to take you to the hospital and when Mummy is feeling better you can go in and see her.'

'But what about Daddy's tea?' Clare burst out, without a moment's thought. 'Who'll make Daddy's tea if Mummy's in hospital?'

The Principal took out a large, white handkerchief and mopped his brow. He looked even hotter, despite the fact that his office had no south-facing window and was always cool, if not actually chilly, even in summer.

'Don't worry about Daddy's tea, Clare. Daddy was feeling a bit sick too, so he's gone to the hospital as well. He'd want to be with Mummy wouldn't he? So they're both quite safe and sound with nice nurses to make their tea. Why don't we go off and see them?' he said encouragingly, as he waved them through the door of his office. 'Now we don't want any arguments about who sits in the front seat with me, so why don't you both sit in the back like grown-ups in a taxi,' he added as they went down the steps.

'I want to sit in the front,' muttered William sulkily.

Clare didn't even nudge him for being rude, she just followed him to where the Principal's Austin sat gleaming in the sun. It

17

was so hot you could smell the petrol and when she got into the back seat the leather was so hot she thought it might burn her legs.

William marched round to the front seat and to her surprise the Principal just opened the door from the inside and let him climb in.

They drove across the empty playground and down the hill to the Courthouse, but instead of driving up College Hill and going on up Abbey Street to the County Infirmary, the Principal turned along English Street.

'This isn't the way to the hospital,' cried Clare, who was very near to tears.

'No, Clare, it isn't. We're going to a different hospital from the one you know. It's a hospital where you can stay till Mummy and Daddy are better.'

Clare watched him wipe his perspiring face again. She could see his face in the rear-view mirror and he seemed quite different from his usual self. Daddy knew him well because they were in the same lodge, which was a kind of club men went to one Friday night in the month. He said he was a good sort, always ready for a joke. But today he didn't look as if he could even smile, never mind make a joke.

The Principal was indeed a good sort. It was because he knew Sam Hamilton so well that he was in such distress. It was not his job to tell his children how bad things were, that Ellie Hamilton had aborted the child she was carrying and was in a critical condition and that Sam himself, as fine a man in his prime as you might wish to see, had collapsed in the street outside the shop where he worked.

He drove quickly along the empty road and turned right about a mile out of Armagh. He slowed down on the wide sweep of gravel that swung away across empty acres of grassland towards a hard-faced, grey building set on a slight elevation in the low, undulating countryside.

He was expected. As the car drew up, a white figure came down the steps to greet them, took a child by each hand and said the briefest of goodbyes to the man who stood towering over them, quite at a loss for anything to say.

As the Principal of the Armagh Primary School made his way back from the Fever Hospital, one of his senior boys collected the bell from his office and walked up and down the corridors, ringing it vigorously.

The clangour echoed round the empty corridors and escaped through the open windows. It was now half past three.

2

Two days after Ellie Hutchinson lost her unborn child the hot weather ended in thunderstorms and torrential rain. Rainwater streamed down the tall window of the bare, half-tiled room where her children played ludo and tiddly-winks on the white surface of one of the two small beds that stood on the highly polished floor. Whenever Clare raised her eyes from the game in which William was completely absorbed, the view over the surrounding countryside appeared only as a blurred wash of green and dark grey. For Ellie, her mother, the sun never stopped shining. As she moved in and out of consciousness, responding sometimes to the nurses who bathed her face and hands or coaxed her to drink, she was aware only of the light, a warm golden light that spread all around her.

Late on the morning of her third day in hospital, she began to move towards the light. Suddenly, she found herself standing under the rose-covered arch that framed the front door of her parents' home. On the fresh morning air she caught the hint of smoke from the newly lit fire in the forge. Somewhere nearby, a blackbird sang a joyous celebration of the new day. For a moment she felt reluctant to step outside, to break the deep sense of peace and stillness all around her. Then, quite suddenly, she heard Sam's voice from the orchard. There was a burst of laughter from the children. At the sound of their voices she stepped through the doorway without another thought and was gone, the light enfolding her. By her bedside a young nurse stared in amazement at the sweet smile on her pale face and the tiny indentation made by her lifeless body on the surface of the high white bed.

The children were not told of their mother's death that day. After much discussion with her staff the Matron decided it would be better if their father told them when he himself had recovered enough to do so. In the meantime, the younger nurses were sent to play with them when they could be spared from other duties. They were brought books and toys. Each time a nurse appeared in the children's room the little girl asked to see her parents and each time the nurse, as she had been instructed, told her gently that it would have to be a little longer before she could see either of her parents.

The little boy seemed indifferent to what was happening. His only wish was to go outside. As it was now clear that neither child had been infected, they were allowed out as soon as the lawn adjoining their ground-floor room had dried after the rain. As long as Clare would kick back the football which one of the male orderlies had brought for William, he seemed perfectly happy, paying not the slightest attention to where he was, or to the comings and goings of nurses and doctors, or the fate of either of his parents.

It was a shock even to the most experienced of the nursing staff when later that same day, before he had yet been told of his wife's death, Sam Hamilton, who had been holding his own with the fever which had struck him, had a heart attack. The Fever Hospital was not equipped for such an event and though they acted promptly and did what they could, phoning the infirmary in Armagh for immediate help, it was of no avail. While the doctor was driving between the city hospital, perched on its hill in the centre of Armagh and the isolated building only a mile or so away, Sam had a further attack and died.

Standing in Matron's office as he wrote out the death certificate, Dr Adams from the infirmary heard the unexpected sound of children's voices. Puzzled, he went to the window and saw Clare and William playing on the lawn. He asked who they were and to his amazement received no answer. It was the first and only time in his long association with the Fever Hospital that he had seen its formidable Matron overcome by tears.

Both the Scotts and the Hamiltons were local families with large connections. Brothers and sisters of Ellie's parents and of Sam's had married both within the city itself and in the villages that had grown up in the last century within walking distance of the various Armagh markets. Sam was a respected member of the Masons and had recently been made Master of the Orange Lodge that he had joined when he moved to Armagh. The entire lodge paraded at his funeral, their sashes decorated with large black rosettes. And when colleagues, friends and family took up the formal method of expressing grief by making insertions in the newspaper, the *Armagh Gazette* had seldom had so many columns of text under any one name.

But the rituals of funeral and wake did little to mitigate the shock to the whole community that an illness, long-absent from the catalogue of everyday maladies, should strike so suddenly, so unpredictably and so tragically. Nor did those rituals do anything whatever to help the two children who had suffered such grievous loss. They remained in the care of the hospital, carefully excluded from all the public expressions of mourning.

Clare wept as if her heart would break when the Matron herself took on the task of telling them what had happened. But almost before that kind lady had offered her clean handkerchief to the child she began to ask questions. In the long hours of the night and in the small spaces when William did not insist on her total attention, she had feared the worst and had already begun to think what would have to be done.

'I'll have to look after William now,' she said quite firmly, 'but what shall I do about shopping for the groceries? I won't have any money and I'm too young to get a job . . .'

She looked anxiously at William who had gone to the door and would have gone outside had Matron not called him back.

'Clare, would you like me to send Trissey to play with William so that you and I can have a talk?'

Clare nodded and breathed a sigh of relief when the young nurse arrived to collect him. She had tried so hard to keep him amused because she knew her mother would want her to look after him, but the hours had been so long. Now she thought she'd have to do it forever because Mummy wasn't there any more. And at the thought of Mummy not being there any more she broke down and wept again on the Matron's starched bosom, appalled by the world that was opening up in front of her, a world full of William and no Mummy, or Daddy, to make it seem worthwhile.

Matron let her cry, stroked her dark curls with one hand and surreptitiously wiped away her own tears with the other. What was there to say to the child that wasn't a pathetic platitude. She'd hear enough about the will of God and doing his bidding when the minister got to her after the funerals. What she needed right now was an aunt, or a grandmother, to step into the aching space the loss of her parents had created. So far, her own enquiries about the family had not been very productive. No one had contacted her about the children as yet, but then both families were busy making funeral arrangements and they knew the children were in good hands. Besides, it was unlikely that any of them had a telephone and it was a hard thing to have to use a call box at a time like this.

'Will we be going home now, Matron?' Clare asked, quite forgetting that she and William could hardly live in an empty house.

'Well you *are* now free to leave here,' Matron began slowly.

She wondered if Clare would understand if she explained about incubation periods and carriers. She liked the child but had had little time to spend with her, for Ellie and Sam were not the only victims to be brought to the hospital during the last week. There had been no other deaths as yet but if the rate of admission continued to increase as it had in the last week, then it was only a matter of time before there were.

'Did you think William and I would get the fever too? Was that why we had to stay indoors?' she persisted.

23

'Yes, it was. But you're both all right now,' she said reassuringly.

The small forehead was wrinkled in thought. It was clear that her reassurance had been irrelevant. Whatever was shaping in the child's mind it had clearly moved beyond the question of being ill.

'Will William and I have to go to Dr Barnardo's?' she asked politely.

Matron smiled in spite of herself.

'No, I shouldn't think so. Dr Barnardo's is for children who have no family, but you have lots of aunts and uncles, haven't you?'

'Oh yes, lots and lots, but we could only go for a week. When we go to Granny Hamilton or Auntie Polly for a holiday Mummy always says that a week is quite long enough. She said you can't go imposing on people just because they are your own family. It's just not fair.'

'But I'm sure some of your aunts and uncles would like to have you, Clare. Has Mummy got any sisters?'

'Oh yes, but they have their own troubles,' she replied promptly.

'What do you mean?'

Clare tried to remember which aunts were real aunts and which were just Mummy's girl friends. Sometimes she got a bit mixed up and once at school she'd had a very embarrassing time when she said she had six grannies. One of the other girls in her class said you couldn't possibly have more than two, so Clare had recited off the names of all six.

'Oh you *are* silly,' said the girl who had challenged her. 'It's only your mother's mother and your father's mother that are proper grannies.'

This time she would be more careful. Mummy had three sisters and two brothers, but Daddy had nine brothers and sisters altogether and she couldn't even remember all their names.

She looked up at Matron and decided that she must be

thinking one of her aunts would come and collect her with William and take them away to a new home. That was what usually happened with orphans in books unless they went into an orphanage like Anne of Green Gables. Then you got sent out as a servant to work on a farm when people like Marilla and Matthew needed a boy to help. Anne had been so lucky to get sent to them by mistake. She wouldn't mind helping people like Marilla and Matthew.

She took a deep breath and began counting on her fingers: 'Well, Auntie Polly has a heart of gold, but Uncle Jimmy has a bad back since he fell off the scaffolding at the aircraft factory. He's on the Boru most of the time and Auntie Polly has to work very hard to pay all the bills. She has three big sons but two of them only think about number one. That's why she can't get up to see us very often and we only see her when Daddy borrows Uncle Harold's car. Auntie Mary is in Michigan and has four children of her own and Auntie Florence is a glamour girl. Auntie Polly says she's great fun but she lives in London and she says she's never going to marry.'

Matron listened fascinated as Clare continued to list the various members of her family. She discovered that Clare's Granda Scott was a real gentleman but he had no hands. This might have been alarming had not Clare immediately explained that outside his forge he was no use at all and couldn't even fry bread without it sticking to the pan. He did his best to help Granny with her jobs because she had bad legs and her chest had never been right after all those years at the Ring Spinners, but he wasn't much good at it and Mummy worried about the bed linen and the curtains.

'I could go and help to look after Granny Scott,' she went on, 'But William wouldn't like it. There'd be no one to play with him while I was busy and he'd get himself so dirty in the forge. If there's somewhere to get dirty then William'll find it,' she added sadly.

The strange thing about this child, thought Matron, is that although she's repeating what she's heard her parents say, she has thought about it and she understands what she's saying in her own way. If she makes the Unemployment Bureau sound like the High King of Ireland it's hardly her fault. That's what she's heard so that's what she calls it. A very sharp ear for what people say, Matron decided, as she listened to Clare's account of her family.

The large black telephone on Matron's desk rang so loudly it made Clare jump.

'Yes, I'll come immediately,' Matron said, standing up as she put the receiver back. 'I'm sorry, Clare, I have to go, but as soon as I can we'll go on with our talk. Why don't you go and have a wee walk to yourself while William's busy. If you see the gardener he'll give you some flowers if you ask him nicely.'

Clare had never seen so many flowers in her life. Formal wreaths in great circular mounds, crosses and emblems with words and mottoes picked out in individual blooms, sprays and posies from local gardens of every colour and hue. In the shady greenness of the Presbyterian burying ground the spill of colour washed so far beyond the newly cut graves that from the moment her father's youngest brother parked his car and opened the heavy iron gates at the end of the long beech avenue to let her and Auntie Polly pass through she could see quite clearly where her parents lay.

She walked quickly, her own flowers in one hand, a shopping bag with a jampot and a tightly screwed-up bottle of water in the other. She wondered where she was going to put her bunch of marigolds and asters with all these other beautiful flowers spread everywhere. She looked over her shoulder and found that Auntie Polly and Uncle Jack were now a long way behind.

Jack and Polly had met for the first time two days earlier, the morning of the funeral, when Jack had met Polly's train at Armagh station and taken her to the church on The Mall. Now Clare observed that they were walking very slowly, talking quietly, nodding towards other graves they passed, people they both knew though their own lives had been separated by Polly's fourteen years of absence and by Jack being sixteen years her junior. As they moved towards the double burial Clare saw Uncle Jack point out to Auntie Polly how the grass for yards around had been tramped flat by the feet of hundreds of mourners.

The wreaths all had little cards with messages written in black ink in beautiful handwriting, except for some that said Interflora on the back and had messages in ball-point from London and Toronto, Michigan and Vancouver. 'In loving memory of a valued and respected colleague – The Staff of Harold Mitchell Ltd, Scotch Street.' 'Safe in the arms of Jesus – a beloved sister and brother-in-law, Robert and Sadie Scott and family, Ballymena.' 'We shall met again on the other side of Jordan – John and Sarah Scott and family, Enniskillen.' 'With fond memories of Ellie and Sam – Armagh Lawn Tennis and Archery Club.'

Clare read every single label, puzzling over names she had never heard of before, cousins of her parents from places that were quite unknown to her both in Ulster and abroad. She had to guess at some words smudged by a light shower of rain the previous evening. All these people, known and unknown, must be very sad about Mummy and Daddy to write such lovely messages. The flowers blurred and she wiped her eyes on the sleeve of her cardigan.

She heard Uncle Jack's voice behind her. He was speaking very quietly but in the deep silence that lay under the tall trees it was impossible not to hear every word he said.

'Polly dear, I wouldn't for the world want to hurry the wee lassie but if ye want to get back to Belfast the night we'd need to be gettin' a move on for that train ye wanted.'

'Right enough, Jack, it's after five. Sure I'd clean forgot what time it was. I'm all through meself. I don't know whether I'm comin' or goin'.'

'Ah sure we're all the same. But you've the hardest job with wee Clare. I don't think it's hit her yet. She seems as right as rain.'

'I don't know. I just don't know. The Matron says she cried a lot when she told her but she seemed to be more worried about William than about herself. D'ye think your mother and father have done the right thing taking him in? They're not so young any more and he can be a wee handful at times.'

'Aye, he's a funny wee lad. I don't know who he takes after but the father said it was up to the Hamiltons to have him. And Mammy agreed, though she did admit to be honest that she'd had her fill of we'eans. Of course, it's part of what they believe in, the Friends that is, they're supposed to help each other at times like this.'

'Sure I'd forgot they were Quakers,' said Polly quickly. 'When Ellie and Sam were married they went to the Presbyterians. Why did Sam not stay with the Quakers? I've always thought they were very good people.'

'They are, Polly, indeed they are. I wisht there was more like them, but Sam was very keen to join the Masons and the Lodge. Ye see ye can't join any o' these organisations if you're a Friend. It's against what they believe. There's none of us boys has followed them to the Meeting House, its only some of the girls that still go.'

Clare unpacked the jampot and filled it carefully with water. So that was why Uncle Jack had taken them all out to Granny Hamilton and then left William there. Granda and Granny must have consulted their consciences about William. That was what Quakers did. They didn't sing hymns or say prayers, they just sat quietly and waited for the Spirit to move them.

'Granda, what happens if the Spirit doesn't move you?' she'd asked her grandfather one day, as he sat by the window, his finger marking his place in the large Bible he read every day.

'Well, that's a matter of faith, Clare,' he said, looking at her very directly. 'If you believe that there is help for you, then it is likely to come, but if you are weak in faith you may have to wait and try again.'

Perhaps now if she consulted her conscience God would tell her what to do with her flowers. They seemed such a tiny bunch compared with all these wonderful wreaths. And she hadn't even got a card. She sat down on the kerb of the grave nearest to where her parents lay and closed her eyes.

'Uncle Jack, can I borrow one of your pens?' she said, getting up quickly and running towards where they stood, their backs slightly turned away from her. Uncle Jack was a bookkeeper at the fruit factory in Richhill and he always carried a row of pens in his top pocket.

'Ye can surely,' he said, taking out a ballpoint and handing it to her.

'Have you a wee piece of paper in your bag, please, Auntie Polly.'

Polly scuffled in her bag and produced a brown envelope, the latest reminder from the Electricity Board. She removed the red notice from inside and put it in Clare's outstretched hand.

Clare sat down again on the granite kerb and wrote leaning on her knee. It was difficult, for without something flat underneath the flimsy paper it would tear if she pressed too hard. She wrote slowly:

> Dear Mummy,
>   You always said it was better if men died first because women manage better but that you'd be heartbroken if Daddy died. It is very sad and I shall miss you but you are with Daddy. That is what you would want.
>   All my love to you both,
>   Clare

She placed her message under the jampot of flowers on the kerb where she had been sitting.

'I'm ready now, thank you,' she said as she walked back to where Jack and Polly stood and gave Uncle Jack his pen.

Neither Polly nor Jack felt it proper to go and look at what Clare had written but some days later one of Jack's brothers, Billy, arrived back from visiting the grave to tell the Hamiltons that the message Clare had written on the flimsy brown envelope was now mounted on some very nice, cream-coloured pasteboard and covered by a layer of clear plastic.

29

Billy had wondered who could have taken so much trouble, for the mounting and covering had been beautifully done. He'd turned the board over and found a message written in a very shaky hand. It read: 'I have taken the liberty of protecting this message that others may read it and pray for this child, as I shall do in the time that remains to me.'

There was no signature, but for some months afterwards, the jampot in which Clare had left her flowers was regularly refilled with sprigs of rosemary.

3

There were few passengers on the last train to Belfast that evening so Clare and Auntie Polly had a carriage all to themselves and didn't have to bother putting all their bags and parcels up on the rack high above both their heads.

Clare dropped her things gratefully and studied the faded sepia pictures above the long, lumpy seats that ran the full width of the carriage.

'The Glens of Antrim, The Great Northern Hotel, Rostrevor and The Ladies Bathing Place, Portrush,' she read aloud.

She had seen them before, last year, when she and her mother had gone on The Mall Church Sunday School excursion. The train jerked violently and squealed, preparatory to moving off. On the platform side, the stationmaster strode past, banging doors and trying handles to make sure they were really shut. As the guard blew his whistle, Clare hurried across to the other side of the train, knowing that in a few minutes' time when they got up steam she would be able to see all the places she knew on the Loughgall Road.

'That's Richardson's, isn't it, Auntie Polly, over there?' she asked, as they gathered speed.

She pointed to a fragment of eighteenth-century chimney-pot just visible over a planting of mature beech trees and the curve of a low, rounded hill.

'Yes, yes, it must be,' Polly replied, getting up wearily from the seat where she had subsided just inside the carriage door. She came and joined Clare at her window. 'And that's the back of Wiley's and Compston's. Look, there's Charlie Running on

31

his bicycle just going up the hill past Mosey Jackson's. Maybe he's going down to see your Granda at the forge,' she went on, making an effort to be interested.

Clare peered down on the figure pedalling steadily up the slight incline. At this point, where the railway bridge crossed over a lane, the track ran right beside the road. For a moment, she was so close to the figure on the bicycle she could have called to him through the open window. Then, just as she was about to wave, a great cloud of steam blew back from the engine. By the time it had gone the road had disappeared and the track had dropped into a shallow cutting where only the bright, white clouds in the paling blue sky were visible above the shaggy line of the full-leafed hedgerows.

She waited patiently for the level crossing but there were no children to wave to anywhere in sight. Although it was a lovely summer evening and the sun was still shining brightly, she knew by the long shadows cast by the trees and even by the cows who were grazing peacefully in the fields that it must be getting late. Perhaps it was past the children's bedtime.

'What time is it, Auntie Polly?' she asked without turning away from the window.

When there was no reply, she turned round and found her aunt was asleep. Settled by the far window she had leaned her head against the rough fabric of the seat and was now thoroughly out for the count.

Clare sighed and wriggled herself more comfortably into her own corner. It was no wonder Auntie Polly was so tired. She'd been busy trying to sort everything out since she'd fetched them from the hospital. Uncle Jack had taken a day of his holidays from work so that he could drive them round in his car but even with the car it had been a very busy day. He'd done everything he could to give a hand, he'd even come with them to Lennox's to buy clothes and underwear because all their own things had had to be destroyed.

'Jack, what would we have done without you?' Auntie Polly said, as they drove out of the town at the end of the morning.

'Sure it was the least I could do,' he replied easily.

Granny Hamilton had made them a very nice stew for their lunch and afterwards they said goodbye to William. Auntie Polly kept looking at William as they were getting ready to go and Clare wondered if he might cry, but William didn't seem to mind staying behind at all. He hardly even bothered to say cheerio and Granny Hamilton had to tell him to wave goodbye to the car as it turned out of the farmyard and up the hill to the main road.

They drove back into Armagh again, this time to the solicitor's office. They'd been there for ages. It was a big, three-storey building in Russell Street opposite the Cosy Cinema and the RUC Barracks. With tall pillars outside, Clare thought the entrance looked more like the outside of a church than the way in to business premises. She'd had to sit for ages on a very hard chair in the outer office with the clerks.

Behind the counter where they worked there were files and folders everywhere, stacked on shelves and desks, piled up on the tops of cupboards and even heaped up on the floor. There were three typewriters all chattering away at once and going 'ping' at the end of every line as well as two big black telephones which rang every few minutes or so.

'Roan Anersin,' said the youngest clerk, who wore a black skirt and a rather crumpled white blouse.

'Row Anderson,' said the middle-aged lady with the spotted blouse and the grey cardigan.

'Munro and Anderson', said the Chief Clerk, the lady who sat nearest to the partner's door. She had silver-grey hair and spoke very correctly. Clare wondered if she had been to elocution classes and whether she spoke like that when she was at home making her tea. She looked as if she might be a single lady. Perhaps she had no one to talk to except a pussy-cat. That must be very lonely and sad, to have no one to talk to.

'Here you are, my dear, you've had such a long wait.'

Clare was amazed to find the silver-grey lady standing in front of her with a glass of orange squash and two biscuits on a little plate. One of the biscuits was a pink wafer, one which she particularly liked.

'I'm afraid this is very boring for you. Solicitors are very careful people so everything they do has to be just so.'

She had such a nice way of clicking her fingers together when she said, 'Just so,' and such a lively smile that Clare wondered if sometimes she got bored too, working in this dusty old office.

Then Auntie Polly and Uncle Jack reappeared. They said thank you and goodbye but then began to talk business all over again. The tall gentleman with spectacles said everything at least three times but although she could pick out words like 'intestacy' and 'deed of family arrangement' and 'residue', she couldn't understand any of it. But he did seem to be very helpful and they all smiled as they shook hands and he came and shook hands with her too and called her Miss Hamilton. No one had ever called her Miss Hamilton before, except as a joke.

She wondered if orphans were called 'Miss' if they were girls. She tried to remember what that man who ate the pudding called David Copperfield when he was an orphan. But that probably didn't count because it was such a long time ago. She couldn't imagine William being called Mr Hamilton.

She wondered what William was doing now. He was sure to get himself in a mess if he played in the yard, which was always muddy after rain. It would be even worse if he went into the fields where the cattle had been. She hoped he would behave himself and not trail around at Granny's skirt tail like Uncle Jack had done all those years ago. William always wanted attention. Maybe that was what Uncle Jack wanted as well. But he must have grown out of it for he was really a very nice uncle now. He'd been so helpful and kind. He'd even bought her a little handbag with a purse inside and given her a whole half-crown to put in the purse as a luck-penny.

She leaned back in her seat and watched the hedgerows stream past the dust-streaked windows. In a few minutes, she too was asleep.

The Great Northern Station was full of smoke and steam. As

she climbed down the steep steps of the train her eyes began to smart so badly that she almost missed seeing a trolley piled high with mailbags that rattled past only a few feet away from her. High above her head the great arches of the train shed shut out the sunlight and created a dark, noisy cavern full of hurrying figures. Clare felt very small and would have taken Aunt Polly's hand if they hadn't both had so much to carry.

'Porter, porter. Carry yer bags, lady?'

Clare drew back as the burly figure blocked their path and shouted at them.

'No, thank you,' said Polly, nudging Clare in the back with the edge of her suitcase, to tell her to walk on.

It was difficult to keep up with Auntie Polly's hasty trot. Clare lost her twice when she got stuck behind people with huge suitcases. Once, a porter walked straight in front of her and caught the edge of the shopping bag Granny Hamilton had lent her to put her things in. It wasn't like this when they went on the excursion to Bangor.

Outside the station there was so much traffic they had to wait ages to get across the cobbled forecourt and the street beyond. Then it seemed as if they walked for miles on broad, crowded pavements leading to a huge white building with green towers on top. Clare's arms got sore from trying to keep her bags from catching in the legs of the people streaming backwards and forwards. Auntie Polly walked faster and faster and she was soon out of breath.

By the time they arrived at the bus-stop she was longing to sit down and so exhausted that she couldn't understand what Auntie Polly was telling her about double-deckers and trolley buses. It sounded as if the trolley buses were far handier and there were more of them but they didn't go all the way. As they went on standing at the double-decker stop, Clare began to wonder what the point was waiting for a double-decker to take you all the way, if it didn't come in the first place.

The bus was very full and there was no room to leave their luggage in the proper luggage space so they had to struggle upstairs with it while the bus lurched out from the stop into the traffic. Thankfully there were two seats right up at the front and when they both sat down Clare told herself that things were bound to be better now. She looked out at the shops and houses that lined the streets. Some of the streets had trees which brushed the roof and windows as they went past, but most of them didn't. They all seemed very dirty and empty, with newspapers blowing along the gutters in the little evening breeze that had sprung up. Here and there, where a house had fallen down, rubble was piled up high and bricks spilled out of the empty windows. There were open spaces with piles of rusted metal and patches of tall weeds and boys kicking tin cans between goalposts of old buckets or rusted-through dustbins.

They went across a bridge and she looked down into a wide, grey river that swept in a big curve between broad, gleaming mud banks. The thought of the mud made Clare shudder. She thought of the little stream at the Dean's Bridge where her mother sometimes took them for a walk. It was shallow and the sunlight glinted and sparkled as it tripped over the bigger stones in its bed. Pebbles were always so much nicer when you looked at them through the water. They weren't the same at all when you took them out. She often thought how nice it would be if the pebbles you picked out could stay wet and keep their lovely colours for ever.

'Not far now, Clare,' said Auntie Polly brightly. 'Look, there's the school you'll be going to next week. That's where Ronnie went before he went to Inst. and he thought it was great. You're sure to like it.'

At that moment Clare was equally certain that she wouldn't like it, a red-brick building set in among the shops and houses that lined the road, with no playground that she could see and not a tree in sight. But she said nothing about her new school and just thought how nice it would be to arrive home to Auntie Polly's house and to see Ronnie again.

It was a long time since she had last been to Auntie Polly's house. Last Christmas. Not Christmas itself when they always went to Granny and Granda Scott on Christmas Day and Granny and Granda Hamilton on Boxing Day. It must have been the Sunday after that because school still hadn't started and it didn't matter that they were so late back that both she and William were asleep in the back of the car.

'Harold's offered me the car for Sunday, Ellie. The weather's so mild he thought we might take a day out. What d'you think?'

It was her mother's idea that they would visit Auntie Polly for she'd said it was ages since she'd seen her. Daddy said that was fine by him. Would she drop her a line or would he give her a ring from work?

Auntie Polly had a telephone, a big black one that sat on a table in the hall at the foot of her stairs. She had to have it for her work. Polly had served her time to a dressmaker and she made lovely things. Once, when they visited she showed them a wedding dress all wrapped up in a sheet with shiny decorations like silver pennies stitched to the skirt.

'I copied the neckline from a dress of Princess Elizabeth's I saw in a magazine,' she said proudly.

'Well, all credit to you, Polly. It's like something a film star would wear. You've hands for anything,' said her sister warmly.

Later that year, Auntie Polly had brought Clare a Princess Elizabeth doll. It was actually one of her own old dolls her mother had been about to throw out, but Polly had said she knew a place where you could buy faces for dolls and the body was still all in one piece. She said she'd make it a dress out of scraps.

Clare was thrilled with her doll. It had a new face and ringlets and a long, white tulle wedding dress. And on the skirt there were three of the beautiful, shiny decorations she had so admired. They were made of tiny, tiny beads threaded on fine wire and then curved round and round and joined up till they made a gleaming circle about the size of a two shilling piece.

'A shilling each, those were,' said Mummy when the doll was unpacked and they had both said how marvellous it was and

37

how kind it was of Auntie Polly when she was so busy. 'The woman that had that dress made for her daughter had piles of money. Can you imagine what it cost, Clare. There were a hundred and fifty of those on the skirt?'

'A hundred and forty-seven,' Clare replied promptly.

Mummy had laughed.

'Not a word about that, Clare,' she warned. 'I dare say Polly reckoned she'd not bother to count them, so she kept you a few.'

Clare felt she was too old now to play with dolls but she sometimes made clothes for them with the coloured scraps of fabric Auntie Polly saved for her, the leftovers of dresses and jackets, frocks and wedding outfits. She still loved looking at her Princess Elizabeth doll.

As the bus turned off the Ormeau Road and into Rosetta Park it suddenly struck her that she couldn't make dresses for her dolls anymore even though she would have unlimited pieces of fabric. Her dolls were all gone. And not just her dolls. Teddy too. Tears sprang to her eyes and she had to pretend she was blowing her nose so that Auntie Polly wouldn't notice.

The Princess Elizabeth doll, the knitted golliwog with his black face and button eyes, the china baby doll called Ruby who cried when you laid her down, the square dog with the velvet nose that Daddy had bought from some American soldiers during the war when you couldn't get toys and Teddy, her very first and only Teddy, that she'd been given as a small baby, they had all been taken away and burnt with her clothes and her books. Matron had explained it all and said how sorry she was and how sad it was for Clare to lose her special toys, but until now she had forgotten. Until they went to the Fever Hospital she had never spent a night without Teddy before.

She tried to think of something different and remembered that the Christmas visit to Auntie Polly's in Uncle Harold's car had been a very happy one. Uncle Jimmy was in much better spirits, he had just started a new job with the Ormeau Bakery and was feeling very pleased with himself. Auntie Polly had gone to such a lot of trouble to make them welcome. The decorations were still up and the house was bright and shining. What Clare loved most was the Christmas tree in the sitting room, a lovely big tree with tiny, gilt-wrapped boxes hanging as decorations in among the silver bells and the gleaming coloured baubles. There were little lights that winked on and off. All different colours. Fairy lights, Daddy called them when he and Uncle Jimmy had sat down with glasses of the funny-smelling dark brown stuff with the foam on top they always drank when they met.

Daddy said he was amazed they'd been able to get fairy lights, with everything in such short supply. He hadn't expected there to be any in the shops. But Auntie Polly explained that she'd brought them back from Toronto with her in 1939.

'I suppose it was kind of a silly thing to bring, but I so loved Christmas in Canada and Jimmy and I were so happy those Christmases we had out there when Davy and Eddie were small. I packed up all the decorations and the garland that we used to put on the door, but the mice got that in the roof space of our old house, before we got the mice,' she said, laughing.

Clare's two big cousins, Davy and Eddie, weren't at home that Sunday. Polly laughed and said they both had girls now, they'd gone off dressed to kill and were having their tea with them, but Ronnie, the youngest, who was still at that school called Inst. and wanted to go to the university, came down from his room where he was studying for exams and talked to them. He'd given Clare some books he'd picked up for 3d each in Smithfield and insisted they were a present.

Clare was thrilled. *Coral Island*, *Little Women*, *Swiss Family Robinson*, *Black Beauty* and *Heidi*. She'd read *Little Women* and *Black Beauty* from the school library box, but she loved to have her favourite books so she could read them until she knew them almost by heart. The other three she had seen in the library but hadn't read. She could hardly wait to begin.

'That'll keep you busy for a day or two,' said Daddy as Ronnie handed them over.

'Don't believe it, Sam. There's no stopping her once she starts. She'll be finished in no time,' said Mummy, turning to Polly who was watching Clare turning the pages to see if there were any pictures or drawings.

They sat in the sitting room with the tree and then had a most marvellous tea in the living room. With both flaps of the table up, it was terribly crowded because of the big settee and the brown tiled hearth of the fireplace, which stuck out rather. Clare and William had to sit on the settee on a pile of cushions because there wasn't room to bring in two more chairs. Clare thought it great fun, but William slipped off sideways and cried until Mummy took him on her knee.

'My goodness,' said Daddy, as Polly set down steak and chips for Ronnie and the grown-ups and bacon and baked beans and chips for Clare and William, 'have you had a win on the pools?'

'No such luck,' said Uncle Jimmy, 'but it's not often we see you. To be honest it's a put up job, Sam. Ronnie has a favour to ask you and we thought if we gave you a good tea you'd have to say yes.'

Poor Ronnie was embarrassed but everybody else laughed for what Ronnie wanted was for Daddy to fix his radio. He'd taken it to pieces because he couldn't get the foreign stations and now he couldn't get anything at all.

'Aye, surely Ronnie,' said Daddy. 'It's just a pity I haven't one of Clare's feathers with me.'

But that worked out all right, for Ronnie had a wee brush from an old paint box he'd had when he first went to school and Jimmy had plenty of oil in his toolbox. After tea, Daddy took the radio to pieces and sorted it out. Clare had watched and held some of the tiny gold screws in her hand in case they dropped them and when it was all finished and switched on it went beautifully.

Ronnie was delighted and showed her how to tune to the

different wavebands and they took it in turns to pick a station and see what it was doing. They found all sorts of different music and foreign stations broadcasting in different languages. Ronnie could pick out French and German but there were others he couldn't make out at all even when they got the call signal and he looked it up in a special magazine he had.

'Here we are, Clare, down you go. Mind you don't fall now.'

The bus drove off leaving them on the pavement near where two roads went off at an angle to each other. Between them was a white building with black paintwork that called itself the Tudor Stores. Clare looked around wearily.

'You know where you are now, don't you?' said Auntie Polly encouragingly.

But Clare didn't know where she was. There were just houses everywhere, semi-detached and detached and a road leading on through yet more houses. As they began to walk, she saw a street sign saying 'Mount Merrion Park'. She knew that was where Auntie Polly lived because she had written the addresses on the Christmas cards while Mummy wrote the message inside, but she still didn't see anything she remembered or recognised.

All the houses looked the same except that half of them had the front door on the left and the other half had the front door on the right. Only when they came to a bend in the road and she saw a gate, unlike any of the other gates she had passed as they tramped up the park, did she recognise something that she knew.

The gate was one of Granda Scott's. She'd seen gates like this one lying in bits on the ground outside the forge while he cut the pieces of metal to size, she'd seen them propped up on billets of wood while he coated them with red lead and then, a couple of days later, with silver paint. She'd seen him hammer the twists and curlicues on the anvil before they were welded on to the topmost member. Never before had she seen a finished gate anywhere except in the fields and farms near Salter's Grange where most of Granda Scott's customers lived.

She felt a sudden overwhelming longing to go straight back to the station they had left over an hour earlier.

Tired and weary and wanting only to go to bed she stood on the doorstep waiting for Uncle Jimmy to come and let them in.

'Ach, hello Polly, hello Clare. Sure we weren't expectin' you till tomorrow,' he said, taking Clare's shopping bag as he stepped back awkwardly into the hall and edged his way round a brand new bicycle which was parked against the banisters.

'Sure I rang you las' night from the box at Woodview,' said Polly, an edge of irritation in her voice. 'An whose, might I ask, is this?'

'It was an awful bad line, Polly. Ah coulden' make out the haf o' what ye were sayin',' he said sheepishly. 'An that's Davy's,' he went on hurriedly. 'He says he'll put it in the shed when he gets a chain an' lock for it. He doesen' want it pinched. It cost a fortune.'

There was a funny smell at the bottom of the stairs and as they went into the living room Clare was sure she smelt bacon and egg. The kitchen door was open, she could see the draining boards were stacked with dishes. There were saucepans parked on the floor and on top of the meatsafe. It looked as if no one had washed up for days.

In the living room, Eddie sat with his feet on the mantelpiece, a stack of *Picturegoer* magazines beside his chair. The table was covered with sporting newspapers where Uncle Jimmy had been studying form before he filled in his Pools coupon. A teapot, an almost empty bottle of milk and a couple of large mugs had been parked on the polished surface of the sideboard. Clare knew what her mother would say if she saw the room in a state like this.

'Can I go to the bathroom, please?' she said, grateful she had remembered that Auntie Polly had a proper bathroom and not just a lavatory outside the kitchen door.

'Yes, love, you know where it is.'

Clare nearly caught herself on the pedal of Davy's bike as she hurried past the table where the telephone sat.

As soon as she stepped into the bathroom she sneezed. She saw immediately what it was she'd smelt the moment they came through the front door. The bath was full of sheets steeping in Parazone. Auntie Polly must have been in such a hurry to get to Armagh when she heard about Mummy and Daddy that she hadn't time to rinse them out. They'd be very clean by now, but as her mother always said, 'Overnight is one thing if they're in a bad way, but more than that you're just wearing them out.' These must have been here for days.

The bathroom was in a mess. There were shaving things everywhere, foam on the mirror and shirts and socks lying all around the laundry basket. It was true Uncle Jimmy had a bad back, but surely Davy and Eddie could pick things up. And where was Ronnie?

There was no toilet paper left so she had to do without and she felt very damp and uncomfortable as she went back downstairs. She had to squeeze past Auntie Polly at the foot of the stairs because she was in a hurry too.

In the living room, Uncle Jimmy was gathering up the things on the sideboard, but Eddie hadn't moved. He hadn't said hello either.

'I'm sure yer tired out, Clare. Would ye like a drop of milk before ye go tae bed?'

'No thank you, Uncle Jimmy. I'm afraid I don't like milk. Mummy says I'm a nuisance because it means William won't drink it either. She gives us orange juice instead. We get bottles of it from the Dispensary on The Mall and you have to mix it with water. It's really quite nice.'

'Is that so?' asked Uncle Jimmy kindly.

He looked at the child perched on the settee, her legs dangling inches above the floor and reminded himself that Ellie and Sam were dead. Gone. He couldn't rightly take it in. Maybe he should have gone to the funeral, back or no back, they could have scraped up the second train fare somehow.

Auntie Polly hurried in and Uncle Jimmy grasped his newspaper as if its flimsy pages might deflect what he feared was to come.

'Could you not even have done that much?' she began crossly. 'I told you the wee bed wasn't fit to sleep in. Where's Ronnie? I thought at least he'd do it if none of the rest of you could be bothered.'

'Sure he's away at camp with the school, Polly. Had ye forgot?'

She shook her head and muttered under her breath.

'Come on Clare dear,' she said, putting an arm round her, 'come on away upstairs, these big men might want to rest themselves, they've been so busy all evening.'

Ronnie's room was beautifully tidy. He had lined up his books on the windowsill and the mantelpiece, and his radio still sat on the small table where she and Daddy had helped him to mend it in the Christmas holidays.

'You can sleep in Ronnie's bed tonight. You won't mind, will you? The bed in my wee work room is covered with sewing and there might be the odd pin there as well,' she explained, as she took out the new pyjamas they'd bought only that morning. 'Will I come and tuck you up when you're into bed?' she whispered, as she kissed her.

'Yes, please.'

It was longer than she intended before Polly got back upstairs to tuck Clare in. By then Clare was fast asleep. Polly noticed that she had fallen asleep clutching Ronnie's copy of *The Swiss Family Robinson*. What Polly didn't notice was that the pillow below the much-loved book was sodden with tears.

Clare woke next morning refreshed in body but sadly depressed in spirits. As she lay looking up at the unfamiliar ceiling, she listened to the sounds of the household as it began its morning round.

'What's keepin' you in there? I haven't all day to stan' here.'

She recognised the voice though she had not seen its owner for a long time. Davy must have been out with his girlfriend last night. There was a hasty but muffled reply from the bathroom. Later, the door banged and there were trampings up and down the stairs. Clare would have liked to go to the lavatory but the thought of bumping into Davy or Eddie intimidated her so she waited till all was quiet before she slipped out of her room and across the landing.

On her way back she saw that the two older boys had left the door of their bedroom, the largest bedroom of the three, wide open. The beds were unmade. Beside each bed a high-backed chair was draped with clothes which spilled down on to the floor which was already covered with random shoes and odd socks. Surely they tidied up before they went to work. Even William, who was not the tidiest of little boys, knew not to leave shoes for someone to trip over.

As she walked away from the open door it dawned on Clare that Auntie Polly and Uncle Jimmy must sleep downstairs. That big settee on which she and William had perched at Christmas, must be one of those put-you-ups she had heard Mummy and Daddy talking about. Poor Auntie Polly. She had the living room to clear every morning before breakfast and then all this mess waiting upstairs even before she started her sewing. Mummy would be so upset when she told her how Davy and Eddie behaved.

And then she remembered she wouldn't be telling Mummy. She knew she could manage Davy and Eddie for a week if she was going home at the end of it, but she wasn't going home. She had been so looking forward to seeing Ronnie but now she thought about sleeping in the tiny sewing room and walking down to that bus-stop, past all those houses, and going to that awful school with no playground and no trees for ever and ever amen.

She climbed back into bed and buried her head under the bedclothes so that no one would hear her cry. It was no use, no use at all. However kind Aunt Polly was she couldn't live here with these large figures and their loud voices and all these grey houses. She'd far rather go to the orphanage. At least in the orphanage there'd be other children and she'd have a teddy bear.

When the lady from Dr Barnardo's had come to school to receive all the money from their collecting boxes, she'd brought pictures of the children to show to them. They looked so happy playing together in a garden with a swing. They each had a little bed and there were toys and books beside each one.

She made up her mind, came out from under the bedclothes and started to get dressed. She'd just have to explain politely to Auntie Polly that she really couldn't impose on her kindness and could she take her to the orphanage right away.

4

Whenever Polly McGillvray looked back on the weeks that followed her sister Ellie's death, she wondered how she had found the strength to go on during that awful time. In those weeks she came to know a despair that was quite new to her. There were moments when the woman who had always seen herself as easy going and optimistic was shocked to find that she would be only too grateful to join her sister under a mound of flowers.

It was not that Polly expected life to be easy or without grief. From her earliest years she had been well acquainted with both hard work and sudden losses. As the eldest girl in a family of six, with a mother often disabled by illness, she bore much of the burden of running the household. She rose early to light the stove, carried water from the well before she went to school and came home to sweep and scrub the stone floor of the big kitchen where the day to day life of the family went on. In the month of her ninth birthday, her own much-loved grandmother died and later that same summer, her playmate, Dolly, from the farm just down the hill was drowned in a flax hole. Two years later, her baby brother died suddenly when only a few days old to the great distress of her mother who continued to lament for years because he had not even been baptised.

The Scott family were not poor for her father, Robert, was a skilled craftsman. Although there were several other black-smiths within a few miles distance, he was never short of work and he willingly toiled all hours for the sake of his young family, but until Ellie and Mary and little Florence were able to help in

47

the house, the burden of keeping the place clean and making sure the younger children were presentable for school was often a full time job for Polly.

Bob and Johnny, her two brothers, had an even greater talent than most small boys for tearing their trousers, scraping their boots and arriving home marked with the results of their activities. Long before Polly left school at fourteen to be apprenticed to a dressmaker in Armagh, she was an expert on mending.

In the cramped back premises of the shop in Thomas Street, Polly worked six days a week. The hours were long and wearisome, the pay during her apprenticeship almost non-existent. But Polly always had the capacity to make the best of any situation. It was she who made the other girls laugh when they were presented with yet one more batch of sleeves to make up, a job they all hated, and it was she who suggested dances and parties and picnics on their rare days off.

But any hardship there might have been in her early years was completely forgotten when Polly met Jimmy at a dance in Belfast while she was staying with her aunt on the Lisburn Road.

Jimmy, who was some years older, wanted to go off to Canada and make his fortune and he made it quite clear that he wanted Polly to go with him. At nineteen, she was delighted with the prospect. Polly, who had never been further from home than her annual visit to Belfast, organised her wedding and set out for Canada a few weeks later as if she were going to the Isle of Man for her holidays. She simply assumed she would come home regularly to visit her family as so many Canadians and Americans appeared to do.

Life in Canada in the 1920s was not as easy or as luxurious as the letters of emigrants often made out. Two years after the local band had played her and Jimmy the two miles to Armagh station and ranged themselves to play 'Will ye no come back again' on the platform where her family and friends were to say their goodbyes, life in Canada was not as rosy as the picture Polly had painted for herself.

With two babies and a husband who could not always find work despite his skills, the prospect of coming home to visit her parents had receded into the far distance. She was homesick and often short of money, but only the most perceptive of her new friends would have guessed at either. Polly always managed to stay cheerful and she had the gift of spending a very small amount to create a treat, or some small outing for her family however bad things were. She began sewing at home and the moment Eddie went to school she found a job in a dress shop.

It was only months after they had bought their first modest home on the outskirts of Toronto that the prospect of the coming war forced a difficult decision upon them. They had been in Canada for fourteen years and had never made the return journey to Ulster. Both sets of parents were ageing and Jimmy's mother was dying of cancer. If they crossed the Atlantic that summer they might not be able to get back again. But if they didn't go now, with war in sight, they might never see their parents again.

Finally, they decided they would return home. They arrived back in Belfast in August 1939. A month later they opened the newspaper to find that the ship on which they had travelled back had been torpedoed as it made the return journey to Canada.

There was no problem with Jimmy finding work. As a skilled mechanic he was taken on at Shorts immediately. Within days he was assembling parts of the fuselage of the Sunderland flying boats which were to patrol the western approaches. Finding a house was another matter. Houses were in very short supply in the city and Polly found that living with her McGillvray in-laws was even worse than being homesick. Davy and Eddie were resentful and unsettled and complained continually about the absence of candy and ice-cream parlours. They compared everything in Belfast with what they had left behind in Canada and hadn't a good word to say for anything.

When the Blitz began it was poor Ronnie who was terrified. Always the quietest and most thoughtful of the three, he became anxious when the first barrage balloons appeared in the sky. Although Polly tried to explain they were there to protect them, Ronnie was oppressed by the great, grey shapes and remained even more anxious about them than about the planes that were soon making raids on the docks, shipyards and aircraft factories.

Night after night Polly lay awake listening, for when Jimmy worked a double shift, he would be at work when the raiders came. She learnt, as everyone in Britain learnt, to fear moonlight, those beautiful clear nights when the raiders could find their targets more easily. But the worst night of all, the one that would remain forever in the minds of those who lived through it, Jimmy was at home, asleep by her side in the new house they had finally acquired.

In the morning they smelt the smoke and the taint of rubber on the air. When they listened to the radio at six o'clock, before the boys were awake and heard the toll of dead and missing, they kissed each other and shed a few tears. Hours later the phone rang and a neighbour of Jimmy's parents told him that his brother was missing. The police had called on his father and suggested that someone should go down to St George's Market to see if he was there. That was where the bodies were being laid out for identification.

Jimmy had found his brother's body, undamaged and unmarked, a victim of blast. By a strange chance he lay beside three of his old school friends whose battered remains had been dug from the rubble of the back-to-back houses down by the docks where Jimmy and his brother had begun their lives. He was looking down at them unable to grasp how four of the five wee lads who kicked a tin can round the street together, should be together once again, when the mother of one of them appeared, bent over and leaning on a stick. Jimmy had stood and wept and the bereaved mother had comforted him.

Although she worried about her family, the war years were

not as hard on Polly as they were on many other women. She was practical and cheerful, coped with shortages and rationing better than most and although she seldom got up to Armagh to see her family she drew such comfort from knowing that they were there, that they were safe and that she was no longer thousands of miles away.

Disasters, it seemed, always struck unexpectedly. One night when Jimmy was cycling to work he was caught by a sudden raid. Before he could find an air-raid shelter, he was knocked out by a lump of flying wood. Lying in the road, lit only by the flickers from burning buildings, a fire engine just managed to avoid his unconscious body at the last minute. That night he escaped death and suffered only a bad headache the next day. He was not so fortunate at the beginning of 1945.

It was with peace already in sight that Jimmy had his accident, as he worked on a plane that might never be needed. No one ever worked out exactly what happened. Jimmy remembered only that his feet went from under him and the next thing he knew he was in hospital. It was likely that engine grease had been the cause of his fall. There shouldn't have been engine grease on that scaffolding, but if there was and Jimmy was concentrating on the job as he moved slowly along the fuselage, he certainly wouldn't have seen it. There was a long argument about compensation which was never resolved. Jimmy was on his back for two months at Musgrave Park Hospital and in too much pain to join in the Victory celebrations. The doctors admitted that he would seldom be without pain for the rest of his life.

That, Polly decided later, was the beginning of her own bad time. After Jimmy's accident, life had been understandably harder and Polly felt it more than all the other hard times she had endured. But when Ellie died, it seemed as if this was the final blow. She felt that the loss of the one bright star that had always shone in her sky, even if she seldom had the opportunity to go out and look at it, was the one thing too many. The rest she could bear. She could struggle with dirt and poverty, hard

51

times and fractious children, sudden grief, illness and the misery of pain and weariness, but for Ellie to be taken away was for the light to be shut off. She had no wish whatever to live in the darkness that followed.

Ellie had been the pretty one in the family and she had a sweetness of nature that matched her soft looks. Polly had loved her younger sister more than either of her other sisters or her two brothers. From the moment the news of her death came, it never occurred to her to do anything other than to make a home for Clare, for Clare was dear Ellie's child and had something about her of her mother though she was a far more robust and lively child than Ellie had ever been.

She was anxious about separating the two children, but she had guessed that the Hamiltons would feel it their duty to care for their grandson and she was grateful when her brother-in-law had told her of their decision. She had always found William a difficult child to love and while she could imagine being able to treat Clare as her own child, she was honest enough to admit that she was unlikely to manage it with William.

The death of her favourite sister would have been disaster enough for Polly, but that heartbreak came at the end of a long series of other sad and unhappy events in her life. In May of that year, 1946, Jimmy, who had held down the job at the Bakery since the Christmas of 1945, had been listed for an early morning shift. He had protested that there were no buses on his route at that hour, but when his protests were ignored, he'd got out his ancient bicycle and cycled to work. It was only a couple of days before his back played up. The doctor had given him a sick note and the Bakery had given him his cards.

Polly's relief when Davy got a new and better-paid job only a week later was short-lived. When he brought home his first pay packet, he said he could only afford two pounds a week for his keep because he was now saving up to get married. When Eddie heard that Davy was paying only two pounds a week he wanted to know why he should pay more. He was saving up for a bicycle so that he could look for the better jobs out on the new industrial estate where there were no buses at all yet.

Only Ronnie, who seemed to take after the more kindly natured Scotts and not the generally hard-headed McGillvray's, came to her with his five shillings a week from his paper round and asked if he could give her a hand with anything.

She refused to take his money, knowing full well he needed it to buy the books the school couldn't afford to provide, but his generous act made it even harder to bear the selfishness of his brothers. For the first time, she saw that the way she had gone on caring for them as they grew up meant that they now simply expected her to do as she had always done. They left a trail of things lying around wherever they went, never did a hand's turn for themselves and, worst of all, never even thought of doing anything for anyone else.

And Jimmy, for all his good-nature, had dropped into bad habits. There was so much he couldn't do because of his back that he often didn't do anything at all. He never even seemed to notice when she was tired or harassed, as once he'd done. He'd taken to sitting by the fire in the small back living room reading his newspaper and looking out the window at the abandoned garden which once had been his pride and joy. As often as not Eddie was there too, a pile of magazines by his chair. She had never yet seen him bend to pick them up when she came into the room to pull the table out for a meal. He never even moved to help her when she opened up the settee at night and tramped back upstairs to carry down the heavy pile of bedding which had to be stored in a corner of Ronnie's room during the day.

The hardest part for Polly was that she knew it was her own fault. Long ago, in the letters she had written so faithfully to her, week by week, when she was in Canada, Ellie had said that she did too much for the boys. Ellie had been right. It was one thing doing your best for your family but she should have made them do more for themselves and more to help her, especially when she was working as well. Now Davy and Eddie would be looking for a wife who would do just what she had done and wait on them hand and foot.

With no help from anyone except Ronnie, the struggle to keep the place decent was a daily battle and now, on top of everything, she began to suffer hot flushes both day and night. Often she got little sleep. Weary of lying in the dark, trying not to twist and turn and wake Jimmy, she'd get up and clean the kitchen or do the ironing. Sometimes she would even go upstairs to the tiny third bedroom that overlooked the road and hand-finish a hem by the light of the lamp built-in to her electric sewing machine.

With her husband and sons asleep all around her she often felt quite desolate. Those were the times she always sought comfort by thinking of Ellie, wondering when they could manage to see each other again, making some plan to save a few shillings each week so she could afford the train fare to Armagh.

Sometimes Ellie rang her from the phone booth in the Post Office.

'It's me, your little sister,' she would say, laughing. 'How are you, Polly? I've only got fourpence worth. Tell me quick.'

Ellie could only ever afford three minutes, but the sound of her laughter would brighten Polly's life for days. Her laughter, like her sweet smile, made you feel the world was a wonderful place to live in.

Whether it was the hardship of the war, or the cheerlessness of the months that followed, Polly didn't know, but it seemed that her customers too were all through themselves. Certainly they had never been so hard to please. However much work she put in, however quickly she had a garment ready for fitting, they were never satisfied. They complained about the prices she charged though they were unexceptional. They insisted they wanted their item ready tomorrow. Some of them came so early for fittings that she had to keep the sitting room permanently tidy. That way there was somewhere for them to wait while she dealt with the client left standing in Ronnie's room in front of the wardrobe with the full length mirror.

Some customers didn't show up at all. Then they rang and wanted to come when she was already booked up. Some even arrived when she was out shopping and rang later to complain. Where was she, they had come and she was out. How did she expect to keep customers if she was never there?

There were days when the phone never stopped ringing and she was up and down stairs all day. She could come no speed with anything. Whatever she started to work on in the morning was still on the ironing board at the end of the day, ready to sew, when it should have been hanging up, ready to fit. Even when Jimmy was reading his newspaper with nothing else to do, she still had to come down to the phone because these days he felt too uneasy to answer it and take a message.

But all these distresses and frustrations were as nothing when three days after Clare's arrival Polly heard a small voice outside her door.

'Please, Auntie Polly, I know you are very busy, but could I have a word with you. It's most important.'

'Of course you can, sweetheart,' she said, jumping up so quickly she nearly tripped over the flex of her machine. 'Are you fed up with that jigsaw? I'm sorry, I wanted to take ye to the park this afternoon but this big, fat lady is coming tomorra and I hafta finish her dress. Come inta Ronnie's room, we can sit on his bed.'

She gave her a hug as they sat down together in the small, tidy room that seemed even smaller because of the huge wardrobe that had come from McGillvray's after Jimmy's mother died and his father went to live with his eldest daughter.

'Auntie Polly,' she began, taking a deep breath, 'it's very kind of you and Uncle Jimmy to have me to stay with you, but I don't want to impose on your kindness. Mummy always says that families shouldn't impose just because they are family. So I've come to tell you that I'd like to go to the orphanage as soon as you have time to take me. Perhaps, if you are very busy, Ronnie could take me, when he comes back from camp tomorrow.'

55

Polly looked at the small, pale face and felt as if her heart would break. What could she say? What could she do? She could see the child was unhappy and was doing her best not to show it. How could she be anything else, shut up in this unfamiliar house with these noisy young men and nowhere to play except the sitting room and that only when there was no one waiting.

She'd had words with both Davy and Eddie about their behaviour towards their little cousin but beyond the odd hello neither of them could be bothered to talk to her and the idea that they might play card games or read stories with her had fallen on deaf ears. She'd even pointed out to Davy that if he was going to get married maybe he should find out a bit about children and their needs. But he hadn't paid a bit of heed to what she'd said. It was just water off the duck's back.

'Clare, lovey, I don't think you'd like it very much in an orphanage. They do their best and they're very kind, but you really need people of yer own who know all about ye and all about your dear Mummy and Daddy. I'm sorry I've been so busy and Uncle Jimmy had to go to see his father. Did you get lonely? Ronnie'll be so glad to see you whin he comes home. Would ye not give it a wee bit longer?'

Clare looked up and found to her surprise that her aunt was near to tears. She was such a very kind aunt but that wasn't the problem. She didn't know what the problem was, but she felt as if she was shut up inside a box and couldn't get out. If it wasn't for Auntie Polly she'd just run away into the forest and live with the animals until someone came and found her and she could live happily ever after.

'Clare dear, are you worried about goin' to school on Monday? Is that it?'

Clare shook her head and looked down at her fingers. That was only a little bit of it.

'Has anyone said anythin' to upset you?'

'Oh no,' she replied promptly. 'Davy's always out and Eddie

never says anything at all. Uncle Jimmy has always been quiet, hasn't he?'

'Yes, love, he has, but he's even quieter since he lost his job.'

'Mummy says pain is very wearing and Uncle Jimmy must get very tired.'

The thought of Ellie talking to her child and explaining Jimmy's problem was too much for Polly. She could see Ellie's fair head bent towards Clare's dark one and Clare listening with that intent look she always wore when she was taking in every word. But Ellie was gone, her child was without a mother, and she, Polly, couldn't even give her the time she needed, never mind a room, or a place to play, or even a few toys to replace all those she had lost.

Polly wept.

'Don't cry, Auntie Polly. I'll stay if you want me too,' said Clare quickly, as she threw her arms round the sobbing figure. 'I could help you hem the dress for the fat lady and when Ronnie comes back he'll show me where everything goes and we can both tidy up for you. And I can answer the phone if you tell me what to say.'

Polly hugged her tightly, lost for any words to speak and for any way to resolve the conflict in her mind. This dear child had brought her something she thought she had lost forever when Ellie died. While she was near, Ellie would not be gone from her. But even as the thought came to her she saw that she couldn't begin to give the child what she needed to so she could begin to heal her own loss.

'Don't cry, Auntie Polly. Mummy would hate to see you cry.'

'You're quite right, Clare. I'm a silly old auntie,' Polly replied, sniffing and wiping her eyes.

'No, you're not. You've been so kind. You're a lovely auntie and Mummy always said I was lucky to have you. Would you like a cup of tea? I know how to put the kettle on, I saw Uncle Jimmy doing it.'

'But that's Polly's job,' her aunt replied, managing a weak smile.

Clare laughed and jumped up from the edge of the bed. She began to sing, 'Polly put the kettle on, Polly put the kettle on, Polly put the kettle on, And let's have tea.'

It was one of the first nursery rhymes Mummy had taught her and every time they read it or sang it she would remind her that her Auntie Polly was really called Margaret, but because when they were all little she was always putting the kettle on she'd got nicknamed Polly and now no one ever called her anything else.

They made tea together and sat drinking it in the quiet sitting room. For an hour or more no one called, the telephone didn't ring and neither Uncle Jimmy, nor Davy, nor Eddy arrived back. Polly and Clare talked about many things, Polly's childhood, her sisters, especially Ellie, about going off to Canada with Uncle Jimmy in a big ship, so big you could go for a walk, or go shopping just as if you were on dry land.

Clare's eyes rounded in delight as Polly described her first winter in Canada, driving in a sleigh with real jingling bells, just like the song, and rugs to wrap yourself in and the swish of the runners over the snow. She took it all in and asked question after question, wanting to know every little detail of Polly's Christmas treats, the presents she had and the decorations she put up in their tiny apartment.

For a little space of time for both the child and the woman, the pain of loss and loneliness was comforted and eased. But it was not healed.

5

C lare tried, she really tried, to like the school that Ronnie had once attended. But actually, she hated it. It seemed such a noisy place with buses and lorries rushing past outside and crowds of children pushing and shoving in the corridors. Worst of all, her class teacher was a young man who waved his arms and shouted at them if they didn't put up their hands the very moment he asked a question.

Some of the children made fun of the way she talked and called her 'La-di-da'. She'd never heard the expression before and didn't know what it meant but she knew it wasn't a very hopeful sign that she might make friends with these rowdy children. She wondered what Miss Slater would say if she saw them elbowing their way into the queue for the lavatory or the canteen. But Miss Slater was far away in Armagh and it looked as if she would never see her again.

Every time Clare thought about her home, her school and the places she knew, she felt tears trickling down her nose. Even when she was trying her hardest not to cry they just seemed to escape without her knowing and once they got going there didn't seem much she could do about them.

Once, a girl who sat near her, caught her wiping her eyes and called her a cry-baby and she thought how angry Mummy would be at someone being so unkind. But thinking about Mummy made her cry even more, so she ran away and hid in the lavatories until a teacher came calling her name and she had to come out.

Every day when Auntie Polly hugged her outside school, she

made up her mind to do better, but every afternoon as she was swept downstairs and out to the broad pavement where she waited for her to take her home, she knew she hadn't managed one little bit better than the previous day.

Apart from Auntie Polly, the only brightness in Clare's life was her youngest cousin, Ronnie. The very first thing he did the Saturday after he came back from camp was to take her into Belfast and walk her round all the booksellers in Smithfield Market looking for any of the books she had lost and any others she might want to read.

He had only two shillings to spend but whenever he found something she wanted he'd tell the man in charge that there was a missing page and that no one else would want to buy it. That way they ended up with a whole bag of books. What did the odd missing page matter if you knew the story anyway, Clare said, as they came back on the bus. But Ronnie only smiled.

Every evening, just before her bedtime, he'd come down from his room and say: 'How about tuning in?'

They worked their way up and down the dial, short wave, medium wave and long wave, laughing when all they got was a sudden ear-splitting blast of static. One night they picked up a radio cab in New York and another night an ambulance in Belfast.

Sometimes they listened to music, pop music from the Light Programme and Radio Luxemburg or classical music from the Third Programme. When they tuned in to the Third Programme, Ronnie liked to guess what the pieces of music were called, so often they had to wait quite a long time till the orchestra, or pianist, had finished playing so they could find out if he was right. Clare heard Schubert and Mozart and Strauss for the first time.

Classical music, as Ronnie called it, was very strange at first. To begin with, Clare found it very loud and often there were such sudden explosions of noise that she jumped violently. But as time passed she was less surprised at what the music did, she began to expect certain things to happen and then to feel very pleased with herself when they did. She always knew when the end of a piece was getting near because the musicians seemed to play faster and faster and get very agitated. Often they ended up with a huge noise and the moment they stopped the audience would clap furiously. That, she enjoyed. It really did sound as if they were having a wonderful time.

But some music was sad. One night there was something playing that was full of violins and before she knew what was happening there were tears dripping down her nose again and Ronnie had to lend her his hanky.

'What's wrong, Clare? Why does the music make you so sad?'

But even to Ronnie she couldn't explain that it was because of walking past the grey houses every day. The music just jumped over them and ran away, far, far away to somewhere wonderful. It was the thought of that somewhere wonderful and not being able to go there that made it more than she could bear.

The worst experience of all was the evening when they heard the announcer say that they were about to hear a piece by Shostakovitch. Ronnie wanted to try it because he'd never heard the name before, so while the audience coughed and the orchestra made funny noises, they settled down to listen. It was only moments later that Clare clamped her hands over her ears.

'Ronnie, Ronnie, turn it off. Please, turn it off,' she begged.

'Does it frighten you, Clare?' he asked, as he turned it off quite cheerfully.

'It's so cross, so angry. It's angry with everything. Even me,' she said, shuddering.

'You *are* a strange one, Clare Hamilton. When you're a big girl I'll take you to a symphony concert but I'll make sure it's not Shostakovitch.'

'Will we go to that funny building near your school?' she asked, her distress forgotten, her eyes shining.

'That "funny building", my dear little cousin, is the Royal Opera House. But I have to admit it is rather idiosyncratic in style.'

'Idiosyncratic? What does that mean?'

Ronnie laughed and reached for his dictionary, found the place and gave it to her.

'Idiosyncrasy. A peculiarity of temperament or mental constitution,' she read out cautiously. 'But you said "idiosyncratic", didn't you?'

'I did. I did indeed. You have very sharp ears. Most little girls of your age couldn't even manage to say a big word like that.'

'I love big words,' she replied giggling. 'Daddy says the bigger the jawbreaker the better I like it.'

'Right then, tomorrow night we'll have the odd jawbreaker. It pays to improve your word power, you know,' he said, as he put the dictionary carefully back in its place. 'But it's bedtime now. Pop down to Mum for your orange juice and I'll see if I can find any pins in your bed. If I can't find any I'll put some in myself,' he said, teasingly, as he opened the door to the tiny sewing room where she now slept.

Much to Clare's relief, school in Belfast ended the last week in June just as it did at home. July began with rainstorms and the thunder of Orange drums. Auntie Polly took her to Great-aunt Annie's house on the Lisburn Road on the Twelfth so she could watch the procession to the field at Finaghy.

Clare leaned out of the upstairs window and wondered how even the biggest field in all the world could accommodate the endless marching figures. She liked the bands, especially the silver flute bands and the lively tunes they played. She loved the plumes and kilts the bandsmen wore and the brilliant colours in the banners, the very white horses crossing very blue streams against vivid green fields on their way to the Boyne.

Best of all were the tall figures who twirled great silver sticks, throwing them up in the air and catching them one-handed as they fell. Her heart was in her mouth every time they sent them soaring above their heads. If they didn't catch it as it fell the whole procession would tramp over them as they bent to pick it up. Clare decided they must have been practising for a long time, for not one of them ever showed the slightest anxiety.

What she didn't like were the big drums. The Lambegs. Daddy had once explained that there was music in drums if you listened, but Clare couldn't bear to listen. When a group of perspiring men arrived below the window, their arms bare, their faces red with effort, she put her hands over her ears. If Ronnie had been there she might have said the drums were angry like that Shostakovitch man, but Ronnie was working in the newsagents for the summer months and today he would be very busy selling ice creams from the freezer, for very few shops were open.

'D'ye not like the drums, childdear?' said Great-aunt Annie kindly. 'Sure ah niver liked them meself an' me father usta make them, so I have no excuse. I growed up wi' them, but the only bit about them I liked was the paintin' o' the pictures. Oh aye, I'da had a go at that if anywan had let me. Shure they'll be past in a minit, niver worry yerself.'

Great-aunt Annie was Granda Scott's eldest sister, a tiny bent-over lady with wispy, grey hair and a thin, high-pitched voice. She made them both very welcome and told Clare the story about Auntie Polly meeting Uncle Jimmy and asking him to come for his tea the very next day. Annie hadn't minded, but her husband had been shocked. He insisted that when he had started 'walking out' it was a year or more before you thought of asking someone to come home to tea.

'Shure yer Uncle Thomas was always very particular, God rest his soul. Ye know he useta swear that the only cocoa he could drink was Bournville and that anything else diden' agree wi' him. That was all very well, but wi' the war on you was lucky to get what you coud lay yer hans on. So what I useta do was always keep an empty tin of Bournville and whatever cocoa I could get, I'd put in it.' She paused. 'An' ye know, childdear, he niver knew to the difference.'

She laughed her thin little laugh and Clare wondered if when you were very old your voice wore out like your eyes and your hair and your teeth. Her great-aunt didn't seem to mind that her voice was funny and her legs were stiff and her hands had funny-looking bumps on them, not like Granny Scott, who seemed to mind everything. Mummy said it was a pity to be such a complainer but everyone's temperament was different and her mother had always complained, even when she was a young woman and was no worse off than any of the other mill girls, who had been breathing tow for years and all had trouble with their chests.

'Och, it's a thousand pities about your Mummy and Daddy, childdear. Your poor Granda is in a bad way about her,' Annie began, when the three of them came downstairs to make a cup of tea.

Clare shivered and wished the kettle would hurry up and boil for the kitchen was chilly and dim. Only a feeble north light penetrated the tall, dirty window that looked out over the jawbox into a yard bounded by a high brick wall with fragments of glass on top. The gas pressure was low, so the kettle was sulking, a few spilt drips of water hissed as they fell on the wavering blue flames. Clare perched on a kitchen chair out of the way, looked around her and wondered how Auntie Annie ever got anything down from the top of the huge cupboards that climbed up the walls, or how she managed with her thin arms to pull the rope for the clothes airer that hung suspended over the sink. Everything in the kitchen was either dark or greasy and there was a smell of drains mixed with the odour of unburnt gas. Clare longed to go back upstairs into the sunlight.

'He actually wrote me a letter, Polly, and ye know yer father's no scholar, saying how he missed his wee Ellie,' she went on. 'An' now, of course, he has this other trouble. It's looking very bad with yer mother. Have ye heard anything more recent-like than me?'

At that point Clare was despatched upstairs with the tray and cups while Polly made the tea, but the sound of Aunt Annie's voice was surprisingly penetrating. As Clare put the tray down, her thin, piping tone echoed in the narrow, uncarpeted stair-well.

'Am afraid, Polly, if she gets the pneumonia again with the state of her poor lungs, we can't hope for much.'

Clare rattled the cups as she put them on their saucers for she knew she hadn't been meant to hear what they said. But she had heard. Suddenly, as if a great dark cloud had rolled away, she knew she would be able to go home. When Granny Scott died she would go and look after Granda just like Heidi had done. She would pick flowers in the orchard and in the old overgrown garden that had once been her great-grandmother's, she would feed the hens and brush the old black spaniel and hold the reins of the big horses when they came to be shod. And she would cycle to school in Armagh and be back in Miss Slater's class again. When she sat beside Margaret Beggs again she would tell her all about the awful school in Belfast.

When Polly and Annie came back upstairs they were sur-prised to see Clare leaning out of the window, smiling to herself, as if enjoying the lively music, when, in fact, the band that was passing on the road below was having a rest, with only one of its kilted and beribboned members playing a single note on a side drum to keep the brothers of their lodge in step.

If it hadn't been for the thought that she would be going home again one day, July would have been an even worse time for Clare. The weather broke again after the Twelfth and day after day was wet and sodden. Ronnie had found a holiday job at the Tudor Stores. It wasn't far away and Auntie Polly let her go and do messages for her there, but the hours were long. Often Ronnie didn't get home till almost bedtime. She would look forward all day to seeing him and then the time they had went so quickly.

Auntie Polly had two wedding dresses to finish for the second Saturday in August and they were not going well. The awk-wardly shaped sisters arrived for fittings at regular intervals, leaving Auntie Polly anxious and agitated. At night, the dresses hung from the picture rail over Clare's bed. As the linings went in to support the heavy brocade of the crinoline skirts, they grew larger each day, taking up more and more of the space in the small room. When she woke in the night, Clare had to remind herself not to be frightened of the ghostly shapes that loomed over her.

When the rain stopped and the sun came out, Clare had the idea of digging the garden and planting some seeds. As soon as Uncle Jimmy had finished helping his neighbour to rewire his house she'd ask his advice about where to start. She was sure that if she did the digging he would be happy to get some plants from his friends' gardens like her father used to do. But the lull in the wet weather was only temporary. Before the rewiring job was finished she could see water lying in all the hollows between what had once been Uncle Jimmy's potato rigs. There was nothing else to do except go back to her reading, lying on the sitting room floor, ready to jump up and answer the phone should it ring or slip her book neatly under the sofa if someone should arrive early for a fitting.

When she ran out of library books and had to wait till someone could take her down on the bus to get some more, she read whatever she could lay her hands on. Uncle Jimmy's few books were all about biplanes and monoplanes and had been written before the war. Clare marvelled at the pictures of the flimsy craft that had first flown across the Atlantic, so different from the deep-bellied Sunderlands Uncle Jimmy had worked on at Shorts and the famous Flying Fortresses he so admired.

She finished Uncle Jimmy's handful of books and started on Eddie's copies of *Picturegoer*. She was amazed to find that film-stars kept getting married and divorced. Some of them had had as many as seven husbands. The idea struck her as very confusing. She wondered how they managed when they all lived in the same place in Hollywood, starred in the same pictures and appeared to go to the same parties.

But Eddie's magazines came in handy when Ronnie took her

to see *The Wizard of Oz* on his Saturday afternoon off. She thought Judy Garland was so marvellous that she looked up the address of her fan club in England and wrote her a letter asking nicely if she could have a signed photograph. She sent it off with a stamped addressed envelope and watched every post for it to arrive. She was so disappointed when it never came. She felt particularly upset as it had needed two tuppenny-halfpenny stamps which Ronnie had bought for her.

When there was nothing else to be found, Clare read the women's magazines that one or two of the nicer of the customers brought for Auntie Polly. Some of the stories were quite interesting and she liked the descriptions of rocky coastlines and heather-covered slopes and dimpled fields with streams babbling along. The stories always seemed to happen in quaint little villages by the sea, or overlooking the lough, or in a hollow in the hills where the heroine had grown up. Now she was famous but unhappy, or rich but unhappy and had come back to be by herself. Usually she fell in love with her childhood sweetheart who was a farmer, or a postman, or a struggling artist, but whatever he was, it always ended happily. Clare did wonder why so many of these pretty, young women hadn't found a boyfriend in the city where they lived, as there were bound to be far more young men there than in their own village, where there only ever appeared to be the one.

Ronnie teased her one evening when he arrived back from work and found her sitting at his table reading his mum's magazines.

'How about this, Clare,' he began, opening the newspaper he had brought home with him and turning to the Beauty for You page. 'Doris Gibb says that "despite the shortages of beauty products in the shops you can still look your best by using simple remedies and a little ingenuity. Eggs are a wonderful asset in the beauty battle." Do you hear that, Clare? Pin your ears back. "For a reviving and stimulating face pack take the whites of two eggs, whisk briskly and cover the face lightly avoiding the eyes. Leave in place for thirty minutes."'

Ronnie raised his face from the newspaper, fluttered his long, dark eyelashes at her and collapsed into helpless laughter.

'How about it, Clare? Shall I whisk for you?'

'I'd rather have my egg boiled. With toast,' Clare replied with a perfectly straight face.

'Yes, I thought you might. You're distinctly weak on vanity. Shall we have a jawbreaker from V tonight? How about vainglorious, verisimilitude, versification? Take your pick, as the gaffer said to the navvy.'

'What's a gaffer?'

But before Ronnie could reply, the phone rang loudly, but not loudly enough to be heard over *ITMA*, which he knew his Mum and Dad were listening to in the living room.

'Hang on a minute, Clare. I'd better answer that,' he said, crossing the room in two of his long strides.

It might only be a customer – some of them did ring in the evening, which annoyed Auntie Polly, but something told Clare that it wasn't. It was a strange feeling she got sometimes, as if she knew something important was going to happen next, except that she didn't know what it would be.

She leaned over the banisters and saw that Ronnie was listening hard, his body very still, quite unlike the way he usually stood when he was answering the phone. She'd watched him often, seen him move from one foot to the other, scratch his back with his free hand or make faces at himself in the mirror that hung above the telephone table.

'Yes, yes. I'll get her right away.'

Clare waited and listened as Auntie Polly emerged from the living room.

'It's being so cheerful as keeps me going.'

Clare recognised the familiar complaining tone of Mona Lot. Daddy so enjoyed Mona Lot and he could imitate her perfectly. Every Saturday at lunchtime he would listen to the repeat of his favourite programme even if he'd heard it at its usual time. 'Some of the jokes are so quick, you can't catch them the first time,' he would say.

There was a burst of laughter from the audience, cut short as Uncle Jimmy managed to pull himself to his feet and turn the knob on the wireless.

'Is that you, Bob? And you're in Armagh?'

If it was Uncle Bob then it was bad news, for Uncle Bob and his wife seldom visited either Polly and Jimmy or his old home at Salter's Grange. Mummy said Bob was the best at all but his wife was a social climber. She hadn't much time for Bob's family but Bob was good to his parents in his own way. A phonecall could mean only one thing and it was only moments before Clare heard what she had been half expecting from the moment the phone rang.

'What did the doctor say? Daddy always lets me know when the chest starts up. He hadn't sent me any word.'

Ronnie had slipped back upstairs and now sat down beside her on the top step. He put his arm round her.

'Poor old Granny,' he whispered. 'Looks like her ticker packed up.'

They listened together as Polly asked about the details of the funeral. Clare wondered if she should be crying, but she didn't feel at all like crying. Perhaps, after all, she hadn't much liked her Granny Scott. Not that she knew her very well. Whenever they went to see her she never talked to her, she always spent the time complaining to Mummy about her legs and her chest and someone called Jinny who was nothing but a sluter but who could close her hand on her money as quick as the next one.

Auntie Polly wasn't crying either as she put the phone down and when Uncle Jimmy came and put his arm round her she just said, 'Up early tomorrow, Jimmy dear. I'll have to go up and give Bob a hand before the funeral. Do you think one of your shirts would fit my father? He might not have a clean one to his name.'

Clare missed her aunt badly while she was away in Armagh at Granny's funeral, but she missed her even more when she arrived back tired and anxious and shut herself up in her room

69

every day with the wedding dresses not yet finished and the bridesmaids' dresses not even begun. Even at meal times, when she came down and cooked for the family, she was silent and unapproachable, not her normal self at all.

Clare waited and watched. Whatever was upsetting Auntie Polly would make it more difficult for her to talk about her plan. She would have to be good and wait till Auntie Polly felt better. Perhaps it was just the wretched wedding dresses. She'd be very glad herself to see them gone.

She found the days passed very slowly. Nothing interesting ever happened, unless you could count customers arriving at the door, or phoning to see when they could come. Now that she answered the door and the phone some of the customers knew her name. Auntie Polly said that was something at least. While they were busy being nice to Clare they forgot to be as awkward as possible with her.

One evening, something unusual did happen. Uncle Jimmy arrived back from helping his neighbour much later than usual. Clare knew her aunt was cross from the way she walked and the way her mouth looked smaller, but Auntie Polly said nothing and when Uncle Jimmy handed Clare a paper bag she watched carefully.

'I came across that on me way home. D'ye think it woud be any use to ye?' he said in a most off-hand manner.

Even Eddie looked up from his ham salad to see what was going on.

'Uncle Jimmy!' Clare exclaimed, as she opened the bag and drew out a teddy bear, a brand-new teddy bear with bright, shiny eyes and golden brown fur.

She went and put her arms round him, meaning to give him a kiss and say a proper thank you. She promptly burst into tears. She cried as if her heart would break and was still crying until Ronnie said: 'Clare, if you don't stop crying, that poor bear will get mildew on his fur. Bears don't like water.'

Then she laughed and said she was sorry she was being silly. Auntie Polly told her she wasn't to mind one bit, that she'd been such a good girl and such a help with the phone and the door, but she did wonder where Uncle Jimmy had found such a lovely bear and him so new too.

But Jimmy just smiled and said nothing.

Things seemed easier after Edward James Bear came to stay. He would sit on the sofa all through the morning and listen to love stories from *The People's Friend*, the latest scandals in Hollywood, or advice on how to maintain your bicycle in peak condition. He was always good company and managed to look interested in whatever she read to him, as she waited, day after day, till the wretched wedding dresses were finally fitted, twitched and tweaked and pinned into place on the two large sisters who had planned a double wedding with the rest of their sisters as bridesmaids.

It was then that events took another unexpected turn. One morning a letter from Canada dropped through the letterbox and lay, a bright blue rectangle decorated with lots of pretty stamps, on the worn bit of the red hall carpet just by the front door. Auntie Polly scooped it up, carried it off to her workroom and said not a word about it. Clare was surprised, for Polly loved getting news from family or friends and always talked about it excitedly at the first possible opportunity.

It was three days later, on another sodden August day, when Polly pushed open the sitting room door and sat down on the sofa beside Edward James Bear. She looked down at Clare, leaning on her elbows on the hearth rug, reading.

'Do you still miss the field you and William used to play in, Clare? And all the walks Mummy used to take you?'

Clare nodded silently. Sometimes when she thought about William and wondered how he was getting on with Granny and Granda Hamilton she thought she wouldn't even mind having to look after him if only she could go back home.

'Uncle Jimmy says he thinks you'd be happier somewhere with gardens and trees. D'ye think he is right?'

'Oh, yes,' said Clare enthusiastically.

71

She could hardly believe it. Uncle Jimmy must have persuaded Auntie Polly that going to live with Granda Scott was the right thing for her after all. She'd talked to Uncle Jimmy about it several times but he hadn't actually said anything either way. And, of course, she'd said nothing at all to Auntie Polly herself. She was still waiting till the dresses were gone.

'D'ye mind when I told you about Canada and the snow and the sleigh rides?' Polly went on.

'And the jingle bells,' Clare added.

'Yes, of course,' Polly agreed. 'But ye know Canada is lovely in springtime too and the summers are lovely and warm. The sky's blue and people go to the shore and out in boats and sunbathe in the parks. Not like grey old Belfast,' she went on, nodding out through the steamed up windows at the rain-sodden houses across the road.

Clare had a funny feeling, funny peculiar, not funny ha-ha, that Auntie Polly was going to say something and she wasn't going to like it.

'Clare, Uncle Jimmy has the offer of a job back in Toronto. It's a nice job with no standin' and no heavy work. An old friend of his has made a lot of money an' he needs someone to supervise some of his property, someone he can trust to keep an eye on things. There'd be a nice little apartment and you'd have your own room with a view out over the park. I think you'd like it.'

'But what about Davy and Eddie and Ronnie?' she cried, so shocked at the whole idea that she hadn't registered her own place in the scheme of things.

'Sure Davy's getting married. He's found a furnished flat and Eddie's goin' to live with them till they save up the deposit for a house. Ronnie wants to stay here and go to Queen's and they'll find him a place in one of these student houses. If things go well he'll be able to come out and see us in a year or two, in the summer holidays. You'd like that wouldn't you?' she said encouragingly.

'I always like seeing Ronnie,' she agreed. 'He's my favouritest

72

cousin and I have an awful lot of cousins, even if some of them I've never even seen.'

'So you'd come with us,' said Polly gratefully, as she settled back on the settee.

Clare shook her head.

'No?' said Polly, sitting upright again.

'No,' repeated Clare calmly. 'No, I can't come with you. Someone has to look after Granda Scott now that Granny's dead. Men aren't very good on their own, Mummy says. So I'll look after him and you can take care of Uncle Jimmy,' she went on, her voice wavering slightly. 'Do you think you could come home sometimes and see us? I shall miss you very much. Both of you.'

Polly didn't know whether to laugh or cry. The whole idea was ridiculous, of course, but the way the child's mind worked never ceased to amaze her. This was the last thing she had expected.

'You were quite right about the orphanage, Auntie Polly. You do need people who know all about you. Granda Scott knows such a lot about Mummy and Daddy. Maybe he'll tell me stories like Aunt Annie did. D'you think he will?' she enquired earnestly.

It was fortunate for Polly that the doorbell chimed at that moment for she had not the remotest idea what to say. Even when she had sewed for several hours in the quiet of her room and turned it over and over in her mind she was no further on. The only thing she was clear about was that she and Jimmy had to go back to Canada. There was no life for him here with jobs short and him with no qualifications for a desk job. Managing Don's property was a great opportunity. Even were the pay not as generous as it was, there was the question of self-respect. Jimmy wasn't an idler, but when he got depressed he had no heart for anything.

'But what about wee Clare?' she asked him, that evening, after Ronnie had taken her upstairs to teach her how to play Monopoly.

'Does she not want to come with us?'

'She says she wants to go and look after her Granda Scott,' replied Polly, shaking her head.

'Well, why not, if that's what the wee lassie wants? Sure she's no town child, she's always talkin' about fields and trees. If you listen to her talkin' to the teddy bear it's all about picnics down by the river or up on the hill. That's what's in her mind all the time.'

Polly had to admit she was surprised. She'd not expected Jimmy to pay much attention to what Clare said, but now he'd seen something she'd missed completely.

'Ach, Jimmy, the forge house is no place for a child. To tell you the truth I was ashamed at the cut of it after the funeral. It's been that neglected since Mammy was poorly and it's worse since Ellie went. She did what she could when she coud get out there without the wee ones. An' sure my father can only use the griddle and make tea. That's about the height of it,' she ended, throwing out her hands in a gesture of despair.

Jimmy nodded sympathetically.

'Aye, that's all very well, Polly, but don't ferget when I was a wee lad, tea and bread was about all we got, an' it did us no harm. Sure she'd have a school dinner,' he added quietly.

'An' who'll pay for the school dinners, an' the bus fares, an' her clothes? My father's gettin' on. By the look of things roun' the house there can't be much money comin' in except his pension. There isn't even the family allowance for Clare. It's only wee William gets that, more's the pity, for the Hamiltons are comfortable enough now with all the family workin'.'

She stopped, aware that Jimmy was deep in thought.

'Are ye really seriously suggestin' we should just let her go?' she asked, her voice full of anxiety.

'We should give it a try.'

'How long for?'

He scratched his head. 'She'll know very quick if she's got it wrong. D'ye remember how she cried that first mornin' here? She was right that time. She's done her best, aye, and so have you, but the city isn't the place for her. Take her up to yer father an' give her a week or two. If she doesn't like it, maybe it'll settle her for Canada. We can't make a move here for a month or more at any rate, till we sell the house. We can only give it a try.'

6

On a beautiful Saturday afternoon, the August sun warm, the sky a fading blue, Jack Hamilton collected Polly McGillvray and wee Clare from Armagh station and drove them the two miles to Robert Scott's at Salter's Grange.

Clare was ecstatic. She had never driven out the Loughgall Road before and being used to the more leisurely pace of walking she tripped over herself as she told her Uncle Jack who all the houses and farms belonged to. It seemed no time at all before they pulled up the short hill and turned left into the bumpy lane that led to the low, white forge with its high-pitched, dark-felted roof.

'Not too far, Jack dear. You might pick up a nail in your tyre. Down here will do nicely,' Polly warned, remembering the slow puncture her brother Bob had discovered after the funeral.

Clare had forgotten how to work the handle of the car door, so Uncle Jack had to come and open it for her. She stuck out one foot, clutched Granny Hamilton's shopping bag in one hand and picked up Edward James Bear with the other.

From the forge, she heard the ring of metal on the anvil. No wonder Granda hadn't heard the car, he was making such a noise. Like a big bell tolling, slowly and regularly with a funny little tap dance of the anvil in between.

She swivelled on her bottom and stood up, bag in one hand, Bear in the other, pushed the door closed with her bottom and began to make her way across to the grown-ups where they stood looking in through the dark doorway of the forge. As she stepped carefully over the scattered bits of metal and wove a path between pieces of machinery, she saw, over on her right, by the hedge, dotted through the rusting harrows and the reaping machines that needed new blades, a whole crowd of dog daisies. They swayed in the slight afternoon breeze, nodding their dazzling white heads, the sun catching their bright, golden eyes.

'Look, Edward James Bear,' she said quietly. 'Just you look over there. Daisies. Aren't they beautiful? You are going to be so happy in your new home.'

Polly would have liked to stay with Clare at the house beyond the forge for a couple of days or more. She reckoned that would give Clare a chance to settle in and herself a bit of time to size up how her father was going to cope. There was no doubt about how much the house needed her attention. It had been looking neglected even before her mother's recent illnesses and now, without Ellie's visits to keep a check on things, it looked as if Jinny, who came on Saturdays to do a weekly clean, was doing as little as possible.

But Polly could stay only one night. It was not just the wedding dresses that preyed on her mind, there were all the arrangements for going back to Canada as well, with or without Clare. Preoccupied as she was, she still put in a hard day's work on the one day she did have. She cleaned out cupboards, boiled up stained and greasy drying cloths and towels, changed both the beds, cleaned the front-facing windows and showed Clare how to wash and rinse her own vest, knickers and socks.

'You can leave them to dry on the elderberry bush round the side of the house, like Mummy and I always did, but if it's wet there's nothing for it but the plate rack above the stove.'

When Polly looked at the rack she found it was thick with grease from Granda's frying and liberally speckled with flecks of soot.

She brought a basin of hot water and a bar of Sunlight and started rubbing vigorously.

'When the wind blows back down the chimney on bad days

ye get the soot on top o' the grease, so mind ye wipe it well before ye put yer clean things on it,' she warned her.

Clare did her best to help. Before Aunt Polly had used up all the hot water from the stove's own tank Clare had filled kettles and saucepans to boil on top of the stove. She fetched water for rinsing from the rainwater barrel and held on tight to one end of each wet sheet while Polly twisted to get the water out.

As Polly worked, she explained important things like making sure there was torn up newspaper in the privy in the orchard when you needed to go there and how it was all right just to nip out behind a bush for a wee-wee but not for anything else. On really wet nights you could use the chamber pot at bed-time but you must be sure to empty it first thing next morning and rinse it out with water from the rainwater barrel.

'Don't on any account put the chamber in the barrel to rinse it. Use the old cracked mug to bale the water out into the pot. Rinse it round and then throw the rinsing water over the flowerbed,' she said as she began to wring out the towels she had just washed. 'Away and see if that old mug is still there in the flowerbed. If it isn't we may find something else,' she said wiping her forehead with her sleeve, as she tipped a saucepan full of steaming tea towels into the metal basin on the scrubbed wooden table under the window.

The old mug, cracked and chipped, with the almost invisible words 'A Present from Belfast' was still there, exactly where Polly expected it to be, inside the stone surround of the flowerbed. It sat in a small depression between the hooped wooden water barrel and a great clump of purple aquilegia that was just beginning to drop its petals on the well-trodden path into the orchard.

'The better the day, the better the deed,' said Polly as they gathered up all the damp sheets and towels and followed the path along the front of the house round the gable and into the orchard. There on an area of shorter grass beneath the tiny back windows of the house they spread everything out in the sunshine.

'That's what your Granny woud call "the gypsies' washin' "','
she said laughing, as she straightened up. 'An' rite cross she'd
be too if there wasn't enough room on the clothes line or if it'd
blown down. "Dacent people hang out their clothes," she useta
say, "'tis oney gypsies lays them on bushes or the groun'." '

'But I can be a gypsy with my knickers and vest,' said Clare,
cheerfully.

'Ye can. But mind, niver put washin' out on a Sunday where
anyone can see it.'

'Yes, I'll mind,' said Clare agreeably.

'No, you'll not,' said Polly quickly. 'You'll *remember*. Just
because I drop back into a country way of speakin' you're not
to do the same. Your mother taught you to speak properly.
Now don't you let her down. It's one thing talkin' to your
Granda, but when you go back to school you remember your
"ings".'

'But I haven't got any rings,' said Clare, perplexed.

'I didn't say "rings",' Polly laughed. 'I said "ings". Like
walking, talking, running. Not walkin', talkin,' and runnin','
she said cheerfully. 'The pot callin' the kettle black, that is, me
tellin' you to mind your "ings". But just remember, won't you?'

It was only hours later when she was sitting in the train to
Belfast that Polly realised what she'd said. School was still
three weeks away and the plan was that she would come back
in a fortnight to see whether or not Clare could stay. Polly
smiled to herself. She knew Clare had her mind made up. She
was a great wee lassie for making up her mind about things.
That was all very well, but what about Clare's Granda? He'd
have something to say about taking on a wee girl and him with
no idea at all about children or about housekeeping. The more
she thought about the whole idea, the more nonsensical it
seemed.

'Are you sure you'll be all right, lovey?' Polly asked, for at
least the fourth time, as they washed up the tea things and
kept an eye through the front window for Uncle Jack's car. He

was coming over from Richhill to take Polly to that same evening train she and Clare had travelled on nearly six weeks earlier.

'Yes, I'll be fine.'

Polly hugged her and thought what a little scrap of a child she was to be left alone with an old blacksmith. Not that her father wasn't a good, kind man but he'd never had the first idea about children. Children were women's work . He must have loved his own children to have worked so very hard to provide for them, but he'd never found any way of showing it. He was never close to them. Indeed, looking back to her girlhood, Polly sometimes thought he looked quite bewildered when he cast his eyes round his own kitchen at the crowd of young people who laughed and joked with each other as they sat at the table, morning or evening.

'Now, Daddy, if the wee one is too much for you, get Margaret Robinson or one of the girls to ring me an' I'll come up,' she said as she walked down the path with him. 'She's a good wee thing but ye might find it too much. Don't be afraid te say. An' if I don't hear, I'll be up in a fortnite to see how ye are. Davy might get the loan of a car, t'woud be awful handy, though Jack Hamilton has been more than kind fetchin' and carryin' us.'

'Aye, he's a good sort, Jack. Like the father. Gran' people the Hamiltons,' he said quietly, as he limped along beside her.

Clare was skipping down the path ahead of them, already beyond the most recent pair of propped up gates and a reaper waiting to be mended. She hopped up and down as Jack got out of his car.

'I've found the place my great-granny had her garden, Uncle Jack, and I'm going to dig it all up and plant flowers. You can come and see it when I've finished if you like.'

'I will indeed, Clare,' he said warmly. 'Have you any plants for it yet?'

'No. I thought I'd better get it ready first so they'd have somewhere to go. Do you think Granny Hamilton could put a

80

few more of her bits in tin cans for me? They take a while to grow, don't they?'

'Aye, but some's faster than others. Yer a bit late this year for flowers, but we could maybe put in the odd wee bush. I'll see what I can do,' he promised, as he turned to greet Polly and her father.

'I see ye have a wee gardener here,' Jack said looking up at the older man.

Robert nodded and raised his eyes heavenward. 'It wouden' surprise me. Sure all the weemen in this family has green fingers an' sure whativer I woud put me han' to, it dies,' he laughed wryly.

After Auntie Polly had hugged and kissed her, Clare climbed up on the bank by the furthest end of the forge and waved to the car as it turned out of the lane and moved slowly down the hill. Then she jumped down and ran after Granda Scott as he made his way back to the house.

'Granda, why do you have a limp?' she asked as he pushed open the door into the big, dark kitchen.

He looked down at her, slightly startled, thought for a moment and replied: 'Ach, an oul' horse kicked me, years ago.'

'Oh dear. Did it hurt badly?'

'Aye, it did. It gave me gip for months an' then it just stopped. But I've had a hippety-clinch ever since.'

Clare was about to ask what that was, when she saw him look towards the door of the sitting room, beyond which lay his bedroom.

'If I take haf an hour on the bed, will ye be all right?' he asked anxiously.

'Yes, of course,' she assured him. 'Anyway, I have the washing to pick up and fold. Auntie Polly said to be sure and do it before the sun dropped too far and the dew fell.'

'Aye, that's right,' he said hastily.

But the way he said it Clare wondered if he really did know about washing and how important it was to have it bone dry and properly aired.

*   *   *

It was the sunshine that woke Clare next morning. Through the fluttering foliage of the climbing rose that had grown far beyond the wrought iron arch framing the front door and now clothed the whole length of the long, low dwelling, a beam of light fell on her pillow, flickered and settled on her pale skin and dark curls. She felt its touch on her eyelids, opened them promptly and looked around her.

She was here. Here, in the bed Mummy had shared with Auntie Polly and sometimes when they were still little with Auntie Mary as well. A big bed with a horsehair mattress. She had thought it rather hard and lumpy when she climbed up into it the first night, but it was all right when you got used to it. She now lay looking up at the ceiling. Its wooden boards had been painted white but she thought it must have been a long time ago for the distemper was flaking. Where tiny snowflakes of paint had already fallen, the previous layer of much-less-white distemper was revealed underneath. As her eyes moved round the whole ceiling above her, she found in different places little suspended white flakes spinning in the draught coming round the door. What could possibly have made the invisible threads on which they spun?

She counted the boards that made up the ceiling. There were twenty-nine and a half by the door but only twenty-nine above the sash window that was set into the thick plastered walls. Some bits of wall were very thick indeed. Just behind the door into the bedroom there was a huge bulge that ran halfway up the wall. The windowsills were nearly two feet deep.

'That's why it's only twenty-nine over there,' she said quietly to herself, when she worked out that the walls were not even. She felt so pleased that she had solved the puzzle.

One day, she thought, when I'm old, I shall remember lying here in this bed counting the boards in this ceiling. And I shall remember what it's like being nine years old. And I promise, absolutely, Brownie's honour, if ever any child I know asks me what it was like when I was a child, I shall tell them all about it and not just say that I can't remember, the way so many grown-ups do.

She wondered if she should get up. Beside the bed was a washstand with a del basin and a big jug. The jug was only half full of water because otherwise it was so heavy she couldn't lift it. She knew the water would feel very cold because she was lovely and warm, so she snuggled down further under the eiderdown and continued to study her new bedroom.

Across the small linoleum-covered space by the bed stood a large dressing chest, a solid piece of furniture with three big drawers and a dark-starred mirror whose screws had worked loose so that it now tilted either too much or not enough. All the drawers had been empty and had smelt strongly of moth-balls when Auntie Polly had unpacked Granny Hamilton's shopping bag and started putting her clothes away.

There was another smaller chest of drawers under the window. They didn't need any more drawers to put her things in because she didn't have very many things, but Clare pulled open the drawers anyway, just out of curiosity. But it was Auntie Polly who got a surprise. She thought one of the lower drawers was full of sheets and that the other one had a spare bedspread and some material for new curtains she had brought up but hadn't had time to make. But all the drawers were empty. Completely empty, but for an old newspaper lining one of them.

'Oh, look Auntie Polly,' she cried pouncing upon it. 'What lovely horses, Granda will love these.'

She spread out the faded copy of the *Belfast Telegraph* on the bed and began to read: 'Three in hand pull their weight in an Ulster harvest field. Eight months ago Ulster farmers heard and answered the "Grow more Food" call. Today a happier note rings out. It is "Reap for Victory". Never before has the autumn beauty of the countryside been so enriched by fields of golden grain. This war harvest promises to be the best in the history of the Province.'

Auntie Polly finished putting the clothes away and sat down

on the edge of the bed. Clare looked up at her, saw how tired she looked and stopped reading.

'Go on,' said Polly. 'Read me a bit more.'

'There may be dark days ahead, times perhaps in which hearts will be heavy, but thanks to the farmers who rallied so well to the "dig" campaign, we shall at any rate have full larders this winter.'

'That must be September 1940,' said Polly abruptly.

'Oh you are clever, Auntie Polly. Look, it's a bit torn but if I hold it together you can see the date: 2, September 1940 – just what you said.'

'It is, it is indeed. I remember it all right. I put that paper there when I did out these drawers. That was the last time this poor old house had a spring clean, albeit it was almost autumn. I left Davy and Eddie with their Granny McGillvray and brought Ronnie up with me. Granny Scott wasn't very well so I spent a whole week going over the place. How long is that ago?'

'Six years, all but three weeks,' replied Clare quickly.

'Long time, Clare, and a lot has happened,' she said sadly. 'The war was far worse than anybody ever thought it would be, even here in the country. You'll understand better when you're older. Often if you knew how bad somethin' was goin' to be you couldn't cope with it atall, but if you take it as it comes you get by. It's only afterwards you wondered how you managed.'

'Ronnie told me about the barrage balloons. He said he was so frightened,' Clare said quietly.

'He was indeed. We were all frightened, Clare, but the grown-ups pretended they weren't to try to help the children. I think maybe Ronnie knew how bad things were. Davy and Eddie never seemed to realise that we might all be dead by mornin'.'

'Did lots of people die?'

'Oh yes, lots and lots of people, not just here but all over the world. So many no one will ever be able to count them all.'

'And children too, and babies?'

'Yes, lots of children and babies too.'

Clare thought she had never seen Auntie Polly looking so sad, even when she talked about Mummy and Daddy.

'Do you think anybody will remember them all, Auntie Polly?'

Polly looked surprised. She stood up and with a visible effort collected herself.

'Yes, Clare, some people will. People like you and Ronnie. Now put that picture of the horses out o' the way in the window to show to Granda and let's get on with our work. If we sit here talkin' we'll never be straight by teatime.'

On the wall beside the door leading into 'the boys' room' was an illustrated text. The colours were rather blotchy and faded but the words were still clear: 'The coneys are but a feeble folk yet they build their houses in the rock.' Coneys meant rabbits, that she knew, but rabbits didn't build in rocks. Surely everybody knew that they had burrows in sandy places, like the Whinny Hills where she'd been for a picnic when she went to Brownies.

She had forgotten about Brownies. It seemed a long time ago now. Her dress and tie and hat would all have been burnt with the rest of her clothes. Gnomes, Elves, Dwarfs and Leprechauns. Those were four groups they had and each one lived in a corner of the big, bare hall where they met. She had been a gnome.

Brown Owl had a campfire that she kept in a big cupboard, a pretend campfire for when they met in the hall. But it did have real sticks and bits of red paper that looked like flames when she put her torch inside it and switched on. Round the campfire they sang songs and listened to a story and then they all promised 'to be faithful to God and the King, to help other people every day, especially those at home. Lah. Lah. Lah.' It was ages before she found out that 'Lah, Lah, Lah' meant 'Lend a hand'.

Well, she could do lots of good deeds every day now for Granda Scott certainly needed someone to help him. Auntie Polly said she thought he never washed up, that he just used the same dishes all week and left them piled up on the wooden table for Jinny to do on a Saturday morning. That was just like one of the neighbours in *Anne of Green Gables*. Mr Harrison used to wash the dishes on Sundays in the water barrel until Anne came to help him and taught him how to do things properly.

From the kitchen, Clare heard the sound of the stove being raked and the rings being pulled back. Moments later, smoke swirled past outside her window, flowing upwards in the beam of sunlight that still threw a bright patch on her pillow. Granda must be lighting the stove.

She climbed out of bed, shivered as her feet touched the cold lino and pulled the small rag rug over to the washstand with her toe. She washed very quickly but did all the bits that Mummy had always done and then put her clothes on as fast as she could. She was just combing her hair, crouched down on the floor so that she could see into the mirror which had now tipped forward, when she smelt burning.

'Clare, are ye up? The breakfast's ready.'

She heard him unlatch the heavy front door which would stand open all day except in the very worst weather or when he went into Armagh on the bus to do his shopping.

'I'm here,' she said, blinking in the dazzling light of the hallway.

She followed him back into the big kitchen. Although great beams of light poured through the newly cleaned, south-facing window and lit up the scrubbed table where all the work of the house went on, its brilliant rays were soon defeated by the smoke-blackened ceiling and the mud-tramped stone floor. Little light penetrated to the further corners of the room, which were made darker still by a heavy, brown-varnished wallpaper covering the lower part of the walls and the darkened wood of the furniture which stood against them.

Clare blinked, confused by the sudden dimness. She was enveloped in wisps of blue smoke that had risen from the frying pan and now oscillated in the movement of air as she closed the door behind her.

'There's no sweet milk,' he said abruptly, as he sat down in his chair, dropped his cap on the fender and poured the last few drops from the jug into his half-pint mug of tea.

'I don't drink milk, Granda.'

Clare sat down at the oilcloth-covered table that stood under the tiny back window of the cottage. Beyond the shorter grass where she and Polly had spread out the washing, the morning light glanced off apple trees that were now weighed down with ripening fruit. Already she could hear the hum of bees happily at work on the windfalls surrounding each laden tree.

On a plate in front of her was some fried soda bread, burnt round the edges and bone dry in the middle. She picked up the first piece and munched steadily.

'What do ye drink?' he asked, glancing at her in amazement, the whites of his eyes in his permanently grimy face making him look even more startled than usual.

'Water mostly,' she replied, judging that there would be no orange juice in a house with no children.

'It's in the enamel bucket in the press.'

She slid down off her chair and crossed to the other end of the kitchen where the tall press ran up to the low ceiling to the left of the scrubbed wooden table. The enamel bucket was nearly empty but she managed to bale out a cupful of water and carry it back to the table.

'Whit'll ye do all day?' he asked, as he finished his fried bread and took a long drink of dark brown tea from his mug.

'I think I shall go exploring first,' she began, 'then I'll start digging the garden and then I want to try out the paint-box Ronnie gave me,' she continued.

It occurred to her that perhaps she should begin with the housework but she wasn't quite sure about what she should do, except, of course, the breakfast dishes.

'Is there anything I can do to help, Granda, any jobs you want doing? I can sew quite nicely if you have any tears or holes in your clothes.'

'Ach, nat atall,' he replied, picking up his cap. 'Away and play yerself,' he added as he headed for the forge.

Clare collected up the cups and plates and took the tin basin from under the wooden table. It really was very dirty under there but Auntie Polly had said that that was Jinny's job and she must have had to leave it so she could do other things to help Granny. Clare decided she must make friends with Jinny when she came and then she could ask her to show her how to do things. There were lots of jobs Auntie Polly hadn't had time to explain to her.

She dried the cups and plates, put them away in the press and was about to throw the dirty water out through the front door, when she saw someone coming up the path from Robinson's, the nearest of the neighbouring farms. The path ran through a flourishing bed of nettles that were so stingy on bare legs that Auntie Polly said she was to go the long way round when she went for the butter and eggs, down to the forge and across the top of the front orchard. But the figure who approached through the nettles was wearing trousers and boots and didn't seem to notice that they were there at all.

He was carrying an enamel bucket of water in one hand and was smiling to himself as he hurried with a strange shuffling walk, towards the open front door. Peeping out of the window, Clare saw he had a flat cap over what looked like a completely bald head and he held the bucket in a funny way with his thumb stuck out as if he didn't want it to get wet.

'God bless all here,' he shouted as he shuffled across the hallway, opened the inner door and came into the kitchen.

'Hello.'

Clare watched him open the bottom cupboard of the press, lift out the almost empty enamel bucket and refill it most carefully from the exactly similar one he carried. He didn't seem to see her or to notice she'd said hello. She wondered how he could have missed seeing her, standing as she was in the middle of the room, watching him. Perhaps his eyes didn't focus very well. They did have a rather strange look about them.

He shut the cupboard door, picked up his bucket and was about to leave when he stopped abruptly, turned and walked towards her. Still smiling, he put out his hand and touched her hair.

'Ach, wee Ellie, I'm heart glad to see ye again.'

Clare smiled warmly at him and was wondering how best to explain who she was, when she heard the familiar, uneven tap of boots hurrying under the arch and into the hall.

'Hello, Jamsey. Are ye rightly, man?' Granda Scott asked as he came through the door.

Clare noticed that his tone of voice was different from usual, louder and brighter. Normally, he was so soft-spoken.

'I am, the best atall,' Jamsey said cheerfully, his smile broadening yet further. 'I've brought you the spring. I'll be over later with the sweet milk.'

'Good man, good man yerself. Have ye said hello to wee Clarey? Polly brought her up yesterday for a holiday.'

Jamsey stared at Clare, a strange blankness replacing his beaming smile.

'Ellie,' he said, softly. 'That's Ellie.'

'Ah, yer not far wrong, Jamsey. Yer not far out atall,' said Robert reassuringly. 'That's Ellie's wee girl. Wee Clarey. Ye'll say hello to her.'

'I will that,' said Jamsey, positively, sticking out his hand so that it looked as if it didn't belong to him.

Clare took it and he shook her hand vigorously up and down.

'I'm pleased to meet ye, Clarey. Your mother was a powerful nice lady. She used to let me play her gramophone.'

'Sure don't you play it still, Jamsey, when we've all our work done?'

'Ach aye,' Jamsey nodded. 'We'll have a bit of a tune later.'

He nodded again as if to himself. Then a sudden look of concentration appeared on his face. He picked up his bucket and made for the door. 'God bless the work,' he called out, without a backward glance.

Robert looked at Clare who had moved to the window and

was watching Jamsey as he disappeared at speed through the nettles.

'Were ye frightened?'

'No. He's a nice man, but he's not quite right, is he?'

'Poor Jamsey, he's kinda simple, but there's no harm in him atall. He'd not hurt you,' Robert said emphatically, 'though sometimes he gets in a mood and ye can't get a word out of him. Other times he'll curse and swear. Pay no heed to that. He doesn't understand the words atall. Sometimes he forgets things, other times he remembers what happened years ago. And he loves music, the gramophone, the radio, songs, bands. Anything like that. Yer mother useta sing to him.'

He stopped abruptly and for one single moment Clare wondered if he might cry. But he just blew his nose on a very dirty-looking handkerchief and said he must away and put more coal on the fire in the forge or it would go out.

After Jamsey's visit, Clare felt she should begin her exploration with the house. She was not very hopeful of finding a forgotten attic in the single-storey building or a secret passage set into the thick stone walls but she thought she ought at least to look at each room carefully.

She stepped into the sitting room, 'the room' as her grandfather called it. It was cooler, but brighter than the big kitchen, its white ceiling and pale-washed walls almost unmarked by soot and smoke. In the alcove to the left of the decorated iron fireplace was a tall built-in cupboard. She climbed up on the armchair by the fire, opened the upper part and found it was disappointingly empty.

The lower one yielded only a string of very battered silver bells which must have been a Christmas decoration a long time ago. She was about to put them back when she noticed that where the silver had peeled away there were marks, rows of little designs with dots and squiggles. It was newspaper, old newspaper, but it was from Japan or China and it had been used to make papier mâché like they did at school.

Some little girl with tiny feet and sloping eyes, the visiting missionaries at Sunday School had told her about, had read the newspaper to her parents and then sent it away to a workshop so that someone could make silver bells. Bells for Christmas on the other side of the world.

She closed the cupboard doors carefully and began to study the pictures in their heavy frames. Haggar and Ishmael she knew. They were from the Bible and they looked terribly unhappy. But who was the big lady with the huge bosom and the big dress, posing against the pot plant?

And then, quite suddenly, she found herself looking at her mother. To the right of the fireplace there hung a framed photograph of a Sunday School picnic. The grown-ups were standing up very straight and the littlest children were sitting on the grass in pretty white dresses. She recognised Granda and Granny at once, so those four children sitting in front of them had to be Polly, Ellie, Bob and Mary. Johnny and Florence weren't there. Perhaps they weren't born yet, or maybe they were too small to come on a picnic. And of course, poor little James who was never baptised certainly wasn't there.

How very tidy everyone was. They must all be wearing their Sunday best. Perhaps, after all, it was an excursion. But then, she could see the baskets of food arranged in the corners of the picture. Granda Scott must have a fob watch in his waistcoat pocket, for she could see a chain quite clearly. His collar looked most uncomfortable but it was snowy white. Granny wore a pleated blouse with a high collar and a cameo brooch and a long dark skirt with frills. Polly was grinning, Mummy was looking wide-eyed at the photographer, Bob had moved, so you couldn't see his face properly and Mary was gazing across the picture at something far away.

'A long time ago and a lot has happened since,' she whispered to herself as she stood looking at all the people she didn't know, friends and neighbours, all the people who went to the little church perched up on top of the hill.

The sun was making dappled patterns on the worn linoleum. The elderly three-piece suite was dark and split in places so that the stuffing leaked out of the arms. It was not a very cheerful room.

Suddenly, she wanted to be in the sunshine. She would go and reap the harvest of the prairies, just like that picture of the three in hand they had found in the bottom drawer of the chest in her room.

She ran down the path to the forge, picked her way carefully through the bits of metal and machinery and climbed up into the seat of the reaping machine that sat awaiting its repair. The seat was slightly springy and she bobbed up and down vigorously to take advantage of it. Below and around her the bright eyes of the dog daisies winked up through the tangled grass, nodding to her, watching her as she prepared to set off.

'Alberta, Saskatchewan and Manitoba, here I come, harvesting the golden acres to give grain to all the world so that everyone, everywhere, will have enough to eat. Whatever darkness there may be to come, the larders will be full. Hey there, Hup there, pull away my beautiful horses, we have a long way to go,' she cried.

In the forge, Robert laid down the callipers and chalk beside the metal bar he was marking and moved silently across to the door of the forge. Out of sight himself, he watched the child set her face to the horizon, gather up the reins in her arms and launch herself across half of Canada. Then, shaking his head and smiling to himself, he went back to his work.

7

B y the end of her first week at Salter's Grange, Clare had put together a new world for herself. She had a room of her own, a home to come back to after her daily explorations and someone there whom she could love. Beyond all this she had the richness of the late summer countryside where the orchards were heavy with fruit and the hay fields lined with stacks ready to bring home. In all the farms and cottages the garden flowers poked up over well-trimmed hedges and spilled through every possible gap to brighten the roadside verges.

From her own front door her view was limited by the trees and bushes planted to give shelter to the house and to define the boundaries of the smith's small parcel of land, but when she scrambled up the old bank by the forge Clare could gaze out and beyond the county road to the low, humpy hills that roll across this part of north Armagh. Green and smooth, they lay peacefully across the horizon, separated from each other by boggy hollows where streams meandered and formed wide, shallow pools. From the windows of the train on her few journeys, Clare had seen the cattle drinking from the muddy edges of these pools amid crowds of the golden flag iris that bloomed every June.

Although she couldn't see very much of it from her chosen look-out point, Clare was aware of the patchwork of fields all around her, of the farms standing on the drier, south-facing slopes, of the orchards and barns and farmyards and the network of narrow lanes and well-tramped paths which wove their way between hawthorn hedges and along the edges of fields to connect up the families that had worked this rich but heavy land for centuries. Often she wished she could fly up into the sky so that she could see all around her. She imagined herself looking down and seeing as far as Armagh and Lough-gall or even further. As far, perhaps, as all the villages and townlands whose names she had heard but which she had never seen.

As the long, sunlit days passed, some of the loss she had suffered from the death of her parents was healed by a sense of their presence. It was a presence she felt but could not have explained. In Belfast, she had felt only their absence and a painful sense of having been taken away from them. But here, she was close to them, she was living in the world that they knew. They were dead and it was sad. She missed them. But here in this place where her mother had grown up, where her father had come to walk the lanes with her, they were still a part of her life.

She felt this most strongly when she stood and looked at her mother's picture in the sitting room. Many of the people in that picture had died, like she had, though mostly because they were old. Granda Scott knew every one of them and she quickly learnt that, if she asked only one question at a time, he would tell her who someone was. Then, if she waited patiently and didn't interrupt his thoughts, he would eventually tell her where they lived and what they did.

What she learnt to watch for was the small smile that meant he had remembered some story, or some expression that person had used or some mischief they had got up to when they were young. Then he would gaze up again at the figure in the photograph, clean and tidy and looking as if butter wouldn't melt in their mouth and laugh at the thought of the day they fell in the bog, or the winter they sledged down a hill on a homemade sleigh and ended up in the hawthorn hedge at the bottom.

Sometimes it was hard to believe that one of the straight-backed figures in a neat black suit and a stiff collar had once

stuffed a potato sack down a neighbour's chimney on Hallow-
een night and that another had frightened the life out of a local
drunk by appearing in a white sheet on the shortcut through the
churchyard, or that the distinguished figure standing beside the
rector had 'scorched' through the countryside on his motorbike
before becoming a mill-owner and making his fortune in cotton
spinning.

She thought then of what people would say now when they
looked at their snapshots and pointed out Ellie Scott and Sam
Hamilton. Sometimes that almost made her cry, but at other
times she was glad that they would look and say what a pity it
was. That way Ellie and Sam would not be forgotten.

Sometimes Jamsey called her Ellie when he did forget who
she was, but she never minded that. She rather liked it. And
every time her grandfather called her 'Clarey' she felt comforted. To begin with, she had been so disappointed by his
silence. He wasn't at all like Matthew Cuthbert in *Anne of
Green Gables* and he most certainly wasn't going to turn out like
Heidi's uncle. Granda Scott just didn't fit in with these people
in books. But when she thought about it, she realised that she
had known that all the time.

In the course of her first week she met the Robinsons from
the nearby farm, the baker who came with his horse and bread
cart on Mondays and Thursdays, the fish man who arrived on
Fridays and some of Granda Scott's many neighbours who
sometimes came to bring a horse to be shod or a piece of
machinery to be mended, but just as often came to sit on the
bench inside the door of the forge to hear the news. Most of the
news of the townland and indeed much further afield was
discussed under the high-pitched roof of the anvil shop or
on the grassy bank outside the shoeing shed.

Not all the people who came to the forge had spoken to her,
many of the older men had just looked awkwardly at her and
nodded, but she wasn't troubled, she knew very well that they
would soon get used to her being there. For the moment she
must just slip away and leave them to their talk.

It was not until Saturday morning that she had her first experience of not being made welcome.

'Ye needen redd up this mornin', childdear, Jinny'll be here in a wee while. She'll wash the delf.'

Clare had already collected up the breakfast dishes, brought out the tin basin from under the table and carried over a kettle of hot water from the stove.

'But Jinny's got such a lot to do today, Granda,' she protested. 'Auntie Polly said she'd got very behind while Granny was ill.'

'Aye well,' he said absently, as he shovelled more coal into the stove so there'd be plenty of hot water.

Before Clare had finished putting the dishes back in the press she saw Jinny marching up the path from the forge. She was a short, thickset woman who strode like a man in her short rubber boots. She wore a dirty cotton skirt and a short-sleeved blouse that strained over her huge, muscular upper arms. Her hair was cropped short and she wore a scowl which made Clare feel frightened before ever Jinny reached the house.

'Who the hell are you?' she demanded as she opened the door and found Clare still clutching two clean plates.

'I'm Clare. My Auntie Polly brought me up last Saturday.'

'A wee Belfast lassie, are ye?' she said sneeringly.

'No. I lived in Armagh till my Mummy and Daddy died.'

There was no flicker of sympathy in Jinny's small, piercing eyes. Clare noticed that she had dark hairs growing on her upper lip like a moustache and stubbly bristles poked out of her chin.

'So now yer goin' to come an' live here with the oul' fella, are ye?' she demanded harshly, as she parked her large, black shopping bag on the wooden settle by the fireside.

'I don't know,' she replied truthfully.

Clare had planned to make friends with Jinny, had expected to help her as she had helped Auntie Polly, but one look at the woman told her that Jinny didn't want her here and that the sooner she made herself scarce the better. She knew she was frightened but she tried very hard not to show it.

'Well, away ye go outa the way. I've me work to do,' she said crossly, as she wrapped a dirty apron round herself and pulled out a floor brush from among a bundle of mops, rakes and scythe handles that stood behind the open front door.

Clare did as she was told, disappeared into the orchard and went to one of her favourite places, the deep pool under the roots of the big pear tree which once supplied the cottage with water until the Robinsons got a pump and offered to send a bucket of drinking water over every day.

The morning was fine and sunny, glints of gold flickered on the surface of the water, but the water itself was so clear she could see the fine silt down at the bottom.

'Sure all wells are bottomless in Ireland, Clare,' Auntie Polly had said, when she'd asked her if it was very deep.

'To tell you the truth, I don't think it can be very deep atall for it useta dry up sometimes in a hot summer and then we had to go all the way to the river and boil every drop forby. I think they tell that to children to frighten them. And don't forget, Clare dear, my wee friend Dolly. Sure a flax hole is not all that deep but it was enough to drown her. Be very careful with water and never be tempted by the flowers. Sure it was a water lily that cost Dolly's life. She reached too far and fell in and couldn't get out.'

Clare stood up and walked on through the orchard up to the very top. There was a gap in the hedge there where she could squeeze through into the lane that ran all the way from the church at the top of the hill to the forge near the road at the bottom. But this morning she didn't feel like going up the hill to meet the children who played on the broad empty space outside the churchyard gates in front of the old schoolroom all the Scott children had attended till they were fourteen.

She tramped back slowly under the trees, avoiding the longest grass where the dew still lay heavy. She had just stepped on to the path by the gable at the back of the house when she saw Jinny throw the contents of Granda's chamber pot into the

97

ashpit and then dunk the empty pot up and down in the rain water barrel.

Fortunately, Jinny didn't see her, so she retreated back into the orchard, made her way through the hedge beyond the privy, and ran quickly down the common and across the big field to the stream.

She sat there under a willow tree for a long time, feeling lonely. She'd really have liked to go and fetch Edward James Bear but she was frightened to go back into the house. Even sitting here, so far away from the big kitchen, she could feel Jinny's presence and imagine her scowl as she filled the kitchen with the dust of her furious brushing.

The morning passed slowly. Clare had another go at digging in her great-grandmother's garden with an old coal shovel, for she had found that though she could lift and carry Granda's smallest spade she couldn't dig with it. The morning got hotter, great white clouds rose in towers above the green fields and became darker. When the first sixpenny-sized spots began to fall she knew she would have to go back to the house. She could hide under a tree or on the sheltered side of the old, ruined house that stood looking across at the front door of Granda's house, but she knew she'd still get a bit wet and though she didn't mind she knew Granda didn't like her getting wet. He always came out and looked for her when the rain came on hard.

As she came into the hall, she saw Jinny's black shopping bag sitting by the door. It was bulging at the sides and was so full that the zip couldn't close properly. Sticking out of the open end, Clare saw the unmistakable ear of Edward James Bear.

Without a moment's thought, she bent down, undid the zip and lifted him out. As she straightened up a blow hit her across the ear.

'Ye wee skitter, what are ye doin' wi' my bag? Thon bag's none o' yer business. Me workin' at this fukin' place for all these fukin' years an' never a word o' thanks. Jinny this and Jinny that. Do this, do that . . . thon aul' woman wi' niver a good word fer me. An' now you, damn you.'

The voice went on but Clare didn't stop to listen. With a cry of pain and blinded by sudden tears she ran for her life, down the lane and into the forge. She dodged behind Robert who stood at the anvil, his hammer poised, and didn't stop till she'd climbed in under the bellows into a small dark space where Jinny could never reach her. She crouched there, crying in pain and fright, clutching Edward James Bear to her chest.

'Childdear, what's wrong wi' ye atall?'

Robert dropped his hammer on the ground and a young man sitting on the bench by the door jumped to his feet and followed him to the corner of the forge where the child had disappeared. They looked in amazement at the small space where the child now crouched.

'Did ye hurt yerself, chile?' asked Robert, getting awkwardly to his knees so that he could see her better.

He leaned towards her and saw that she sat clutching her ear with one hand and holding her teddy bear with the other. For a while he couldn't make out what she said and then she said it more clearly.

'Jinny hit me because I took Edward James Bear out of her bag,' she sobbed. 'She doesn't like me . . . I'm afraid of her . . . she's coming after me.'

'Well, we'll see about that,' said Robert as he pulled himself to his feet with the aid of the bellows.

He turned to the young man who had stood looking down at them both, his face full of concern.

'John, will ye stay with the wee'n till I make an end 'o this. She's gone too far this time,' he said in a whisper as he threw on his cap.

'Would ye not come out now,' said John coaxingly. 'She'll not get at ye here. I won't let her past me,' he went on firmly. 'Ye needn't be feared of her, Robert'll not let her hit you. Come on out now or you'll get your nice wee dress dirty.'

Despite two children and a baby of his own, John felt he wasn't doing very well. The poor wee thing was shivering against that damp old wall and he thought he saw blood on her fingers where she had put them up to her ear.

'Robert wouldn't think much of me if I couldn't keep her away from you. I'm about twice the size of her. I useta be a boxer,' he added, a touch of desperation in his voice.

Clare scrambled out, well blackened with the soot and slack that lay in the bellows pit and wiped her eyes. To her amazement the kindly young man laughed at her.

'You've got two big black marks on your face now,' he explained. 'You'd frighten anybody yourself,' he said, taking off his jacket and putting it round her. 'Now come and sit down here beside me, till yer Granda comes back.'

Clare shivered violently and snuggled into the warm jacket. It smelt of oil, just like Daddy's.

'Were you fixing a motor car?' she asked suddenly.

'Aye, I was. How did you know that now?'

But she didn't get a chance to tell him. From outside the forge came a torrent of shouted abuse. Jinny was screeching at Robert and calling him all the names under the sun. But Robert was not to be shifted. She was to go and not come back.

As John turned toward the open door to see what was happening, Clare clutched her teddy bear fiercely and tried to hide herself behind his broad back. But it was all over in minutes. The shouting subsided and she heard the irregular sound of Robert's boots as he limped back into the forge.

'Yer all right now, Clarey. She's away an' she'll not be back. I told her I'd have her put in jail for stealin' if I iver saw her face here again,' he went on, as Clare emerged cautiously from behind John.

'Now, yer grand again, Clarey. Just you forget all about it,' said John Wiley kindly, as he put an arm round her.

'Was she stealin' on you, Robert?'

'Aye, it's been going on a long time but I thought it diden' amount to much,' he admitted ruefully. 'She an' the aul' mother's that poor I diden' grudge her a bit o' tea or sugar in thon bag as well as her five shillings. But she has the house stripped bare an' me none the wiser till Polly goes lookin' for the scissors, an' the good cups, an' some linen or other she was wantin' for the chile's room.'

'Why did she want my bear, Granda, when she's grown up?'

'She'd take anythin' to the pawnshop for a few shillings.'

Tears rolled down Clare's cheeks and made streaks through the dirty marks that had made John laugh. The thought of Edward James Bear in a pawn shop was too much for her. She sat and howled.

'Leave her be, Robert,' said John gently. 'She's had a shock and a wee cry will do no harm.'

He took out a handkerchief and pushed back her hair where he had seen traces of blood. It was only a scratch. But it was probably one of Jinny's long, dirty fingernails.

'Have ye any TCP, Robert?'

'Aye, I have. I keep it on the mantelpiece behind the tea-caddie so it should still be there. She probably coulden' see it,' he said sharply.

'I'll see if me wife can come down later. She's a great nurse, though she never went for the hospital. She just seems to pick it up.'

'I'm obliged te ye, John, I don't know what I'd have done without you,' said Robert awkwardly, as John rose to go.

'Your coat smells like my Daddy's coat,' said Clare, as she gave it back to him. 'That's how I knew you'd been mending a motor car,' she went on, a trace of a smile appearing on her tear-streaked face.

John laughed and shook his head at Robert.

'That's a good one. We'll have to watch ourselves with this one around,' he said, as he raised a hand in farewell and set off down the lane.

The fire was nearly out when they went up to the house, so it was a while before the potatoes boiled up for their meal. Robert reached up to the mantelpiece high above the stove, found the bottle of TCP and dabbed the scratch. Then he asked her if she had another dress.

'Oh yes, I have two of everything, except cardigans. I only have one of those. And coats, of course. Auntie Polly had to buy me a raincoat.'

He looked helplessly at the blackened ankle socks and the dark marks on the cotton dress. He sighed.

'Maybe ye ought to wash yer face and put on yer other dress. I think ye may use warm water,' he said, handing her the smaller of the two kettles that sat on the stove all day.

By the time she had washed, changed and eaten her mashed potato with a big knob of fresh butter, Clare began to feel more like herself again. She was glad Jinny was gone but she knew Auntie Polly would be worried about the cleaning, even if she had been doing so little. She was wondering what she could do to help when Robert emerged from his bedroom, his face washed and shaved, a sign that he must be going somewhere.

He was still in his stocking feet and he made no noise at all as he limped across the floor and took down the small New Testament that sat on top of the huge family Bible and the two volumes of Bible commentary stacked in the bookcase that hung on the wall in the alcove on the right hand side of the stove.

Clare watched closely as he leafed through the pages. He shut the book abruptly, sat down in his wooden armchair and leaned his head in his hands at the table where they had just eaten their dinner. Clare thought she had never seen him look so upset and angry before. Even when he came back from chasing Jinny away he hadn't looked like this.

'Have you lost something, Granda?' she asked cautiously, for she had noticed that unlike Granda Hamilton, who read his Bible continuously, Granda Scott read nothing but the newspapers that neighbours passed on to him or that he collected when he was in town.

'That . . . woman,' he said, tightening his lips to silence in place of some forbidden word, 'she's taken the few pounds I had in my wee drawer for the shoppin' an' she's cleared the Bible where I kept a pound or two to fall back on. I haven't even got my bus fare to Armagh that I cud borrow a pound from one of me friends and there's not a bite in the house but bread and potatoes.'

Clare had never seen him so upset before. If it had been Daddy, or even Uncle Jimmy, she'd have gone and put her arms round him, but Granda wasn't used to that. Even Auntie Polly only gave him a tiny wee kiss on the cheek when she was going home.

'I might be able to help, Granda. Would you wait a wee minute till I go and see?'

Clare hurried into her room, threw herself across the bed and waved her arm back and forth down the small space between the edge of the bed and the wall. Breathless, she wriggled back across the bed clutching the pink handbag Uncle Jack had bought her on their day's shopping in Armagh. She opened it anxiously, took out her purse and knew from the weight of it that all was well.

'Here y'are, Granda. We're all right,' she said, a note of triumph in her voice as she marched back into the kitchen.

She opened the purse and turned it upside down on the oilcloth in front of him. A shower of coins fell out, half-crowns, florins, shillings, sixpenny pieces, threepenny pieces, a few large pennies and one very battered ten shilling note.

'Where in the name o' goodness did you get all that?'

Clare took his question literally and stood pointing at the relevant coins while he sat shaking his head.

'That half-crown was Uncle Jack, that one was Granda Hamilton, those were Uncle Jimmy, those were Eddy for fetching his magazine every week, that was Davy for cleaning his shoes, that was Auntie Polly for all the sewing I did and that was Ronnie when I was leaving,' she explained, picking up the ten shilling note. 'He said it was for emergencies.'

'An' why did ye not buy sweets?'

'Well, first I had no ration book, so I had no sweetie coupons and then when my new ration book came I gave them to Auntie Polly. I knew she was short because she was always buying sweets for Uncle Jimmy. He gave up the cigarettes when he went back on the Boru and she said sweets helped to take his mind off the cigarettes. So I gave them to her. Anyway, sweets are bad for your teeth, aren't they?'

He laughed to himself and counted out the money carefully.

'That's one pound, fifteen shillings and sixpence I'm borrowin' off ye,' he said. 'Would you like an I OWE YOU?' he asked seriously.

She giggled. It was the first time she had ever heard him make a joke.

He put the note in his empty wallet and the coins in his pocket and went back to the bedroom to find his shoes. He returned shortly with his hat and coat on, an anxious look on his face.

'I can't leave ye here yer 'lone.'

'I could come too,' she said hopefully.

'Aye,' he said, looking perplexed as he considered this new possibility.

'Perhaps,' she offered, seeing his difficulty, 'I could take a little walk and meet you at the bus to come home, while you call in at the Railway Bar and do the shopping.'

'An' who told you about the Railway Bar?' he asked sharply.

'Mummy did,' she replied promptly. 'She says being a blacksmith is very hard work and a few Guinness when you're in town helps to keep your strength up. But children can't go in bars. I could walk down Albert Place and along Lonsdale Street to The Mall and meet you at the bus.'

'Would yer Mammy let you do that?'

'Oh yes, she says I'm perfectly sensible and she never worries about me crossing roads, even when I have William with me.'

'We'd better away then, it's near time she was comin' up the hill. Here, put that in your purse.'

He handed her a half-crown and a long strip torn crookedly from his ration book. 'I've plenty o' points, so buy yerself something nice. Now an' again won't hurt yer teeth.'

Clare was thrilled to be in a bus rattling into Armagh. They sat together on the hard wooden seats that Daddy had told her were called utility. She talked most of the way, checking out the features of the landscape as well as the names of all the houses and farms.

'Why's it called Riley's Rocks?' she asked as they passed the sudden outcrop that appeared beyond the Orange Hall at the end of a long stretch of bog. 'What's that funny thing up on top of the hill, the arch with a kind of monument next to it? Where does that road go to? Is that the mill you and Granny used to work in when you were young?'

She got some answers but not a lot of new information. She noticed a woman give Granda a big smile as they got off the bus together.

'Are ye sure ye'll be all right? How will ye know what time it is?'

'I'll listen for the cathedral clock.'

'An' how will ye put in your time?'

'I'll have a walk and then I might have an ice cream in Geordie Stevenson's and then I might watch the cricket, or maybe visit a friend. But I'll be back for the bus in good time,' she reassured him.

Satisfied at last, he said, 'Mind yerself, then,' crossed the top of Albert Place and pushed open the decorated glass door into the welcoming dimness of the Railway Bar.

Clare skipped down past the red-brick houses of Albert Place and came to an abrupt halt where Albert Place joined Lonsdale Street. The shelter had gone. Where the flat-roofed, solid, grey shape had stood, surrounded by muddy puddles, there was now a space. Only a pile of broken rubble squashed flat by the steam roller marked the outline of the concrete building which she and Mummy had passed every time they went for a walk up Lisanally Lane with William in the Tansad.

It had been a very ugly building when it was first built but it had soon been covered with painted slogans, Union Jacks and V-signs, so you could hardly miss it as you came to the corner and turned up between the seven brick houses and the stone wall of the Pavilion grounds before the lane became a proper country lane. And now it had disappeared. Like magic. It seemed so funny without it.

She walked slowly along the street, smiling at the women who sat knitting in doorways or who had brought chairs outside to catch the sun. She knew some of them to see, but not to talk to.

Halfway along she saw some children who had been in her class at school. They were jumping back and forth over a muddy trickle which flowed under the road in the piece of waste ground between the last of the houses and the Catch-my-Pal Hall.

'What happened to the shelter?' she asked as she came up to them.

'They knocked it down. It was great. They had a big metal ball on a chain an' a man in a machine swung it. Bang! An' the wall just fell down. The dust was somethin awful, but when it was all done there was a bonfire. We had a great time. Better than VE Day. Why did ye not come down?'

'I was away,' she said, hurrying on, because she didn't want to explain.

She bought her ice cream and carried it carefully over to the wall surrounding The Mall, so that she could sit on it and dangle her legs.

You could still see the marks in the stone where the old railings had been. She remembered the day she and Daddy had watched the men taking the railings down, not all of them, but the ones on the outside. Daddy explained that they could use the metal to build more Spitfires and that would help the war effort.

'Like my collecting paper for school?'

'Yes, just like that. How's that going?'

'Very well. I'm doing great. Granny Hamilton is clearing out all the boys' old motorcycle magazines. Every time she comes to town she fills her shopping bag and leaves me some more to take in. I'm a colonel now and if I get to be a field marshal there's to be a party in the City Hall and I'll be asked to go.'

She licked her ice cream all round the edge of the cone so that it wouldn't drip on her dress. It would be awful if she got this one dirty before the other one was washed.

She thought of the party in the City Hall. They'd played games in teams and had prizes and then they'd had a most wonderful tea with sandwiches in neat triangles and small squares, with little flags sticking out of the top one to say what was in them. There were banana sandwiches, which were very nice, and small iced buns with tiny silver balls on top.

Mummy had laughed when she told her about the banana sandwiches and asked whether they could have them for tea. She'd wanted to know what a banana looked like. You couldn't get bananas any more, Mummy had said, but if you mashed up turnip and had any banana essence left from before the war it did taste a bit like the real thing. She'd been really surprised about the dragées. That's what the silver balls were. It was amazing anybody had any left by now. You hadn't been able to get them for ages.

Daddy had teased her about the bananas, he said bananas were marvellous juicy things about three feet long and Mummy had scolded him and said they'd go and see if they could find a picture of one in the library.

She pushed the rest of her ice cream down into the cone with her tongue and began to nibble the crisp edge of the cone itself. Then she saw a boy whiz past on a bicycle and suddenly thought of Uncle Harry. He and Daddy took it in turns to do Saturday afternoon in the cycle shop, for a lot of people came in from the country then and you couldn't afford to miss the trade these days.

She finished the last little bit of her cone, licked her lips thoroughly and decided she'd go and see if Uncle Harry was in his shop. She got off the wall and went down the next lot of steps by The Mall Church so she could walk under the trees. When she came to the White Walk, one of the two paths that runs across The Mall, she was puzzled to see firemen in uniform rolling up hoses and running back and forth.

She laughed at herself. You could hardly have a fire in the middle of all the grass. Of course, it wasn't a fire. They were taking down the huge round pond that Mummy had called 'a static water tank'. It had been there for the war to give the firemen extra water. Where it had been standing there was now a big brown circle in the grass, far too big for a fairy ring, it was more like a hole in a very large, green carpet.

From The Mall she took the short cut up the back luter that brought her out into Scotch Street almost beside Uncle Harry's shop. The door was propped open and the minute she walked in her nose twitched. It always did. As sure as they popped in to say hello to Daddy, she would sneeze and Uncle Harry would say, 'Bless the child.'

A boy behind the counter was rubbing a rusted wheel with wire wool. He looked up but didn't stop.

'Is Mr Mitchell in this afternoon?'

'Aye, he's out the back mending a puncture. D'ye want him?'

'Yes, please.'

He propped up the wheel and disappeared through a door entirely covered in coloured pictures of bicycles.

'Well, look who's here!' exclaimed Harry Mitchell as he came back into the shop, wiping his hands on a piece of cotton waste. 'I wondered who wanted to see *Mister Mitchell*. What happened to yer Uncle Harry?' he asked, beaming down at her.

'I wasn't sure if you'd still be my uncle . . . now I'm an orphan,' she explained a little awkwardly.

'Ach, surely, surely. I'll always be your uncle. Now tell me what yer doing here. I thought you were in the big city.'

Clare explained about her plans to come and look after Granda Scott if Auntie Polly could be persuaded. She told him some of the difficulties Auntie Polly had mentioned.

'I can see her point of view,' said Clare. 'It would cost Granda a lot to send me to school on the bus and pay for school dinners unless I could take sandwiches. He hasn't much money though he works hard. I wondered if I could save up enough for a bicycle. It would be a great help not having bus fares?'

'How much money have you got?' Harry Mitchell asked, looking at her seriously.

'Well, I had one pound, fifteen and sixpence this morning but I lent it to Granda Scott. There was a horrible woman who used to clean every week and she's been stealing his money for a long time and he didn't know. She tried to steal my teddy bear that Uncle Jimmy bought me and Granda told her not to come again.'

'My goodness, that was bad luck on the good man. Did he get the police till her?'

'No, he just told her not to come back. He says she's desperate poor and has an old mother who never let's her alone, shouting and complaining at her all the time.'

Harry Mitchell considered the small figure for some minutes before he spoke again.

'When will you be ten, Clare?

'October the eighth. It was Mummy and Daddy's wedding anniversary. They said I was their anniversary present.'

'Well, Clare, I'll tell you what we'll do. We'll find a child's bicycle for you this time. Not a new one, mind, and I'll do it up for you. And I'll have it ready for your birthday. And when you grow out of it you can trade it in for a ladies' size. And the next thing you'll probably be wantin' a motorbike,' he said with a broad grin.

Clare giggled at the idea.

'But, Uncle Harry,' she protested, 'One pound fifteen and sixpence isn't nearly enough for a child's bicycle. Even a reconditioned one. Daddy said the price of bicycles is something desperate these days.'

'Ah yes, but there is special discounts for young ladies. There's only one catch,' he said, pausing for effect.

'What's that?'

'You have to come and see your Uncle Harry now and again and give him the odd kiss and hug.'

Clare ran round behind the counter and held up her arms to him.

'You are an awfully nice Uncle Harry,' she said, as he picked her up so she could kiss him. 'Just wait till I tell Auntie Polly that I'm going to have a bicycle. Thank you, thank you, thank you. I can't quite believe it. Do you think you might be a fairy godmother in disguise?'

'Well, you never know, Clare, it's something I hadn't considered,' he said, laughing to himself, as he put her gently back on the floor again.

'What time's the Loughgall bus?' he asked, looking at his watch.

'Ten past five.'

He shouted to the boy out in the yard that he'd be back in twenty minutes and came round from behind the counter.

'We'll away down to the bus and I can make myself known to your Granda. I've often heard tell of him but we've never met. Is he a nice Granda?'

'Oh yes,' said Clare, 'though he has no hands. He really needs someone to look after him.'

Harry Mitchell was quite happy to listen, and listen he did, all the way back to where the Loughgall bus sat under the trees, slowly filling up with Saturday shoppers ready to go home for their tea.

8

Breakfast was rather later than usual on Sunday morning and it was not long afterwards that Clare discovered Granda Scott didn't like Sundays. To begin with she noticed he said even less than usual. He sat in his chair and shuffled through the previous day's newspaper, which he had already read. As the morning wore on and he had no fire to light in the forge and no Jamsey to greet he became increasingly fidgety.

Clare was sitting at the table below the orchard window and had just completed her painting of the Canadian prairies when she heard him sigh. She pushed the painting away, stirred the dirty water in the jam jar with her brush and wondered what she could paint next.

'Sunday's a long old day,' he said, as he sat back in his chair after making up the stove.

That settled it. Granda Scott was at a loose end. This was a regular state of affairs with William, who was forever at a loose end, but there were so many games you could play with William it was only a matter of deciding which one. But you couldn't offer to play 'Snap' with Granda Scott. She couldn't suggest taking the dog for a walk when poor old Blackie had been dead for months and hadn't been able to walk very much anyway. And she couldn't suggest feeding the hens, because they too had disappeared, though she hadn't yet found out what had happened to them. For the moment she couldn't think of anything she might suggest.

She began to wonder what Granny Hamilton did with William when he came looking for someone to play with.

All their card and board games had gone and she had a feeling that Quakers didn't approve of playing cards, so they couldn't even play 'Snap' with those. She couldn't imagine Granda Hamilton playing football with William, and Uncle Jack and the other uncles and aunts who still lived at home all had their jobs to do on the farm. On Sundays when they weren't at work they often went off to visit their married sisters and brothers. The trouble was if you didn't do something quite quickly about William when he was at a loose end he would cry and work himself up into a real temper.

While she was still thinking about William, she saw her grandfather scuffle around among his boots and shoes under the side table where the radio sat. She saw him pull on a very old pair and watched as he limped across the floor, stepped out into the sun-filled hallway, pick up a spade from behind the front door and disappear across the front of the house.

She knew perfectly well he wasn't going to dig the garden. Apart from the overgrown flowerbed along the front of the house and the huge tangle of rose that had run wild over by the old ruin, there wasn't a garden any more. If he had a spade in his hand then he must be going to clear out the privy in the orchard. Perhaps that was why he didn't like Sundays. It wasn't a very nice job to have to do.

Just then she remembered Jinny and the chamber pot. She had seen her throw the contents into the ash pit instead of taking it to the privy as she should have done and then she'd dunked the empty pot up and down in the rainwater barrel. Tonight, before dark, they would both have to fill their wash jugs from that water barrel.

'Oh dear,' she said aloud, as she slid down from her chair and went to the door. He had been so very cross yesterday about Jinny that she really didn't want to mention her name again and bring it all back. And it might sound like telling tales as well. But something would have to be said. Auntie Polly had been so precise about the rainwater barrel.

She tidied up her paint box and washed and dried her brush. Perhaps it could just emerge in conversation.

'Granda, what would we have to do if something nasty fell in the rainwater barrel?' she asked, as he came back into the house.

'What like?'

'Like a dead bird. Perhaps one that was just flying past and fell in. Or a mouse,' she added, thinking that perhaps a bird wasn't very likely to be flying over a water barrel that stood so close to the house.

'Ye'd lift it out an' throw it in the bushes.'

'Or perhaps some nasty mud fell off the roof in a storm,' she went on, hopefully. 'You couldn't just lift that out, could you?'

'No, but it would settle to the bottom, it wouldn't do any harm.'

She frowned and tried again.

'What would you do if someone just accidentally forgot and put their chamber pot in to rinse it?'

He laughed shortly.

'Sure ye'd have to drain the whole thing out and hope that it might rain again soon to spare Jamsey bringing two buckets instead of one.'

He turned on his step as if he was about to go down to his room and then changed his mind.

'Ye didn't ferget, did ye?' he asked sharply.

'Oh no, I didn't . . .'

'Are ye trying to tell me that that . . . wuman put my chamber pot in the rainwater?'

'I'm afraid so. I didn't want to tell stories, but Auntie Polly was most strict about it. She said people could get ill if water wasn't looked to.'

'Aye, an' she's right there.'

Without another word he went to the press and lifted out the rainwater bucket. He limped across the front of the house and by the time Clare had caught up with him he had started to bale out the water. Bucket after bucket he poured round the roots of the climbing rose and the trees and shrubs that lined the path to the forge until, the barrel half-empty, he was able to tip it over and drain out the rest of the water and the muddy remains at the bottom.

Clare watched and saw the beads of perspiration break on his brow. It looked like very hard work.

'Would you like a mug of tea, Granda?'

'Can ye make tea?' he asked, looking surprised.

'Oh yes, I can do quite a lot of things but I didn't want to be a nuisance. You might rather do things the way you're used to.'

'Never worry about that. I know I'm no hand in the house. Tear away. A mug of tea would go down well. And put more water to boil while yer in the house, we may scald out the barrel while we're about it.'

The path to the orchard was very wet after they'd finished the job of scalding, so Clare fetched the yard brush and he swept the water aside into the long grass and the nettles. While he was clearing the path Clare pulled out a large weed from the flowerbed. With all the water he had poured on to the dry soil it came away quite easily.

'Look, Granda, it just popped out,' she said, waving a huge head of groundsel towards him. 'Do you think we could get them all out?'

'Aye.'

By the time all the weeds were gone the soil in the flowerbed showed up soft and dark. It looked very tidy but empty.

'Do you like flowers, Granda?'

'Aye.'

'We could plant flowers, there's plenty of room now the weeds have gone.'

'Where woud we get them?'

'You just ask your friends for cuttings. That's what Daddy did and he had our whole backyard full of lovely things. Do you mind?'

'Aye, I mind. Yer mammy was mad about flowers,' he said, walking off abruptly to wipe the mud from the spade and the brush on the long dewy grass of the common.

Clare smiled to herself. Last Sunday, Auntie Polly had scolded her for saying 'I mind', but she knew she wouldn't be cross as long as she didn't say it at school. Mummy had explained a long time ago that there were things you could do at home, like licking the baking spoon, that you must never do anywhere else. It was all a matter of remembering when you could say things like 'I mind' and which people you could say it to.

By the time they had walked up the orchard and filled their wash jugs from the well, it was time to put the potatoes on and fry up the chops that Granda Scott had brought from Armagh.

'Can ye fry a chop?' he asked, as he brought them from the glass-fronted cupboard in the sitting room, the coolest place in the house.

'Oh, yes. Ronnie showed me how. I can do a whole mixed grill if ever we're in the money.'

He laughed to himself and then became anxious again.

'Ye won't burn yerself?'

'No, I'll be very careful,' she reassured him as he pulled back the rings on the stove and swung the heavy griddle on to the fire.

The chops were tender and sweet and there was some gravy to pour over their mashed potato.

'Yer a great wee cook,' he said as he finished his meal with a draught of buttermilk and wiped his mouth on his sleeve.

She giggled and felt pleased as he tramped off to his room for half an hour on the bed and left her to clear the table.

Clare was sitting on the settle by the stove reading his abandoned newspaper when she heard the throb of a car engine. It was seldom enough a car passed on the road below the forge, but this one sounded as if it was much nearer. Before she had even put down the newspaper she heard it stop. Just as she opened the kitchen door she caught sight of Uncle Jack striding up the path.

'Shhh,' she said as he reached the door and bent down to give her a kiss. 'Granda's having half an hour on the bed . . . come on in,' she whispered.

115

'How are ye, Clare, are ye rightly?' he asked quietly as he sat down opposite her.

'Oh yes, I'm very well and so is Edward James Bear, though we've had our adventures,' she said equally quietly.

'Oh have you now? What's been happening?'

Clare told him all about Jinny and showed him her scratch and explained how his handbag had got them out of a pickle. She was just telling him about Uncle Harry and her new bicycle when Granda Scott appeared looking sleepy and rather startled.

'Hello, Jack, is it yerself? Ye've caught me in my dishabels,' he said awkwardly, as he stepped barefoot into the kitchen and held out his hand.

'Never worry, man, sure if we can't do what we like in our own place, what use is it atall?' he said easily. 'I came over to see if you an' Clare would come over for a bit of tea. There's wee ones up from Stonebridge for her and William to play with.'

'Ach no, Jack, thank you all the same. I'm not dressed,' he said uneasily. 'But take wee Clarey and welcome, she'll be glad to see her brother.'

'Sure there's no dressin' to go to Liskeyborough. Weren't two of me brothers in overalls takin' their motorbikes apart when I left, an' me father only in a suit long enough to go to meetin'. He'll be in his old boots walkin' the land by the time we get there,' he said encouragingly.

Granda Scott smiled and jerked his head upwards.

'Well,' he began, 'could ye wait till I put on a collar?'

'I'll wait all day so long as ye come. The father had a mind to ask you about the mare an' I'll not be popular if I come back wi'out you.'

While Granda Scott struggled with the clean collar he felt necessary for his first visit to the Hamilton's farm, Clare collected her grandmother's shopping bag from the bedroom.

'Might ye not need that again, Clare?' Jack asked quietly.

'What for?'

Jack looked at the small, bright face and thought of what

116

Polly had said to him about her staying with her grandfather. He could see it was hardly the place for a child, but she seemed remarkably settled and not troubled at all by the awkwardness of the old man.

He just nodded.

'Maybe you should pop in your socks and dress for Granny to look at. We might need some Thawpit to get the black marks out. She knows about these things more than I do,' he said laughing.

Clare was absolutely amazed by the drive to Liskeyborough. To begin with she thought Jack was going the wrong way. Always when Mummy and Daddy had taken her to Liskeyborough they had gone on the Portadown bus or walked out the Portadown Road, hoping someone would give them a lift before her legs gave out. But Uncle Jack turned left towards Loughgall and not towards Armagh, which was where the Portadown Road began. At the foot of the hill he turned right, drove along past Grange School, through Ballybrannan, under a railway bridge, round the foot of a high hill and in no time at all, there they were, driving into the familiar wide farmyard from quite the opposite direction to the one they usually came. What Clare found even more extraordinary was that the distance was so short.

She was still asking Jack questions and trying to understand how her grandparents had seemed to live so far apart when really they lived so very close to each other, when the Hamiltons all stopped what they were doing and came out or over to greet them.

As well as Granda and Granny there were two uncles whom she did remember, Billy and Charley. They were the ones with dungarees and oil on their hands. There was another one whom she'd never seen before who worked in some remote place called Larne. His name was Bobbie and he had a rather plump wife called Mary who kept saying that everything was 'ni-ice' in a most peculiar way. They didn't seem to have any children, but there was another of Daddy's sisters who had come from

Stonebridge with three boys, the youngest about the same size as William. Her name was Molly and she was rather soft and smiley, but Clare never managed to sort out the names of her boys because they never kept still long enough for her to attach the right name to the right boy.

'Come and say hello to your sister, William,' called Granny Hamilton after she had given Clare a hug and a kiss.

Clare watched as Granny called down the farmyard to where William and his cousins stood eyeing each other. But William didn't hear or didn't choose to hear. Granny Hamilton seemed concerned and called again, but still William didn't respond. Clare knew he wouldn't. If he had someone else to play with he never bothered with her.

'Don't worry, Granny, William's always like that. Mummy told me to pay no attention, it's just the way he is,' she said reassuringly, as they went into the house together, leaving Granda Hamilton heading over to the stable with Granda Scott limping cheerfully beside him.

'I've brought your bag back, Granny. Thank you for lending it to me, it was very useful.'

'What'll ye do when ye go back to Belfast? Has Polly bought ye a suitcase?'

'I'm not going back, Granny. Granda Scott has no one to look after him. I know I'm not very big and I can't lift heavy things, but I can do quite a lot of jobs. He let me cook the chops today, so they weren't burnt.'

'Are they usually burnt?'

'Yes. He doesn't seem to have the knack of cooking. I was going to ask you about making stew and champ. You always give us such nice dinners when we come to see you.'

So Granny Hamilton sat down at her well-scrubbed kitchen table and explained how to fry soda bread without burning it round the sides, and how to prepare scallions to mash with the potatoes for champ and how to cook fish from the fish man slowly in the oven dotted over with a bit of butter and a shake of pepper.

'Childdear, that's enough for one lesson,' she said, stopping abruptly, though Clare had never taken her eyes away from her for one moment. 'Are ye really sure ye want to stay with yer Granda? He's a good man but it's a hard life for a girl or woman, in the country. It'll maybe get a bit easier now the war's over, if we could just get rid of the bread rationing. There's talk that maybe the electric's coming, but sure there'll always be the heavy work, the stove to clean, an' the water to carry. Ye'd have an easier time in Canada you know and Polly would take you as quick as wink. Ye'll need to make up your mind about that on a clear day.'

Clare had always thought Granny Hamilton loved the country and liked being with the animals. She had often helped her to feed the hens or make up the feed for the calves. Sometimes, when she'd come to stay for a day or two there'd been a lamb by the stove in the kitchen who had to be fed from a bottle like a baby. But now she looked at Granny's face and thought that it seemed not only lined with wrinkles but marked with sadness and weariness.

'Would you have liked to go to Canada, Granny?' she asked gently.

'Aye, ah would. I very nearly did. I'd just saved up enough for my ticket when I met your Granda. So I bought a wedding dress instead,' she said, with a regret that made Clare feel very sad indeed.

'It's all very well, Clare, however good the man ye might get, it's hard labour unless yer born gentry with people to fetch and carry for you and nothin' to do but ride about in a carriage or a car, like the Cowdys or the Copes or the Richardsons. For an ordinary girl, there's a better life in the town. At least it's clean, it's not scrubbin' and cookin' and feedin' animals all the time. An' if ye do well at school sure there's a whole lot of things ye can do these days. Ye needn't even get married at all,' she said leaning on the table, as she pushed herself awkwardly to her feet.

Clare remembered that Granny had arthritis in her hips. The

119

doctor had said there was nothing he could do for it. The only thing he could suggest was that she rest. Granny had told Mummy and Daddy what he'd said one Sunday when they'd come out to tea.

'So I'm goin' to lie on the settle there and wait for the fairies and the little people to come and do my jobs for me,' she'd said with a funny laugh. Clare had seen the worried look on her mother's face.

'Now then, Clare, that's enough of women's talk. Yer Auntie Molly wants to go for a walk up to the obelisk. I can't mind, have ye been up with Mummy and Daddy, or did they think it was too much for you? It's a brave steep climb.'

'No, I haven't been. What's an obelisk? Whereabouts is it?'

'Away and find Jack and Molly and Bobby and Mary and tell them if they're goin' to go now while it's fine an' I'll have the tea ready when they come back. See if ye can read the words on the obelisk, I've half forgotten them meself.'

'What about William and the wee boys from Stonebridge?'

'Sure they can go if they want to, if you can find them. I never see William when they come up for the day,' she said, half to herself.

Clare thought she sounded quite relieved at the thought of not seeing William. She went to the door and looked all around. But there was no sign at all of either William or his cousins. She stepped out of the long, low house and saw a small group of adults standing round a young chestnut mare. They were watching carefully as Granda Scott examined her feet.

'I'm much obliged to you, Robert,' said Sam Hamilton warmly, just as Clare appeared at the edge of the group. 'I'd never have thought of that bein' the problem if ye hadn't pointed it out to me.'

Granda Scott was looking pleased and when Clare passed on Granny's message about them going up to Obelisk Hill while it was still fine, he seemed perfectly happy to walk on down the yard with Granda Hamilton, talking about horses and the fact that there were already far fewer of them on the land since the war. She heard Granda Scott say that once he used to have as many as forty horses a week to shoe and now he only had three or four. He admitted that it was no bad thing in one way, for horses were heavy work and he wasn't as young as he used to be, but it was a sad thing to see the machinery come in and take their place. A lot of older animals were being put out to grass where they didn't need shoes and they were simply not being replaced when they died.

'Come on then, up the hill we go,' said Jack, as they set off down the lane and along past the Hamilton land.

Clare looked around her on the warm summer's afternoon and saw the very first hint of yellow on a couple of heavy-leafed chestnuts. There were already rose hips in the hedgerows and long feathery grasses on the narrow verges of the lane which wound along beside the floor of a small stream and then twisted its way higher and higher till it came up the brow of a large, rounded hill.

'D'ye think we can make it, Clare?' said Auntie Molly, Jack's youngest sister, a very thin, pale woman, who seemed amazed by the fact that she had produced three noisy and vigorous boys.

'Oh yes, we can do it, can't we, Clare?' said Uncle Bobbie, who talked very loudly and liked to sound jolly. 'Do you good, Mary, get the beef off.'

Clare didn't think she liked Uncle Bobbie very much and when she saw the look on his wife's face after his remark, she wondered if Mary liked him very much either.

The hill was steep and the ground roughened from the tramping feet of sheep and cattle. Clare trailed her hands across the heads of tall, branching buttercups and kept her eyes on the worn stone finger that stood at the highest point. She got there first and stood looking in amazement.

She had never been anywhere so high before. She spun round like a top, trying to see in every direction all at once. Under an almost clear blue sky the green, sun-dappled countryside swept away to the far horizons. She could see houses and farms tucked into small windbreaks or huddled down in sheltered hollows, orchards with trees running like lines of children in a gym class and great sweeps of pasture, dark green or gold, depending on where the shadows fell from the few towers of cloud welling up in the warmth of the afternoon. Between the humpy hills little lanes appeared and disappeared again.

She turned slowly now and discovered she could see Armagh quite clearly, its two cathedrals perfectly outlined on their respective hills, the pale metal domes of the Observatory reflecting the light. But best of all, was something she had never imagined she might see, the blue, shimmering mass of Lough Neagh stretching to far mountains. Beyond those mountains, more mountains, the furthest away like pale ghosts of those nearer at hand.

It seemed that the whole world lay at her feet. All the places she had ever been, or ever heard of, Salter's Grange and Liskeyborough, Tullyard and Drummond, Lisnadill and Kilmore. She had only to listen to the four adults who pointed their fingers and argued as to who lived in which farm and where that lane led to and she would hear all the names she had ever heard her parents speak throughout her whole life. It was like seeing a story laid out in front of you, in colours and shapes instead of words.

There was a breeze up on the hill, not cold, but strong enough to catch her breath and bend the tall buttercup stems. She walked away by herself and looked up at the crumbling stone face of the obelisk. She tried to read it and finally managed to fit the words together. But it was not the words written on the obelisk that seemed to stay in her mind, it was something Granny had said when they were sitting together in the well-scrubbed kitchen of the farm now tucked out of sight on the other side of the hill.

Granny had said that she'd need to make up her mind what to do on a clear day. Well it must be a clear day when she could see every house and tree for miles and the outline of mountains she knew were far away.

'I'm staying here,' she said quietly to herself, as she walked across the top of the hill to have another look at Armagh. 'I'm not going back to Belfast or over to Canada. I'm staying here, with Granda.'

She stood listening to the breeze and the song of the birds and only when Uncle Jack came and tapped her on the shoulder did she realise that the distant sounds she'd heard were her aunts and uncles calling to her because they thought it was time now they were all going back down to the farm for their tea.

9

T he second week of Clare's stay at the house beyond the forge passed so quickly she could hardly believe it was Saturday when she woke on yet another fine, sunny morning, the one on which Auntie Polly was due to arrive from Belfast.

She lay looking up at the ceiling and listened for the sounds that would tell her it was time to get up. Granda Scott would light the stove, put the kettle to boil and carry the heavy griddle from its place in the cupboard. Then he would call her and she would fry the bread for breakfast and make the tea. That was just one of her jobs now.

All week she had been trying to see what she could do now there wasn't even Jinny to do any work in the house. She had found plenty she could do. She'd even managed to wash and iron one of Granda's shirts after she'd found a whole collection of flat irons mixed in with broken tools and old shoes under the corner cupboard in the kitchen.

'Granda, why are there *four* irons?' she asked as she lifted them out and began to blow off some of the dust and cobwebs.

He looked at them and tried to remember the last time he had seen a woman smoothing. Suddenly, a smile lit up his face. Clare thought he looked extraordinarily pleased with himself.

'Well, ye see, ye have to heat the smoothin' iron on the stove and then ye pass it over the clothes. But the heat goes away awful quick so you take another iron an' put the first one back. An' I mind ye have to give the iron a wipe as you lift it from the stove for fear there's dirt on the end of it to drop on the clean clothes.'

'You haven't got an ironing board, have you, Granda?'

'No, there's niver been one o' those. I seed yer Granny fold up a sheet or an old blanket that had got kinda thin and put it on the table. That's how she useta do it. Were ye goin' to give it a try?'

'I was, but I'll have to take a sheet off my bed and use that.'

'There was sheets . . .' he said uneasily.

'That's all right, Granda, it'll do my sheet good to be ironed. Clean sheets always feel lovely when they've been freshly ironed.'

It had been an awfully slow business. To begin with the top of the stove was so dirty and greasy she had to rub for ages to make a clean bit before she could put the irons to heat. One of the irons must have had a bit of rust on it but she didn't notice until she'd ironed it on to the shirt. Fortunately it was only on the tail at the back which would never show. And they did cool so quickly. You'd only just got down the front when the wrinkles stopped coming out and you had to go back to the stove for another one. No wonder Mummy always said her favourite wedding present was her electric iron.

She'd had a go at cooking herrings in the oven. That was nearly a disaster for the fire was too low. When she opened the oven at dinner time they were just as they'd been when she put them in. But then Granda came and made up the fire and gave it a good poke and when she looked again the butter was making a little fizzling sound and they agreed they just needed to wait a while longer and keep the potatoes warm on the side of the stove.

On Tuesday, when Granda Scott went into town she'd gone to spend the afternoon at Robinson's next door. Going there the first time was nearly as bad as visiting Granny Hamilton because there were so many people and she couldn't get all their names sorted out. Old Mrs Robinson was easy because she just sat by the stove in the farm kitchen and gave orders and young Mrs Robinson was fine because she had lovely dark hair and eyes, but apart from Jamsey, she couldn't work out which of the men were Robinsons and which were the hired hands. They all came and washed their hands at the pump and tramped into the big kitchen for their tea laughing and talking together.

Old Mrs Robinson asked her a lot of questions. She looked rather cross with her funny little spectacles and her habit of wrinkling up her forehead if she didn't understand, but actually she was quite nice and when Clare said she had to go home to get Granda's tea ready she told young Mrs Robinson, who was called Margaret, to give her some extra eggs as a present and some scallions from the garden to make champ.

'Sure the scallions is running wild in the garden, childdear. Wheniver ye want a few, come and take them. Don't bother to ask anyone, just help yourself. An' the next time ye come Margaret'll have a cutting of thon red geranium that ye admired. Yer welcome any afternoon Robert's in town.'

It was only a little cutting, but when she went back on Thursday Margaret had put it in a proper flower pot she'd found in one of the outhouses. Much nicer than a tin can they'd agreed as they stood in the dairy together washing eggs.

Clare thought it looked quite perky already though Margaret warned her it would take a while to root. Then it would be another while before it produced a flower bud. It might bloom this year if the weather stayed mild till Christmas as it often did, but it might not and then she must bring it indoors and keep it in a cool room so that it didn't get the frost that would kill it, nor be forced into growth by the warmth which it wouldn't like either.

Clare was quite surprised that geraniums were so particular. When Mummy and Daddy visited Granny Hamilton or some of their own friends who had gardens they used to bring back bits and pieces of plants in a paper bag and just push them into the soil in the flowerbed Daddy had made with concrete blocks all down one side of the backyard. Everything grew and bloomed all over the place, especially some pretty blue stuff that trailed down and covered the concrete blocks so that they didn't show at all. She wished she could remember its name but it had gone right out of her head.

There always seemed to be flowers in the backyard, even in winter. Indeed, when she thought about it, she remembered Mummy saying that she'd like a garden that would give her a posy in every season of the year and last Christmas Eve she had a tiny, wee vase of flowers on the table for Christmas Day.

'Look, Sam, we've managed it. Winter jasmine and a few rose buds. I think they may open yet in the warm. Not many people have garden flowers for Christmas like we have.'

She still cried sometimes when she thought of Mummy and Daddy but then she reminded herself that they were together and she was sure Heaven would have lots of flowers. That helped too.

She slid out of bed and began to wash. They'd been so lucky with the weather on Sunday. It had stayed fine all afternoon while they were at Liskeyborough but then after she went to bed, she'd heard the rain drumming on the roof. Granny Hamilton had said it would rain and it certainly did. It must have rained all night for next morning there was a huge puddle right outside the front door. She was just coming out of her room when Granda opened the front door and a blackbird who was having a bath just looked up at him and then went on with his bath.

'Ach that one's been here for years now,' he explained when she asked why he didn't fly away. 'I call him George. He coud next thing to talk to you, that bird. He'll be back in the kitchen lookin' crumbs when he gets useta you. Niver throw the crumbs to him, that frights him, just drop them at yer feet an' he'll come right up to you an' eat them up. Ye won't have to sweep up after the same fella.'

The rainwater barrel was overflowing and the water was so clear you could see right to the bottom. And the earth in the newly weeded flowerbed looked dark and inviting. When she was putting away the breakfast dishes, she saw Granda Scott turn aside on his way to the forge and stand looking at it. She

127

was sure he looked pleased as he limped on down the damp path where the pear tree still dripped bright drops after the night's downpour.

The secret of not burning the bread was making sure it hadn't curled up in the first place. And that meant seeing the lid was on the bread bin which Granda usually forgot. Then you had to make sure the fat was spread all over the pan and wasn't just sitting in patches. It was so dark over the stove it was always hard to see the melted fat unless you tipped the griddle and made sure it was shiny all over.

Mummy had a flat thing called an egg slice for turning over bread in the pan but Granda hadn't got one. There were no cooking tools left so she decided she would just have to pretend. She found a big spoon and picked out the largest of the surviving dinner knives and between squashing and flipping she managed to get each piece properly coated in fat before it had time to burn.

'Yer a dab hand at that. Ye'll make someone a powerful wife,' he said, watching her later that morning.

She giggled. She couldn't possibly marry anyone even if she wanted to because she'd have Granda to look after when he got old.

She'd finished washing her own vest, knickers and socks and had just hung them on the elderberry bush when she heard Jack's car. She ran down to the forge to greet them.

It was only when she saw Auntie Polly that it came back to her that the fortnight had been a trial, to see if it would work. She had no doubts at all in her mind that she wanted to stay, but what would she do if Auntie Polly said she couldn't, or if Granda got all anxious and uneasy and was too afraid to think that they could manage somehow?

She was so upset that for a moment she just stood and watched Polly and Jack getting out of the car and didn't say a word.

There were kisses and hellos and Jack told Granda Scott that the mare was as right as rain again and the father was very grateful to him. Polly wanted to know what Jack was talking about and Clare told her all about their Sunday visit as they walked up to the house.

'Somebody's been gardening,' said Polly as she came up to the front door.

'Aye, we pulled out a weed or two last Sunday. I think maybe we can find a few more about the place if we chanced to look,' said Granda, laughing wryly.

'I have stuff in the back of the car for Clare, a few wee shrubs and some bits of perennials me mother split up for her. Will I away an' get them?' asked Jack, as they stood looking at the empty flowerbed.

'Oh, yes please, Uncle Jack, I'll come and help you,' said Clare as they set off back to the car.

They brought the carefully wrapped bundles and packets and put them in the shade and then went into the house where Polly was making a cup of tea.

'You've been a busy girl, I hear,' she said, as Clare came back into the room with the sweet milk she'd fetched from the sitting room.

'Aye, she's wrought hard,' agreed Granda.

'Well, I've got great news for you all,' said Polly as she poured for them. 'Jack here phoned me up last Monday and told me about Jinny and the very next day I'd a call from Bob asking me if there was anythin' wrong at home.'

She paused, put down her own cup of tea and scuffled in her handbag.

'So, I told him the whole story and look what he sent you, registered post,' she went on waving a bright envelope at them. 'He says I'm to buy anythin' you need immediately an' I'm to make him a list of anythin' else for the winter.'

She took out four five pound notes from the envelope and held them up. Clare had never seen a five pound note before and even Granda Scott looked amazed.

'Ach, sure he shoulden a done that. It's far too good,' he said awkwardly.

'It's good enough, Daddy, I agree, but don't forget Bob is a bank manager now and he's just been promoted. It took a brave few horseshoes to keep the backside in *his* trousers.'

Everybody laughed and Clare put out her hand for a note.

'Why's it got a piece of silver paper down one side,' she asked, as she studied the flimsy paper with its delicate scrollwork and engraving of the King.

'That's to make sure it's proper,' explained Jack. 'It's very hard to forge a note if it has a wee stripe like that down it.'

'Well, it looks as if we need to go shoppin',' said Polly as she emptied her cup. 'Will ye come to Armagh with us, Daddy, or will ye let us do the stuff for the house and you to do yer usual this afternoon?'

'Ach, sure I'm no use on linen an' suchlike. Tear away. I'll come on the bus and sure maybe ye'll still be there.'

'Very likely, indeed,' said Polly cheerfully, as she produced another less exciting-looking envelope. 'This is for Clare, from her Auntie Florence in London. "A pair of shoes and a winter coat or whatever she most needs," she says, and she sends you both her love. Isn't that nice?'

Clare couldn't quite believe it. It looked as if, suddenly, not just one, but two fairy godmothers had appeared. But it struck her then that it was awfully funny people never talked about fairy godfathers. After all, Uncle Bob was a man. And so was Uncle Jack and he had brought her all those exciting-looking things to plant in the flowerbed.

'I'll see yez later, then,' said Granda Scott, as Polly collected them up and got them moving. 'Don't buy up all Armagh,' he laughed as he saw them to the car.

Clare guessed that after all the excitement he might have half an hour on the bed before he went back to the forge.

Shopping was hard work and Clare wasn't much interested in blankets and sheets, but it was nice to be in Armagh again and go into shops that she used to go into with Mummy. Some of the people behind the counters remembered her and she made Auntie Polly promise faithfully they would go down Scotch

Street and say hello to Uncle Harry and ask how her bicycle was coming on.

Buying a winter coat in John M. Wilson's looked as if it was going to be very easy. The first one she put on fitted perfectly and was such a pretty dark blue that she didn't want to take it off again.

'Only one problem, sweetheart,' said Auntie Polly. 'I may not have enough clothing coupons. I tried to get extra ones for you but they haven't come through yet. I've filled in at least three forms explainin' what happened to your clothes and why you have to have new ones. But there's such a lot of red tape these days.'

'You mean I can't have it, even with Auntie Florence's money?'

Clare's eyes filled with tears and she felt quite ashamed of herself.

'Excuse me,' said the assistant, who'd been pretending not to hear, 'But are you Miss Scott of the Grange?'

Auntie Polly laughed and admitted that she was, but not for a brave while now. And the assistant nodded and said she thought she recognised her and forby she knew very few people called Polly.

'Do you remember Florrie Patterson?' she went on, a broad smile on her face.

'Of course, I do,' said Polly. 'Florrie and I served our time together in Thomas Street. How is she? Is she well?'

'She is, aye. She's gran'. She's my aunt an' she useta talk about you an' some of the jokes you had down in Thomas Street. She works up the stairs here. She's our alteration hand. Now if you have a word wi' her about the coupons, an' she has a word wi' the Boss, I wouldn't think ye'd have much bother wi' the wee coat.'

So they left Jack in the men's department to buy some socks for Granda Scott and trooped up the narrow wooden stairs to where Florrie was working away on her sewing machine.

'D'ye mind Her Ladyship we worked for?' asked Polly.

131

'Could ye iver ferget her?' replied Florrie. 'An' d'ye mind the way her voice useta change on the way from the front of the shop to the workroom. She could curse and swear at us somethin' ferocious but if you heerd her in the shop or the fittin' room you'd think she was Lady Muck.'

Clare thought Florrie was great fun and she'd have sat listening to them talk all day if Polly hadn't remembered how much they still had to do on their list.

'We must go, Florrie. We've left Clare's uncle in menswear and he'll think we've fell and forgot. We're away to Leyburns for shoes now. I'll think of you as I pass the shop. I'm sure she haunts it still.'

'Aye. I could imagine that rightly. An' never worry, Polly, about them coupons. I've got more than I need. I'll see to it for the wee lassie.'

She turned to Clare who was already clutching her coat in the parcel the assistant had wrapped up for her. 'Health to wear, Clare, strength to tear, Clare, and money to buy more, Clare.' She took a shiny sixpence from the drawer of her sewing machine and gave it to her. 'Put that in your pocket the first time you wear yer coat and say three times: "May my pocket never be empty."'

'May my pocket never be empty,' said Clare solemnly.

'That's right,' said Florrie. 'Don't ferget.'

They said their goodbyes, collected up Jack and made their way up into Marketplace. The day was getting very warm and the pavements were crowded. On the steps in front of the Technical School a nurseryman had laid out his wares, shrubs wrapped in sacking and flowers blooming in pots. Clare wanted to go and look but Auntie Polly said they'd have to go to Whitsitts first. There wasn't a decent saucepan you could make a drop of soup in and even the old saucepan for boiling eggs looked as if it was ready for the dump.

'Could we buy an egg slice, please?'

'Why d'you want an egg slice, Clare?'

'Well, it would be easier to turn over the bread at breakfast.

Mummy used to have one and I remembered it. It's quite difficult with a spoon and knife though I can manage it now.'

Clare noticed that Auntie Polly looked very thoughtful as she walked up and down the display stands trying to find an egg slice. Perhaps egg slices were too expensive.

'And it would be nice to have a sharp knife for the scallions. The dinner knives are all very blunt,' she added, as Polly found what she was looking for.

By the time they had tried on shoes and found a pair of lace-ups for everyday they were all hungry. Jack said he knew a good place for dinner down in the old horse market and they set off down Scotch Street carrying all their parcels.

It seemed to be further away than it usually was and Clare was so glad to get there. She sat herself down on the wooden bench and let Auntie Polly stack all their shopping in the corner. The smell of roast meat and cooking potatoes made her feel very hungry indeed.

'Are you still not drinking milk, Clare?' asked Polly, as Jack prepared to order their meal.

Clare smiled sheepishly and shook her head.

'Not even the Robinsons' nice fresh milk?' she persisted.

Clare shook her head again and then leaning towards her, whispered to her that she needed the lavatory quite quickly.

'Just over there. Through that door and up the stairs,' said Polly, who knew the place from long ago.

She turned to Jack, about to say something about how nice it was to come to a place after such a long time and find it had hardly changed at all.

'Does Clare not drink milk?' he asked, before she'd had time to open her mouth.

'No,' she said, quietly. 'I've tried my best but it's no use. Ellie never forced her, so neither have I.'

Jack looked so very upset that Polly was quite amazed. He had been in such good spirits all morning but now he seemed quite distraught. She'd got so used to his relaxed, easy-going personality that for a moment she was completely taken aback.

133

'Jack dear, what's wrong?' she asked, her voice full of concern. 'Are ye worried about wee Clare stayin' with her Granda and not gettin' the right food? D'ye think I should take her back with me after all? What is it atall, Jack? You look as if ye'd lost all belongin' to ye.'

For a moment, Polly thought Jack might be going to burst into tears, but then she saw him make an effort to collect himself.

'Polly, I didn't know about the milk till this minit,' he began. 'That's why the wee lassie's still alive and not pushing up the daisies with Ellie and Sam. They've only found out in the last week or so. It was the milk that brought the typhoid. This woman from Donegal came to Armagh to stay with relatives. She didn't know she was a carrier an' she was helpin' them with their milk round for that was their livelihood. They had a horse and cart that took the churn and delivered every morning. All the people that got the typhoid was on that one milk round and there was sixty or more people died as well as Ellie and Sam. It's been kinda hushed up, but I heard from the gardener up at the hospital that there was that many ill, they had to send ambulances full to Belfast and even to Dublin. We might well have lost the wee one as well,' he said abruptly, as he got up and went to fetch them lemonade from the bar.

Clare was so tired when they finally got back from Armagh that she said she would take 'half an hour on the bed'. She was still fast asleep at teatime but when Auntie Polly wakened her she was fine again. She helped to make the potato salad to go with the cooked ham and tomatoes from Armagh and then when they had tidied up and put the tea things away they found proper places for the new blankets and sheets and hung her new coat on a hanger on the back of the door with an old shirt over it to keep the dust off.

It was a lovely summer evening and Auntie Polly wanted to pay a short visit to the Robinsons. It was getting late, but she said Clare could come too for they wouldn't stay very long. They walked down the lane and across the top of the orchard and Clare told Polly all about her two visits to the Robinsons, how much she had liked them but how confused she'd been. Could Auntie Polly help her to sort out which were Robinsons and which weren't.

The family were very pleased to see Polly and they asked her how she thought her father was. Clare heard old Mrs Robinson say that they'd all been concerned about him after Ellie died, even before he'd lost his wife, but he seemed to them to be well improved recently.

They'd heard about Jinny from John Wiley's wife, who was the sister of one of their helpers, and they all agreed it was no bad thing she was not coming back. If Robert needed some help in the house there were girls and women a-plenty who'd be glad to help out and who could be trusted.

Margaret told Polly that Clare was a great hand at washing eggs and they were thinking of offering her a job. Everybody laughed at that, but Clare thought it was a good idea. She'd been thinking about how she might earn some money like she had in Belfast in case they might have another emergency.

Auntie Polly still hadn't said whether she could stay or not and Clare tried to pluck up courage to ask as they left the farm kitchen and stepped out into the cobbled yard where the whitewashed farm buildings gleamed in the fading light. They turned out of the farmyard between high white pillars and crossed the gravel at the front of the house where the big monkey puzzle tree stood in the middle of the small, enclosed lawn and threw long shadows on the path that led up to the front door that no one ever used.

But Clare couldn't think what to say. Polly had fallen silent and everything was so still all around them it almost seemed wrong to say anything and spoil the peacefulness of the evening. All she could hear was the distant lowing of cattle down by the stream and the scuffle of birds beginning to roost for the night in the nearby trees and hedgerows.

They tramped silently past the horse trough and the cart shed and the potato house and the big hay shed, already filling up with bales of straw from the harvest. It was as they were about to walk on across the top of the orchard to the forge that Clare suddenly noticed in the fading light that someone had taken a scythe to the nettles on the short cut.

Where before there had been a narrow track, passable only to people wearing trousers and boots, there was now a broad swathe of dying vegetation just waiting to be raked away. Moments later they walked through the front door which still stood open to the cool of the evening.

'Did you scythe the nettles, Daddy,' asked Polly as he heard their footsteps and looked up.

He was leaning over the table, lighting the lamp, the soft glow from the newly trimmed wick showing up his face in the now dark kitchen.

'What nettles?' he asked absently, as he warmed the mantle and then put back the globe.

'On the shortcut?'

He thought for a moment and then nodded at them.

'Ach no, I'm no han' with a scythe. That was Jamsey. After ye went off to town this mornin' he came and did it and when I spoke to him he said it should have been done long ago for they'd sting the legs off wee Clarey.'

'Wasn't that kind of him,' said Polly, as she turned towards Clare, a thoughtful look on her face. 'I think Jamsey must be hopin' you'll stay,' she added casually.

'Aye,' said Granda Scott more forcefully than usual. 'An' he's not the only one. Sure what woud I do now without her ?'

10

T he morning had been wet. Heavy, thundery rain swept across the front of the cottage, blurred the prospect of fields to a green wash and sent rivulets of water running down the path to the forge where the trees and shrubs threshed in the blustery wind and released the first shrivelled leaves of the approaching autumn to lodge in the rich grass that had flourished through a warm summer.

Towards noon the rain eased, the clouds began to lift, and by late afternoon when two figures appeared cycling out of Armagh along the Loughgall Road, their arms were bare under hot sun and their light cotton skirts billowed and flapped with the following southerly breeze.

'Race you to Richardson's gates,' shouted the older girl, her words carried off by the movement of air, but her meaning clear from the jerk of her head.

'Right, you're on,' replied Clare, as they spun down the Asylum Hill and bumped through the bad bit of road at the bottom, where the even more broken and potholed Mill Row joined the main road.

Along the wall of the asylum, past the mortuary chapel and under the line of sycamores that lay beyond Longstone Lane they flew, pedalling furiously on an open road with neither sight nor sound of a vehicle. Inevitably Jessie drew ahead. Clare made a half-hearted effort to catch her, but she knew of old Jessie's longer legs always had the advantage of her, even on a day when she wasn't tired and just starting her period.

'You win, as always,' she said laughing, as she skidded to a halt, laid her bicycle down on the grassy verge and joined her friend who was already sitting on the low wall adjoining the handsome gates of the Richardson estate. 'Will we go down to the stream?' she asked as soon as she'd caught her breath.

'Aye, c'mon, let's go down.'

They left their bicycles propped against the wall, crossed the road and climbed through a gap in the hedge. The slope was steep and they had to stop talking and concentrate on finding tufts of grass to use as footholds and handholds, but after a few minutes they were standing on a minute patch of sand beside a tiny, noisy rivulet, well swollen with the morning's rain.

Once down into the deep ravine, it was an easy matter to choose a big stone and step across the flow. They made their way to a tree which stretched a branch across the stream and obligingly provided two seats, side by side, completely out of sight of any passers by on the road above.

'I love it here,' said Clare, swinging her legs and looking down at the threads of vivid green water weed shaped by the strong flow. 'Do you think we might still come here when we're old?'

'Why not? Sure, if we're both in wheelchairs, we'll be so rich we can hire a team of fellas to lower us down on ropes.'

Clare giggled. One of the things she loved about Jessie was the way she just came out with things. You never knew what she'd say next. She sometimes wished she was more like her friend, more easy with things, less considered. That way, she'd be much more fun. Sometimes when she was teased for her seriousness at school, she thought it would be such a relief to be like Jessie and take everything in her stride.

'But if we had a whole team of fellows, it'd defeat the object of the exercise, wouldn't it?' she said with a smile. 'This is where we talk secrets, isn't it?'

'Yes, but what's the chance of havin' any good secrets when we're old?'

The strong sunlight fell through the leaves of the beech tree that provided their seat and dappled their skin and hair. It cast a golden halo on Jessie's wavy, shoulder length tresses and picked up the freckles on her creamy skin. Jessie's eyes and hands were always in motion and they caught the light, while Clare sat still, absorbed in the motion of the water, her skin paler but clear, her hair a mass of dark curls, her eyes distant, but quick to light up and gleam with pleasure whenever she turned to her friend.

Their meeting had been a strange chance, though they lived not a mile apart as the heron flew, from the stream beside Jessie's home to the pool in the water meadow beyond the forge.

Clare had had her new bicycle from Uncle Harry for her tenth birthday as he had promised and on a lovely October day she cycled to school. But despite the new bicycle, the day was no happier than the days of the preceding weeks when she'd travelled into Armagh by bus. Having longed to go back to her old school in Armagh, having thought about it through all her time in Belfast and looked forward to it during the final week of the summer holidays, she had been bitterly disappointed on her first day back.

Miss Slater had gone. 'In the family way' was the phrase she heard the older girls use. In her place was a new class teacher, tall and thin, with a hard face and no sense of humour, who was preoccupied with the state examination for which the brightest pupils in her class would be entered.

She had written to Margaret Beggs, her best friend, to tell her she was coming back but Margaret was not one bit interested. She'd moved house and wanted to forget she'd ever lived in Edward Street. Her new friends all lived on the Portadown Road and Clare's company was no longer wanted.

As if this were not bad enough, Clare found herself utterly bored by the work they were doing for the benefit of those wanting to take 'the Qualifying' and go to the local Grammar School. She came to dread the blue text-book with the medical cross on the cover. *First Aid in English* it called itself. Inside, there was a long, long list of things to be memorised. 'The adjective from eagle is aquiline, the female of monk is nun, the opposite of ingress is egress . . .' Learning by heart, spelling tests and practice in copy books left her miserable and frustrated. There were no more stories, no more geography lessons, no more nature table or library box times. It was all English and arithmetic, spellings and sums. She couldn't bring herself to learn her spellings each evening, so she ended up at the bottom of the class.

Where this state of affairs would certainly have led, Clare never found out. One afternoon when she went to collect the bread ration, Clare found herself in the baker's queue behind a small, white-haired lady. She thought she recognised her, but she couldn't be sure. While she was still thinking about it, the old lady fumbled and dropped the dark-toned loaf she'd just been handed. Clare jumped forward and caught it before it fell on the floor.

'My goodness, that was quick thinkin',' said the baker, as he leaned across the counter to help the old lady open her shopping bag.

'Thank you very much indeed, my dear. I'm afraid it's my hands. They don't work very well these days,' she added apologetically.

The loaf was safely loaded into her bag and she was about to leave the shop when she turned, looked at Clare, and said: 'You wouldn't by any chance be Clare Hamilton, would you?'

'Why, yes,' admitted Clare, as she handed over the money and coupons for her own loaf.

'I taught your dear mother at Grange school and your uncles and aunts as well, but your mother I remember best.'

She stood waiting until Clare had collected her change and they walked out of the shop together.

'Eleanor was a very able girl. You look very like her, though she was fair and you are even darker than your father. I knew him too, for my aunt lived at Hockley and I used to go there a lot. Come over here, dear, we mustn't clutter up the entrance,' she said sharply. 'Thank you, Mr Farmer, I'll see you again on Friday,' she added, turning back to address the tall figure behind the counter.

They stood talking for a while and then Mrs Taylor arranged for Clare to come to her house on The Mall for a cup of tea after school.

'I'm afraid the tea will be hardly worth coming for, my dear, but perhaps I may have something else to tempt you with,' she said thoughtfully.

Mrs Taylor had been widowed for many years and her only daughter was nursing in Canada. She admitted she enjoyed company and Clare was soon a regular visitor. Each week she would choose books from Mrs Taylor's small library and each week they would talk about what she'd been reading. During one of these conversations Clare found herself admitting how bored she was at school and how she was now bottom of the class, because each Friday morning the class was rearranged in order of merit after the weekly spelling test and she hadn't been learning her spellings.

'Oh dear,' said Mrs Taylor looking most anxious, 'I wonder if I can explain to you, Clare, why something like learning your spellings could make an incredible difference to your whole life.'

Clare was quite taken aback by the sad and serious look on her new friend's face. For all Mrs Taylor's formality of manner, Clare found her a lively person. She smiled at Clare's comments about the characters she met in the books which moved back and forth in the waterproof carrier bag Uncle Harry had so thoughtfully provided behind the saddle on her bicycle. And often she told funny stories about her early days in teaching when, as young Miss Rowentree, she thought she knew quite a lot after her training course in Belfast and then discovered that knowing things didn't help in the slightest, unless you could get the better of the very assorted group of children you had to teach.

Clare listened, fascinated, as she described the school room beside the church, a room continually criticised in the inspector's reports for not possessing a map of the world or a globe, for having structural cracks and only one 'office' for both boys and girls. She'd heard stories of pupils who'd emigrated, who'd died, or been killed in the war, but she'd never seen Mrs Taylor looking as sad and as thoughtful as she looked when she confessed to being bottom of the class.

Mrs Taylor set down her teacup and sat up very straight.

'You see, my dear, people make judgements based on their own preconceptions. They look at your clothes and decide whether you are rich or poor. They listen to the way you speak and decide whether you are educated or ignorant. They look at the results of a spelling test and decide whether you are intelligent or stupid. And based on that judgement, a judgement which can be utterly false, they make decisions. Do you understand?'

Clare nodded. Jane Austen's novels were full of that kind of judgement and so was *The Mayor of Casterbridge*, which she had just put back in its proper place on the shelf. Just because poor Elizabeth-Jane used country words like 'leery', her father was ashamed of her, even though she was actually a very thoughtful and observant person.

'Clare, I'm sure your mother would have wanted you to do well at school.'

'Oh yes, Mrs Taylor, Mummy always said it was very important for a girl to have a good education.'

'But, Clare, my dear, if you are bottom of the class, you will not sit for the Qualifying. And if you do not sit for the Qualifying, you will not have a chance of going to the Grammar School. Is that what you really want?'

Clare had been about to reply that, no, it wasn't what she wanted, when there was a vigorous *rat-ta-tat-tat* at the front door. Mrs Taylor laughed wryly.

'Here's someone come to meet you who wouldn't have an idea in the world about Jane Austen or Thomas Hardy. But she does have other qualities. Would you go down and open the door to save my legs.'

'Hallo,' said Clare, shyly, as she looked up at the figure on the doorstep, a girl a year older and at least a foot taller than herself.

'You're Clare,' the girl said, as she tramped down the hall and paused at the foot of the stairs. 'That's great. I'm Jessie. Is Auntie Sarah all right?' she asked as they went upstairs to the sitting room.

'Yes, she's fine. I'm just saving her legs.'

'She could do with a new pair. I think this pair's worn out. That'll learn her to be a teacher!' she said cheerfully, as she marched into the crowded room, bumped her way through the close-packed furniture and gave her aunt a big kiss.

They had cycled home together and been friends from that moment on. The following year, when Clare did pass the Qualifying, at her first attempt, Jessie just managed it on her second. After Clare had collected up her year's savings, the egg money, some dollars from Auntie Polly and a withdrawal from Granda Scott's bank book, Jessie's mother had taken them both to Armagh and supervised the buying of their school uniform.

Clare would never forget that day. They had each put on the tunic and blouse, tied the tie, donned the three-quarter socks and the blazer. They stood staring at each other while Mrs Rowentree made sure there was letting-down on both the hems and room for development in both the blouses. The assistant came back into the fitting room and handed them each a black beret and a large pair of green knickers.

Jessie had taken one look at the huge bloomers, held them up in front of her, and then deftly wound them into a turban for her head.

It had been a ridiculous and happy moment. Even the assistant had laughed. And although Mrs Rowentree had made some protest, it was half-hearted, for she was laughing too.

'You've gone very quiet. What mischief are ye plannin' now?'

At the sound of her friend's voice Clare jumped, laughed at herself, and came back to the present.

'I was thinking of the day your mother took us to get our uniform.'

Jessie grinned and made a gesture with her hands as if she were lowering the imperial crown with great solemnity on to her head.

'I'll probably be out on my ear tomorrow when the results come out, so ye can have anythin' fits you.'

'Oh don't say that, Jessie. Please don't say that. You didn't think you'd done so bad at the time.'

'Ach well, sure what does it matter? I never thought I'd get the Qualifying and I've had a great time these four years since. If I'm out, I'll get a job and have lots of money an' then we can go to the pictures whenever we like. It won't make a bit of difference to us except for sittin' in the same classroom and not being able to say two words the whole day. Are you goin' into school in the mornin' or waitin' for the post?'

'I'll go in,' said Clare quickly. 'I couldn't stand waiting for the post. Anyway, it mightn't come on the post tomorrow. If I had to wait till Monday, I'd go mad.'

'You'll be all right, Clare. What are ye worryin' about? You'll sail through. I'd bet you five pounds if I had it, I'm that sure.'

Whether it was her friend's words, or the sudden warm pressure of her hand on hers, Clare couldn't tell, but she found her eyes filled with tears. She felt herself suddenly wondering if she would ever sit here with her friend, ever again.

'I suppose we'd better go,' she said reluctantly.

'Aye, I have stuff for the tea in my bag, so there'll be no tea till I get there,' said Jessie laughing and swinging herself deftly back on to the bank.

'Me too,' Clare added, as she followed more cautiously behind. 'Though Granda never notices the time when he's in the forge. It's not tea time, till I tell him it is.'

'That's handy.'

Clare followed Jessie up and across the steep bank until they had almost reached the gap in the hedge.

'Jessie!' she whispered hastily.

'What?'

'There's someone doing something to our bicycles.'

'Is there indeed? Well, I'll see to them,' she said angrily, before she had even raised her head to look.

Without further ado, she pushed through the hedge, marched across the road and confronted the offender.

'And what do you think you're doing to my friend's bicycle?'

Clare paused halfway through the hedge and surveyed the scene. Jessie stood, hands on hips, glowering down at a fair-haired boy in an open-necked shirt who appeared to be unscrewing the valve cap on one of her tyres.

'Trying to put this valve cap back on, but it's fiddly and I'm not much good at it. Here, you have a go.'

Clare had an irresistible desire to giggle when she saw the look on Jessie's face. But Jessie was not to be charmed.

'Are you a Richardson?'

'Yes, I'm Andrew. How do you do?'

He stood up and held out his hand politely, as Clare crossed the road to join them. Jessie shook his hand and turned to Clare.

'Clare, this is Andrew Richardson. I'm not sure he wasn't lettin' your tyres down.'

'No. I don't think so,' said Clare as she shook hands. 'There are better ways of letting tyres down.'

'Are there?' he enquired, looking at her directly. She was amazed to find how startlingly blue his eyes were.

'Yes, a good poke with a penknife or a spike of some sort,' she replied honestly. 'I'm sure he's got a pen knife,' she added turning to Jessie.

'Don't put bad in his head, Clare. He's maybe done damage enough.'

'Not guilty, madam,' he declared, looking at Clare again. 'There were some boys here when I came down to open the gates. They ran off when they saw me and I noticed the tyres were flat. I've pumped up one, but the other was more difficult,' he explained.

'That was very kind of you,' said Clare, feeling strangely uncomfortable.

He was really a rather friendly boy, though he did have a peculiar accent and was wearing very posh jodhpurs and riding boots.

'Well, if you've managed to get any air back in, I think we must be going,' said Jessie, firmly.

He nodded, straightened up Clare's bicycle and gave it to her.

'Have you far to go?'

'No, not far. Only the Grange.'

'Should be all right that far.'

'Thank you. Thank you very much for pumping it up,' she said as she wheeled it out on to the road and stretched herself up into the saddle.

'Not at all. It was a pleasure,' he said, with a grin, as he turned towards the heavy iron gates on the driveway and swung them fully open just as a large car approached at a leisurely pace from the direction of Armagh.

They stopped by the pump opposite Charlie Running's cottage, had a drink and splashed their hot hands and faces. They always stopped by the pump to make plans for the next day even when they weren't thirsty, because Jessie's road home left the main road just a little further on, where Riley's Rocks poked their hard-edged shapes through the soft greenness of Robinson's bog. It ran downhill, struck westwards through Tullyard and then wove its way onward between scattered farms and cottages cut off from each other by the undulations of the hilly countryside and the small plantings of orchard and woodland.

Clare remembered the September morning, four years ago now, when they met up at just this spot for the first time, dressed in the new uniforms that still had some of the original creases from the manufacturer's box. Clare's three-quarter length socks wouldn't stay up and Jessie insisted she'd got bigger since her blouse was bought. It had rained suddenly and violently as they struggled slowly up the Asylum Hill. There was nowhere to take shelter and no time to waste. They pressed on and arrived at Beresford Row at a quarter to nine, new Burberrys damp, hair dripping beneath the sodden berets, to search for their labelled pegs in a minute cloakroom full of perfectly dry girls, who had walked from Barrack Hill or Railway Street and missed the rain completely.

'Are ye workin' for Margaret tomorrow?' asked Jessie, as she pushed her hair back from her damp face.

'Yes, I'm looking after the children. She wants to go into town.'

'Pity. No Ritz this week,' she said sadly.

'I can't afford it anyway, Jessie. I'll need black stockings if I go back. The forge is very quiet.'

Jessie nodded and said nothing. She was a lot better off than Clare. There was pocket money from her father every week, regular bits and pieces of money from her mother for doing jobs and the occasional half crown from Auntie Sarah, but as often as not Jessie was broke too. Unlike Clare, who always had an eye to the future, never knowing what she would have to find money for, or where it was going to come from, Jessie was unthinking. If the money was there, she spent it. Come easy, go easy was her way. If she had it, that was fine, but if she didn't, she never complained.

'Will we go for a walk tomorrow evening?'

'Aye, why not? I'll call for you about seven. We'll maybe pick up a couple of good-lookin' fellas and go off to a dance.'

Clare giggled. The chances of meeting anyone on a Saturday evening were so small, even bumping into an elderly neighbour was a major event.

'Make sure you put your nylons on, Jessie,' Clare laughed, knowing that Jessie, like herself, had never even seen nylons, let alone be able to afford the price of those smuggled over the border from the Republic.

'Time I was away,' said Jessie, looking at her watch.

'What time is it?'

147

'Quarter past five.'

'Me too. See you tomorrow,' called Clare as she swung herself into the saddle.

She caught sight of Jessie's flying figure for a moment before she was hidden from view by the scatter of young trees around the old quarry. She felt suddenly sad and anxious. Tomorrow the exam results would be out. If she did well, her scholarship would be renewed and she would stay at school. If she didn't, she must leave and get a job.

If Jessie failed to get Junior, her family could afford to pay for her to stay on in the hope that she might scrape through Senior Certificate in two years' time, but that was out of the question for Clare. Thirty pounds a term was an enormous sum to find and then there was the lunch money and all the other expensive things that kept cropping up, from hockey sticks to educational outings.

She made a final effort on the hill past Robinson's. Perhaps it was just her period and the pain in her back that was making her feel so low. She'd have to put herself in better spirits before she looked in the door of the forge.

She wheeled her bicycle up the bumpy lane and smiled as she glanced up at the house. In one of the window boxes Uncle Jack had made for her, something new was blooming. It was too far away to see exactly what it was, but it certainly hadn't been in bloom when she left just after their midday meal.

'Hello, Granda, are you dying for your tea?'

'Ach, yer back. Did ye see Jessie?'

'Yes, we did our shopping and then we sat and gossiped.'

'Any news?' he said, putting down his hammer and leaning against the bellows.

'I brought you the *Guardian* and the *Gazette* both so you'll be well newsed,' she said with a laugh, 'and I saw Mrs Taylor, who was asking for you. And Jessie's father's had his tests done. Good news. They say his heart's all right. He had to go to the hospital again today though.'

148

Clare saw how tired he was. He had a way of leaning against the bellows, even when they didn't need pressing and there was a look below his eyes that made him seem pale, though his skin was always brown beneath the layer of grime his sweat trapped as he hammered. So often these days, she knew he was glad to stop work when she appeared, so she tried to think of anything else that would prolong his brief respite.

'Have you had any callers yourself?'

'Aye, one or two. Mosey Johnston paid me for his gate, so we're all right for the rent for a week or two. Ah thought he wasn't goin' to pay me atall, he's been that long. And yer friend John Wiley was here. He says there's some big bug from across the water comin' to Richardson's for the weekend. His wife's landed him with the childer for the whole time an' he's not well pleased.'

Clare laughed. Dear John. The older the children got, the less he liked looking after them, but June was chief helper to the housekeeper at Drumsollen and working all weekend would be extra money for the family.

'I think maybe I saw the big bug arriving, Granda. There was a very posh car coming out from Armagh and the gates were open at the foot of the drive.'

'Aye, that's likely it, for John said he had to away back quick once I'd done the bit of a weld for him. He asked for you. He said to ask you how your flowers were doin'.'

'I hope you told him they're doing well. Something else is out since that rain this morning, but I can't see what till I go up and look.'

She paused, suddenly made anxious by the dragging weariness come into his face now that the pleasure of her return had passed.

'Would you like a glass of the spring to keep you going till the tea's ready?'

'Ach, no. I've near finished. I'll not start anither job the day. I'll be up shortly. Did ye say ye'd got both papers?'

'Yes. I was lucky. There were still some left. I think I should

149

order them, then we'd be sure of them. Whoever's in town could collect them, Jessie, or me, or the Robinsons.'

'Well . . .'

Clare smiled warmly, said the tea wouldn't be long, picked up her bicycle and manoeuvred it past a field gate for Harry Nesbitt. Of all the expressions and customs she'd had to learn since the day she and Edward James Bear walked up the path to the house for the first time, Granda Scott's way of saying 'Well' had puzzled her most and taken her longest to work out. But once she'd observed for a while there was no further difficulty. 'Well' said with that slight upward inflection, meant exactly what most other people meant by 'Yes'. So she would order the Armagh weekly papers and a Sunday one as well. It would mean going in especially to fetch it, but what did that matter? It was one of his few pleasures, and surely they could find tenpence a week.

She unpacked her shopping on to the hallstand and parked her bicycle under the elderberry bush beside the far gable. So thick was the canopy of a huge beech tree arching above the bush itself that even in the wettest weather she seldom had to wipe the saddle dry in the morning, and if she forgot to collect her underwear, hung there to dry, then it'd be no worse off than leaving it over the back of a chair in 'the boys' room'. This was the small room beyond her own bedroom where she had set up the old washstand under the window, so she'd have a place to do her homework should anyone come to call on Robert before she'd finished, or when she was able to find him brass band music or a talk about Ulster customs to listen to on the radio.

The dazzling splash of brightness she'd seen from the forge was in the green-painted box on the sitting room windowsill. In a moment, she was close enough to see it was a fuchsia. As she put out a tentative finger to touch it, she laughed, and remembered precisely what fuchsia it was.

'What a strange coincidence,' she said quietly to herself as she stroked the waxy petals.

The cutting that had produced its first glorious bloom, a

purple corolla with long orange stamens, surrounded by a milky white skirt like that of a ballerina, John Wiley had brought her from the small bush in his own garden.

'Here ye are, Clarey. Niver say where ye came by that fellow, but I promise you, you'll like him. Most beautiful thing I iver saw in a garden in all my life.'

'Why can't I say where I got him, John?' she said, taking the moss-wrapped fragment from his large hand and settling herself to listen to the story she was sure he had to tell.

'Well, d'ye see, Major Richardson, he went off to England on some business or other and when he came back, he had this bush. Said it was a new variety. Made a great fuss about it. Wouldn't let Old Harry touch it. Had to plant it himself. And I can see why he was so particular. Ach, when it first came out up at the house, I thought it was lovely, so I asked Old Harry for a wee cutting. But he said it was more than his life was worth an' he wouden' give me as much as a leaf.'

John hung his head in despair, then grinned at her mischievously.

'Well, that's all right, thinks I, and waits my time. And sure enough one day Harry's mowing the lawn an' somethin' goes wrong with the mower. It jumps outa his hands and knocks a brave wee branch off the fuchsia an' then stops dead. Well, when he called me to get the mower going for him, I saw the branch in a jar of water. I knew rightly what it was, so we "did a deal" as they say at the pictures. I'd not say a word about the damage to the bush an' he'd not say a word about the bit of that branch in my pocket.'

Clare wondered what Andrew Richardson would think if he knew a piece of his uncle's precious plant was growing on the windowsill of the forge house at Salter's Grange. And that cuttings from it would soon be found in every cottage and farm where there was someone with an eye hungry for colour and fingers green enough to coax one more to grow.

Strangely, she didn't think he would mind. Despite his strange accent and his posh clothes, he'd been very kind. If those boys he'd seen were from the Mill Row, they'd not be beyond pinching the pumps and her precious back carrier bag, though they wouldn't risk lifting the bicycles themselves.

She stood looking down at the exotic bloom resting against her fingers so softly.

'Something beautiful,' she said quietly, as she wondered what its name might be. 'Until I find out, I shall call you Clare's Delight.'

She spent a few minutes removing faded blooms and yellowed leaves from the rain-battered plants in the flower bed below the window and then, remembering she was supposed to be getting tea ready, she dropped her gatherings in the old bucket hidden behind the aquilegia and headed for the kitchen.

As she reached the open front door, she was greeted by 'The Yellow Rose of Texas', being played with a needle that should certainly have been thrown away long ago. Her heart sank and weariness swept over her. She would be pleased enough to see Jamsey most afternoons, but today it was late, her back ached, and her mind was so preoccupied with her talk with Jessie that the effort of talking to him intimidated her.

She paused, her hand on the latch. It was a bad sign that he was still here this late in the afternoon. Usually, he was gone long before this. He came often to play one or other of the two ancient gramophones which had filled the house with lively noise when Polly and Mary, Ellie and Florence, and Bob and Tommy were still at home. When he was having a bad day, he would come over from the farm to escape whatever had upset him and play records, often going on playing the same record over and over again. Sometimes she managed to cheer him up, but sometimes it was not till Robert came up from the forge and found some message for him to take to the farm that he was prompted to go home.

The music died away, but Jamsey did not lift the playing head and the needle went on scratching in the groove.

'Hello, Jamsey,' she said, quietly slipping round towards the window so that he could see her.

'Up yer cock.'

As bad as that, she thought, looking at his face, pasty, white and immobile. His eyes regarded her, but did not see her.

'No, Jamsey, don't say that. Robert doesn't like you to say that,' she said firmly.

He stared at her and seemed to be about to repeat the forbidden words.

She put her finger to her mouth.

'Shh. Lemonade and sasparilla, Jamsey. Say lemonade and sasparilla, for me.'

'All the same price, take your choice, lemonade and sasparilla,' he said, tears springing to his eyes.

'There now, don't cry, Jamsey. What'll we sing?'

He looked at her blankly as if he hadn't even heard, but she saw him straighten himself as he always did when he sang. It was the only time he ever lost the sad droop to his shoulders.

Clare began, her light voice a thin thread in the large room where the last of the afternoon sun had retreated and shadows gathered in all the corners.

'The pale moon was rising above the blue mountain
The sun was declining into the blue sea
It was then that I went there and walked with my Mary
My Mary, the loveliest Rose of Tralee.'

Halfway through the first verse, a strange, half-strangulated noise began to accompany her. Jamsey knew the words well enough but couldn't sing them, though he was able to mime their cadence.

Clare turned towards him and conducted him with both her hands. She was so delighted when suddenly he broke into a broad grin. Conducting him while they sang had never yet failed to make him smile.

'One for the road, Ellie,' he said, the moment they stopped.

'Name your pleasure,' she replied promptly.

'Once in Royal David's city,' he said, without hesitation.

For a moment, she wondered if she could manage it, but there was something about the way he looked at her, the way he leaned slightly towards her, the way he called her 'Ellie', that gave her courage. She sat down opposite him and conducted him through all the verses. They were still singing when Robert came in for his tea.

'I'm sorry I haven't even started yet,' she said apologetically, after Jamsey had raised a hand and suddenly departed. 'He was in a bad way.'

'Poor man, it's hard to know what goes on in his head. Sometimes I don't think it's anythin' anyone says or does, it's just inside him.'

She put the kettle back on the stove and poked it up while he unfolded the newspapers she'd left by his chair. He never read the papers before his meal, but he liked to look them over, squinting down through the tiny round glasses with their springy earpieces that gave him such trouble when he went to hook them round his ears.

She cut slices of bread from the grey-brown loaf and brought out the small cheese ration from the corner cupboard. There were two sorts of jam, gooseberry from Liskeyborough, and damson from the orchard behind the house. 'Not worth picking this year,' the Robinsons had said. 'Take what you like.' And Margaret had told her you could get extra sugar coupons for making jam if you asked for them. So she'd dug in the rubbish dump for jars, scrubbed them and boiled them, picked the fruit and made her own jam for the first time. She felt so proud of the full jars standing in 'the room' to cool. Even if it was a bit runny, it tasted wonderful.

After their meal, Robert took half an hour on the bed and Clare settled to read at the table because the light was better there than by the fireside. But she found it hard to concentrate though the library book, a copy of *Pride and Prejudice*, was one of her favourites.

She stared out through the tiny orchard window. Then she ran her eye over all the assorted objects in the thick embrasure, the salt and pepper for the table, a bottle of ink for the accounts for the forge, a few old penholders with a paper bag containing threepence worth of shiny gold and silver nibs from Woolworths. The Tilley lamp lived there too, when not in use, and a packet of candles for when they ran out of paraffin. There were matches and shoelaces, a pair of scissors and an airmail writing pad with envelopes.

'Are ye studying again?' he asked as he padded over to his chair where he'd left his boots.

'No, this is for fun,' she said, moving back to the settle on the far side of the stove. From there, he could hear her better, because he could see her face.

Just as Robert stretched up from putting on his own boots, they heard the scrape of someone approaching on the path outside. Usually they could guess who the visitor might be, but tonight they looked at each other in surprise. It was early yet. Not many men finished their work before dark and women usually visited during the day.

Clare jumped up, pulled open the kitchen door and saw Margaret's husband, the eldest of the Robinson boys, standing there, a look on his face that had to mean bad news.

'What's wrong, Eddie? Is Margaret all right?'

'She's all right in herself.'

Eddie raised a hand in salute to Robert, pulled off his cap and sank down on the settle.

They waited for Eddie to collect himself. She felt a sick nausea sweep over her as the seconds dragged by like minutes.

'I'm the bringer of bad news to yez both, an' I'm sorry for it. Jack Rowentree is dead,' he said, his voice as firm as he could manage. 'Yer wee friend Jessie found him a while ago when she got back from town,' he added, as he turned towards Clare, his voice breaking down as he spoke.

'Oh no!'

'Ach, man dear, that's desperate news. Was it the heart after all?' asked Robert, his eyes staring, his face a stiff mask in the fading light.

'No, it wasn't,' said Eddie, collecting himself and sweeping his hand back over his shock of brown hair. 'That's the worst of it, Robert. I have to tell ye, Jack had bad news from the Doctor. He came home and shot hisself.'

Robert Scott wished he'd a drop of whiskey in the house for Eddie Robinson looked as if he'd seen a ghost. But the last time there'd been a bottle in the house was the previous Christmas when Bob had brought him some. Whiskey was hard to come by these days, even if you had the money to pay for it, as Bob did.

'Margaret said I was to ask your opinion, Robert,' Eddie began, taking a deep breath and looking up at the older man.

'Aye,' said Robert encouragingly.

Clare stood watching them in amazement. Eddie Robinson was such a brusque, lively character, never at a loss for a quick word or a witty remark. The transformation was startling.

'By right we should go an' pay our respects,' he said, beginning firmly enough. 'If the man had died natural I'd 'ave put the mare in the trap meself an' sent Jamsey over to see if yez wanted a lift. But I don' know rightly what to do the way things are.'

Robert nodded and looked at Clare.

'I'll have to go and see Jessie, Granda, whatever you decide,' she said hastily, aware that tears might suddenly stream down her face.

'We must go as usual, Eddie,' said Robert quietly. 'We coulden' leave that wumman in her grief to think her neighbours had turned their backs on her.'

'I can go on my bike, Granda, that'll leave more room in the trap,' Clare began. 'Will Margaret face it, Eddie, she's not got long to go, has she?' she asked anxiously.

'No, she hasn't. She said she'd maybe not go to town tomorrow after all, but she's for going over to Rowentrees, if Robert here thinks it's the right thing.'

'Aye, Eddie, ye can't turn yer back on need. Woud ye give me a minit to see if I've a clean collar.'

'There are some in the top drawer,' said Clare in a whisper as he passed her on his way to his bedroom and left her alone with Eddie.

'It's not even that I know the man well, Clare. Sure he's been away for years, all through the war. An' even when it was over he was a long time gettin' back. Torpedoed twice an' then a prisoner of war,' he went on, his hands outstretched. 'An' he comes back safe from all that and then this. Sure there's no sense in it. No rightness at all.'

Clare stared at him. For the first time in the five years she'd known him, she saw a face unsmiling, shoulders hunched in despair, hands that struggled in the air to express a hurt he couldn't put into words.

What could she say, what words of comfort were there?

She remembered that day, so long ago now, when the minister of the church her parents had attended, came to visit her at the hospital before Auntie Polly took her away. William had been excused the minister's visit, which made it slightly easier because she didn't have to worry about him fidgeting or walking off. She'd sat on a high-backed chair in a waiting room with heavy furniture and a highly polished table covered with years-old magazines.

The minister had talked and then he had prayed. There wasn't much difference between the two. What he said when he arrived, he said again in the prayer before he left. She'd wondered then if he thought God wasn't listening because he said everything at least three times and it couldn't be for her benefit for she was paying attention to every word.

'God gives and God takes away. Blessed is the Lord. We cannot see what is best for us, but He sees. In His wisdom he binds and looses. Mummy and Daddy are in a far better place. A place with no pain and no distress. They will be in the company of angels singing and praising the Lord. She wouldn't want to call then back to this vale of tears when they could be united in fellowship with the Lord, now would she?'

He'd gone on for a long time and then read the twenty-third

psalm which was nice because she liked it and knew it by heart. And then he'd told her that the Lord would comfort her and he had to be going.

She couldn't really tell whether the Lord had comforted her or not. She couldn't imagine how He would do it. She did wonder if He knew how to comfort little girls who had lost their parents. When she went on feeling so unhappy through all those long weeks in Belfast she'd wondered if perhaps the Lord was too busy. She hadn't blamed Him because it probably wasn't His fault, but she felt afterwards that it was always better not to expect too much help from anywhere and then you wouldn't be too disappointed.

'It's an awful shock, Eddie,' she began, 'I don't know what I'm going to say to Jessie. I can't think of a single word of comfort, can you?'

He shook his head sadly.

'Whin me father died I diden' shed a tear. He'd had a good life and he'd started to ail, so in a kind of a way I was glad he diden' linger and fail. An' it was the same wi' the mother, though she did go kinda unexpected. But Jack Rowentree is a man in his prime. That's not right, Clare. I can't figure roun' that atall,' he said, standing up as Robert emerged from 'the room' looking uncomfortable in the fiercely starched collar from the laundry which he felt obliged to wear on any occasion that called for an expression of formality.

'I'll see you both there,' said Clare, glad to be able to escape before her tears let her down.

She set off back up the road to the turn where she and Jessie had parted not three hours earlier and skimmed down the slope where Jessie had disappeared from view when their roads diverged. She pedalled hard, indifferent to the fine, warm evening and the golden light that spread across the lush meadows and made them glow. She overtook a couple of ponies and traps and didn't even glance up to see who else was travelling in the same direction and on the same sad errand. On the final slope up to the two-storey house where Jessie had been born, a car passed her. It pulled into the farmyard ahead of her and found a place to stop among the crowd of traps and vans and bicycles already there.

The front door stood wide open and voices reached her as she leaned her bicycle against the wall of an outhouse. The thought of going into those crowded rooms appalled her. But she must. She had to find Jessie and her mother and say that she was sorry and ask if there was anything she could do. That much, at least, she knew she had to do.

But she couldn't bring herself to move. Pressed against the wall of the barn, she stood staring across at the house, its windows all thrown wide to let the spirit go, its blinds all drawn, so that it looked as if the dwelling itself had closed its own eyes and was trying to shut out the memory of what had happened.

It was then that Clare thought she heard someone crying. She listened and was sure. The sound seemed to be coming from the outhouse behind her so she pushed open the worn half door. She saw Jessie lying on the straw, her arms over her head, her shoulders shaking as she sobbed.

'Jessie, Jessie, my love, don't cry, please don't cry or I'll start and I'll never be able to stop,' she pleaded, as she put her arms round her friend.

'I'll see him, Clare, I'll see him every day of my life, lying here with only half his head left and the blood running round all the bumps in the cobbles and making a wee lake over there,' she gasped, nodding to a damp patch on the barn floor.

Clare stroked Jessie's hair and abandoned her own attempt not to cry. Her tears poured down unheeded on to the soft, brown hair as she knelt in the fresh cut straw where her friend had thrown herself again.

Neither girl heard the door behind them open, nor did they notice the small, weary figure who stood there looking at them intently as they clutched each other wordlessly.

'Jessie. Clare.'

Clare was the first to hear. Startled, she looked up and saw

159

Mrs Taylor, Jessie's aunt, standing very straight, a dark outline against the brightness of the sunlit farmyard behind.

Sarah Taylor walked towards them, bent down and kissed Jessie and then, to Clare's surprise, kissed her too, her lips dry against her wet cheeks.

'Now, my dears, I have to ask you a favour. I take it, Jessie, this is the place where my little brother died.'

Jessie nodded and drew the sleeve of her cardigan hastily across her eyes.

'Well, there is something I should like to do, but I fear I have neither the strength, nor the skill,' she began. 'I would like to leave flowers here for Jack. When he was a little boy he used to bring flowers for me. He knew I loved flowers, no matter what kind they were. Buttercups or daisies, things from the garden, honeysuckle from the hedgerows, leaves or berries. Anything that grew. And I'd like to acknowledge that. Will you do that for me?'

They got to their feet and looked down at her.

'Lots of flowers, Mrs Taylor?' asked Clare who wanted to be sure she understood.

'Yes, an extravagance of flowers, Clare. So many it will take you both to carry them and the rest of this lovely evening light to find them,' she said, turning on her heel as if to depart. 'I'll tell your mother, Jessie, that you've offered to do something for me. I'm sure she can spare you with all these other people who are so anxious to help her.'

Together they rode the lanes. There was plenty of late honeysuckle twining its way through the quickset hawthorn and climbing the branches of the larger bushes and trees planted to give body to the hedgerow. From the damp tangled grass in the hedge bottoms, tall spikes of meadowsweet scented the air. They gathered armfuls of both and then thought of garden flowers they might add. When they called with Charlie Running to ask if he could spare a few roses, he cut them his best, added dahlias as well and sent them on to his cousin Dick Compston for sweetpeas. They filled their baskets and carrier bags and tied bundles of foliage across their handlebars to save themselves a second journey back to Jessie's home.

Dusk was gathering when they arrived back, but to their surprise there were candles burning in the darkness of the barn. Some old stone jars filled with water had been left ready for them together with a cluster of two pound jampots and an extra bucket of water.

'Do you think she's gone a bit funny?' asked Jessie, as they carried the flowers into the barn and saw the candles flicker in the draught from the open door.

'Who? Your Aunt Sarah? No, I don't think so,' said Clare quietly, as she chose the biggest stems to put in the tallest of the stone jars.

'What'll I do with these?' asked Jessie, doubtfully, holding up a handful of roses with very short stems. 'They'll not sit in a jar, wi' stems that wee.'

'Did your father like roses, Jessie?'

'Aye, he did. Said it was his favourite flower.'

Suddenly, it seemed obvious to Clare what she had to do.

'Why don't we put them here, on the floor itself,' she said, tipping out water from one of the jars.

The water splashed down and ran into the damp hollow where earlier someone had washed away Jack Rowentree's blood.

'Look, we can make a kind of floating bowl, just here,' Clare went on, taking some of the roses from her friend's hand.

She placed them with care, the short stems between the cobbles where the water was deepest, and waited while Jessie did the same with those she still held.

'Smell, Jessie, smell,' she cried, as the last dark red bloom found its place. 'Charlie said they'd such a great smell it made up for the poor stems.'

Clare watched her friend as she drew in the heavy perfume and then stood up and looked down at the jars and jampots overflowing with summer flowers.

'Mmmm. They're lovely,' Jessie said, nodding.

The candles threw light against the massed flowers and spilled over to wink back from a few drops of water lying like raindrops on the petals of the small pool of dark red roses that smelt so wonderful.

Clare waited and watched.

'I think it looks great,' said Jessie with a great sigh. 'Will we away and get Aunt Sarah and show her what we've done for Daddy.'

11

W hen Clare woke next morning she could hardly believe she'd slept the whole night through undisturbed by dream or nightmare. Her mind was still full of the sight and smell of flowers and of the stillness of the lovely summer evening she and Jessie had shared in the lanes they knew so well.

She decided there and then that Jessie's Aunt Sarah was a very wise lady. Whether or not what she had asked them to do was what she actually wanted for herself, she couldn't tell. What she was quite sure about was that the evening had brought healing to the awful hurt Jessie had suffered when she found her father lying dead in the barn. However sad Jessie was going to be, however much she missed her father, Clare felt sure what she had seen would not now haunt her.

She was so absorbed in thinking about Jessie and the difficult time ahead of her it was some minutes before the significance of the day for herself and her own future swooped up into consciousness and had her out of bed in seconds.

'Today's the day,' she said to herself, as she poured rainwater into her wash bowl, a few little fragments of elderflower swirling round in the clear water.

She knew she was anxious. It was all she could do to eat breakfast normally, so that Robert wouldn't be concerned about her. She could hardly wait to be on her way into town, so that she could be alone with her thoughts.

It was shortly before ten when she bumped over the level crossing and pedalled steadily up Railway Street. There weren't many people about. Saturday mornings were always quiet in the city. The horse-drawn Wordy carts that delivered coal and wood and the heavy items that came by train from the Belfast docks, didn't deliver on Saturdays. The shops at this end of the town were small and very limited in what they had for sale. There were no queues to be seen.

She smiled as she cycled past the fruit and vegetable shop at the top of Albert Place and free-wheeled down into Lonsdale Street. She remembered the day when the little shop had its first consignment of bananas. She'd heard about them on the way from school to the bus and had walked back to join the long queue, sure that Granda Scott would be thrilled to have bananas again. But they'd run out just as she got to the counter. A woman saw the disappointment sweep across her face and gave her one from her own ration. A strange, curved, pale green object. She had said thank you most enthusiastically, taken the precious fruit home to Granda Scott and been told that it wasn't ripe yet. It never did ripen. It just changed colour slightly and then went bad. Bananas, she decided, had to be added to her list of life's disappointments.

But what never disappointed her was her new school on The Mall. The buildings were old. Two Georgian stone houses separated at ground level by a carriage entrance that led to the stables behind. Inside, the narrow staircases in both houses connected only at first-floor level. There were ancient bathrooms, tiled corridors and open fires that had to be looked after throughout the day. Not the ideal housing for a school, some would think, but its limitations never mattered to Clare. From that first morning when she'd struggled to dry her hair in what had once been a maid's pantry, she'd been happy there, happier than she'd ever been, since she had lost her parents.

It didn't matter to her or to Jessie that much of what went on during the school day, actually went on somewhere else. They played hockey on The Mall itself, their pitch marked out to avoid the cricket crease that was used all through the summer. Tennis involved a long cycle out along Lisanally Lane to the courts belonging to the local Lawn Tennis and Archery Club. Gym took place in green knickers in the Temperance Hall in Lonsdale Street. Science meant a walk back up College Hill to her old primary school and when Jessie began Domestic Science she would hurry across the White Walk and up into the town to the old market house, now the technical school. For really special events like Prize Day, the whole school wound itself in a long, dark green line, across The Mall, up Russell Street and down English Street to the City Hall, where they climbed the wide, shallow staircase and sat on blue plush seats laid out in rows on the highly polished and beautifully sprung dance floor, juniors at the front, seniors behind, parents up on the balcony above and staff and governors on a stage, hung with wonderful red velvet curtains that swept aside dramatically when the proceedings were about to begin.

As she wheeled her bicycle up the entry she saw a blackboard propped up outside the steep steps leading down into the maid's pantry. The results had been delayed. Would girls please return at eleven o'clock, or expect them to arrive in the post on Monday.

Clare moved on to the old stables, now a bicycle shed, and found a crop of bicycles, most of which she recognised. She parked her own and stood looking around her. Since the end of June, the small plants that made their homes in the crevices of the old walls had really come on. Herb Robert cascaded down the rough, worn stones, its leaves already tinged with red. Ivy-leafed toad flax showed minute purple blooms, and here and there, with a fine disregard for the season, bright bunches of wallflower flourished wherever the mortar was loose or a piece of coping had fallen away and left a gravelly hollow in the top of the wall.

She climbed the steps which led on through the stable block into the open space of unkempt grass where they walked and talked in the lunch hour on fine days. It was only a broken path now, through what had once been a productive garden, but on either side neighbouring houses still kept their fruit trees and currant bushes, their cloches and cold frames, their patches for vegetables and their lines of flowers for cutting, sweet peas and dahlias, roses and chrysanthemums. Watching their progress from day to day was one of the delights of the summer term.

She found she had the old garden all to herself. All the other girls in her class must have gone to sit on The Mall or spend their sweet coupons at the little shop on the far side, beside the five-storey warehouse that had just reopened as a slipper factory.

So glad to be alone, she picked a tussock of grass in a sunny spot and sat down.

'What's the worst that can happen, Clare?' she whispered to herself.

That's what Ronnie would say. Dear Ronnie. What a good friend he'd been to her. He'd written her letters and sent her books. Once when he was on a cycling holiday with some friends from Queens, they'd arrived to visit her and Granda Scott and thoughtfully brought their rations with them. He'd wanted her to come up to Belfast for his graduation just last month, but it had been too difficult. Though he'd found somewhere for her to stay, she'd had to think about the train fare and what to wear. But what settled it was the July date so close to The Twelfth. She knew Granda Scott needed her to get him ready for the one great occasion in the year when he wore his stiff collar, his one and only suit and his well-brushed hard hat.

Clare heard the cathedral clock strike the half hour. The morning was so fine and pleasant the chimes seemed as close as when she heard them from the field on the Cathedral Road where she'd played with William, long ago.

The thought of William made her feel both sad and uneasy. She had tried to keep in touch with him for she was sure that was what her parents would have wanted, but her efforts hadn't been very successful. After the first visit to the farm when Uncle Jack had come and taken her and Granda Scott over for tea, there had been other Sunday visits when Uncle Billy or one of the visiting brothers came and collected her on their motorbike. As far as seeing William was concerned those were just as unsuccessful. If William had anyone else to play with he ignored her. Indeed, whenever they joined the other cousins at the tea table both her grandparents had to check him for being rude to her.

That was nothing new with William and Clare felt she should 'make allowances'. Her mother had always taught her that some people have difficulties that we don't really understand, like Granny Scott who had always complained all her life, even when she was young and hadn't anything wrong with her at all. But after Clare's next attempt to visit William she felt that even her mother might be upset by his behaviour.

One Saturday at the end of October she set off for the farm on her newly delivered bicycle.

'Yer sure ye can find yer way?' asked Granda Scott, anxious as always when she did something she hadn't done before.

'Oh yes,' she replied, spelling out the route with all the landmarks and the names of each of the larger farms she would pass.

She remembered now how he had laughed and said she'd a powerful memory. He couldn't mind the half of what she'd just told him.

As she turned into the yard, she spotted William poking a stick down one of the gratings that drained water away from the house. Although she'd rung her bell and called hallo as she came through the open gate, he didn't bother to look up.

'Whose is the bike?' he asked abruptly as she got off and wheeled it over to where he was standing.

'It's mine,' she said, propping it carefully against the white-washed wall of the house so that the handlebars wouldn't scrape.

'Where did ye get it?' he went on, crossly.

'Uncle Harry reconditioned it for me so I could cycle to school and save the busfares.'

167

'Where's mine?'

At seven and a half William was small for his age and certainly too young to go to Richhill school on the much busier Portadown Road, but Clare knew from long experience that William never listened to reasons. She could see he was angry and was still wondering what to say when Granny Hamilton appeared.

'Ach, hello Clare. Is that the new bike? Have you come to give William a ride on the pillion?'

Clare had agreed warmly that she had. She was grateful that Granny Hamilton had worked out that William always had to be the centre of attention. But her relief was short lived.

'I want a bicycle too,' he said quite quietly, as if he was talking to himself.

Clare shivered as she thought of him and the way he began to stiffen himself.

'I want a bicycle too,' he repeated, an ominous tone in his voice as he began to chant, his voice getting higher and higher.

Granny tried to get him to stop. She caught his arm, but he punched her and she was so taken aback that she let him go. He went racing up the yard still shouting and disappeared into the adjoining field, scattering in all directions the cattle who had been peacefully grazing there.

'I'll have to go after him, Granny!' she burst out.

'No, you won't. Let him be. Run down to the workshop and see if your Granda or your Uncle Billy is there. Tell them William is off again and I can't run after him. I'll away an' make us a cup o' tea. A nice welcome that an' you took the trouble to come over t'see him,' she muttered, as Clare ran down the yard as fast as her legs would carry her.

William would soon be twelve but he hadn't improved much over the years that Clare could see. These days he usually did what Granda Hamilton told him. Her grandmother said that she didn't know where Granda found the patience to deal with him for William never did anything without being told. You could tell him a hundred times to wash his hands or tie his shoes, she said, and he still wouldn't do it unless you stood over him and told him again.

Suddenly, a large ginger pussycat appeared. Clare sat quite still and watched it as it walked along the top of the wall dividing the school grounds from the garden of its nearest neighbour. It walked as if it knew just where it was going, stepping delicately over the occasional projecting branch and bending its handsome head where the boughs interrupted its pathway. Almost at the top of the garden it paused, turned, and retraced its journey, a determined look on its face. Clare was intrigued. What could it have been up to? Had it some inner plan or was it just patrolling its territory?

Time had slowed down. She'd discovered that it did that sometimes. Like when you were bored, or when you were unhappy, or like now, when you were waiting for something to happen. When you were busy, or engaged, and especially when you were happy, time just slipped by. It disappeared before you could even look at it. It happened with the minutes, the hours, and even the days of her own life. She wondered if it might even be able to happen with the years.

She thought of the way Robert would say to some visitor, parked on the settle by the fire on a winter's night, 'Ach, sure you'd wonder where the time goes.'

'Aye, it seems no time at all since we were trying to set a trap to catch Master McQuillan on his way to school,' would come the reply.

Sitting quietly in her corner, she'd heard stories enough of Robert's childhood escapades. She treasured them. From them she'd put together parts of his life that through a mixture of shyness and reticence he never thought to speak of, even when she encouraged him.

The theme of all these conversations with his contemporaries was always the same. Life sweeps you forward and before you've really got the measure of it, you find you're getting old. As she listened on the long, dark evenings, she observed how some of those who sat by the stove were wryly regretful about growing old, others were resigned, while some few were angry and bitter, behaving as if somehow life had cheated them. It often seemed that a single event was the focus of all their discontent. It kept coming into whatever story they told. Always they spoke as if the whole of their life would have been different, so much more to their liking, had the particular event not happened.

'Sure if I had my time over again, I'd not do . . .'

Almost like a refrain, the same phrase ran through her winters at the cottage.

Some of the men who sat back on the settle laid the blame on marriage and the demands of rearing a family, some spoke of the lack of opportunity in the countryside, even in the Province itself. There were those who like Granny Hamilton had planned to emigrate and changed their minds. There were some who had come back home in the end, but now wished they'd stayed away. There were men who blamed the war for taking away the jobs that were beginning to open up for them when it began and women who said that it was children tied you to a grindstone of hard labour.

From beyond the steps, floating up from the entry, Clare heard the sound of voices and high, forced laughter. It must be almost time. She felt so reluctant to move. It was such a short distance, the path and the entry between where she now sat and the doorway where the school secretary would pin up the results on the old blackboard, but once she travelled that short distance, the world would change for ever, one way or another.

The cathedral clock struck the hour just at that moment. It didn't take her by surprise. Having no watch, she'd grown so practised at judging time she was seldom wrong. If she was paying attention that was. Only when she felt free to let her mind follow its own paths did time steal away on her unobserved.

As she stood up, collected herself, and began to walk steadily down the path, she remembered that Uncle Jack had promised her a watch if she passed. He insisted he'd been saving up for some time now.

The disorderly mass of girls clustered around the board in front of her suddenly dissolved, as they dived into the building to collect their individual slips of paper. Heart in mouth, she stared at the scatter of F's in the right hand column. There were quite a few who had failed and as Jessie herself had guessed, she was one of them. A distinction in Art, which she loved, a credit in domestic science, which she was good at, a scraped pass in English; and then the single figure percentages in the subjects she hated or found boring.

Alison Clare Hamilton came just above the crease across the middle of the big sheet of paper. For a moment, Clare wasn't sure if the black stars beside some of the marks were hers or belonged to the person above. Gradually she made out that they were indeed hers. She had distinctions in six of her ten subjects, good credits in the rest, even in geometry, which she always found difficult. And as if to confirm the obvious, at the end of her row, it said PASS in big letters.

Jessie was right. Only yesterday she'd said: 'If I had a fiver, I'd bet you'd pass, I'm so sure.'

. She stepped down into the back entrance of the left-hand house in which the headmistress had her rooms and made her way along the dim corridor to the staircase that led to the office. The girls ahead of her had dispersed. She heard their footsteps echo on the bare boards of the Art room as they followed the one way system across into the other house and down its matching staircase into its maid's pantry which led out through a tiled lobby into the carriage entrance.

'Well done, Clare. I knew you'd do well, but you've done even better than I expected. How did you manage those wonderful marks in French and German?'

Clare shut the door with a clatter, surprised to hear the familiar voice when what she'd expected was one of the office staff. A slim, dark-haired woman with bright, mobile eyes held out a brown envelope with her name written on it.

171

'I think we might apply for one of the overall prizes on those results,' she went on cheerfully. 'I can't imagine many people doing better than you've done. Especially in German. After only two years. There are some very nice, *large*, book tokens,' she went on, knowing only too well Clare's weakness for books and her slender means.

'I haven't quite taken it in yet,' admitted Clare weakly.

'But you *are* coming back, aren't you?'

'Oh yes, I wanted to come back. But I knew I had to have a scholarship.'

'Well, you have that now. No doubt about it. And really, on those results, you ought to start thinking about a University Scholarship. If you go on like this, they'd certainly have you at Queens,' she added, as she turned to greet the next girl who had just pushed open the door.

She freewheeled down the Asylum Hill, as she always did. As she began bumping fiercely on the rough surface opposite the Mill Row, suddenly the penny dropped.

'I've done it,' she said to the empty road. 'I really have done it,' she announced, as she whizzed past Richardson's gates. She was glad there was no one about, for she knew she was grinning like an idiot and she couldn't do a thing about it.

'I must write to Ronnie tonight,' she declared for the benefit of a large crow who regarded her thoughtfully from the road-side verge and made no attempt to fly off.

It was because of Ronnie she'd managed such good marks in French and German. He might not believe her, but she'd tell him anyway.

She slowed down as the road steepened and passed between the railway bridge and the low mound where Mosey Jackson's cottage stood hidden among the trees.

A few months after she'd begun at the High School, Granda Scott's wireless packed up. He'd been very upset about it. The wireless was an important part of his life. He listened to the news first thing every morning and then again at midday. At

172

night, he set his erratic, old alarm clock by the time signal at nine o'clock. They both knew it couldn't be the battery, for Clare had taken it into Armagh to have it recharged quite recently. And if it wasn't the battery, it had to be something in the works. That meant getting the wireless itself into town for a repair and there was no knowing how much that might cost.

'There might be dirt in around the valves, Granda,' Clare said tentatively.

'Aye,' he replied, in a tone which wasn't so much agreement as a hope that he might receive some further information.

'If it was, we could clean them with methylated spirit and a feather,' she went on, watching him closely.

When he was anxious the whites of his eyes always seemed more prominent and she was more conscious of the stoop of his shoulders.

'Daddy showed me how to do it,' she went on firmly, 'but we'd need to bring it on to the table for the light.'

'Well, sure we could do that,' he said, sounding relieved.

He lifted the wireless from its dark corner on to the table by the window and then looked at it helplessly.

'It was yer father got this wireless for me,' he began. 'He bought it off some man second-hand an' did it up. The wood of the case was all scraped an' he revarnished it. Made a lovely job of it,' he went on, running his hands over the greasy but undamaged surface. 'I'm sure he took it to pieces as well.'

'Oh yes, he did. I remember it now. There's four wee screws so you can take the whole back off.'

'Well . . .'

Poor dear Granda, Clare thought as she pedalled on. He was always so afraid of things being broken, for he had never succeeded in fixing anything very much himself. However skilled he was in the forge, he was no use at all at mending even the simplest household object. Over their years together she had seen him try but in the end she had to agree with what her mother had said long ago and admit that he had no hands.

Clare had cleaned the inside of the wireless exactly the way she'd seen her father clean Ronnie's. Robert watched anxiously. When she switched on and produced a blast of sound much louder than she'd expected, he'd shaken his head and laughed.

'Sure you've great hands, Clarey. You can put them to anythin' takes your fancy,' he said, beaming with delight.

They moved the wireless from its old place on his table by the stove and put it on top of the floor-standing gramophone, which had finally given up the ghost. Away from the stove, it wouldn't get so dirty. And it was much easier to see the numbers on the dial.

Some days later, alone in the cottage, Clare turned the knobs, found dance music, classical music and a babble of foreign languages. She remembered her evenings with Ronnie in Belfast and the fun they'd had trying to pick up foreign stations. On this set, she found Paris was amazingly easy.

From then on, when she was alone, or in the evenings when Robert dozed by the fire or read his paper, she would tune in to whatever French or German station she could best pick up. News broadcasts she particularly liked, for after a little while she was able to work out what was going on. She made a game of picking up new words and searching for them in her dictionary. Often, she'd get distracted and end up making a lovely collection of new words, but forget the one she'd set out to find in the first place.

Robert was curious. No longer anxious she'd break the precious wireless by twiddling the knobs, he wanted to know what she was listening to. Sometimes, she'd turn the volume right up so that he could hear for himself. He would sit, his best ear cocked toward the set as if he were taking in every word.

'D'ye mean to say ye know what them people are sayin' to each other?' he asked in amazement.

'Not all the time,' she replied, laughing. 'But you get used to words if you keep on hearing them. The French are having

awful trouble with their government. I hear about that so often,
I can nearly always follow it.'

'Aye, I've heard tell o' that. But you're hearin' it from the
French themselves, aren't ye?'

When she had the chance to join the German class, a year
later, Clare jumped at it, her ear already familiar with the sound
and pattern of the language, even if she knew only the call
signals of a few stations, the names of the broadcasting orches-
tras and a handful of words.

'Well, what's the news?' Robert asked, putting down his
hammer and leaning against the anvil as she reached the door of
the forge.

By the smile on his face, she was sure he'd guessed.

'I passed.'

'Aye, ah know. An' came out up at the top of yer class forby?'

'Who told you that?' she asked in amazement, as she sat
down on the bench inside the door.

'I heerd it on the wireless.'

She laughed in pure delight. She could see he was as pleased
as Punch.

'Missus Rowentree phoned the school to see about Jessie an'
she knows that teacher ye talk about, so she asked how you'd
done an' got all the details. She says yer language teacher is
powerful pleased.'

'Did she come down to see you?'

'Aye, she came to leave a message to say thank you for
helpin' Jessie out last night. She says she's a differen' wee girl
the day. But she's askin' if you'll sit with her at the funeral on
Tuesday.'

'With Jessie?'

'Aye. An' why not? Sure the pair of you might be sisters for
all yer that different.'

'Jessie didn't get her exam, Granda,' said Clare sadly.

'No, she diden'. An' the mother's not one bit put out. She
says Jessie is no hand at the books, but it did her no harm to
have her four years at the High.'

'How *was* Mrs Rowentree? I hardly got speaking to her last night.'

He considered for a moment. She saw him make up his mind to speak and turn to look her straight in the face.

'She was rightly considerin'. She said Jack had an awful fear of illness, an' that his own mother died in agony with cancer. If he had to go it was better for him. She'd been in a bad way over Jessie findin' him, but she's over that now. Missus Taylor is staying with her an' is a great help to her, she says.'

'Mrs Taylor has been very kind to me too, Granda. If it hadn't been for her encouraging me I'd not have got the Qualifying.'

'Aye, an' now I heer ye can think of the university,' he said, looking pleased again.

'I doubt if we could afford that, Granda, even with a scholarship,' she said matter-of-factly.

'Not at all. Sure we'll get what'll do us. Haven't we managed fine since ye came with yer Auntie Polly and Uncle Jack and yer wee bag o' clothes an' the teddy bear? We'll manage fine,' he said with surprising firmness.

He moved across to the bellows and leaned gently on the long, smooth handle. The fire on the raised hearth had dropped so low that only a fine thread of pale smoke showed it was still alight. He pressed again and the embers glowed briefly. She watched as his arm rested on the shaft. The gentle pressure increased, the glow strengthened. In a few moments, the fire would be ready to work again.

'Did you have any other callers?'

'I did indeed. Sure I've two bits of news for you,' he laughed, pushing his cap back and scratching his forehead. 'Eddie Robinson was here and had great news. The we'ean arrived at breakfast time. It's a wee girl and ye'd think Eddie had won the Irish Sweepstake, he's that pleased.'

Clare clapped her hands together.

'Oh, that's great! Just great! Margaret was afraid it'd be

another boy and her with three already. She says three was quite enough, but Eddie was mad for a wee girl.'

'Well, he's got his wee girl an' Margaret's fine. She's expecting you after dinner as usual.'

'It's all good news today, isn't it, after such bad news yesterday,' she said slowly, as she got to her feet.

'That's always the way. It's always a mix. Never all bad, but never all good,' he said as the fire broke into an orange and gold cavern ready to take the half-finished decoration for the top of a garden gate.

'If I'm going to Margaret as usual I must get the potatoes on.'

'D'ye not want the other message I was bid give ye?'

'What other message?'

'The one from the young man on the chestnut mare?'

She giggled.

'D'ye think I'm jokin'?'

'I do.'

'Well, I'm not,' he said with a grin. 'A nice young man, well-spoken. Knew yer name an' that I was yer Granda. D'ye not mind him?'

Clare was baffled. Apart from Jessie's older brother John, and Eric, the youngest of the Robinson brothers who was about her own age, there were no young men in Clare's life. There were certainly no young men with chestnut mares.

'He came to ask if you got home all right. He said you had a wee bit of a problem with your bicycle.'

'Oh . . . Andrew Richardson,' she gasped, as light dawned. 'Some boys from the Mill Row let our tyres down when we left our bikes up against the wall by the Richardson's gate and he pumped them up again.'

'Aye,' said Robert, as he pressed the iron bar into the heart of the fire. 'Well, it's good for business. He said he was for England in a day or two, but when he was next back he'd bring the mare for her new shoes.'

He looked at her sideways and smiled to himself.

'To tell you the truth, I don't think it was shoes for the mare he was after atall. But we'll see. We'll see,' he said cheerfully. 'Give us a shout when the dinner's ready.'

Clare wheeled her bicycle up to the house. As she parked it under the gable, she wondered whether or not, given the dimness of the forge, Robert had managed to see that she was blushing.

12

The autumn of 1951 was wet in Ulster. Morning after morning, Clare cycled to school in pouring rain. Day after day, the return journey in the late afternoon was just as bad. But often, during the hours between, the clouds opened. From great patches of blue sky, the sun poured down with enough warmth to dry the leaf-strewn paths across The Mall. The golden radiance flickered through the lightly clad branches where the surviving leaves, bronze and gold, fluttered and fell. They caught in the uncut grass that edged the saturated rugby and hockey pitches, grass so lank with growth and so sodden with the regular downpours that it seldom dried out at all.

In these golden intermissions, when strong shadows fell on the worn paintwork and dusty mouldings of whichever classroom she found herself in, Clare would gaze out through the rain-spattered windows, restless and strangely discontented. She felt such a weariness upon her. She longed to be free to sit in the sun or cycle down the quiet lanes with nothing to do but please herself.

At moments in the school day, as she changed into hockey boots, or collected her books before walking up the hill to the science laboratory, or ran her finger along the shelf of foreign language literature in the tiny library, she found herself trying to imagine life beyond the present. Would there ever be a time without the endless cleaning, the collecting of rations, the preparing of food, the mending of clothes? Would a day come when she didn't have to puzzle and calculate how to make the

179

little that she and Robert could produce between them stretch to meet their very modest needs?

Though her work for Senior Certificate was heavier and more demanding, Clare didn't feel it was the cause of the weariness that dogged her. She enjoyed the challenge of the French and German books they were reading and the struggle to make her writing and speaking as good as her understanding was already. And she loved moving into the different world opened up by the French and German magazines that arrived each week. She dreamed of walking down the Champs Elysées in springtime, or standing in the nave of Notre Dame, or drinking coffee in the place du Tertre and watching some budding artist struggle with a canvas. She would cruise down the Rhine, visit the vineyards on the south-facing slopes, gaze up at extraordinary castles on rocky outcrops and walk in the Black Forest. Her imaginings delighted her and the work itself gave her a comforting reassurance that dreams could become reality if you gave your mind to them.

No, it was not school that was making her feel so low. She knew she carried a heavy burden of responsibility, for Mrs Taylor often spoke of it in a most kindly way. But, what really troubled her and made her both anxious and sad was Robert's failing vitality. She saw the distress in his face every time he had to go and take half an hour on the bed. Even quite simple tasks tired him these days and he had to stop and rest more and more often. When he couldn't be physically active, he had little to occupy him, for work had been the complete focus of his life. As the activity of the forge became less and less, so Robert retreated ever further into himself and grew more and more silent and withdrawn.

His earnings from the forge were shrinking all the time. Nor was it simply a matter of his failing strength. The changes that began during the war were now very obvious throughout the countryside. Repairing farm machinery and shoeing horses had been the mainstay of Robert's work. But the move from horses to tractors had really speeded up in the last few years and the old horse-drawn reaping machines and harrows that needed regular repairs had almost disappeared. Most of them were rusting in barns though one of them still stood in the long grass opposite the forge, because the owner had never bothered to collect it. Years ago, Robert had admitted to Granda Hamilton that he couldn't shoe forty horses a week any more, but now there were weeks when the shoeing shed was never used at all and the once familiar smell of singeing hoof no longer lingered on the afternoon air.

Robert still made gates, a job he enjoyed doing and Clare often watched with pleasure the familiar sequence of creating from the narrow iron bars the twists and swirls and curlicues, the signature of his work. But apart from the gates and the odd tool to repair there were very few jobs coming in. Farmers and neighbours came to the forge as before to exchange news, but Clare knew Robert didn't charge when these old friends brought some small job to be done. Worse still, when he did do a big job, like a pair of gates for a driveway, or a couple of field gates for one of the local farms, he might wait weeks for payment. Several times in the last year, he'd not been able to order more iron from Shillington's in Portadown, because he was waiting for money to pay their last account.

Clare found herself continuously doing sums in her head. Robert's pension was their only regular source of income, though she herself usually managed to add at least five shillings every week to the small drawer in the dressing table where he kept his pension book and his money. She looked after the Robinson children on Saturdays so that Margaret could go to town, did all the family's mending, washed the eggs when Margaret was behind hand and the collection van was due, and sometimes delivered meals for her to an old aunt down in Ballybrannan. Margaret wasn't generous with money, but she was very fair. If she didn't produce cash, then at least there'd be no bill for the milk, butter and potatoes Jamsey brought over to them in the course of the week. When the farm was very busy at harvest, or when the thresher came, there was so much extra work that Clare had no spare time at all but she never minded, because then she would arrive home triumphant, with money, credits for future weeks, home-baked bread and often a boiling fowl or a piece of home-cured bacon as well.

Whether on her solitary journeys to and from school, or sitting by the stove in the evening when Robert dozed or talked to some neighbour who had called, however often she thought about it, she came to the same conclusion. There was no immediate problem with paying their rent, nor with feeding them. The trouble started when something had to be bought for the house, or for the forge, or for themselves.

Robert's only coat, an old gabardine raincoat, was so thin it had no warmth left in it. He hadn't had new underwear since the end of the war and his vests and long johns were so worn the darns were the most substantial part of them.

'If you don't stop worrying about it, you'll only make it worse,' she said to herself, as she pedalled home one Friday afternoon.

She thought of Jessie and smiled to herself. With any luck, she'd appear sometime during the evening.

'The food's awful and there's a list on the back of the bedroom door of all I'm not to do that's as long as yer arm,' she'd announced, on her first visit home after going to Belfast to stay with a distant relative as a paying guest while she did a secretarial course. Each Friday night visit brought a stream of complaints and stories that made even Robert shake his head and smile.

'The typin's not so bad, ye'd get to kinda like it, but thon oul' shorthan' would put ye baldy,' she told them a week later.

The thought of Jessie's presence revived her, but day by day, Clare felt very alone and missed her sadly. She sometimes remembered what Auntie Polly had said about missing her sister. As if a bright light had gone out. Jessie wasn't dead like her mother, thank goodness, but their brief meetings at weekends were a sad substitute for all they used to share.

The great thing about Jessie, she decided, was her capacity to see the funny side of anything. It was a gift and she didn't have it. Apart from her own escape into dreams there was little light in her life and not a lot to look forward to. Everything she did seemed so very fixed. The same thing, at the same time, week after week.

As she got off her bicycle and wheeled it up the lane, she wondered sadly if things would look any better by the time she reached her sixteenth birthday. A week earlier, her fifteenth birthday had passed almost unnoticed. Jessie had remembered and so did her Aunt Sarah, but not Granny Hamilton, who was supposed to have such a memory for dates, nor Aunt Polly, though she would remember eventually and send her some dollars which would help with Christmas.

Clare found the winter months a real struggle and it was only in the spring when she felt more like her old self again that she remembered the one person who had actually put her finger on at least part of the cause.

'Holy Moses, Clare,' Jessie had said, on one of her visits. 'Is that my old tunic yer wearin'? If it is, ye must have grown again since lass week! Another inch an' I'll get a good look at yer knickers. Here, stan' wi' yer back to me. Sure yer near as tall as I am, all of a sudden.'

Christmas came and with it the annual visit from Uncle Bob and Aunt Sadie. Sadie had acquired a fur coat when Bob became the manager at his bank's branch in Ballymena. It made her even more patronising than when he'd only been deputy manager. Ballymena itself had been a step up from Antrim and now he was manager Sadie was hard at work cultivating 'the right people'. But Clare was relieved to discover that Bob remained his usual kindly self.

Finding a quiet moment he asked her if there was any talk yet of getting the electricity. When Clare said it looked as if it would be a couple more years yet, he said she was to be sure and let him know, so that he could pay for having it put in. He was sure the landlord couldn't afford to do it and it would be a great help. In the meantime, he slipped her an envelope and said casually there must be one or two things they were needing.

Because there was so much flooding on the roads in Fermanagh at Christmas time, Uncle Johnny and Auntie Sarah didn't appear until the end of January. Johnny had been saving up his wastage allowances from the shop for months and the result was a whole box full of groceries, tinned food that was only available on points and enough tea to help them through till August when the ration was due to be increased by another half ounce each. Sarah presented Clare with a Bible and a set of twelve booklets each setting out a programme of daily readings with detailed commentary, so she could study a passage of scripture every day and an extra one on Sundays.

Robert was glad to see his visitors come and even gladder to see them go, for he was shy with his sons and thoroughly uncomfortable with their wives. Clare was painfully aware how cold the sitting room felt, even though she'd lit the fire hours before they were due to arrive. She noticed, too, how uncomfortable both the women appeared to find the wooden settle when they had all retreated to the comforting warmth of the big kitchen.

'Sure company's very nice, but it wears you out,' said Robert, leaning back in his chair and hitching his bad leg up on the fender. 'Did I see ye get a present from Sarah? The same lady doesn't give much away,' he added tartly.

'I've four Bibles now,' she said grinning. 'Five, if I count in your big one. She gave me one when I came and another about three years ago. Now this one. She must think I wear them out very fast,' she went on, glad to see Robert looking more relaxed. 'I never use hers at all for the print is so awful and the paper's so thin the pages stick together. I think she must have got a job lot cheap. I use the one Granda Hamilton gave me that first Sunday Uncle Jack took us both over. Do you remember that day?'

'Aye, the first Sunday I met him in his own place. The day he says I cured his mare,' he laughed. 'Sure the better the day the better the deed, he said when I wondered if he were afeard I was breaking the Sabbath and him a thoughtful kind of a man in that way.'

Robert lit his pipe and waved the match up and down to put it out.

'He's a very well-read man, yer Granda Hamilton,' he went on. 'Knows his Bible a lot better than those who go around talkin' about it all the time,' he added sharply. 'D'ye think Sarah reads all them passages and so on that she's always talkin' about?'

'She might, but she doesn't let anything they say put her off what she's made up her mind to do anyway. I think Uncle Johnny gets a bit fed up with it all.'

'Johnny's no scholar, no more than I am,' said Robert, shaking his head sadly. 'An' a right tear away he was afore he got married. I'll never understan' how he took up wi' a woman like that.'

'Maybe she took up with him.'

'Aye, ye might be right there. There's many a man ended up at the church door wonderin' how he come to be there.'

He fell silent and Clare watched the blue haze of his pipe smoke swirl up to the blackened ceiling, borne on currents of warm air from the stove. She sensed his thoughts moving far away from their fireside to a different world, a world long gone, where he was a young man, a husband, and very soon a father, fifty years ago, or more.

Clare didn't know exactly what age Robert was and had never liked to ask.

'Would ye read a bit o' the paper or have ye studies to do?'

There was always school work to be done, but he so seldom asked for anything that she never had the heart to refuse him. She took up the local paper, shuffled the pages and wondered where she had left off.

'What did it say about the King? Ye were readin' that last night when Eddie called in an' I don't rightly mind what the conclusion was.'

She found the item again and read it out to him. The King was clearly recovering well from his operation. He had been to Heathrow Airport in London to say goodbye to Princess Elizabeth as she left for her visit to Kenya. He had stood bareheaded on the January day and waved cheerfully at the departing plane, watching it until it was completely out of sight.

Robert shook his head sadly. 'Whatever it says, I don't think that man'll do. He didn't sound himself at Christmas. Never mind the stammer, sure he has that near beat, it was his voice. It wasn't right. Poor man, he has hisself wore out with the war an' him niver trained up to be a King. T'was desperit hard on him when his brother let him in fer it. Sure I read somewhere he's only fifty-seven and here's me seventy-five an' in better health than him.'

He knocked out his pipe and pulled off his boots.

'I think I'll take half an hour before we hear the news. Ye can maybe have a word with them people in Paris to see if we're missin' anythin',' he said with a short laugh as he headed for the door of 'the room'.

The King died the following week and Robert could not have been more upset if it had been Bob or Johnny. As if to make up for not going to pay his respects, he listened to every news broadcast, even though they all said the same thing. He perused all the newspapers Clare brought home for him and then asked her to read them aloud as well. He seemed anxious he might miss some detail he felt he ought to know.

Clare felt sad for Princess Elizabeth. It was all very well being a princess, but she'd lost her daddy. Losing someone you loved was the same thing, whoever you were. But it must be awful having to say the right thing and do the right thing as she had to do, when she must be feeling so unhappy. With that schedule she was given every morning, there wasn't much hope she could have a quiet cry when she needed to.

Standing in the cold wind in front of the Courthouse in Armagh, the High School neatly lined up in the space allocated to them behind the children from the Armstrong Primary, Clare tried to remember that this was a historic moment, a moment one would recall for one's grandchildren. Or so everyone kept saying. But as she listened to the proclamation that Elizabeth was Queen, all she could think of was a young woman who had lost the father whom she clearly loved, just as she herself had lost her father and her mother, six years earlier.

The week of the King's death was a long, sad week, it felt as if life had come to a standstill. Jessie's college closed and she came home unexpectedly. She wanted to take Clare to the pictures as a treat, but the Ritz cinema had closed too. On Thursday evening when Clare read the paper to Robert, she found that a meeting of the Drum Unionist Association in Drumhillery, a few miles down the road, had also been cancelled because the King had died. Until after the funeral, although Robert had visitors enough in the forge by day, anxious to talk about the news, not a single person called in the evenings.

On the following Friday, the day of the funeral itself, while all thoughts turned to London and the silent crowds waiting near Westminster Abbey, Robert limped down the frosted path to the forge and instead of opening the lower part of the half door and starting work, he closed over the upper part and put a padlock on the end of its large bolt. Robert hadn't bolted and padlocked the door of the forge since the day of his own father's funeral in 1920.

Between the bitter cold weather and the sadness that lay like a shadow after the King's death, February passed slowly. March roared in with westerly gales that tore a branch from the big pear tree halfway down the path to the forge and ripped up a corner of the dark felt that covered the low building's high-pitched roof.

When the storm passed, leaving the felt flapping but still in place, Clare gave thanks for Uncle Bob's Christmas gift. Robert had expected to have to tackle the job himself, but instead a young man came with a long ladder to do it for him.

On a mild Saturday morning with sudden bursts of warm sun and the very first daffodils showing signs of unfurling in the

187

sheltered corner by the old house, Clare carried mugs of tea to the forge and watched him as he climbed down into the pool of sunshine where she stood waiting.

'Do you take sugar?' she asked, as she held out his mug.

'Ah do, if ah ken get it,' he replied promptly.

'I *do* have some,' she said laughing, as she offered him the sugar bowl from the tray. 'Not more than two, please. I have to make it last.'

He took two well-heaped spoonfuls and stirred them vigorously.

'How's it going?' she enquired, nodding up to the exposed lathes where he had pulled back the torn felt.

'Rightly. Great view from up there. Ye can see Armagh.'

Clare looked at the long ladder and the steep pitch of the roof against the blue of the sky in which the last fluffy white clouds were dissolving in the warmth of the sun.

'Could I go and have a look?'

'Aye, if ye've a mind to. Yer not afraid of heights? Some women bees scared.'

'I'll have a try, if that's all right with you.'

'Aye surely,' he said agreeably, as he took a great gulp of his tea. 'I'll keep a hold of it down here an' steady it fer you. It's a bit whippy as ye get to the top.'

Clare gathered up the ends of her skirt, tied them in a loose knot above the knee and checked that she could still step from tread to tread. She thought of all those women in long skirts she and Jessie had watched at the Ritz, hopping in and out of covered wagons, trekking across the prairies, fording rivers and organising themselves for sudden attacks by Indians. No wonder Annie Oakley chose to wear trousers.

Her eyes focused on the damp, green-streaked gable in front of her. She climbed slowly and steadily, until she could grip the edge of the roof itself. Only then did she let herself scan the horizon.

To the west, Armagh was outlined against the brilliant blue of the sky, the twin spires of the new cathedral so sharp they seemed to have been etched in with the aid of a ruler. On the hill opposite, less dramatic, more earth-bound, the square tower of the old cathedral rose out of its enfolding trees, its heavy stonework dark with age. Around both great buildings, like currents of water eddying where they will, the small stone houses and later brick terraces curved and wove as they followed the contours and the slopes of the hills on which they stood.

In the brilliant light, everything looked fresh and beautiful. Across the road from the forge, Eddie Robinson's fields were a rich, velvety carpet, on which his cattle, a motley collection of different breeds, appeared trim and well-fed. The Robinsons' square farmhouse was dazzling white. Beyond its stables and byres, long, low, whitewashed buildings with red doors and shutters, the mossy branches in the orchard stretched their thickening grey buds skywards. And everywhere the hawthorn hedges were misted with green.

Most of the road to Armagh was visible, but to her surprise Clare found she could see part of Drumsollen House, on the Richardsons' estate. Usually only its tall chimneys were visible, rising clear of the surrounding trees, but from her viewpoint, she could actually see its gardens splashed with sunlight, though normally they were completely hidden by the long, curving driveway which led up from the gates on the Loughgall Road.

She twisted round carefully till she could see Grange Church pointing its spire into the blue, well clear of the ancient yews in the churchyard, where at least three generations of Scotts lay buried. Cottages marched, one beside the other down the hill, low-roofed, the wispy smoke from their fires rising vertically in the still air.

She shaded her eyes and looked south-eastwards across the main road and beyond Eddie's water meadows. The hedges were white with the earliest of the flowering thorns, but the low hills blocked her view. She wished she could climb higher, for somewhere over there, below Cannon Hill, lay the farm at

Liskeyborough, only a mile or two away for the jackdaws who played round the church tower. Her grandmother would be feeding the hens or the new calves, or peering at the old wooden barrel in which she'd planted daffodils to have them near her front door.

If she could have seen Liskeyborough, the whole of her world would have been spread out before her, from her own front door to the furthest points of her travels. And on a clear day, too. A day for making up your mind, Granny Hamilton would say.

She remembered the young man drinking tea and leaning against the ladder to steady it. With a last glance behind her, down at the cottage itself and the tumbled ruin opposite where she shut up the chickens at night, she began her descent, her eyes still dazzled by the light, her mind preoccupied by the map of her world her climb had set out before her.

'What'd ye think?' he asked, giving her his hand on the uneven ground.

'Great, just great. I wouldn't have believed you could see so much. The forge isn't that high,' she said easily, as she took his empty mug and put it back on her tray.

'No, it's not, but it's clear of trees and suchlike. You only need a wee bit a height to see a brave way if there's nothin' comin' between you an' it. Especially on a clear day.'

She smiled and thanked him for holding the ladder and left him to go back up and finish securing the new piece of felt.

'You only need a wee bit of height to see a brave way if there's nothing coming between you and it,' she said to herself as she went back into the kitchen to get on with the weekly scrubbing of the floor.

'Especially on a clear day,' she added as she filled her bucket.

It wasn't a very exceptional remark, but it echoed in her mind, stirring up feelings she couldn't properly place. After this long, weary time with all its troubles and sadnesses, she felt as if something had been cleared out of her way on this lovely spring-like morning.

It might be the turn of the season, or her own joy in the springtime to come. Whatever it was, there was no point puzzling about it. When the young man spoke about seeing from a clear space, she'd felt her heart leap, her spirits rise. For the next hour, she scrubbed her way across the kitchen floor without noticing the dark foam she was producing, the grit accumulating in the piece of old towelling she was using to rinse, or the redness of her own hands from the hot water.

In her thoughts, she was circling the tiny world in which she lived and giving thanks for a decision she had made nearly six years ago, on just such a clear day.

13

The apple blossom had come and gone. With its falling petals passed the first warm days of the year and the first of the long, quiet dusks that seemed to go on for ever. Clare found it heartbreaking to have to sit at her table, evening after evening, shut up with her revision for the June exams. She thought of the times, now long past, when she had slaved over her spellings and what a difference that had made to her future. But it wasn't easy.

The sun was now so high it slanted through the tiny windows of 'the boys' room' at the back of the house, where she worked, her books and papers spread out on the bed that had been Bob and Johnny's, a long time ago. As the hours passed, the heavy shadows under the old trees in the orchard deepened and a blackbird sang his heart out from the highest branch of the one pear tree that threw its branches up and over the surrounding apple trees.

When her restlessness and the beauty of the evening got too much for her, she would walk out to the front door and stand under the rose-covered arch, the pale petals of Albertine unfolding around her. She would breathe deeply, grateful to escape for a little the confinement of the small, back room where the window hadn't opened for years and the aura of damp and dry rot never faded, even in summer.

The evening air was so full of scents and perfumes the heavy smell of elderflower from the huge flat blooms on the tree by the gable, the tang of cut grass from Eddie's meadows, the lingering aroma of turf smoke from the sunken metal circle in front of the forge, where an old cartwheel had been rehooped earlier in the day. There were hints and murmurs of forgotten aromas, the dark perfume of the old roses her great-grandmother had grown and the tang of herbs whose names she didn't even know. Behind her on the hallstand stood a great jug of double white lilac from the tree by the old house, to judge by its size, a tree her great-grandmother might well have planted.

Sometimes she wondered what she herself might leave behind, what trace of her life, of her being, in this place, a grandchild might find, something she had made, or planted, or set going. And then she would remind herself of the exercise book open on the old washstand, the novel in English or French or German she was currently studying, the notes to be gone through, the dates and definitions to be learnt by heart.

The month of May, Clare decided, was a wistful month, a month that stirred up longings one couldn't even name and made the longings one could name even harder to bear. But, as Mrs Taylor always said to both her and Jessie, 'All things pass, both pleasant and unpleasant.'

And May and June did pass, the exams safely and successfully completed. Term ended and suddenly she was free. She could do whatever she wanted to do. She had time. Time that felt like a huge legacy of hours and days, weeks and weeks of them, to spend as she chose.

'Great, just great,' said Jessie. 'You've been a right pain this last six weeks. Gettin' you out of that room was like gettin' blood out of a stone. C'mon we're goin' to live it up. Roy Rogers in *Trail of Robin Hood* Monday or Tuesday, *The Underworld Story* Wednesday or Thursday, *Tomahawk Trail* on Friday. An' we'll go to the field in Armagh on the Twelfth an' make sure Robert doesn't have one too many while he's listenin' to the speeches.'

Clare laughed and thought how wonderful it was to have Jessie home. She too, had her summer holiday, nearly as long as her own.

'I take it you've won the pools,' she said wryly as Jessie finished outlining her plans for the following week.

'No, I've done far better than that. I've made a fiver,' she announced triumphantly. 'My treat. We're goin' upstairs. Ice cream in the interval and chips on our way home. How about that?'

Clare was intrigued. Since Jessie's father died her mother had gone back to teaching and one or two relatives had contributed towards the cost of Jessie's secretarial course, but Jessie certainly hadn't appeared to be any better off than before, for she still had her old habits of spending money whenever she got her hands on any.

'So how did you manage that?' she asked, smiling. 'Tell me the secret. I could do with a fiver or two myself.'

'Ach, sure it was the cat did it?'

'What cat?'

'Yer woman that I stay with. Mad about that cat, she is. If you heard her talkin' to it you'd think she was mental.'

'Yes, but what about the fiver?' Clare persisted.

'I was at a loose end one evenin' an' I did these sketches of dear pussy. I left them lyin' in what she calls the "guests' lounge" an' when she sees them, she wants them. I told her I only do sketches on commission and that I charge five pounds a sittin'. I was only pullin' her leg, but she's that daft she thought I was serious, so she asked me to do a sittin'. D'ye believe me or do you want to see it?'

'Of course, I believe you. You always were marvellous at sketching. But I can't let you spend your money on me.'

'Why not?'

'It's not fair.'

'Would you do it for me, if you had a fiver?'

'Yes, of course, I would.'

'Then what are you bletherin' about? Now which nights are we goin' to the Ritz? I can't go tomorra night, worse luck. Mammy's for Hockley to see the other oul' aunt an' she says I've to go with her.'

Clare laughed at the wry look on her friend's face. Jessie never minded going to visit Aunt Sarah with her mother,

194

though she said the crack was always better if she went on her own, but visiting Sarah's older sister Florrie was definitely not Jessie's idea of fun.

'We might see each other on the way there. I'm heading Hockley direction to go to a dance,' she said lightly.

'Yer not? Where's the dance?'

Jessie's face fell, her disappointment so clear she looked an absolute picture of misery.

Clare relented. She'd intended to tease her friend a little, but seeing her looking so let down, she hadn't the heart.

'Oh, it's nothing much, Jessie. Only the Orange Hall. Uncle Jack's lodge,' she began. 'That's why I couldn't ask you to come with me. It's invitation only. I only got one because Aunt Minnie wants me to help her with the sandwiches and Jack said if I stayed for the hop he'd run me home. I'm really sorry I couldn't ask you to come with me.'

Jessie shook her head and looked at her sharply.

'You'll tell me next they're unfurling a new banner.'

'Yes, they are indeed,' said Clare, surprised. 'How did you know?'

Jessie shook her head impatiently.

'Ach, it's the season for it. Sure they're all at it, any that kin afford it. Have you any idea what one o' these dos is like?'

'No,' said Clare honestly. 'I've never been to anything like that before. I thought it might be rather interesting.'

'Interesting,' Jessie repeated carefully. 'They say there's one born every minit,' she went on raising her eyes heavenward. 'Sure they'll speechify half the night, ye'll be starved by the time ye even see a bully beef sandwich an' there won't be a man there under forty. Or if there is, he'll be with his Daddy and he'll hide in a corner till it's time for them both to go home. I think I'll be better off with Florrie.'

Uncle Jack collected Clare the next afternoon, waited patiently while she put her freshly ironed dress across the back seat and drove her off at speed to Liskeyborough. He had to see a man about a lorry for the field, he said, as he dropped her in the farmyard, her dress over one arm, Jessie's new Louis-heeled shoes and her purse in Granda Scott's shopping bag.

Aunt Minnie was already installed at the broad table under the kitchen window, bowls of mixture and a pile of sliced loaves at the ready. At the far end of the table, Granny Hamilton sat and watched, her hands so bent now with arthritis that she could no longer grip a knife.

'Hello, Clare, how are ye?' she said, smiling up at her. 'Is that the wee dress you were tellin' me about? The one Polly sent you?' she asked, her sharp eyes running over the navy blue fabric with its pattern of white spots. 'Away an' put it in the bedroom before we get butter on it. There's a wire hanger on the back of the door.'

Clare got to work, grateful for Granny Hamilton's company for Minnie was a large, silent woman whose most frequent conversational utterance was 'Really'. She was, however, a dab hand at making sandwiches. She'd reduced the first stage to two efficient movements. One spread the butter generously and evenly across the slice from crust to crust, the other removed as much as possible while leaving a layer sufficient for the filling to stick to. It was some time before Clare mastered the technique, but after all, she reminded herself, Minnie had been doing it for years.

Granny Hamilton entertained them as they worked. She passed on the news from the aunts and uncles scattered around the province and brought them up to date on the large number of cousins now leaving school and finding their first jobs. Every so often she interrupted herself to comment on the assorted men who came to the kitchen door enquiring for Jack or one of his brothers, in connection with the preparations for the evening.

'Sure that poor man has himself worried silly about the night,' she began, as she craned her neck to see who it was that was tramping down the yard, knowing that the most likely place to find Jack was in the workshop. 'If he'd known he'd be

196

Chairman in the year of a new banner, he'd never have taken it on. But there was no talk of that until a few months ago and now he can't get out of it. He's that shy, he'd go half a mile out of his way to avoid speakin' to a stranger.'

'Will he have a lot of speaking to do?' asked Clare, as she carefully cut open the waxed paper on a sliced loaf so they could reuse it for the finished sandwiches.

'Ach, yes. There'll be thanking brother This for the loan of the field and brother That for the loan of the lorry to stan' on. An' then he'll have to thank the Reverends for dedicating the banner and addressin' the assembled company. After them, he'll have the bands to thank for comin' from Rockmacreaney, or Richhill, or wherever indeed they're comin' from. An' after that he'll have to thank the lady that cuts the cord an' give her a wee box with a pair of silver scissors in it. And then he'll have to do the Women's Committee and thank them for makin' the tea.

'That's about half the Women's Committee you're buttering bread with, Clare, in case you didn't know,' she added with a grin, when she saw the very serious look on Clare's face as she took in all she was saying.

The kitchen had grown warm and stuffy, even with the stove low and the door propped open. Clare looked out. The sunshine had disappeared since she'd arrived. Dark clouds were piling up on the horizon. It would only be a matter of time before it rained. And it would be heavy.

'Aye,' said Granny Hamilton, looking up at Minnie, 'forby your Harry, there's his cousin Sam from Stonebridge and his other cousin, Billy Hamilton from Four Lane Ends. Oh, they're well pleased at the way the lodge is growin' and bringin' in the young ones,' she said, pressing her lips together and nodding sharply. 'That, I heer tell, was why they made the effort for a new banner. The aul' one would have gone on a while longer, but some of the senior men in the lodge made a brave bit in the war. Sure the prices was sky-high for farm produce, an' one or two did a nice wee sideline with men from Belfast who had their own customers, if you understan' me. It didn't hurt them to put their han' in their pockets,' she went on, looking out the window where the first sixpenny-sized drops were beginning to fall.

'It'll be a big night for the young ones, shakin' hands with the Chairman and the County Grand Treasurer,' she went on, one thought leading to another. 'But they'll have their fathers with them to keep them straight,' she added thoughtfully.

She frowned at the rain and turned back to Minnie, who had not uttered a word for the last hour.

'Is your young Harry nervous about tonight?' she asked agreeably.

Minnie twitched, pushed back a straggling lock of greying hair and added another slice to the pile in front of her.

'Not really,' she said slowly, as she buttered the next.

Clare bent her head lower and spread faster, because she was afraid she might laugh. It wasn't just Minnie, poor thing, who'd never uttered two words if she could manage with one, it was the whole prospect of the evening as it now unrolled before her. Jessie was going to have such a good laugh.

Not that she ever minded when Jessie laughed at her for getting things wrong, for Jessie wouldn't know how to be unkind, but sometimes Clare was glad Jessie didn't know the half of what went on inside her head. It meant she felt less of a fool when her imagination got the better of her.

The longer Clare went on buttering and listening to Granny Hamilton, the more she could see that she really had let her imagination run away with her this time. She been so excited that Sunday afternoon when Granny asked her if she could come and help Minnie.

'You'll stay for the do, won't you?' said Jack, who'd just come into the kitchen. 'I'd like a dance with my young niece.'

Although she and Jessie were practised dancers, neither of them had ever danced anywhere but the Temperance Hall in

Lonsdale Street where the High School girls went for gym and games. The thought of wearing a dress and dancing with a proper partner instead of another girl in green knickers was very appealing. Clare could imagine the band playing a lively quickstep, herself spinning round the lamplit hall in the arms of a handsome young man, raising the dust from the wooden floor as they wove expertly in and out of the other, less practised dancers.

She had entertained her dreams on many a boring journey home from school and across many a yard of dirty floor to be scrubbed, but it had never entered her head that Auntie Polly would send her a dress for her birthday a whole three months early.

'My dearest Clare,' she read, when she found the note in the parcel.

I'm sorry it's so long since I sent you anything. I know how little you and my father have and I'd love to do more. Life is being kind to me but I've been short of money because we heard of a specialist who could help Uncle Jimmy's back. It's just great. He'll never lose the pain completely but he feels a new man because most of the time he can move quite freely and when there is pain he can take tablets which actually ease it so that he can sleep. When I think of all those nights he used to just sit and read the paper when he was tired out but couldn't sleep with the pain I can hardly believe it. It was worth any money.

If this dress doesn't quite fit, take it to my old friend in Walkers, where we bought your blue coat. She'll alter it so you won't even know. I enclose some dollars to pay for the alteration. Let me know exactly what she has to do so I can do it for you myself, next time.

You'll soon be sixteen, Clare, and Daddy says you're a fine girl, that I'd hardly know you since you've grown taller. He's so proud of you and says your Mummy and

Daddy would be too. He says you work so hard, both at
school and at home. See you enjoy yourself as well.
    With much love, hurrying to get this in the post,
        Your loving Auntie Polly

Clare held the dress against herself, almost certain it would
fit. And it did. When she'd slipped into Robert's room to look
in the big mirror inside his wardrobe door, she could hardly
believe it.

She adjusted the white collar on the high, buttoned-up neck
and pirouetted in her bare feet to see the swirl of the generously
cut skirt that flared out from the neat waist. With the brightness
of excitement in her dark eyes and her even darker curls setting
off the creaminess of her skin, Clare hardly recognised the face
that looked back at her in the dim light of the heavily furnished
room. She was wondering if she dare use lipstick for the big
occasion when suddenly she remembered she'd no shoes she
could possibly wear with such a smart dress.

'I don't think this rain's goin' to give over,' announced
Granny Hamilton firmly. 'I think it's settled in for the night.'

Startled, Clare came back to the present and looked out
through the open door. Broad puddles were spreading across
the uneven surface of the yard. Huge falling drops of rain raised
spikes of water in them like tiny, pale flowers.

'What'll they do about the banner, Granny?' she asked
quietly.

'Nothin' for it, they'll have to use the hall. Sure, they'd all get
soaked and the banner would be well christened. They can take
a wee shower an' be none the worse if they're kept movin', those
banners, but not a downpour like this. Especially when they're
new and the paint not that well settled.'

She surveyed the table, the finished and wrapped sandwiches
lined up in battle order ready to be packed in a big box.

'Minnie, ye may make us a cup o' tea. Goodness knows when
you an' Clare will get a bite to eat. Can you make up some of

those thin crusts with a bit o' jam? There's new raspberry in the cupboard Mrs Loney brought me a present the other day.'

The rain didn't stop, it got heavier. Minnie, Clare and two cardboard boxes of sandwiches were squashed unceremoniously into the back of Jack's car for the short drive to the hall. In the front seat, the Master of the Lodge kept up a stream of anxious questions about what was going to happen. Jack tried to answer him while swerving between the worst of the flooding from the springs in the hedge banks of the deep-set lane above the farm. The journey was uncomfortable but mercifully short.

They parked as near the hall as they could, but between the driving rain and the muddy path outside, Clare abandoned all further thoughts of her first glorious appearance on a dance floor. Clutching her half of the sandwiches, she splashed through the puddles, deposited her box in the minute kitchen and retired into the adjoining lavatory to dry her wet hair on her handkerchief.

As she stood in front of a small, starred and spotted mirror, drawing a comb through her wet curls, she thought ruefully of the time it had taken with the flat irons to get out the creases her new dress acquired crossing the Atlantic. They were nothing to the creases just made by her close confinement with Minnie and the two boxes of sandwiches in the small back seat of Jack's Austin.

She peered at herself in the mirror and made up her mind. Holding her breath and with great care, she outlined her lips with Perfection Pink and rubbed them together as Jessie had instructed her. Having nothing else to hand, she blotted them and left a perfect print on her wet hanky.

'At least I can tell Jessie I wore her lipstick,' she said to the mirror as she turned her back on it and went out into the hall.

The hall was bleak and chilly. Two men were struggling to install the banner in an upright position on the narrow platform of the low-ceilinged room, while others brought out stackable chairs, discovered there weren't nearly enough of them to seat the expected company and went off in search of more. Clare shivered and wished she'd brought a cardigan. It was July and the afternoon had been hot and sunny, but she ought to know better by now. As Granda Scott always said, 'There's many weathers in an Ulster day!'

Tonight felt like winter as the rain pounded on the corrugated roof and the grey light filtered through the small sash windows. The empty, echoing hall was gloomy, the wooden floor, just like those she and Jessie had seen in countless barn dance scenes at the Ritz, became damper and dirtier as men with chairs, men with ladders, men with supports for the poles of the banner, all tramped back and forth by way of the muddy path to the main road where they had parked their assorted vehicles.

The men's voices echoed as they called instructions to each other. The furled banner leaned drunkenly on its poles, first one way and then the other, till someone decided it would have to be unfurled. If it wasn't supported properly unfurled then the whole thing might fall over on the platform party when the lady with the silver scissors did her bit.

Clare wondered how the said lady was to have risen the twelve feet off the ground to where the banner was lashed around its crossbar in order to unfurl it, but no one seemed to have considered this difficulty. More urgently, they now faced the immediate problem of getting a field full of people into the hall, in company with two pipe bands, the special guests and the members of the lodge itself.

As the evening wore on, however, it seemed to Clare the bad weather itself was helping out. Many guests stayed at home. But even then, the hall was packed. The press of perspiring bodies, mixed with the odour of damp clothing, rubber boots and Brylcreem, made Clare long for fresh air. But she could see that was a long way off.

Finally the proceedings began. There were prayers and exhortations from the ministers, followed by strong words about courage and loyalty. Clare was puzzled when the elder of the two clergyman made lengthy reference to the Battle of the Somme and the great sacrifices made by the Ulster Division in the cause of freedom. As she went on staring at King William on his shiny white horse, it suddenly came to her that the Battle of the Somme must be the image on the other side of the banner.

'I hope and pray that this example may inspire you to live lives worthy in God's sight and that the freedom that has been passed down to you will still be yours . . .'

His voice tailed off ominously as he looked down at the young men lined up below the platform, three of her cousins in their midst, wearing new suits and looking acutely uncomfortable.

He spoke as if he expected another war to break out at any moment. Surely he couldn't really mean it, she thought. Didn't everyone expect the last one to be the very last one of all. If enough people didn't want another war, couldn't they stop it happening?

To keep herself occupied, she studied the detail of exotic flowers all round the border of the banner and the vivid landscape of little hills, the background to William's portrait. The horse, she thought, was very good. And horses were difficult to draw, so Jessie said. Especially in that rearing position. But William wasn't very inspiring. Short and rather podgy, he looked as if he was cross-eyed. Or perhaps that was just the light of battle in his eye.

The clergyman was now speaking of religious freedom.

'The Orange Order will not abide anyone interfering with the way in which we worship. All those who march behind this banner stand for freedom of worship,' he pronounced firmly, shaking his finger at the assembled company.

Clare yawned discreetly behind her hand and looked around her. The rows of faces were impassive. They gave no hint as to whether they thought he was inspired or talking a lot of nonsense. And they applauded every speaker with equal courtesy, including the whole list of votes of thanks Granny Hamilton had so accurately predicted.

A second clergyman was now getting to his feet. He smiled genially at the assembled company and said that the unfurling of a banner meant that a lodge was flourishing. This was a good sign. Long may it continue. He then pointed out the fact that Roman Catholics went to Mass before eight o'clock. They must admire them for that and be prepared to make the same effort.

'Week after week you have the good example set by the Royal Family attending Divine Worship. They are fighting against Communism. But we here in Northern Ireland have another battle to fight as well as the fight against Communism. We have to fight the enemy that never sleeps, We must never forget Rome. The Church of Rome is ever ready to exploit weakness. We must be vigilant. We must be ready,' he warned, as he waved an emphatic finger and sat down.

Clare was confused. She couldn't quite see how Northern Ireland was involved in the struggle against Communism. She'd never heard of anyone she knew being a Communist or even knowing anybody that was. Perhaps the lodge had inside information about these mysterious people. As for the encroachment of the Church of Rome, the only conversion she had ever heard off was the joke about the elderly Protestant on his death-bed, who decided to be converted, because he thought it was better if one of them went than one of his own side.

She would have to ask Granda Hamilton what it all meant, she really would. He wasn't a member of a lodge because of being a Quaker, but he always knew what was going on and would answer her questions as well as he could. Every one of his sons had joined the lodge and now his grandsons were just waiting to be seventeen to apply for their sash.

She'd so missed seeing him today. A cousin in Castlewellan had died and he'd gone to the funeral taking William with him. Whenever Granda went anywhere now he always took William and Granny breathed a sigh of relief. She was quite open about it. William was as difficult as ever, she said. If he hadn't someone or something to keep him occupied he was a pain in the neck. His grandfather was the only one who had the patience to keep on at him and make him behave properly. He'd always worn her out from the first day he ever came, but now when she was so tired and often in pain she just couldn't cope with him at all.

Clare sighed. She had done her best but nothing seemed to work with William. Sometimes she imagined he would find something that really interested him, football, or chemistry, or bird-watching. But so far there was nothing that had engaged him in any way. She wondered if William would join the lodge when he was seventeen, like the rest of his cousins. But that wasn't very likely to solve the problem.

The Chairman had finally got round to thanking the bands and the Ladies Committee. While he was expressing his deep appreciation of all the ladies did for the lodge, Clare slipped from her seat close to the kitchen door and moved silently inside. She lit the Calor gas under the copper. It had just come to the boil when the band launched into the National Anthem and the assembled company leapt to their feet and sang all three verses.

It was almost eleven o'clock by the time everyone had been fed and provided with innumerable cups of tea. There was an awkward pause when it seemed that neither of the bands present expected to play for dancing. Eventually, a few brave souls from each offered their services and the piano was retrieved from its hiding place in the cloakroom.

They struck up a quickstep that set Clare's feet tapping, but no one moved. A thick knot of men at one end of the room kept their backs turned to the women and girls sitting round the walls at the other. Clare waved hopefully to her cousin Sam. He blushed and looked the other way.

Finally, after three more numbers, the Chairman took the floor with his wife, a large lady with tightly permed hair, who nodded over his shoulder to the younger men and mouthed to them to 'Go and dance'.

Clare waited patiently. Someone was walking towards her. A large man in a navy striped suit and brown leather shoes. He said nothing, just nodded at her and held out his hand. She stood up. He pressed two fingers to the small of her back. Holding her at arm's length he walked her backways along the side of the room. At each corner, he twisted his body to accommodate the new angle and then continued as before.

'Big crowd,' he said after the first circuit.

'Yes,' agreed Clare, unable for the moment to think of any more promising response to this conversational effort.

'Are you a member of the lodge?' she enquired, thinking it a pretty poor attempt on her part.

'Na,' he said, dismissively. 'No time for all this marching and so on. Encourages bad feelin'. I'm agin it.'

'So how do you come to be here?' she asked promptly, quite unable to contain her curiosity.

'Wanted to see how the banner looked,' he said, as the music stopped. 'I painted it,' he added, walking away as silently as he'd come.

After that, she did take the floor with Uncle Jack, who was a great dancer, though he tried to tell her he was past it. But they only managed two dances. Just as they were getting into their stride, someone came and proposed a vote of thanks to the musicians and they had the National Anthem all over again. It being Saturday night, the hall had to be empty and closed up before the Sabbath.

In no time at all, Clare was saying goodbye to Jack at the bottom of Granda Scott's lane. The rain had stopped, but she still had a job picking her way through the familiar puddles in front of the cottage.

To her surprise, the front door was not closed and when she pushed open the kitchen door, she found the lamp still lit.

'Did ye enjoy yerself?' Robert asked, as his half-closed eyes flickered open.

'I did indeed, Granda. I had a great time,' she said, with as much enthusiasm as she could manage. 'Granny says we're both to come over for our tea next week, it's far too long since she's seen you.'

'That's very nice of her, very nice indeed,' he replied, nodding to himself. 'Did she like yer dress?'

'She did. She said it suited me real well,' she went on, glad to be able to tell the truth.

'I had a young gentleman askin' for you this afternoon,' he said as he leaned over to pull off his boots.

'Who was that?' she asked, amused by his habit of teasing her.

'Oh, one that's been here before,' he said firmly. 'I think you mind his name. The one on the chestnut mare.'

He winked at her as he headed for his bed.

'Goodnight now. Sleep well after your first dance.'

14

W hen Clare woke next morning to the quiet of a summer Sunday, Andrew Richardson was the first thought that came into her mind. Twice now he'd come to the forge and she'd been away. It did seem such bad luck. Apart from going to school and the occasional outing with Jessie, she was almost sure to be at home, studying or cooking or doing housework. Why couldn't he have come then?

'Third time lucky, perhaps,' she said to herself, as she slid out of bed and poured rainwater into her basin.

But the first week of the holidays passed without a further visit from the rider on the chestnut mare.

'Stop being so silly,' she muttered, when she caught herself glancing out the kitchen window as she scrubbed the table, peeled the potatoes or washed dishes.

'He's not going to come, you know,' she told herself severely when she'd been lingering at the front of the cottage, slowly dead-heading the flourishing perennials over by the water barrel, the spot which gave her the best possible view of the road beyond the forge.

Before she set out to scrub the floor, she made sure her blouse was clean. She took care that she didn't wipe her perspiring face with a grubby hand when she was doing dirty jobs. Her dark curls were combed much more often than her usual once a day and a tumbler from the corner cupboard in 'the room' had been brought through to the kitchen cupboard and was left well polished in case Robert should send the visitor up to the house for a drink of spring water.

When she went to look after Margaret's children on Saturdays, she took them to play in the small field in front of the forge. With the main road on one side and the lane to the forge on the other, there was no possibility of missing a visitor. But none of her efforts were of the slightest use. No one came. She just knew the more she watched and hoped, the less likely it was he would appear.

'He won't come now,' she told herself sadly, as a new week began and there had been no sign of him while she'd been at home and no teasing word from Robert when she came back from the expeditions Jessie had planned for them.

To make matters worse, John Wiley hadn't come to the forge for nearly a fortnight. Normally, he turned up every two or three days to tell them about the comings and goings at Drumsollen House. Just when he might have news of Andrew Richardson, John was enjoying one of those rare periods when none of the Drumsollen vehicles broke down and not even one of his tools needed a repair.

The weather was heavy and sultry, the dense foliage of the trees and shrubs hung dark and motionless by the roadsides. In the deep shadows, myriads of insects rose and fell in the warm, still air. The last of the early summer flowers had gone and although the cottage gardens were a blaze of colour, the countryside itself was dull, weary with heat and growth, dim under the pearly skies when the cloud was high, and sodden when the continuous warmth generated heavy, thundery showers.

Clare felt restless and impatient. She was thoroughly irritated with herself for spending so much time on her vain imaginings. Thinking about an encounter with Andrew Richardson only made the unexciting character of her life yet more obvious. Each day, she made up her mind she'd not waste another moment wondering if he might turn up, thinking what they might say to each other, or asking herself why he'd come in the first place. But it was not until a letter arrived from her cousin, Ronnie, that she was able to put Andrew Richardson to the back of her mind.

Anne Doughty

Letters from Ronnie were frequent enough and always welcome, but taking the slim envelope from the postman one Monday morning in late July, Clare felt apprehensive. Ronnie's letters were usually long, often enclosed newspaper items he thought would interest her. Recently, he'd put in his own articles about the state of agriculture and industry in the Province. He'd spent hours in the Central Library looking up material and then he'd cycled out into the countryside to talk to farmers and visit factories. She couldn't remember when she'd last had a letter from him in an ordinary-sized envelope.

She tore it open hastily. As she'd guessed, there was only a single sheet of note paper. Carefully folded inside it were two very battered pound notes.

Dear Clare,

You know how hard I've been trying to find a job in journalism. Well, I've finally given up. Belfast is hopeless. I've just had an offer from a Liverpool newspaper and I'm going to take it. But I've decided I'm not coming back. I'll try to get a second job in Liverpool, probably in a pub, and as soon as I've saved my fare I'm heading for Canada. Mum and Dad have said they'll help me raise the money.

The last year has made it perfectly clear that there's nothing here for me and from the papers Mum sends I can see there are plenty of openings in the Toronto area. It's all rather sudden I know and I'm sorry to spring it on you. I do so want to see you before I go. Please will you come up to Belfast for a couple of nights? My landlady says you can have her daughter's room as she's away at guide camp. I'll show you the sights of the city and then you can help me pack! I'm off this Saturday. Leave me a message with Mrs McGregor and I'll meet your train. I know it's dreadfully short notice, but I can't afford to miss this Liverpool job even though they say it's only temporary and I really can't bear to go without seeing you.

Give my love to Granda. I'd have liked to have come up

210

to see him properly and then I wouldn't have had to steal you away, but I've some things that just have to be done before I go. Please come if you possibly can. Remind me to tell you how you helped me to earn the cash enclosed which is for you whether you come or not!
　　As always, with love,
　　　　Ronnie

She stood in the laneway, the torn envelope and the pound notes in one hand, the single blue sheet in the other. She read it a second time as if reading it again would make it easier to grasp. But it didn't. She'd grasped it perfectly well the first time. Ronnie was going. Her dear cousin was taking the Liverpool boat and he wasn't coming back. She'd seen him only twice in the last six years, but he had been a comforting presence through all that time. Tears sprang to her eyes.

She couldn't possibly blame him. He'd worked so hard and got a good degree but he'd still not been able to find a job. He'd had to work weekends at his uncle's butcher's shop on the Beersbridge Road, a job he hated, just so he could go on paying his rent to Mrs McGregor, for the room he'd had as a student. He'd done all sorts of temporary jobs while trying to find something on a newspaper, but there'd been so many disappointments. In his position, she reckoned she'd have ended up doing just the same.

But the thought of his going made her feel desolate. She shivered as she went back into the dark kitchen even though the morning was warm and the room steamy from the soot-streaked shirts she'd set to boil on the stove in the biggest saucepan they possessed.

She was surprised to find Robert so philosophical when she told him about Ronnie's plans.

'Sure that's the way, childear,' he began, 'it's always been the same as long as I've heerd tell. There's young ones that'll niver be able to settle. If their minds are fixed on somethin' they want to do, or if they have an ambition to make money, sure there's

211

no stoppin' them. An' why woud one stop them? Haven't we all to make our way with what's given to us?'

He dropped off his cap by the side of his chair and waited till she set his midday meal in front of him.

'Boys, that looks good,' he said, as he made a hole in the middle of the pale green mound of champ and sliced a knob of butter from the dish to put in it.

'Did you ever think of America, Granda?' Clare asked as she pulled her own chair up to the table.

'Aye, ah did. I was all for it at one time. My brother William went out to Montreal and started up a business, got on his feet in no time and sent back saying he'd have any o' the family that was interested out t' help him. The ticket woud be seen to if we just said the word.'

He nodded to himself and took a deep draught of his buttermilk.

'My mother was always the one that wrote the letters an' she says to me "Robert, are ye for off. We'll not stan' in yer way. Will I send word to William that you'd like your ticket?" An' I says to her, "I'll tell ye the night, Mam."'

He paused again and made hungry inroads into his champ, mixing the melted butter with the well-mashed potatoes and chopped scallions. Clare waited, watching the flickers of memory touch his eyes and lips with the faintest of smiles.

'I went back down to the forge, for I was my father's helper in them days, an' as I was goin' in the door I sees this white mare comin' up the loanen with a neighbourin' man. So I went to meet him an' give him the time o' day. An' as I was standin' there the mare nuzzled up to me and blew down me neck. They do that sometimes if they like ye. An' I thought to meself: What woud ye be doin' behind some counter in some shop in Canada, Robert? Sure ye'd be far better makin' shoes for a mare.'

He finished his buttermilk in a long swallow and laughed a short, hard laugh. 'Did ye iver hear anythin' so daft in your life?'

He pushed back his chair and began to undo his bootlaces.

212

As he tramped across the kitchen in his stocking feet, Clare turned from the table and answered him.

'I don't think you were daft at all,' she said firmly. 'And where would I be if you were in Canada?'

He stopped on his step, turned and laughed again.

'Aye, well . . .' he said, looking pleased, as he headed for his lie-down, leaving Clare to her thoughts and her plans for going to see Ronnie.

15

A s she stepped down from the worn and shabby carriage of the Armagh train, two days later, Clare decided that the Great Northern Station hadn't changed much in six years. She walked briskly along a platform as noisy, crowded and dirty as the one she remembered from the evening of her arrival with Auntie Polly.

The brilliant sunlight that had drawn out the rich greens in the passing countryside and cast lengthening shadows from the higher points of steeple, farmhouse and barn all the way from Armagh, now struck the worn brickwork and the soot-covered pillars and accentuated the shabbiness of the high-arched train-shed with its handsome wrought-iron work and leafy decorations.

She strode along, aware of the crisp rustle of Auntie Polly's dress. Already far ahead of the other occupants of her carriage, she remembered the struggle she'd had to keep up with Auntie Polly's hasty trot, the way suitcases and porters' trolleys loomed up in front of her, major obstacles to be negotiated.

The thought of the child she had been cast a shadow over the excitement that had grown steadily as the miles passed and the time of her arrival drew closer. Even after all these years, thinking of Ronnie still brought back the awful memory of her weeks in Belfast after her parents died and how desperately unhappy she had been.

Suddenly, she felt overwhelmingly grateful for the life she now had. However hard it might be, however dull and boring, at least she was free to try to make things better. She did have

214

choice in her life and choice was something the unhappy child she'd been could never have had. Children might have good luck or bad luck, but they had never had choice. She had just been very lucky.

She spotted Ronnie almost as soon as she set foot on the platform. Standing beyond the barrier, his hands in his pockets, his dark eyes appraising the people who streamed by, his face seemed thinner than she had remembered, his hair thicker and darker, his eyes more strikingly brown.

'Hello,' she said, coming up beside him as he craned his neck to scrutinise the last few passengers now making their way down the platform.

He stared at her in amazement, put an arm round her and kissed her cheek.

'You've grown,' he said accusingly.

'Well, what did you expect? A wee cousin with a teddy bear?'

He grinned broadly and looked her up and down.

'On balance, I think I rather fancy this one,' he said, as he took Jessie's new weekend case from her hand and propelled her towards Great Victoria Street. 'Come on, or we'll be late for our tea.'

'Mrs McGregor has taken a fancy to you,' he began, as they queued at the bus stop. 'She said you sounded "vairry pleasant" on the phone.' He raised his eyes heavenwards. 'How do you do it, Clare? My father always said you could charm ducks off water.'

Clare blushed. She blushed even more as Ronnie took her hand and led her upstairs and she saw the bus conductor eyeing them. He winked at Ronnie and said something she just couldn't catch. She wondered if he thought she was Ronnie's girlfriend.

'Shaftesbury Square, Clare. Do you remember? We passed through it on our way up and down to Smithfield to find books.'

'I don't think so,' she replied doubtfully, as she looked down at the crowded pavements. 'I remember Ormeau Park and the bridge over the river and the smell of the gasworks,' she added more confidently.

215

'That hasn't changed. Still stinks.' His voice changed and a bitter edge crept into it. 'The immediate environment has the highest incidence of bronchitis and chest complaints in the British Isles. And bronchitis is one of the areas of research that can't get funding. It's too unglamorous.'

She turned to look at him, startled by his tone, but before she could say anything he grabbed her hand again, pulled her to her feet and hurried them back downstairs.

'What about this?' he asked, waving his hand at an extensive red-brick building set beyond impressively smooth lawns and a flourishing line of trees.

'No, I don't remember it,' she said, as she stepped back on to the pavement, 'but I know it's Queen's University. When you asked me to your graduation you sent me a postcard. I have it stuck in my mirror, so I see it every morning.'

'Good, I'm glad to hear it. My Alma Mater as they say. Yours too, I expect. Unless you head for Oxford or Cambridge.'

'Oh Ronnie, don't be silly. How could I ever go there?'

'Perfectly well, if you get a scholarship,' he said matter-of-factly. 'But you mightn't want to be so far away from Granda,' he added thoughtfully.

'I couldn't possibly go to England,' she said firmly. 'I'm not sure I could even manage Belfast unless I travel every day,' she went on, surprised that she had even thought of the possibility in the first place.

'No, you can't travel every day. You'd miss too much. You have to be here. As near as possible. That's why I'm so pleased you've charmed Mrs McGregor. Now what do you think of the outward appearance of this dwelling?' he asked, stopping under a lime tree opposite the garden gate of one of the tall, terrace houses on Elmwood Avenue.

Clare ran her eye along the row of red-brick dwellings with their tiny walled-in square of shrubs and flowers. The fluttering leaves of the mature trees cast dappled shadows on the brick-work and stroked the projecting roofing and sills of the first-floor bay windows. Despite all the comings and goings of this late afternoon hour, the avenue seemed to have an air of quiet about it, as if nothing could disturb the solidity of either these long-established buildings or their accompanying trees.

The house Ronnie was regarding with such concentration had roses trailing along the garden wall and a clematis by the front door. It had been newly painted. The window frames, a startling white, stood out in contrast to those of its neighbours, which might once have been green or brown but were now indistinguishably peeling and dingy. The front door, a dense, shiny black, looked as if it had been polished as thoroughly as the brass knocker and letterbox that decorated its solid shape.

'Very smart, indeed,' she said enthusiastically. 'Is this the house where you live?'

'Yes, this is where I reside, as journalists are wont to say. This is my domicile, my fixed abode, my pied-à-terre. Until Saturday, that is. I painted it myself. Two weeks' freedom from rent and a fortnight's evening meals. What I lost in sweat up the ladder I put back at six o'clock tea. Wait till you try Mrs McG's scones and cake,' he laughed, as he pushed open the tiny gate and took out his doorkey.

Clare decided that Ronnie had been very fortunate indeed to find Mrs McGregor and not just because of her cooking. In person, she was exactly as Clare had pictured her after their brief conversation on the phone, warm, friendly and direct, one of those sensible and kind-hearted women who take a real pleasure in caring for others. Over tea, it emerged that her husband was a merchant seaman who was away for months at a time on the South America run. Mrs McGregor used her time and energy to visit the elderly, housebound people who still lived in the avenue and ensure that the six students who occupied her upstairs rooms were as well fed as rationing and the vagaries of her ancient gas cooker would permit.

'But how *do* you manage to get the sugar and butter, Mrs McGregor?' Clare asked, after she and Ronnie had done justice to both the scones and the cake.

217

'Well, ye see, I do a bit of a Robin Hood,' she replied, with a wink as she poured more tea for them. 'These old folk o' mine, poor dears, they canna' eat a lot. I take them wee bits an' pieces of home baking an' then whin they offer me their points, I say thank you and use them to feed up my hungry wee students.'

After their meal, Ronnie took Clare up to his bedsitter.

'My goodness, isn't this posh?' she gasped as he opened the door.

She stepped into the spacious first-floor room and ran her eye round the decorative mouldings on the ceiling, the worn but still handsome furniture, the framed prints and pictures which filled the wallspace not already occupied by bookcases.

Beyond the bay window with its faded velvet curtains, the heavily leafed trees broke up the sunlight so that it flickered and fell in dappled patterns on the scarred leather surface of a large desk. The desk was piled high with books and papers. There were books everywhere. Some carefully arranged on bookshelves, others neatly stacked in small piles on the floor. A small group had been packed already, for a pile of boxes stood in a dim corner, tied with string and labelled, 'Store, Ronnie McGillvray – July 1952 until further notice!'

She moved between a well-polished table and a huge sofa to stand by the handsome marble fireplace and finger some of the smallest books in the room. Propped between heavy wooden bookends on the chill, white surface of the mantelpiece, the slender volumes had gold lettering on faded leather covers. As she twisted her head to read the titles she suddenly found herself thinking of Saturday, of the Liverpool boat standing by the quay below the Queen's Bridge, its gangways still in place, just like the travel advertisements in the window of the Guardian Office in Armagh.

'Goodness, Ronnie, what are you going to do with all your books? These are so lovely. But you can't take them all, can you?'

'That depends on you,' he said firmly.

'On me?'

'Yes, you. The one and only, original Clare Hamilton.'

She giggled.

'You wouldn't have a sixpence by any chance?' he asked, after a search of his pockets had proved unsuccessful. 'It can be a bit chilly in here even on summer evenings.'

She found one in her purse and watched him while he fed it into the gas meter. She studied him carefully while he turned knobs and struck a match. In so many ways he was still the cousin to whom she had been so devoted as a little girl. He still teased her and made her laugh. But he had changed in some way she couldn't quite define. There was a tension and a sharpness about his face. There was something different, too, in the way he moved and the way he sometimes spoke, almost as if he were quoting from a text book or a political manifesto.

When he put the match to the fire it hissed and plopped in protest, but after a moment or two it settled down to a comfortable roar. As Clare studied the broken, cream-coloured honeycomb of the gas fire, the flames changed slowly from blue to orange. Soon the roar subsided to a gentle, soothing murmur.

When they settled in the two ancient armchairs in the now shadowy room, Ronnie began to talk about his books and about his time at university. He said a little about his hopes for the future and went on to talk about the two days that remained before he returned her to the Armagh train and departed himself in the opposite direction to begin the longest journey he had ever made.

Yes, he agreed, there did seem a lot to do, but he had made some contingency plans. Mrs McGregor had been most helpful. She'd said he could store his books in a small boxroom at the top of the house for as long as he liked. It would be a shame to have to sell them, especially if his little cousin could use them.

Clare was just about to ask which of his cousins he meant, for all the McGillvray's were tall, when she realised he was thinking of her. She opened her mouth to protest.

'Now, Clare,' he interrupted, 'as your only relative with intellectual pretensions on this side of the Atlantic, I think I ought to make clear what you ought to do about your future. Just in case you hadn't thought of it for yourself, that is,' he began, as he stretched his long legs out comfortably over the fender.

He outlined briefly the advantages of going to university and then pointed out the further advantages of making up her mind now, even though it would be two years before she had her scholarship. If she decided now, then she could take over this room in two years' time, bring his books back down from upstairs and be within walking distance of all the main lecture theatres. Mrs McGregor herself had suggested it when he had talked to her about Clare's exam results last year. Now, she'd gone so far as to say that the quiet young man on the next floor would be a good person to use the room until Clare was ready to come, as he still had two years to do.

'But me no buts, tonight, Clare,' he said, when he saw she was about to protest again. 'I won't say another word about it till tomorrow's morrow, as they say in the best of the old romances. I'll give you a guided tour of the environs first thing in the morning and then I thought I'd take you up to Stormont. Uncle Harry is one of their bouncers. He's about to retire, so he's offered a tour on the quiet before he goes. You can tell me what you think of my plan while I'm packing my suitcases on Saturday morning.'

To her surprise, he stood up, turned towards her with a dramatic gesture and launched into song. His light baritone voice was so tender and full of feeling as he sang 'The Leaving of Liverpool' that she was hard pressed to keep tears from her eyes.

'That was lovely,' she said quietly, when he finished and strode across the room to draw the curtains and put on the lamps. 'I didn't know you could sing.'

'Neither did I, till I had a few too many one night at a friend's stag party,' he said laughing, as he dropped a pile of newspaper cuttings into her lap.

'Beauty begins with cleansing,' she read aloud. 'The importance of moisturisers? By Doris McGilloway?'

She looked at him in amazement, knowing from the sparkle in his eyes that he was teasing her and was delighting in her puzzlement.

'Who *is* Doris McGilloway?' she asked sternly.

He clutched his hand to his heart.

'I cannot tell a lie. It is I,' he began. 'But I got the idea from you,' he went on. 'Don't you remember Doris Gibb and the beaten eggs to put on your face?'

She nodded silently. Eddie and his *Picturegoer* magazines, Uncle Jimmy and his piles of newspaper, the copies of fashion magazines the customers brought, the battered books from the library, all came into her mind simultaneously.

'You used to read everything you could lay your hands on, even the beauty hints. It was all a bit advanced for a nine-year-old. Well, I have news for you. The Doris Gibb who wrote those beauty hints was a man. I met someone on the *Belfast Telegraph* who knew him. He had a whole collection of noms de plume. Which one he used depended on what he was writing. He used to do household hints as Dorcas Something-or-other. "How to look after your fur coat", "How to remove iron stains from your marble work surfaces", "How to make your own beeswax polish". You name it, he did it. So, I thought: McGillvray, you need to eat. If he can do it, you can do it. So I did. I used Doris in memory of our past inspiration and McGilloway to conceal my real identity.'

Clare shook her head and laughed. In this mood, there was something so direct about Ronnie. He was so open and without guile. And yet she sensed he was not as easy as he liked to pretend. It seemed to her his dramatic style and lively manner was one way of distracting attention from his true feelings. The more she saw of him, the more she thought he'd begun to be very unhappy indeed, that something had made him really uneasy, even downright angry.

'But, it wasn't enough to get you a job, Ronnie?' she said softly as she leafed through the pile of articles.

221

'Nope! You don't want people asking questions unless your sure they'll come up with the appropriate answers and I might have had some answers that didn't suit. Quite reliable on the beauty front, but a different cup of tea if you let him loose on anything that matters.'

'Like your research on bronchitis?'

'How did you know about that?' he asked sharply, a startled look on his face.

'You mentioned it in the bus when I said I remembered the gasworks and it sounded to me as if you knew quite a lot about it.'

She watched him look away as if something at the far side of the room required his immediate attention. In the low light from the two lamps he'd made from old wine bottles, his face looked almost haggard, quite unlike the person who'd re-minded her of a wartime beauty recipe.

'And what you knew had upset you,' she added quietly.

'You don't miss much,' he said wryly, as he turned back towards her and stared down at the black marble hearth. 'That was the last straw, when they wouldn't publish that particular article. "It wouldn't look good," they said. "Controversial", "Might offend the Ward councillors." If journalism is about anything, surely it's about the truth, about pointing out human misery and exploitation. How can you ever change what needs to be changed if all the unpleasant things are swept under the carpet, if only the people who are well-fed and comfortable have a voice?' he said, making no attempt whatever to conceal his bitterness.

'That's why you're going, isn't it?'

'Yes it is, Clare. Part of me doesn't want to go one little bit. I love this grim, old city in a funny way. I don't mind being broke. I don't even mind the place being run down and behind the times, but I mind not being able to say so, not being able to try to change things, to make things better. I thought I could stick it out, but I can't. I'm getting nowhere fast. And that's wrong. If you've got something you can do then you have to

222

find a place and a time where you can do it, otherwise you let yourself down. And if you let yourself down, then ultimately you let others down.'

He looked into the glow of the gas fire, defeat on his face.

'You won't let anyone down, Ronnie,' she said firmly. 'You never have, so you're hardly likely to start now. At your advanced age,' she added lightly.

To her delight, he smiled. He reached out, took her hand and squeezed it.

'My father once said you were a lot older than your years. I think he has a point,' he said, nodding to himself. 'I shall miss you more than anyone else in Ulster, even though I've only seen you once in a blue moon. Don't forget that.'

He drew her to her feet and kissed her gently on the lips. Without another word he led her downstairs and brought her through to the kitchen where Mrs McGregor was filling hot water bottles on the scrubbed wooden draining board beside her ancient gas cooker.

16

C lare collapsed gratefully on to the vibrating front seat of the double-decker bus and stared down at the continuously changing pattern of pedestrians on the crowded pavements below. Across the square, beyond the heavy-leafed trees, the dazzling white stone of the City Hall expanded outwards in pillared porches. Exotic, turquoise-capped turrets reached upwards from its solid mass. Silhouetted against a pure, blue sky they made her think of rock outcrops projecting from a limestone cliff.

Beside her, Ronnie waited till two women sat down in the seat across the way, then arranged his long legs as best he could in the aisle between. It had been his idea to walk down from Queens to their city-centre bus stop. That way, he said, they could get a proper look at interesting buildings like the Moravian Church, or pause at the junction with the Lisburn Road to cast an eye down the terraces of Sandy Row towards the redbrick mass of Murray's Tobacco Factory.

Although his tour of Queens had been very thorough and they'd been on their feet since nine o'clock, she'd been happy enough to walk when they emerged from the main gate and turned towards the city. In the previous two hours, he had shown her all the buildings on the main university site. He'd taken her into the Great Hall to look at the ceiling and the portraits, marched her round the Quad and pointed out the various lecture theatres. He bought them a cup of tea in the Students' Union, then walked her back to the Library and upstairs to the Reading Room.

Not satisfied with his whispered tour of the main subject areas and his brief guide to classification, he'd approached a small, grey-haired lady, deployed his considerable charm and got permission to take her into the stack.

The warm, musty atmosphere of the book stack was totally intriguing. Fascinated by the endless rows of books on subjects she had never even heard of, Clare realised she wasn't paying attention to what he was saying. But when she did manage to say something, she was quite surprised to discover he'd been watching her closely and didn't mind at all that she'd missed what he'd just said.

Curious about the circular windows beside the small work areas beyond the metal walkways, she stepped towards one, pulled out a chair and sat peering down at the sunlit lawns and pathways below. The only noise she could hear was the distant mutter of the central-heating system keeping the temperature up for the sake of the books and the quiet footsteps of a librarian loading a trolley with the requests from the reading room.

'Did you work up here?' she asked abruptly, aware she hadn't said a word for ages.

'In my Final year, yes.'

She saw him look at her quizzically, but he said nothing. He just waited till she stood up, then said: 'Come on, I told Josephine we wouldn't be long.'

'Is that her name?' she asked, surprised they should be on such intimate terms.

'Shouldn't think so,' he replied, smiling, as she followed him back towards the entrance. 'But the Chief Librarian is known as Napoleon. He's not on this morning or you'd see why.'

She grinned back at him as they came through the door of the stack and headed for the request counter. The top of a grey head was the only sign of the lady in question.

'Thank you very much,' said Ronnie, as the head responded immediately to the sound of their approach. 'I'm touting for new business so you won't be out of a job,' he added cheerfully, as she cast an appraising glance at Clare, then attempted to look severely at him.

As they were crossing Shaftesbury Square to get to the Dublin Road, Clare realised she shouldn't have worn her best shoes. The little pair of Louis heels had had several recent outings, but visiting Aunt Sarah, or going to the Ritz with Jessie, didn't exactly involve much walking.

'Queen's Bridge,' said Ronnie quietly as they crossed the Lagan. 'That's the Liverpool boat berthed down there. They're probably checking out their red carpet for tomorrow night,' he added.

'Don't say things like that, Ronnie,' she replied hastily. 'You'll make me cry and I mustn't. I'm a big girl now.'

'Yes, you are,' he said seriously. 'I wasn't expecting you to be so grown up.' He paused a moment and added, 'Sweet sixteen and all that. It's not even your birthday till October,' as if his problem with her grown-upness was a matter of arithmetic.

She looked away and studied the rows of tiny shops lining the Newtownards Road. Sweet sixteen and never been kissed. Was that what he was thinking? But she had been kissed. He'd kissed her himself last night and now he looked as if he might like to kiss her again if only they hadn't been on a bus surrounded by women with shopping bags.

As the thought struck her, she had no idea what to say.

A moment later, Ronnie had to give his attention to his legs as the two large women in the nearby seat began to manoeuvre their persons, bags and parcels into the narrow aisle. As the bus juddered to a halt, Ronnie collected himself and continued his commentary on the passing scene.

'It gets posher as you get further out,' he began. 'Higher density of trees whacks up the property prices. By the time you see Castlehill Road leading to Massey Avenue you're in Nob's Hill. Minister of Education, Under Secretary of This and That, you know. They live there to be near the job. Walk to work on the chauffeur's day off,' he added casually. 'If you see police-men around, then some big shot has been sent from Head Office to make sure they're doing it right. But mostly in July they all go on their hols. That's why it gets so quiet the likes of us can sneak in the back door and get a shufti.'

'Golly, is that it?' Clare asked in amazement.

Suddenly they were past the substantial suburban houses with neatly trimmed hedges and old roses and a huge building perched high on a hillside shone white in the brightness of the sunlight.

'Yes, that's it. The seat of what this benighted province chooses to call "democracy". Looks quite impressive now they've got the cow dung and black paint off. You probably don't remember that.'

'Remember what?'

'Camouflage. During the war. They wanted to put the Air Force and a whole lot of top brass in there. Sounded like a bad joke. The place made a wonderful target. Absolutely marvel-lous bomb run up any of the approach avenues and a vast, shoe-box of a building gleaming white in a bomber's moon.'

The bus stopped. They got off and stood gazing up the long, tree-lined drive that climbed steadily towards the imposing front of the building beyond the heavy wrought-iron gates.

'So they painted it and covered up the avenues with cinders,' he went on. 'It's taken them years to get it cleaned up again.'

'Did they really use cow dung or are you pulling my leg again?'

'Yes, honest Injun. I do not tell a lie. Uncle Harry was in on the job. He'll tell you. Some chemist or other worked it out. But the mix didn't come off as well as it was supposed to. They'd awful trouble with streaks.'

Clare looked longingly at the green slopes running parallel to the handsome avenue and the grey pavement now growing steeper by the minute.

'Do you think we could walk on the grass?' she asked tentatively.

'Don't see why not,' he replied promptly. 'They can't put you in jail, you're under age. I'm being transported anyway. What the hell!'

Clare stepped on to the grass, took off her shoes and felt the soft, cool turf under her hot, swollen feet. She felt better immediately.

'Ah, these country colleens,' said Ronnie, looking down at her with an exaggerated sigh. 'I'm sorry we're late for the morning dew. You could have bathed in it.'

She giggled and trailed her feet as they slowed down on the steepest part of the slope. Ahead of them, the right arm of a huge statue was raised against the blue of the sky in a fierce, menacing gesture. A few vehicles loaded with tree prunings and gardening equipment were parked on the roundabout at his feet, indifferent to his protest.

'Worth it for the view, isn't it?' he said, as they stood catching their breath on the wide stone terrace in front of the main entrance.

The city with its encircling hills was laid out below and beyond them. Only the beginnings of heat shimmer softened the sharp outlines of the edge of the Antrim basalts, the strong lines of factories and mills, churches and warehouses, docks and gantries and the massed ranks of back to back houses that had spread outwards from the flat land around the docks and the city centre as industry demanded more and yet more labour.

From this distance, the unhealed gaps left by the bombing were almost invisible, the shabbiness of buildings untenanted or awaiting demolition masked by sunlight and trees. Clare looked up at Ronnie and saw his face crumple. He'd said last night that he loved this city, but now she saw so clearly just how much it meant to him. She turned away and looked along the terrace towards the car park in case her seeing his distress would make it even worse for him.

Ronnie gave his uncle's name to the doorman and they went inside. She took in the vast sweep of the entrance hall, stared up at the elaborately decorated ceiling and looked longingly at the marble tiled floor. She couldn't quite believe it. She thought of ballrooms on the screen at the Ritz Cinema, remembered the Churchills' ball in *Emma*.

'Just perfect for ten couples,' she whispered, as the doorman disappeared in search of his colleague.

'*Da-ta-da, ta-ta-ta-ta,*' sang Ronnie loudly.

To her utter amazement, he caught her in his arms and swung her across the floor to the unmistakable rhythm of 'The American Patrol'.

'Ronnie,' she gasped, as he executed a skilful reverse turn in the midst of the empty space.

But his only answer was to move them in even wider circles towards the impressive staircase at the far end of the brightly lit hall.

She had no idea Ronnie was such a good dancer. The further they went, the more elaborate his footwork became, but his hand on her waist was so firm that she reckoned if she missed her step he'd just pick her up and put her down again. Ronnie swung her towards the foot of the great staircase just as a figure appeared on the half landing and began to make his way down.

As they came to a halt, she followed Ronnie's gaze. A young man in a very white shirt was descending slowly, his jacket hooked on one finger over his shoulder, his eyes flickering casually around the empty space behind them. For one moment, Clare thought she was imagining things. The figure stopped beside them.

'Hello, Clare,' he said, smiling at them both.

She was quite sure now from the quizzical look in his eye he'd seen them dancing.

'Hello, Andrew,' she just managed to reply. 'This is my cousin, Ronnie McGillvray. Ronnie, this is Andrew Richardson. He lives up the road from us.'

Ronnie looked doubtfully at Andrew Richardson and then smiled suddenly.

'Clare and I are about to have a free, conducted tour of the premises,' he began. 'Would you like to join us or have you done it all before?'

'No, this is my first time here,' he said easily. 'I'm on chauffeur duty for Grandfather and I'd love to see round the place.'

'Well, now's your chance. That tall, grey-haired man by the entrance looking this way and wondering what on earth's keeping us is my uncle. The bigger his audience, the better he likes it. What we lack in numbers, we must make up for in intelligent interest. Come on.'

Taking Clare's hand, he walked her back along the pillared hall as Andrew fell into step on her other side.

Uncle Harry's tour of Stormont was an event Clare was sure she'd never forget. Apart from the fact that he insisted they see every corner of the building from the basement to the top storey, he was full of stories about the well-known personalities who had come and gone over his long years of service. Names she knew only from the more up to date history books or from Granda Scott's avid perusal of the newspapers were Uncle Harry's 'regulars', faces he recognised, striding figures who said, 'Good morning,' or stopped for a friendly word as they headed for their respective chambers.

Harry McGillvray sat them down at the back of the empty lower chamber and described exactly how it looked when it was in session, who sat where and how the various members related to each other. As she listened, it occurred to Clare you might do worse than read an account Uncle Harry and some of his colleagues could put together if you really wanted a history of the political events in the Province.

'There wasn't much we diden' know about up here,' he said, nodding to himself, as he led them into the Senate Chamber.

He pointed up at a recently carved inscription recording the gratitude of the King for the use of the chamber as an Air Force Headquarters during the war.

'Me an' young Bill Murray were on duty the night o' the big

Blitz. He was on this door here, an' I was down at the entrance. All I coud see whin I luked out was the whole sky lit up an' the city afire. I couden' tell whit parts was hit though I knew for sure the docks woud get it. I was thinkin' o' course 'bout the wife an' the boys, fer we lived York Street way in them days,' he explained, turning to Ronnie.

Clare watched Uncle Harry as he nodded up towards the inscription, his face deeply lined, his eyes bright with moisture, his recall pin sharp. Ronnie was standing very still beside her, the gaunt look suddenly strongly marked on his face. But, as Uncle Harry continued, it was Andrew's appearance that changed most dramatically. His relaxed manner, his fresh, sun-tanned look disappeared. His skin paled and his features became immobile. He grew ill-at-ease and fidgety.

'Bill could see nothin' outside atall because o' the black out,' Harry McGillvray continued. 'But he coud see the big table that was jus here. The wee Waf girls was puttin' the bombers on it, comin' in over the city. The telephones were ringin' from the batteries and the look-outs an' the fire brigades an' suchlike. An' he was thinkin' jus' the same as me: Ah wonder is the missus and the we'eans all right?'

As she stood listening, Clare became aware that they were in the room where the devastation of the city had been played out with models and counters on a broad, spotlighted table.

'And were they?' she burst out, unable to bear the tension any longer.

He pressed his lips together and shook his head silently.

'The house was gone the next mornin' when he got back. Like as if ye'd taken a knife an' cut a piece out of the row. The neighbours next door was hurted, but not bad. Bill lost his whole family, even his aul' granny that'd come to stay to be comp'ny fer his wife whin he was doin' nights up here. Bad times,' he concluded shaking his head sadly.

'Yes, Mr McGillvray, very bad times,' said Andrew with feeling.

Clare was startled by the unfamiliar note in his voice. As the

231

older man drew them over to the benches on the right of the chamber and pointed out where they should sit, she felt Andrew move towards her. A moment later, he sat down abruptly, so close she could feel the warmth of his skin through the thin fabric of his shirt.

'Aye, they were, Mr Richardson,' he responded, with a sharp look at the young man. 'I've maybe said too much about that night,' he went on, a note of apology in his voice. 'I'm rememberin' now about yer father. He wasn't long elected so I diden' know him well. It were the start of the blitz in London, weren't it?'

'It was. They'd only arrived that day from leaving me at school,' he replied, no trace of emotion in his voice.

'Your mother too, Andrew?' Clare asked, before she even thought about it.

He nodded and turned to smile weakly at her.

'And my grandparents, a passing uncle and my youngest aunt,' he went on. 'It was always open house in London. It could have been even worse. I do still have some family scattered about the place.'

'There's been a lot more scattering since the war,' agreed Harry McGillvray. 'We thought the war was the worst thing coud happen, but it's not over yet. We've not seen the end o' the changes it'll bring. An' not all for the better either.'

Clare followed his pointing finger and obediently studied the three painted roundels that decorated the Strangers Gallery. Two women with generous bosoms and flowing hair bent over a sickle and a spinning wheel, while a third sat, her skirt spread across her knees, looking uncomfortable, a ship perched across them.

'In the 1920s when this chamber was decorated, agriculture, the linen industry and shipbuilding were the basis of Ulster's wealth,' Harry McGillvray continued, moving back to his more formal tone. 'I doubt if there's more than a few hundred acres under flax these days,' he added sadly. 'There's a desperate shortage of work for all the pullin' strings they do up here to get new industry. We're way behind the rest of the UK in livin' standards, even wi' the new Welfare State. It'll be a brave while afore we make up to what they have across the water, I'm tellin' ye.'

As she listened to Harry McGillvray's sharp comments, Clare remembered Ronnie's bitterness over the articles on asthma and bronchitis he couldn't get published. She thought of all the items she'd read to Granda Scott in the last months about dangerous houses that hadn't been condemned, huge numbers of school children who'd been in contact with tuberculosis, and the high figures for rural unemployment.

Even before Ronnie had talked about his reasons for leaving Ulster, she'd sensed all was not well. Now, the pieces were fitting together and making a picture she must pay attention to. She needed to understand what was going on. This was such a good opportunity to find out more but no matter how she tried, she simply couldn't pay proper attention to what Ronnie and his uncle were saying. What Andrew had just revealed repeated itself over and over in her mind. It was the most important discovery she had made today. An orphan just like me, she kept saying to herself. An orphan just like me.

They each thanked Harry McGillvray for his splendid tour and wished him a happy retirement. When Clare left Ronnie to say his goodbyes to his uncle and went outside, Andrew followed her. They stood together for a moment, blinking in the brilliant light. After the cool interior of the marble-floored entrance hall, the heat struck fiercely.

They moved slowly across to the edge of the terrace. The shimmer had increased over the city and some small white clouds were beginning to bubble up on the horizon, but overhead the sky was still an unmarked blue. Against its vivid backdrop, the mass of the building towered up behind them like an impregnable fortress, dominating the landscape in every direction, thrusting its ruler-straight avenues outwards with the same strong gesture as the raised hand of Sir Edward Carson's statue.

'It's quite a view, isn't it?' said Clare abruptly.

Andrew was standing close beside her, as if it was the most natural thing in the world. He remained perfectly at ease, but she suddenly felt awkward and self-conscious.

'Yes, it is. Very impressive,' he said agreeably. 'But it's not my favourite view in these parts,' he went on cheerfully. 'That's a few miles down the road. Scrabo Tower. Just outside New-townards. D'you know it?'

Clare shook her head and smiled, grateful for a simple question.

'No, I don't. This is my first visit to Belfast,' she admitted. 'I came when I was a little girl, but that was just after the war, so no one took me anywhere. Except Ronnie, of course,' she corrected herself. 'He used to take me to Smithfield to look for storybooks, because I'd lost all mine.'

'How did you lose them?'

Clare felt the colour drain from her face as she looked away. He had only asked a simple question, but somehow she couldn't bring herself to look at him. She thought of saying something ridiculous like, 'I left them on a bus.' Then she glanced back at him. When she found his eyes were watching her steadily, she couldn't bring herself not to give him a proper answer.

'All my things were burnt after my parents died. They had typhoid,' she said hastily.

'I thought there was something different about you,' he said matter-of-factly.

'What sort of something?'

'I don't quite know,' he began. 'I'll tell you when I find out,' he added quickly, as he heard a footstep behind them.

'Admiring the view?' asked Ronnie sharply.

Clare thought he looked very near to tears and was about to say that they were when Andrew got in first.

'I was telling Clare that my favourite view is a few miles down the road. Scrabo Tower. Do you know it?'

234

'Oh yes,' replied Ronnie, 'I had a great-aunt used to live half a mile away. D'you remember me telling you about Pretty Kitty?' he asked, turning to Clare.

Clare nodded, grateful that the bleak look had gone from his face.

'Wasn't she the one that used to take you on the route marches?'

'That's the one. Thought it was uplifting to the spirit. It may have been, but it was hard on the legs. She was a tough old lady. Used to march me up the hill and then up to the top of the tower as well.'

'If Clare has never been, we could go there,' said Andrew casually. 'Grandfather will be closeted till after four and it's only a few miles.'

'That's very good of you,' said Ronnie awkwardly. 'Would you like to go, Clare? How's your head for heights?'

'I'd love to go and my head's fine, but I'm terribly hungry. I think we've walked miles this morning.'

Ronnie laughed and looked almost easy again.

'Well, if Andrew doesn't mind, I think I know where we can get some lunch. Fish and chips?'

Andrew nodded cheerfully.

'It's an unpretentious little establishment, as they say in the guide books. It's called Jim's Place. Only it's spelt P L A I C E, and it comes in newspaper,' he added, looking questioningly at Andrew, as if he expected the newspaper to create some difficulty.

'Let's go,' said Andrew promptly. He turned on his heel and led the way across the terrace to the nearby car park.

Clare had difficulty keeping up with his long strides, but he stopped by the nearest car, a large, well-polished Rover, whipped out his keys, opened the passenger door and waved Clare into the front seat. She caught a look of irritation on Ronnie's face as he climbed into the back, but Andrew didn't seem to notice.

*   *   *

235

The lane up to the tower was steep, rough and deeply rutted. Clare made a mental note that next time she wanted to wear high heels she would at least try to imagine what the day might bring. Her legs and back were aching again and she was dripping with perspiration, but she knew the effort was going to be worth it. She'd promised herself she wouldn't look back till they got to the top, but with every step she was aware that more and more countryside was spread out around them.

As they climbed higher, a tiny breeze sprang up and the birds hiding in the heavy patches of shade began to stir. Little flocks of linnets flitted across their path from one patch of gorse bushes to another. From high above their heads, skylarks, almost imperceptible dots against the blue, suddenly began to pour a cascade of sound into the heavy, quiet air.

'Hail to thee blythe spirit,' said Andrew, stopping up ahead of her and shading his eyes to look upwards.

Ronnie stopped too and wiped his face with the back of his hand as he waited for Clare to catch up. For a moment, Clare saw the two of them look at each other across the deeply rutted path, Andrew, fair-skinned and freckled with a gleam of red in his fine blonde hair, his body slim and at ease, Ronnie, dark-haired and sallow, his face angular, his limbs taut with tension.

'Bird thou never wert. Wert thou?' demanded Ronnie, as he peered up into the sky.

Clare smiled to herself and wondered why they were so wary of each other.

'How much further?' she asked, just to keep them occupied.

'Not far,' they replied, speaking at the same time.

She was glad they both laughed simultaneously. It broke the tension.

They threw themselves down in the shadow of the tower to cool off and were still sitting there exhausted when an elderly lady appeared with three glasses of water on a tray.

Andrew jumped to his feet immediately.

'Miss Millin, how are you?'

'My goodness, it's Andrew. Goodness, how you've grown! How is your Aunt Charlotte? Still gardening?'

'Yes, she manages to do a bit. Still carries her secateurs in her knitting bag wherever she goes! Do you think we could possibly go up the Tower. It's not one of your tea room days, but Clare has never been before and she's going back to Armagh tomorrow.'

'And I'm leaving the country tomorrow, so it's my last chance,' said Ronnie, as he got to his feet more slowly.

The old woman looked at him sharply.

'I'm sure I know you, but I can't remember your Christian name,' she said quietly. 'You used to come, years ago, with old Miss McGillvray from the back of the hill. I remember she could never understand why you always wanted to look at Belfast when you went up.'

Ronnie blushed. In that single moment, Clare grasped one of the biggest differences between Ronnie and Andrew. While Ronnie had begun to expect the worst, Andrew still hoped for the best. It seemed to make a difference to everything they said and did.

'Of course, ye can, an' welcome,' she said, waving her hands at them. 'We may open the tea room later if there's many about. We're our own boss, as they say. But if we're not open, come round to the kitchen for a drink. You'll be needing it, I think, by the time you do the steps.'

'All one hundred and twenty-two of them,' laughed Andrew, as he put their glasses back on the tray and carried it back to the kitchen for her.

'Well then, was it worth the climb?'

Clare leaned against the rough stone of the parapet and gazed away to the south. Beyond the gorse-covered rock outcrops below the tower, all the way to the furthest point of the horizon, the gentle, undulating countryside was ribbed and seamed with hedgerows. Bathed in sunlight, the little fields thus divided lay like a patterned counterpane over the bumpy surface of the drumlin swarm, moulded by the flow of an ice sheet, aeons ago.

The waters of Strangford lough lay shimmering at the edge of the fields, its calm surface dotted with the same humpy little hills, now islands lapped by blue water, the green of their summer grass yet more vivid by contrast with the encircling lough.

'What did you say?' she said vaguely.

Her eyes were held by the varied patchwork, the contrast of new-grown pasture with the pale colours of cut meadow, the rich brown of recently ploughed stubble set against the heavy bluey-green foliage of potato fields. Farms and cottages were scattered among clusters of trees and along narrow winding lanes. All was still but for the clacking movement of an old reaping machine, a strange insect-like creature moving steadily up and down a nearby field of wheat.

Ronnie smiled to himself and moved on, his respects paid to the three sides of the tower on which his aunt had lavished her enthusiasm. Miss Millin was right. He wanted to look back at the city, as he always had.

'Can that be the Mountains of Mourne?' Clare asked herself, as her eyes focused on the furthest point of the horizon.

'Yes, that's them all right.'

She turned round, startled to find she'd actually spoken out loud. Andrew was standing behind her, gazing at the same misty outline.

'That's Donard, I know,' he said, without looking at her. 'And I think that's Commendagh, but the others to the west I'm not sure of. I climbed Donard once hoping I could look north and see Scrabo, but it wasn't a clear day. Not like today.'

'My grandmother always says you should make up your mind about things on a clear day,' she began, surprising herself. 'I've never been sure whether she means it literally or not.'

'What do you need to make your mind up about, Clare?'

'Nothing very much at the moment, I don't think. I don't lead a very exciting life. Visits to Belfast apart,' she said smiling, as she moved a little further along the battlements and looked out over the lough to the Ards Peninsula on the other side.

'Perhaps you could make up your mind to write to me when I go back to Cambridge,' he suggested. 'I get homesick for Drumsollen and for Ulster and I seem to spend less and less time here,' he said matter-of-factly.

'Why's that?'

'Family mostly. My mother's family are all in England, London and Home Counties. They've paid for my education so they expect to see me. Grandmother Richardson finds young people tiring, so even when I am allowed to come, she farms me out to cousins, the further away the better. I've been in Fermanagh for the last two weeks. Tomorrow I'm off to Cavan. From there to Dublin. From Dublin to Holyhead. And back to Cambridge. I probably won't see you again till next summer,' he added sadly.

Clare was completely taken aback. So he'd want to see her this summer if he weren't going away, would he?

'How long have you been at Cambridge?' she asked quickly when she realised she'd not said anything for several minutes.

'Two years. I've done Part 1 History. I enjoyed that. I start my Law when I go back. Not so sure about that.'

'Then why did you choose it?'

'I didn't. I wasn't sure what I wanted to do so Uncle William decided. He's a solicitor, wants me to come into the firm.'

'In London?'

'No, actually. He lives in Winchester.'

'So you'd not come back to Ulster?'

'Oh yes, I'll come back. I just don't know how I'll manage it. This is still my home.'

'Even though you've been away so much? You seem to have got around a lot.'

'Yes, I have. Since I was seven,' he agreed. 'Friends in prep

239

school and then at Haileybury. I went out to Kenya one long vac with a friend whose Dad was in the Foreign Office. And I spent another one learning French in Brittany. Grandmother was horrified when I came back, she said I sounded like a peasant.'

'I'd love to hear you lapse into peasant,' she said, laughing at the thought of Andrew without his public school accent.

'If I come back in two years' time, where will you be?'

'Where I always am, except when you call,' she said, grinning at him. 'Getting ready to go to university if I get my scholarship.'

'You will,' he said, firmly.

'How do you know?'

'I know, because you've made up your mind to get it. That's what's different about you. I said I'd tell you when I'd worked it out. You make up your own mind about things. I don't always manage to. Some things, yes, but others no. Like doing Law. But you make up your own mind about everything. Say you'll write to me, please.'

He slid his arm round her waist, drew her towards him and kissed her.

'And over there on the south side of Greyabbey is where my Aunt Charlotte lives,' he said, pointing with his free arm as they heard footsteps approaching.

'Time's getting on,' said Ronnie tartly, as he noted the position of Andrew's right arm. 'I think I'll head down.'

'Yes, indeed, be with you in a moment,' said Andrew agreeably.

'Can I take you to the Mournes when I come back? And to see Aunt Charlotte? And anywhere else you'd like to go. Please.'

'You seem to have made up your mind about it.'

'Yes, I have.'

She nodded briefly and cast a long, wistful glance out over the countryside below.

'I wish you didn't have to go to Cavan tomorrow.'

'So do I, Clare. But there will be other times. I shall be back. You can be sure of that,' he said firmly.

She nodded and smiled back at him. Even when he took her hand and they began the long descent together, she didn't quite recognise the fact that she had made up her mind about two very important matters that would shape her whole future life.

17

A lthough Clare made up her mind she wouldn't cry when Ronnie took her to the Armagh train on Saturday afternoon, tears trickled down her cheeks as he swung her little case up into the empty carriage. When he put his arms round her, the tears flowed even faster.

'Now then, don't cry, Clare. It may never happen,' he said, brightly. 'I may make my fortune in Liverpool, take over the paper and pop across at weekends to see you. I'll send my Rolls Royce up to the Grange to fetch you,' he said as he fished out his handkerchief and dried her eyes.

She sniffed and tried to smile. It was no use pretending. She was quite sure he would go on to Canada and it would be years before he could afford to come back however successful he was.

'I couldn't possibly give you that trouble,' she said, pulling out her own hanky and blowing her nose. 'I'll make sure my chauffeur gets his time off during the week. Just let me know when you're coming.'

He gathered her in his arms again and kissed her. He was still kissing her when the guard blew his whistle and doors banged shut all around them. He caught her by the waist, half lifting her up into the carriage, closed the door and walked beside her as the train began to move very slowly along the platform. She struggled awkwardly with the window, let it down and reached out her hand to him.

'You'll go on writing to me, won't you?' she said as the train gave a sudden jerk.

'I'll always write to you,' he promised, releasing her hand as it

242

gathered speed. 'Please take care of yourself,' he called as they neared the end of the platform.

She stood at the window waving, until the train clattered across the tracks and a trolley piled high with mailbags obscured his tall figure. She sat down with a bump and cried all the way to Lisburn.

Two hours later, she got off the Armagh bus opposite the gates of the Robinsons' farm, walked quickly up the hill and turned into the lane leading to the forge. To her surprise, the smoke of a freshly made-up fire swirled above the roof of the cottage and the half door of the forge was still propped open. Granda Scott hadn't gone into town. She wondered what could have happened to prevented him. She'd never known him not go into Armagh on a Saturday unless he was ill.

Avoiding the propped-up gates and the stray bits of farm machinery, she walked quickly up the lane, anxious he might be unwell. Just as she reached the smoother path under the trees and shrubs beyond the forge he appeared at the front door, a basin of water in his hands. She breathed a sigh of relief.

'Ach, there ye are. Yer back. It's great t' see ye,' he said, setting the basin down on the windowsill.

There was a shake in his hands and his eyes moved around distractedly.

'I was wonderin' if I had a clean shirt an' a collar.'

He stood by the wrought-iron trellis, his narrow chest exposed where his short-sleeved vest lay open, his bare arms pale above the elbow, his shoulders drooping. Suddenly, she was aware of the way he was standing there. It brought her heart into her mouth. Not only was he old, he had become frail.

The vulnerability of his body was bad enough, but what upset her most was his distress. He was always anxious when something upset him and he could find no way of speaking about it. But she was especially alert whenever he asked for a collar. Collars were seldom anything but bad news.

'Now, Granda,' she said gently, 'you know you've always got a clean shirt. Don't we keep the two Uncle Bob gave you the

243

Christmas before last in the bottom drawer so we're never caught?'

He glanced upwards and gave an awkward half smile.

'Sure I clean forgot. I never thought o' lookin' there.'

He studied the basin and the shaving things he'd already lined up on the kitchen windowsill.

'Charlie Running's wife died lass night. The funeral's tomorra. I was afeerd maybe ye'd stay another night to see Ronnie off.'

'I wouldn't do that and not let you know,' she said firmly. 'I'd have phoned Margaret and Jamsey would have come over with a message.'

'Ach, I forgot all about the phone, an' them must have it a year or more. Eddie's thinkin' o' buyin' a car. He was over this mornin' to tell me about Kate,' he said, dropping his eyes and studying the broken tarmac round the front door.

'What happened with Kate?' she asked quietly.

'Ach, what happens to all bedrid people sooner or later. She got pneumonia an' it ran its course in three days. Sure she's been an invalid these five years. D'ye not mind, Charlie useta come down on his bicycle to see us of an evenin'?'

'I do remember now, but it was only once or twice.'

'Aye, once Kate took to her bed he had too much to do lookin' after her an' the house and the goats and the chickens forby. He coulden' leave her at night for she got lonesome. They say it was her nerves more than the arthritis but she went to skin an' bone. An' a lovely lookin' woman she was too. She an' I are the same age to the day but Charlie is ten years younger. I haven't laid eyes on him for months. But I'll go up to the wake tonight.'

'Will Eddie give you a lift?'

'Aye, he's a good neighbour, Eddie. I must pay my respects to Kate. Sure she was my sweetheart for two years till Charlie came along,' he added abruptly, as he went back into the house for a towel.

'D'you really want to wear a collar tonight?' she asked, as he came back out again. 'Wouldn't the best of your everyday shirts not be all right? You'll have to wear the collar tomorrow for church.'

'Well.'

He set up the mirror against the window frame and dipped the brush in the warm water to moisten his bristle.

'Woud'ye ever come with me?' he said awkwardly. 'Ah know ye diden' know Kate but I'd like fer Charlie to meet ye. He'd maybe be loathe to come visitin' again if he felt someone strange was here, but if he knowed ye he'd not think twice.'

Of course she'd go, she said. If there wasn't room in the trap, she'd use her bicycle and meet up with him at the pump opposite the house. She left him to his shaving and went indoors, to change her dress and get their tea ready.

After standing in the sunlight, the big kitchen was dark and oppressive, full of steam from the kettle rattling its lid on the stove. She moved it to one side and surveyed the familiar room from the hearth. She felt as if she'd just returned home after a long absence in a far country.

Robert had been born in this house in the same bed he now slept in. Most of the better furniture was what his father had bought in the 1870s, when he married a girl from Battle Hill. After years as a journeyman he had rented the house and forge from the present owner's father and set up on his own. They'd prospered and produced six children, but only Robert, the youngest, had stayed at home and followed his father's trade.

'Robert and Kate,' she whispered to herself, as she refilled the kettle and put it back on the stove.

She wondered how different Robert's life might have been had Kate become the woman of the house, all those years ago, and not Ellen. What made Kate reject good, steady Robert and choose Charlie, a man younger than herself, unusual in those days?

'A lovely lookin' woman,' she said in a whisper to the quiet room, where only the heavy tick of the wag o' the wall clock and the first murmurings of the freshly filled kettle broke the silence.

Perhaps Robert was too steady, too reliable. Charlie must have offered Kate something Robert just didn't have. Certainly, he'd loved her all her life, cared for her till the very end.

She spread a cloth on the table under the window and fetched butter, jam and cheese from the cupboard. She slipped into Robert's room, brought out a clean shirt, left it on the bed for him and went and changed into a blouse and a cotton skirt. She hung up her dress on the back of the door and turned to the mirror to run a comb through her hair.

Some day she too would be old. Instead of dark curls, the face in the mirror would have grey hair. Or white. Her creamy skin would be dry and wrinkled and darkened with age. Somewhere beyond that day she would die, suddenly, from a heart attack, or slowly, like Kate, from some disabling disease.

She stood rigid in front of her mirror, the comb still clutched in her hand. It was such an appalling thought. And it must get worse as you got older. At least now it all seemed so far away you could reasonably forget about it, but how would it feel if you were forty, or sixty, or in your late seventies like Robert and Kate? Could it possibly be you actually got used to the idea as the years passed?

She heard the startled call of a blackbird, splashed by Robert's shaving water as he threw it under the nearest shrub.

'Standing here isn't going to get the tea made,' she said sharply.

She turned to her suitcase, unpacked her overnight things and the few special books Ronnie insisted on giving her, so that she couldn't possibly forget him, he said. Small, leather-bound volumes with gold titles. She couldn't imagine ever forgetting Ronnie. Nor Andrew either.

Clare left her bicycle by the pump and waited at the open gate to the Runnings' bungalow until the trap caught up with her and Eddie had tethered the mare in a nearby lane. Charlie's dahlias were looking wonderful. Clare remembered the night when she and Jessie plucked up courage to ask if he could spare a few roses for putting in the barn where her father had shot himself. That was the only time she'd ever spoken to him. He'd been so kind and gentle that night.

'Aye, roses. Certainly,' he said. 'Yer more than welcome. But they'll not be much good in a vase for all they've a great perfume. I'll cut you some dahlias. Sure I cut them for Kate every day or two an' it only encourages them to flower more.'

The small house was packed and Eddie led them into the less crowded of the two downstairs rooms. Along one wall the coffin stood on trestles. From where Clare stood, the white tip of Kate's nose was clearly visible above the silk and lace draperies that lined the small, narrow casket.

She followed Eddie reluctantly. She'd been to more than one wake with Robert but never before had she ended up so close to an open coffin that she couldn't avoid seeing the worn and wasted face of the woman who lay there.

'I'm sorry for yer trouble, Charlie.'

A few yards ahead of her, she saw Robert speak to Charlie Running. He held out his hand, but to her surprise Charlie ignored it. He simply put his arms round Robert and hugged him.

'Sure I know you are, Robert,' he said warmly. 'Who would know better than you what I've lost? She was askin' after you only last week an' I told her what news I had of you from Eddie here. Sure it's months since I've laid eyes on you yourself. How's your wee lassie?'

'She's here herself,' Robert replied shyly, as Charlie released his grip and a glass of whiskey was thrust into his hand.

'Are you Clarey?' Charlie asked in amazement, as he stepped towards her and held out his hands.

Clare nodded and wondered if she should offer her condolences now or later. But Charlie was beaming at her.

'Sure I didn't know it was you. Didn't I think you were some connection of Jessie Rowentree,' he said laughing, as he turned back to speak to Robert. 'Haven't I been watching your wee Clarey growing up these lock o' years past an' diden' know it

247

was her. Maybe it was the uniform. But sure I used to see her regular down at the pump if I was working about the front of the place,' he said cheerfully.

'I'm very sorry about Mrs Running,' said Clare quietly.

'I'm sure you are. But don't be too sad, Clarey. Kate had suffered a lot. She was ready to go. She told me so,' he said steadily enough. 'But I don't know what I'm goin' to do without her,' he went on, his voice breaking, tears suddenly streaming down his face.

'Here, drink a drop of this man,' said Robert promptly, passing over the whiskey. 'Yer not without friends an' she has ye well learned how to look after yerself. An' ye've the books forby,' he said firmly.

Charlie took a good swig of the whiskey and wiped his eyes roughly on the sleeve of his jacket. Eddie had slipped away and the small room was empty now but for the three of them standing in the space between the window and the foot of the well-polished coffin.

'Yer Granda, Clarey, was always the sensible one,' Charlie began, looking directly at her. 'Many's the spot he got me out of years ago. I always went to him whin I was in trouble. An' sure he doesn't change. God bless him. Now come on, Robert, till I get that glass topped up again an' see if there's a lemonade or a cup of tea for Clarey.'

He took them by the arm and marched them down the hall into a large kitchen with people wedged into all the corners. The centre of the room was filled by a huge table covered with rows of open bottles and plates piled high with sandwiches and cake.

'Make a space now for the three of us. Ye all know my auld friend Robert. This is his wee granddaughter, Clarey, an' right glad I am to see them both. Drink up now, drink up, there's plenty more where that came from.'

At the time, Clare never imagined the death of poor Kate Running could make any difference to her own life, but, as the late summer moved towards autumn, Charlie Running's frequent visits produced such an improvement in Robert's well-being that Clare was able to put out of mind many of the worries and anxieties that had pursued her through the previous winter and spring.

Charlie blew into their lives like a fresh breeze. His presence fanned embers of recollection that brought a light to Robert's eyes Clare hadn't seen for longer than she could remember.

'God bless all here. Erin go brach,' he would salute them, as he pushed open the kitchen door and seated himself on the far end of the wooden settle.

'What sort of a day have ye's had?'

As often as not, he didn't wait for an answer, but launched into some story about his own. Robert would put down his paper and peer over the tops of his National Health glasses. Next morning Robert would be sure to point out that Charlie's stories always had a bit added on to them, like fishermen's stories, but in the evening it was never long before Charlie's humour drew a wry smile out of him. Clare always knew when Robert was in particularly good spirits because he'd go as far as having a sly dig at Charlie, or make some veiled reference to past misfortunes or miscalculations.

From the end of the settle nearer to the stove, Clare would observe them closely. Certainly, there was a tension between them, but even if some old antagonism still expressed itself in the continuing banter, she sensed the source of the trouble was long since healed.

'Sure ye may go up to Stormont and sort them out yerself, man dear,' said Robert, with a twinkle in his eye. 'They haven't the way of it at all. Ye may have to put them right,' he went on, with a perfectly straight face.

Whenever Charlie launched into one of his regular political diatribes, Clare listened hard. Robert always shook his head at the radical suggestions Charlie made, but after listening to Ronnie, Clare knew Charlie had information Robert would be loathe to acknowledge, even if it did come his way.

Charlie had left the schoolroom by the church on the hill

249

when he was fourteen, like all the rest of the boys and girls in the area, but he had been devouring print ever since. Once he got his first job in Armagh as a junior clerk with the City Council, he beat a path to the library. He went to evening classes at the Technical School, sent away for correspondence courses and read everything he could lay his hands on. By the time he had to retire a few years early to look after Kate, he'd worked in so many different areas of local government and stored up so much information in his prodigious memory it wasn't really surprising Robert thought he was a walking encyclopaedia.

'Sure is it any wonder that blacksmiths are being put out of work,' Charlie began, one evening. 'In 1939, there were over 75,000 horses in Northern Ireland and only 858 tractors. By 1948, the horses were down below 60,000 an' the tractors was up till 11,222. An' if I'm not mistaken in the last four years since I studied the figures, the trends have continued. Numbers of tractors and vehicles have continued to rise, the horses are disappearing from the workplace. They'll only survive where there's money to keep them for pleasure.'

'An' what about the auld blacksmiths, Charlie? What'll ye do wi' them?' asked Robert.

'Ah tell ye what I'll do, Robert, if this young lady here will give me permission,' he said, turning to Clare with a very serious face. 'I'll call roun' for you tomorra night about seven an' take you over to Loughgall for a couple o' pints of Guinness. They do say that older equipment benefits from extra lubrication.'

Charlie bought a little car with the money from a legacy Kate had put away for him. It gave Robert the first outings he'd had for years and something to look forward to as the weather got colder and damper and the dark evenings longer and longer. However much he complained to Clare about Charlie's political views and his way of 'talking as if he'd swallowed the dictionary', he always acknowledged how generous and good-hearted Charlie was. More than once, she saw the look of disappointment on his face when the kitchen door opened in the early evening and the visitor wasn't Charlie.

She enjoyed the regular, quiet evenings when the two of them went off together. She was able to spread her work out on the table under the window in the soft, yellowy light of the Tilley lamp, the comforting glow from the stove all around her and revel in the pleasure of having space and warmth. Usually, as winter came on she had to do her homework sitting up in bed, fully dressed, a board across her knees, a rug around her shoulders in the unheated room, the older Tilley lamp perched precariously on the washstand, which sloped away from the wall at the same angle as the slope of the floor itself. Often, by nine thirty, when she emerged to make a cup of tea for whoever had called, her hands were so cold she could barely take the lid from the teapot without dropping it.

She studied hard all through the long autumn term. As the weather got worse, Saturday night visits to the Ritz became few and far between and she saw Jessie only on Sundays, when they rode into Armagh to go to church, a ritual Robert and Mrs Rowentree always insisted on.

'Have ye heard from yer man yet?' demanded Jessie afterwards, as they propped their bicycles outside the paper shop and got out their purses.

'Which one?' Clare replied unthinkingly.

'Woud ye listen to it,' Jessie cried, raising her eyebrows and staring into the heavens. ' "Which one?" ' she mimicked. 'How many boyfriends d'ye have these days?'

Clare laughed.

'Come on, Jessie,' she said, still grinning. 'Even you can't make a boyfriend out of a cousin in Liverpool and a boy I met once who's sent me two postcards in three months.'

'Well, it's better than nothing.'

'I wouldn't call the Ritz in Belfast and a meal afterwards "nothing",' Clare retorted promptly. 'Especially not when repeated at regular intervals,' she added slyly.

Jessie blushed and tossed her hair.

'There's nothin' in it, I told you. He's just at a bit of a loose end, that's all. He hasn't been long in the Belfast shop and he's lonely.'

'And who's been getting all their art materials at way below cost and their framing done for nothing?' Clare added, as they went into the small, front-parlour shop where the Sunday papers were laid out beside racks of wrapped bread, packets of bacon and sausages and trays of eggs from the hen run out at the back.

'Bet ye a fiver ye end up with yer man Andrew,' pronounced Jessie, as they put their newspapers into their carrier bags and struggled into plastic raincoats ahead of the heavy shower gathering itself over the cathedral.

'And if I had it, I'd bet you a fiver on your man Harry. As it is, I'll make it a prediction. Can I be your bridesmaid?' asked Clare, as they pedalled out of the shelter of the houses and into the rain.

When they parted at the pump opposite Charlie's, Clare made sure to look up at the house and wave, but Charlie must have been out at the back with the chickens or the goats.

She watched Jessie disappear at speed towards Tullyard and began pedalling slowly homewards herself. The rain cleared as quickly as it came. The sky opened and through great rents of blue the sun poured down on the wet countryside. In the hedgerows, the few remaining leaves, tattered fragments of russet and gold, each carried a shimmering raindrop on its sodden, downturned point.

Suddenly and unexpectedly, Clare was overwhelmed with sadness. Jessie would marry Harry. She was quite sure of it. It might be a year, or two years, or even more, but it would happen. It was perfectly clear Harry had fallen for Jessie. He'd taken one look at her bright face, listened to what she'd said about paintings she'd never before laid eyes on and started to teach her about colour and brush technique. Already, she was producing saleable work of her own and his genuine delight in her success could mean only one thing. Everything she'd told

252

her about him spoke of his interest and commitment. Her disparaging comments were only caution. She couldn't yet believe her good fortune, because Harry was not only tall and good-looking, he was heir to a family art and antique business well-known throughout Ulster.

Term ended so close to Christmas Clare had to work very hard indeed to get everything ready for the annual visits of her uncles, Bob and Johnny. Apart from writing all the letters and cards to the family in Canada, a job she had taken over from Robert many years ago, there was the extra cleaning she felt necessary when the aunts were due to appear, their cautious glances preceding any descent into a chair or on to the settle by the stove.

With no long-learnt skills in the area of housework, Robert knew he was not much help. As if to make up for this, he regularly exhausted himself clearing up small jobs in the forge or at the front of the house. Just before Christmas itself, after a long afternoon's work outdoors Robert decided on a lie-down before his tea. Charlie called unexpectedly to deliver a crate of stout and one of mineral water, his contribution to their Christmas festivities and she was left to entertain him alone.

'God bless all here. *Erin go brach*,' he roared as he came round the door.

'Shh.'

Clare put her finger to her lips and saw an anxious look wipe away the grin on Charlie's face.

'Is he poorly?'

Clare shook her head. 'He's tired himself out clearing up in the forge because he's excited about Christmas. Will you drink a cup of tea? He'll probably be up before you've finished it.'

'A cup of tea woud go down well, Clarey. Oh, it's bitter out there this afternoon.'

The kettle was already boiling and the teapot warm in the rack over the stove. A few minutes later, she poured for them both. Charlie curled his fingers contentedly round the large delf cup.

'Charlie, what does "*Erin go brach*" mean? I went to look it up but there's no Irish dictionary in school.'

'No, there wouldn't be, more's the pity. Why would a good Protestant school give house room to the language that was driven to the bogs and the mountains?' he asked bitterly. 'I wonder how many of yer good, loyal Ulstermen realise that the Gaelic is on their lips day in and day out. If you told them that they wouldn't thank you.'

'How do you mean, Charlie?'

'Tullyard and Drumsollen, Lisanally and Mulladry, Kilmore and Mullnasilla,' he replied quietly. 'All places you know, Clarey. But do you know what they mean? And if I drove you and Robert a few miles north of Granda and Granny at Liskeyborough and showed you Derryloughan, Derryvore, Derrykinlough, Derrytrasna and Derrycarvan would you be able to tell me what particular tree dominated the woodland that once covered that whole area down by Lough Neagh.'

Clare's eyes widened as Charlie warmed to his task.

'Clarey, what does Robert call that wooden object that keeps out the worst of the draught these cold nights?'

'You mean the kitchen door?' she asked, baffled by his question.

'Now think again, Clarey. I asked you what Robert calls it?'

She grinned broadly as she caught his meaning.

'You know very well, Charlie. He always says "Shut the do-er." '

'Aye indeed. "Do-er". And sure what is "do-er" but one pronunciation of the Irish for "oak". And isn't that what doors would be made of? And isn't that why all those wee townlands up by Lough Neagh are all Derry this or Derry that? If ye have a knowledge of the Irish you can take out a map and read the shape of the land, its nature and condition, its history. Ach, a whole world of knowledge is there in the names that were put on the land in the Irish.'

'Do you speak Irish then?'

'I do, I do indeed. And it is not that long ago when there was plenty of Irish spoken in this part of Armagh and not just the Catholic servants in the big houses. And at the same time County Down was full of Scots who brought the Gaelic with them from Scotland and kept it up even when they mastered the English as well. There were Englishmen too who had respect for what they found here. Have ye ever heard of Brownlow?'

She shook her head.

'Great man was Brownlow. An Englishman from the Midlands – a small fault in a good man, as the saying is. Got a grant of land around Portadown, learnt Irish himself and saw to it that all his workpeople could speak it whether they were Catholic or not,' he began, pausing to drink deeply from his tea cup.

Clare watched him twist the cup in his fingers as he stared into the fire, his whole manner more quietly thoughtful than usual.

'That's why my father and mother who worked for him, never let their Gaelic drop. They were Scots and good Presbyterians forby and I admit there are differences between the Gaelic and the Irish spoken in Ulster. But it's no great thing to get over. They taught me the Irish from I was a child. Ye see the world differently if ye can see it through another's language,' he added slowly. 'But ye know that yerself, don't ye, Clarey, with yer French and German?'

'Now that you mention it, yes, I do. But I hadn't thought of it before,' she admitted. 'I suppose that explains why people are so sad when a language dies away. So much goes with it.'

'Aye, a whole world of living and learning by experience. Sure what's stories and poems but the distillation of what one has picked up on the way through life?' he ended sadly.

'Are ye rightly, sir?' he said turning away and hailing Robert in his usual voice. 'I hear you were havin' a rest.'

'I was,' said Robert, yawning hugely. 'But I'm glad to see ye. Stay an' eat a bite of tea.'

Clare smiled to herself as she went to the cupboard to see what they had. It wasn't a lot, but that wouldn't bother Charlie. And more to the point, it wouldn't trouble Robert either. To Clare's surprise, Robert never tried to keep up any appearances with Charlie.

As she laid the table, she thought over what Charlie had said about Irish and how important the language was to him. There was something strange there, as there was about his relationship with Robert. One way and another there were a whole lot of things she'd like to know about Charlie. Perhaps the best time to ask would be when Robert came back from one of their outings. Sometimes after a few Guinness he was more forthcoming than usual.

18

J anuary was never Clare's favourite month. She hated the wild, windy weather that always began just as school started again after the Christmas holidays. On the more exposed parts of the road she sometimes had to get off her bicycle and walk until she reached the shelter of trees or the angle of the road changed, so she wasn't pedalling straight into the eye of the wind. There were sudden sleety showers that stung her face and made the road slushy and dangerous until it melted properly. Whenever the morning bus or an occasional car overtook her, she was sure to get her shoes and stockings soaked with spray.

In fact, everything she did was more difficult in January. It was still dark when she got up in the morning, the candle flickered in the icy draughts under her bedroom door, the lino was as cold as stone if her warm feet missed the thin, rag rug. Although she kept her underclothes in bed with her, there was nothing to be done about her blouse and tunic. They hung on the back of the door and she shivered as she pulled them on. Often she wore an old jacket over them as she cooked breakfast on the smoking stove, her fingers numb from washing in cold water, the big kitchen only a little less chill than her own icy bedroom.

The wind roared in the chimney pots and sent smoke and soot billowing down around her. Depending on its direction, the wind would blow the fire in the stove so that it glowed orange and burnt itself out while Robert was in the forge, or made it sulk and smoke so much the potatoes took twice the time to boil, the oven was slow and the water in the stove's tank was only tepid when she had grimy shirts to wash.

Day after day she struggled back from Armagh and hung her school Burberry to dry on the back of the kitchen door. Despite the plastic pixie hood tied over her beret, her hair was always wet. She got soaked so often, it amazed her she so seldom caught a cold. But that was something to be grateful for. What on earth would she do if she wasn't fit to go to school and couldn't do their shopping afterwards?

She tried to save Robert the journey into town in the worst of the weather because she was so worried about him. Every time he coughed she felt herself wince. Even in summer he'd had a cough, as long as she had known him, but in January it was always worse. She could hardly bear to look at him when he coughed, his cheeks hollowed as he struggled for air. His whole body shook as he fumbled for his handkerchief to clear his mouth. She tried to persuade him to go and see the doctor but he only shook his head.

'Ach sure there's no point, childear. Alfie Lindsay's a gran' doctor. If ye break an arm, or need the hospital, he'll have ye seen to as quick as wink, but he'll tell ye straight what he can't mend an' he told me years ago there's no cure for this cough. It's Miner's disease, he says. It has some other fancy name I can never mind, but it means the same. It's the coal dust in the lungs. There's no cure for it.'

'But he might have something to ease it,' she protested.

'Well . . .'

That was encouragement enough. She made up her mind and went to the surgery the next day after school.

The moment she sat down in Dr Lindsay's room with its big old-fashioned desk and its bright lights over the work surfaces, she was glad she'd come. Dr Lindsay listened to her carefully. He said a balsam would break up the mucus and make the cough less racking and he'd a tonic he was sure would improve Robert's appetite. He asked her if they had any whiskey in the house from Christmas and when she said they had, he told her how to make hot toddy with sugar and lemon and a bit of spice.

'It may not improve his chest,' he said, laughing, as he took the bottles from his store cupboard, 'but if it makes him feel better he may get a good night's sleep.

'Now is there anything else you need? I can put it all on the one prescription so it'll still only cost you a shilling. Thanks be to the National Health. What about some Disprin for headaches? Maybe you might need a couple yourself at certain times of the month.'

She nodded and smiled, touched by his thoughtfulness. She hadn't seen Dr Lindsay since she was a little girl, but he'd changed very little. He had always smiled at her and made little jokes.

'I don't know what we'll do if ever Dr Lindsay retires, Clare,' her mother said one day, when they'd been to the dispensary to have Clare measured and weighed. 'He's always so kind.'

Suddenly, Clare saw herself walking down Russell Street with her mother pushing William in his pram. Ahead of them, the bright sun reflected from the marble slabs of the White Walk, the path that ran between the cricket pitch and the huge circular pond put there for the firemen to use if the German planes came and dropped their bombs.

'Are we going past the status water tank, Mummy?'

'No love, not today. We've to go and get orange juice and Robeline at the dispensary.'

'Why is it called a status water tank?'

'It's not "status", Clare, it's "static". Say "static".'

'Static.'

She'd repeated the word carefully. Her mother went on to explain that 'static' meant 'standing still', 'staying in the one place'. Something static was something that didn't move. She always explained new words to her like this. She loved having new words to remember.

'Wouldn't it be funny, Mummy, if it got up and walked away?'

259

Her mother laughed and said yes it would be very funny, but it wouldn't be a good idea. Because it might be needed where it was. They crossed the road and walked along under the shade of the trees, until they were opposite the red-brick house where Dr Lindsay used to work before he had his new house and surgery on the other side of The Mall.

That lovely summer's day must have been before she went to school. So long ago. Her mother took the two of them out every afternoon, William so small he slept in his pram most of the time. Sometimes there was shopping to do, but often they went for long walks. That was when her mother told her the names of all the different trees and flowers they met by the roadside or leaning over the garden hedges. She learnt the names of the places where they walked, Lisanally Lane, Mullinure, Drummond, Drumadd. She often said them over to herself, or made them into a song when she was playing by herself.

When William got too big for his pram, Daddy bought him a Tansad. Her mother found the pushchair much harder to manage than the pram over broken pavements in town and the bumpy lanes they so enjoyed, but she said it wouldn't stop their walks.

William never liked the Tansad. He cried when her mother lifted him in and did up the straps to stop him falling out. As he got bigger, he just wouldn't sit in it at all. He wanted to walk too. But then, he'd get tired and have to be carried. However hard her mother tried to persuade him, he just wouldn't get back in once he'd got out. Time and time again, Clare pushed the empty Tansad home, knowing her mother was exhausted long before they could see the roof of their own house.

Her mother persisted, hoping that William might grow out of his reluctance. Each day she scooped him up and put him in the pushchair, talking to him all the time. Sometimes she winked at Clare, who knew perfectly well they simply couldn't go for a walk, if William wouldn't sit in his chair. It'd have to be once round the field on the Cathedral Road and even then, he'd probably have to be carried back.

260

One day they set off well enough, heading out the Portadown Road, to visit the stream at the Dean's Bridge. Halfway up College Hill, William began to complain. He screwed up his face and started to pull irritably at the restraining straps. He couldn't talk very well, but he always managed to make his meaning perfectly clear.

'Wan' out. Out, Mummy. Walk. Wan' t' walk.'

Clare's heart sank. If he wasn't let out, he'd scream, but if he got tired and had to be carried, it was such a steep pull back the way they'd come. She was so grateful when her mother bent to loosen the straps, for when he screamed she couldn't bear the noise.

'Now, William, that's a good boy, take Mummy's hand.'

She remembered hearing her mother speak, but what happened next took her entirely by surprise. She heard a screech of brakes. Startled she looked up. A car stood with its back towards her, its bonnet up against the garden wall opposite, and William was sitting in the middle of the road screaming his head off. A man got out of the car, came over and picked him up.

'That was a near one, Ellie,' he said, as he brought a kicking, writhing William back to where they stood by the empty pushchair.

It was the first time she had ever seen her mother smack William. She smacked his legs hard, put him back in the Tansad before he'd got over the surprise and fastened the straps firmly, as he wriggled and twisted to get out again.

'Tom, I'm sorry,' she said, tears streaming down her face. 'You might have killed yourself if you weren't such a good driver. I just don't know how he did it, he was so quick. Are *you* all right?'

'Right as rain, thank God. What about you? You're white as a sheet. Can I take you all home?'

'Ach, Tom I can't trouble you,' she said, wiping her eyes.

'Sure it's no trouble at all for you, Ellie. Wait here an' I'll get the car reversed back on to the road. I'll take it up and turn in front of the Royal.'

261

Even now, she could still recall the funny smell of the leather seat in Tom's car and how he'd asked her would she be all right in the back with the folded Tansad wedged behind the passenger seat, a rug over it in case it might bump against her. And she remembered so clearly that that was the last walk she'd had with her mother.

'How's your brother, Clare?' Dr Lindsay asked, as he helped her put the bottles of medicine into her shopping bag. 'He's with the Hamiltons out near Richhill isn't he?'

'Yes, he is,' she said, collecting herself, the memory of that awful day still vivid in her mind.

She saw him lean back in his chair, ready to listen to her as if he had all the time in the world. She made an effort to respond.

'He goes to Richhill school now.' She hesitated. 'I'm afraid I don't see him very often, though I do go over nearly every Sunday afternoon. But even when he's there he doesn't seem to want to see me. William can be very awkward,' she ended, uneasily.

He nodded and pressed his lips together, recalling the night he had delivered William. The midwife sent for him, because labour had gone on for so long, far longer than she'd expected for a second child.

'Your mother told me how awkward he could be a few months before she died,' he began, looking at her very directly. 'She was worried she mightn't be handling him the right way. But I'm afraid there's no right way we know of for boys like William. It's maybe not his fault at all, but it's very hard on those who have to deal with him. How does your granny manage?'

'She says he wears her out. She can't really stand having him on her own. She leaves him very much to Granda. Billy and Jack do their best, but Granda is the only one can get him to do anything. He just keeps on at him, very quietly. William never does anything he should do without being told, every single time.'

Suddenly, to her own surprise, she found tears in her eyes.

'I think if I had to look after William again I'd go mad,' she burst out suddenly. 'I could manage it when my mother was alive, but I just couldn't do it now, not with Granda, and school, and keeping the house going.'

She put her hands over her face and wept.

'There now, Clare,' he said, standing up and putting a hand on her shoulder. 'No one could possibly expect you to look after William. You've your work cut out looking after Robert. My spies tell me you're doing a great job of it too.' He paused to hand her a couple of squares of gauze to wipe her eyes. 'Now, have you been worrying yourself about not doing enough for your brother?'

She nodded silently, afraid if she said a word more she'd start crying again. Really, she was being so silly and she was keeping him back. It was long after his surgery should have closed. She'd met him on the doorstep, seeing out the last patient when she'd arrived straight from school. It must be at least half past four by now.

'Now, Clare,' he said firmly. 'I want you to listen to what I'm going to say and to remember it. Whatever problems William causes, they're not *your* problems. Just because he's your brother, you must not think it's up to you to cope with him. If all's well at the moment, put him right out of your mind. If the situation changes, come to me and we'll see what can be done then.' He paused a moment to let his words sink in. 'Is your Auntie Polly still in Canada?'

'Yes, she is,' she said, nodding quickly. 'She's very happy. Uncle Jimmy's back is much better and he has a job with no standing or lifting.'

'So there's no word of her coming home?'

'Oh no.'

She wondered why he'd asked about Auntie Polly. She watched him swinging gently from side to side in his swivel chair, rubbing his chin thoughtfully, and waited.

'I was thinking you could do with a nice auntie to talk to. Is there no one you can tell your worries to?'

263

She shook her head.

'No one I can think of.'

'Well, we'll have to see what can be done about that,' he said, nodding to himself. He got to his feet and opened the door. 'Now you're to forget all about William, remember. And that's an order. And the next time you start to worry about something the first thing you do is come and see me. If I can't help myself, I have a nice young nurse here every morning. There are times she might be more use to you than an old fellow like me. But you are *not* to worry. You wouldn't want to give me extra work, would you?'

Outside, on The Mall, she got on her bicycle and slowly pedalled off. For once it was not raining. Stars winked in a clear sky. She shivered in the frosty air after the warmth of the surgery. As she headed out of town and into the velvety blackness of the countryside she began to feel an enormous sense of relief. After all this time there was now someone she could turn to if any of the awful things she could imagine were actually to happen.

Robert's cough improved very slowly, but his appetite picked up quite quickly and Clare was grateful for Uncle Bob's Christmas envelope. She added a few shillings to their grocery money, so she could buy extra bacon and butter and anything she could think of that would encourage him to eat more. A week of bedtime toddies rapidly lowered the level in the whiskey bottle, so she made up her mind to refill it. Once it was empty Robert would never hear of buying another just for a bedtime drink, but if she were to top it up every few days, it might be quite a while before he'd notice.

The barman looked startled as she pushed open the door of the Railway Bar and cast her eyes around the place she knew so well by repute only. He put down his cloth and the glass he was polishing and hurried over to her.

'Were you lookin' for someone belongin' to ye, miss?' he asked loudly, as a group of elderly men drinking porter turned their eyes towards her.

'No, I've come to buy a bottle of whiskey,' she said, wondering why he was trying to edge her away from the bar. 'How much is the cheapest one you have?' she asked, stepping past him and taking out her purse.

'I'm afraid I have no whiskey for sale today, miss,' he announced loudly, as if she were standing at the far side of the dim, almost empty saloon.

She saw him glance furtively towards the solitary group of drinkers, sitting motionless underneath a cloud of cigarette smoke.

'But you've some on the shelf over there,' she said, dodging round him again and moving along the counter. 'It says Bushmills on that bottle and I know that's whiskey,' she protested.

'I'm sorry, miss, I've no whiskey for sale,' he repeated. Beads of perspiration stood out on his forehead as she leaned over the bar and peered at the solitary item standing on the empty shelves behind the upturned bottles ready to dispense measures.

'Are you having some difficulty, Mickey?'

A large, heavily-built man got to his feet and walked over to where they stood.

'No, sir, not at all, sir. The young lady just came in lookin' for her father, didn't you, miss?'

Clare stared at him. He didn't look simple, but really, what on earth was he talking about. With the approach of the tall, florid-faced man, he was positively shaking with agitation.

'Actually I'm looking for a bottle of whiskey for my grandfather,' said Clare, turning towards him. 'The doctor said a toddy might help him get a better night's sleep and the bottle my uncle brought at Christmas is nearly empty. If I don't refill it soon, he's going to notice and then I won't be able to.'

'And your grandfather is . . .'

'Robert Scott.'

'The blacksmith at Salter's Grange?'

'Yes,' she said, nodding to him, as she unfolded a tattered pound note and scanned the silver in her purse, wondering if she'd brought enough.

The heavy face creased and he smiled, exposing his worn cigarette-stained teeth. He looked down at Mickey.

'Sure Robert's been drinking here for years, Mickey. Would he not be entitled to a spare bottle if you have one?' he said, nodding meaningfully towards the bar.

'Oh yes, sir, yes. Indeed aye. But . . .'

'Perhaps this young lady could deliver one to him with the compliments of the house.' He caught the barman's eye. 'I've no doubt you'll recover the cost in the course of plying your everyday trade.'

Before she had time to protest, Clare found herself accepting a heavily wrapped bottle and being escorted silently out through the back premises. It was only as they reached a door leading on to the waste ground behind Lonsdale Street that Mickey caught her arm.

'Niver say where ye got that bottle,' he whispered. 'Niver breathe a word. We're not allowed to sell whiskey over the counter to anyone. An' yer underage forby. Thon man that spoke to ye is high up in the police. Mind yerself goin' home ye don't break it,' he added hurriedly, as he disappeared back up the yard, leaving Clare to stumble her way by the light of a flickering street lamp till she reached the pavement and could follow it all the way round to the front of the Railway Bar where she'd left her bicycle parked beside its entrance.

While Robert was taking half an hour's rest after his tea, she added several inches to Uncle Bob's bottle. She breathed a sigh of relief as she put it back in the corner cupboard and took the new bottle away to hide under her bed.

She'd been not a moment too soon. She'd only just come back into the kitchen when she heard Charlie Running's familiar step at the outer door. As he was getting up to go, a few hours later, after entertaining them with the latest news, Robert stopped him.

'Ah, sure what's yer hurry man. Stay and have a wee night-cap wi' me. Sure Clarey here is the best han' at all at a hot toddy. Woud there still be enough in the bottle Clarey for the two of us?'

'Oh yes, there's plenty left, Granda. You only need a wee, tiny bit for toddy,' she said, as she pulled the kettle over to boil it up and fetched the bottle from the corner cupboard.

She saw Robert look at it as she set it on the table. She was glad to be able to turn away into the dimness beyond the reach of the lamp and fetch the half lemon on its saucer from the kitchen cupboard.

'It's amazing how that bottle's lasted since Christmas,' said Robert, thoughtfully. 'Sure, I thought the nite woud see the end of it.'

Clarey heated the mugs, made the toddies and watched the two men as they toasted each other across the fireplace.

'Good health, Charlie,' said Robert, as he raised his mug.

'Slainte,' replied Charlie, as he bent and took the first sip.

'That's a drop of good stuff, Robert,' he said, looking surprised. 'If I couldn't see the label on the bottle over there, I'd have said it was a drop o' Bush, but sure ye can't get Bushmills these days for love nor money. It all goes for export. Balance of payments, they say.'

'Aye,' agreed Robert, 'it's a gran' drop. I've had no appetite at all wi' the aul' cough, an' I've enjoyed it well enough these lass nites, but I would say the nite I can taste it the best at all. It woud put the heart back in ye.'

'A few more nights o' that stuff, Robert, an' we'll have you fit for a wee outing. Your friends at the pub over in Loughgall has all been askin' for you,' he said, as he handed Clare his empty mug. 'Thank you, Clare, that was great. I'll not feel the cold at all on the way home. May your bottle never go empty, as the saying is.'

Clare laughed as she always did at Charlie's sayings, but later, by the light of her candle, she examined the bottle she'd hidden under her bed. It certainly said Bushmills. But how could that be if it all went for export? And what was the difference between Bushmills and the bottle Uncle Bob had brought? Wasn't whiskey all the same, except it was made by different firms?

As she climbed into bed and blew out her candle, she shivered violently. She could never decide whether to put her hot-water bottle at her feet to warm the empty acres of cold space down there, or clutch it to her bosom where she could really enjoy it. One day, when I'm rich, she thought sleepily, I shall have two hot water bottles in my bed and Granda's whiskey bottle will never run empty, ever again.

19

By the end of January Robert was so much better he was able to go out with Charlie once more. But the weather was no better. It stayed cold and wet, one storm following another, the grey rain clouds so heavy the big kitchen was dim all through the day. Although the path to the forge streamed with water and the overhanging trees dripped on everyone who passed under them, Robert insisted on going down to light the fire.

'Sure the chimbley gets damp if there's no fire an' then where will I be when I'm fit to work?' he said each time Clare protested.

When she went to the surgery for more medicine, she consulted Dr Lindsay. She told him how frail Robert seemed and how easily he tired.

'Let him do a bit in the forge if he wants to, Clare. He's a man has worked all his life. He doesn't know how to sit around,' he said reassuringly. 'What he would gain by resting would be lost by boredom.

'Sometimes it's better to let people tear away, as the saying is, rather than spare them. Tell him to keep himself warm and to go and lie down as soon as he feels tired. If he does that, he'll not go far wrong. Is he in better spirits?'

Clare grinned at him.

'Oh yes. The medicine has been a great help but I think the hot toddy has been even better.'

'Is that so?'

He smiled broadly and looked at her for a moment. Then,

269

with a strange, distant look on his face, he began to tell her a story.

'I remember when I first came back from Medical School in Edinburgh, Clare, I worked with an old doctor here. Ah, he's long gone. And like many young men, I thought I knew it all. I'd won the odd prize or two and I couldn't wait to get to work. But in my first winter we lost a lot of patients. I know now you get times like that – green winters, some call them – but I didn't know it at the time. I really took it to heart. I felt maybe I hadn't done the right thing, or I hadn't done enough.'

He saw she was taking in every word, so he went on.

'The old fellow took me aside one day and said, "Alfie, you've the makings of a doctor, but you look too much to the body." The body will heal itself as often as not, he said, even in spite of doctors, but the spirit is another matter. "Strengthen the spirit, my boy, by every means at your disposal. Sure what use is life if there's no joy in it?" I think he had a point, don't you?'

'Yes, I know you're right,' she responded quickly. 'Since Granda's been able to go over to Loughgall again with Charlie Running he's been so much better. I could hardly believe it the first night he came back and told me a whole long story about how they were making the Queen's dress for the Coronation in the village. He didn't think it was true, but he told me anyway. What really pleased him was having news for me.'

'Yes, I can imagine it,' Dr Lindsay said, nodding to himself. 'And then just think, Clare, how well Charlie has recovered from the loss of Kate, who was so dear to him, now he has Robert to look to,' he said, standing up reluctantly. 'We vulnerable creatures, we all need to care and be cared for. As long as we can do that, life is worth living,' he added, opening the door into his deserted waiting room. He paused. 'You look better yourself. Have you stopped worrying like I told you?'

'Yes, I have. Except about my exams in February,' she said laughing. 'I think that's normal, isn't it?'

'Indeed it is. I wouldn't attempt a cure. Good luck with them,' he added, as he watched her lower her shopping bag carefully into her front basket and wheel her bicycle out on to the roadway where the wind whipped at her coat tails and the rain blew in her face.

As she pedalled slowly along the wet road, she wondered how she could possibly feel so cheerful when she was getting wetter by the minute and had nothing to look forward to at home except an evening's revision and a pile of washing that would have to be dried indoors.

On a mild and bright Saturday morning, a few weeks later, she was washing the breakfast dishes when she spotted the postman coming up the path. Drying her hands quickly, she ran down to meet him.

She felt the colour drain from her face as he handed her an envelope without a word or a smile. It was a perfectly ordinary blue envelope of the kind Ronnie had been using for years, but it was crumpled, the black ink of the address a smudgy grey. Rubber stamped across it in bright blue was the message: 'Damaged by sea water.'

She ripped it open. Inside, all she found was a brief note.

> Dear Clare,
> By the time you get this I shall be on the high seas. I had nowhere near managed to save my fare, but I've been keeping my ears tuned and I've managed to get a working passage on a ship to New York. They were short of a bar steward, so my experience in Belfast has paid off.
> Hope all goes well with you. I'll write again when I can.
> In haste,
> Much love,
> Ronnie

'The high seas,' she said aloud, clutching her hands to her face as she hurried back to the house.

Her mind leapt back to very last day of January. She'd arrived home in the fading light to find smoke rising from the chimney of the forge and stepped in to say hello to Robert. There were four other men there and to her amazement they were all standing or sitting in complete silence.

'What's wrong?' she asked hurriedly, turning from John Wiley to Robert and back again.

One of the older men sitting on the bench inside the door shuffled his feet and looked up at her, his face mask-like in the glow of the fire on the hearth.

'Bad news, Clarey. Robert'll tell ye,' he said, uneasily, his eyes going to her grandfather as he spoke.

'The sea-doors is broke on the Larne ferry an' they say she's goin' down. The weather's that bad they can't find her t' get any help till her.'

'An' there's weemen wi' young childer coming back from England on her,' said John awkwardly, as if he had a lump in his throat. 'What chance woud they have in a lifeboat in weather like this?'

The answer came soon enough. Within the hour, as darkness fell and the wind rose yet higher, Robert turned on the radio for the six o'clock news. There had been no radio message from the *Princess Victoria* since two o'clock. Lifeboats and ships were searching for survivors.

By the following morning, it was certain there were no women or children among them. Only forty of the strongest and fittest of the men from the crew survived. One hundred and twenty-eight people were lost. Clare read the newspaper reports to Robert each evening and tried to hide her tears as the stories of heroism, loss and grief unfolded.

With the damaged envelope in her hand, the full horror of the loss of the *Princess Victoria* swept over her again. Ronnie had decided against the £10 assisted passage, so she'd been sure it would be months before he could save up enough to go. Besides, from what he'd hinted in his letters, she really thought he meant to see her before he left.

But now he was gone. He was 'on the high seas'. If only he hadn't used that particular phrase. 'Mountainous seas' had breached the doors of the car deck on the *Princess Victoria*, flooding her and crippling her. 'Mountainous seas' prevented ships coming to her aid, swept survivors from life rafts, or carried them beyond the helping hands that tried to catch at their lifejackets with boat hooks.

In that narrow stretch of water between Larne and Stranraer, with both coastlines perfectly visible on a clear day, the sea had destroyed a well-made, well-manned vessel. And Ronnie was crossing the storm-ridden Atlantic in winter.

Totally distraught, she ran into her bedroom and sat weeping on her bed.

'What am I to do? What am I going to do?'

As her tears diminished, she shivered violently. Slowly, cold reality took shape. There was nothing, absolutely nothing whatever, she could do. What made it worse, the only person she could have told was Jessie, but she worked alternate Saturdays since she'd got her job at the gallery and this was her weekend in Belfast. If she told Robert, he'd be upset for her sake and she couldn't bear that. She would simply have to bear it, try to put it out of mind and behave as if she didn't care at all, because there was nothing else she could do. Except hope all would be well.

With an effort of will, she gathered herself, filled her bucket with hot water and prepared to face her least favourite job of the week, scrubbing the mud from the lane off the kitchen floor's well-tramped surface.

Ronnie's next letter arrived a week later. His crossing had been unexceptional, he'd made some useful contacts, and he was writing on his knee in a long-distance bus heading towards the Canadian border. He expected to arrive in Toronto in two days' time. He already had the address of a newspaper which might be interested in someone with an Ulster connection.

Clare was torn between relief and pleasure and furious anger at the way she'd upset herself. Since that damaged envelope had arrived, she'd slept badly. She'd not been able to concentrate on her work, despite all her efforts. Once or twice, she'd even caught Robert looking at her as if he were going to say something, but thought better of it.

'Let that teach you a lesson, Clare,' she said firmly, as she added Ronnie's latest letter to the pile she kept at the back of the drawer behind her clean underwear. 'If you'd gone on like that much longer you'd have upset Robert and you'd have made a right mess of the exams as well. No matter what happens you've got to keep steady. If there's no one to help you, you'll just have to learn to help yourself.'

After all the bad weather at the beginning of the year, Clare could hardly believe it when March produced such unexpectedly warm, still days. They brought springtime in a glorious rush of unfurling daffodils and leafing trees. As always, her spirits rose as she looked hopefully at the fuchsia cuttings in the deep windowsills of her own room and the boys' room and began to plan how she'd put together this year's window boxes once the risk of frost was past.

With the evenings now light till after tea, she had time to walk up through the orchard after school and bring back posies of primrose and wood anemone for their table. She cut sprays of forsythia and budding spindleberry from the shrubs on the path to the forge and put them in a jar on the hallstand. As she stood looking at the bright flowers and the tiny leaves, she breathed a sigh of relief. The really bad weather was over. Life would be easier for a while.

Robert was so much improved that he spent most of his day in the forge. He visited the pub in Loughgall regularly again and he enjoyed hearing all the talk about the plans the village was making to celebrate the Coronation. When Clare read him a newspaper report about some thread produced by silkworms kept in the village being accepted by Buckingham Palace, he threw up his head and laughed.

'So much for them makin' the dress single-handed. Coud ye be up to people? The stories they put about that place. They'd try to tell you they was goin' over for the day themselves if you were fool enough to believe them.'

Despite all her work for the examination, Clare listened to the news from the pub and the forge. When she heard Robert shuffling the newspaper he'd already read, she knew he was at a loose end. She'd always come and sit with him and try to entertain him when he felt the time long. But many an evening she was grateful when she heard Charlie's step at the door and his greeting booming into the kitchen so that she could go back to the books laid out in the boys' room.

At the time, all the talk was of the Coronation, the grand preparations going on in London and the many events being organised locally. Try as she might, she could not get excited about any of it. When the day finally came she listened to the broadcasts from Westminster Abbey with Robert during the day and went gratefully back to her work when Charlie arrived to take him out that evening.

The day passed quietly enough for Clare, but it ended with an event that had far-reaching consequences for her. Early in the evening, Robert's landlord for the last fifty years, Albert Nesbitt, complained of indigestion and went off to bed early. Next morning, his daughter found him dead. By the time Clare arrived home after a three-hour paper, Robert had already shaved and donned the white shirt and collar from the bottom drawer.

'Oh dear, who is it this time?' Clare asked, as she came into the kitchen and took one look at his scrubbed and polished appearance.

'Ach, it's oul' Albert Nesbitt. Very sudden. Sure he was up here last week to collect the rent to save you the bother of goin' down with it. Said he knowed you were workin' for the exams and sure the walk woud do him good, forby a bit of crack in the forge.'

'Is Eddie going to the wake?'

275

'No, Eddie doesn't know the Nesbitts very well, though he'll go to the funeral, of course. But our friend Charlie used to work for Albert's father at weekends after he left school. He'll be going for sure and he'll pick me up on his way.'

'You're sure you don't want me to run up on the bike and ask him?'

'No need, no need at all,' he said firmly. 'Sure Charlie and Albert were comrades. It was Albert Nesbitt got Charlie Running to join the IRA. They were in the same unit.'

'The IRA?'

Clare was so amazed, she hung her blazer on the end of the settle and dropped down beside it.

'Aye surely. Whenever there usta be trouble round these parts, didn't the police, or the B-specials, come and collect up the pair of them. They used to get put inside regular. They'd plenty of time to get to know other.'

'You mean Charlie was a Republican?' Clare asked, not sure she could really believe her ears.

The problem was Robert's tone. It was so matter-of-fact, she couldn't rightly take in the enormity of what he was saying.

'Aye certainly. Still is, to the best of my knowledge. D'ye niver notice the "*Erin go Brach*"?'

'Yes, of course, but I thought that was just because he speaks Irish.'

'Ach no. It's a signal. Like the way the Masons shake hands. It lets others know where he stans.'

The wag o' the wall gathered itself, the throaty whirring warned them it was about to strike the hour.

'Goodness, it's six o'clock and you've had no tea yet,' she said, concerned that Charlie would appear before she could get it on the table. 'Will you tell me about this another time, Granda. I really do want to know.'

'He'll likely tell ye himself,' said Robert easily. 'He thinks yer a great girl. Especially since ye started listenin' to Radio Eireann and comin' out with the Irish. Maybe he's hopin' to get you into the movement,' he added with a broad grin.

Clare picked up her blazer, pulled the kettle on to the heat and said she'd be back in a minute. As she hurried into her room and tugged her tunic over her head, a possible explanation for Robert's manner came to her. He must have helped Charlie in some way when he was mixed up with the Republican movement. But it was all very strange. Robert was so very loyal, she'd have thought he wouldn't even speak to a Republican, yet he and Charlie were dear, close friends. It was all very strange.

Clare's exam results were good, so good it seemed there was little doubt she'd get her scholarship the following June if she were to try for it. She was relieved and delighted. She'd been back at school only a few days when the bad news came.

A letter from a solicitor in Armagh informed them of the sale of the late Mr Albert Nesbitt's farm, landholdings and other property to Mr Edward Hutchinson of Portadown and pointed out that, as sitting tenants, they were entitled to remain as tenants of the aforesaid Mr Edward Hutchinson. The rent could be forwarded to the Armagh or the Portadown branch of the above mentioned firm of solicitors. As from 3rd inst, the date of completion of the conveyancing of the property, the amount payable would be increased to ten shillings.

'Ten shillings?' gasped Clare, as she came to the critical figure. She knew they'd never be able to scrape together ten shillings every week.

'But they can't do that. That's a hundred percent increase. I'm sure that's illegal.'

Robert shook his head.

'Sure Albert hadn't put the rent up for twenty years, Clarey. It's maybe reasonable enough if we did but know it.'

'But the new Taylor houses down in Eddie's front field are only seven and six,' she protested. 'It was in the *Armagh Guardian* last week.'

'Aye, but that doesn't include rates. Albert paid the rates on this place and I did all his bits of mending and welding no charge, so he wouldn't be out of pocket. It works all right with someone ye know. But this new man doesn't know us an' maybe has no work I coud do fer him,' he said thoughtfully. 'Or maybe he just wants the money,' he added more sharply.

Clare saw the strained look on his face and regretted her outburst. She didn't want him to be worried about it. It was up to her to find the money.

'You're probably right, Granda. I've been reading too much about wicked landlords and the Land League for history. But I don't know what Charlie's going to say when we tell him. I don't think it'll be popular.'

To her surprise, Robert laughed heartily. The strained look disappeared and he was perfectly cheerful again.

'Charlie was all for shooting the landlords at one time,' he said, still grinning. 'If we're bate we'll send him down to Ballybrannan and see if he can get rid of yer man for us,' he added, as he threw on his cap and headed for the forge, leaving Clare with the stiff, white sheet of paper still in her hands.

She thought about the new rent every time she cycled to or from school or whenever the routine, everyday jobs left her mind free. Over and over again, she went through the details of their tiny budget and tried to see how she could cut their expenses. But she knew perfectly well she couldn't. Even before this latest blow, the rise in food prices had begun to make things difficult. No, there was no doubt about it, the extra money for the rent would have to come from somewhere outside.

She thought of Uncle Bob who had always been so generous and Uncle Johnny, who would be generous were it not for his dear wife. And Auntie Polly, who was so generous by nature she seldom had any money in the first place.

Night after night, Clare lay awake doing sums in her head,

considering the letters she might write. In the end, she decided she needed to save Uncle Bob and Uncle Johnny for real emergencies and somehow solve this one herself. What she needed was a Saturday job that paid considerably more than Margaret's five shillings a week, but few women could afford help and there were no shops in Armagh so busy on a Saturday they'd pay for an extra pair of hands.

She had still not solved her problem when an envelope arrived with a London postmark, the address written in a large, flowing, quite unfamiliar hand.

'Andrew Richardson,' she said aloud. It had to be. She laughed as she tore it open and hastily read the friendly message.

In the year or more since they had stood together on Scrabo Tower, he'd sent her twenty postcards and a Christmas card. Admittedly, when he sent a postcard, he chose a very interesting or attractive one, covered the whole space on the back in tiny writing and put it in an envelope. But he had never written what Clare would call 'a proper letter'. This was the first time he'd even written her a note.

He had been apologetic, explained that letters intimidated him, that he couldn't face the empty pages. He promised he would try but, please, in the meantime, would she forgive him and go on writing, he so enjoyed her letters. They were his only real contact with home.

This time his note said he'd be spending the rest of the long vacation in England and would not be visiting Drumsollen House in the immediate future. She wasn't really surprised, as he'd hinted this might happen. He congratulated her on her splendid exam results and said he was sure she'd get her scholarship next year. He was now off to Norfolk to stay with his Great-aunt Mary, a formidable lady who'd run a field hospital in France during the First World War and now ran her north coast village through her chairmanship of the Parish Council. He was looking forward to getting away from London where he'd been staying with his uncle's family. He hoped to do

279

some bird-watching out on the marshes but his main objective was to paint Great-aunt Mary's kitchen, which looked very sorry for itself. It had been flooded to a depth of six feet when the sea defences gave way earlier in the year.

Clare wondered where Great-aunt Mary had been while the sea was busy flooding her kitchen. As she added the note to the small pile in one of the two tiny drawers below the mirror in her room, a thought struck her. June Wiley was now full-time housekeeper at Drumsollen House. She would go and see if she needed another pair of hands.

'Aye, right enough, Clarey, it was a good thought,' said June warmly, as she sat them down at her kitchen table. 'There's that much work up at Drumsollen I could do with half a dozen girls. An' I'd be right glad to have a sensible one like you at the weekend when these visitors come. But between you an' me the money's tight. There's times John says he's seen old man Richardson clear out his own wallet to make up the wages for the staff on a Friday. An' sure even that's cut down t'half what there used to be when I first went there as a maid.'

'What d'you think's happened, June? Granda says they used to be very well off. Were they?' Clare asked as she sipped her tea.

'Oh aye, Clarey. I remember before the war the big parties there useta be. And whatever was left over, should it be smoked salmon or Irish ham, or meringue pie or trifle, it was shared out for the indoor and outdoor staff to take home. You wouldn't see the likes of that these days even if you could get the stuff. Every wee bit there is left goes into the larder or that big fridge The Missus got back in 1940 before everything got so scarce.'

She reached forward and refilled Clare's teacup, casting an eye out of the kitchen window to make sure her three girls were busy with the jobs she'd given them.

'Here, dear, have another wee scone. Isn't it nice to see a bit of white flour again?'

'Lovely scones, June. John always says he can't understand why he's not fat and you such a good cook.'

June tossed her head and made a dismissive remark, but Clare knew she was pleased. She was sure June and John must be a very happy couple. Although they both worked hard, she'd never heard either of them complain about the long hours up at the house or the jobs waiting to be done by whoever got back home first, except in a light-hearted way.

'I think the beginning of it was when William and Adeline were killed over in London. Oh dear, that was a terrible shock. Old Mr Richardson went roun' lookin' like a ghost for months. He was just devastated. I think William was his favourite, an' he was a very clever man. He'd just got into Stormont like the father an' they had him in Economic Development or suchlike. He wasn't the boss but he was gettin' that way. I think he was the one kept the family right with their money, the investments and so on, for they haven't all that big an amount of land, not in these parts anyway, though there's more down in Fermanagh.'

June gave a complicated explanation of the Fermanagh connections of the Richardsons, which Clare found difficult to follow, and then returned to the fortunes of Drumsollen.

'Not only was William gone, leavin' his son to be educated the expensive way these people think fit, but Edward, the older brother, loses his wife and kinda goes off the rails. They say he drank his way through a fortune before he met this widow with a daughter and a bit of money of her own. He farms out Caledon way and is a great horsey man. Hunts and trains show jumpers. Always back and forth to Dublin. They say if it weren't for the wife, he'd have to sit on an egg less and it's her father pays for their boy's education. As well as the girl, Virginia her name is, they've a boy Edward would be a couple o' years younger than Andrew. Have you ever met young Andrew?' she threw out, as she stood up and had another look out at her girls.

To her amazement, Clare found herself blushing. She was

terribly grateful when June opened the window and asked her elder daughter if they'd finished doing the vegetables.

'June, it's nearly your supper time and I'm keeping you back,' Clare said, recovering herself. She stood up and carried their empty cups to the sink. 'Yes, I've met him twice,' she went on. 'The first time he mended my bike down by the gates and the second time was up at Stormont, of all places. I was visiting with my cousin and he'd taken his grandfather up to some meeting or other. We all went to look at the view from Scrabo Tower while he was waiting for him. We had a lovely afternoon.'

'Aye, ye woud that. Sure Andrew's good company. He coud talk to anyone, high or low. Whether it was the Queen herself or the old charwoman, it's all the same to Andrew. Just like his father. Doesn't go down well with The Missus. That's why we don't see much of him, more's the pity. I suppose travelling is expensive. That's her excuse anyway.'

The door opened and the three girls appeared. The eldest, Helen, carried a bowl of water full of peeled potatoes. The next, Jennifer, had a dish of chopped cabbage and the youngest, Caroline, carried a black kitten with large blue eyes.

June stood back, her hands on her hips, and laughed.

'Are we going to have Kitty for supper then?' she said, picking up the youngest child. 'Didn't I tell you to bring the supper in till we get it on the stove for Daddy comin'.'

The child laughed and threw her spare arm round her mother's neck, while hanging on firmly to the kitten with the other.

'Hope I haven't kept John's supper back,' Clare said smiling. 'Tell him it was my fault.' She thanked June for the tea and scones and for her company.

'Sure it was a pleasure to see you, Clarey, an' I'll not ferget what you told me. I'll maybe hear something woud be a help to you. Now wait a wee minit. Take yer hurry, as the sayin' is,' she insisted, as she lowered the child to the floor and took a paper bag from the kitchen drawer.

'Take a few wee scones for you an' Robert. Tell him I was askin' for him. An' I'm sure somethin' will turn up,' she said reassuringly. 'Never fear, Clarey. I'll keep my ears open an' so will John,' she said cheerfully, as she put the potatoes into a saucepan and set them to boil.

'I'd not be one bit surprised if somethin' didn't just fall inta yer lap.'

John Wiley always thought there was a touch of the fortune-teller about his wife, but when he arrived back from Drumsollen House a few nights after Clare's visit and heard a Saturday job had appeared for her, he reckoned it was little short of miraculous.

'Now draw over an' eat your meal like a good man. Sure ye can take a run down to the forge when ye've had it an' tell her the good news yerself,' June said, as she took a covered plate from the oven and put it on the table in front of him. 'Eat up now, for ye must be starvin' an' it that late. Was it the car again?'

John nodded sharply as he tucked in to his meal. As Old Man Richardson often said, the car, like himself, was getting on in years. These older models needed much more attention to keep them going.

'So tell us what happened, June,' he said, as he hungrily lowered bacon and cabbage with forkfuls of mashed potato. 'All I heerd in the course o' the day was that aul' Martha Robinson had handed in her cards, an' you'd spoken for a girl for Saturdays. I can't see how that's come about atall.'

June laughed heartily and nodded as she put the kettle to boil.

'Ye coud have knocked me down wi' a feather when The Missus came into the kitchen. You'd know somethin' was well amiss fer she niver sets foot beyond the end of the carpets. The long an' the short of it was, Martha's been goin' to the tent mission at Lisnadill, this great evangelist chap they're all talkin'

283

about. Martha's got religion. An' she's got it bad. So the first thing she does is give up comin' to the house on a Sunday to do the lunch. It'll be doun on her knees mornin' and night from now on.'

'Aye, but that's Sundays,' said John looking puzzled.

'It is indeed. But The Missus is no fool. She knows fine well that you'll not get anyone to come an' work like Martha did, so she comes askin' can I make a meal on Saturday she can heat up on Sunday.'

June made the tea and continued.

'So I says to her, "Well, maybe if I had some help meself on a Saturday I coud do a dinner. But what about the rest of Martha's work?" An' I told her all the jobs Martha did while the Sunday dinner was cookin' an' in the afternoon forby. "What about them?" says I.'

John watched as she poured him a mug of tea, a slow smile on his lips. He'd seen what was coming, but he'd not spoil her story.

'I suppose we could get a girl in on Saturday to relieve you and do Martha's jobs,' she says to me. 'Then you could make a casserole or a meat pudding, or something of that kind for Sunday.'

June grinned, poured herself a cup of tea and stood with her back to the stove drinking it.

'So I shook my head an' says, "Ach, sure gettin' a girl on a Saturday will be desperit hard. Ye'll hardly get one for less than fifteen shilling."'

John laughed and finished his tea.

'She wouldn't have liked that.'

'No, not one bit. But by the time I'd finished she'd agreed to think about twelve and sixpence if only I coud find someone.'

John came and put his arm round her, gave her a kiss and a hug.

'Yer a great girl, June. Ye've a head on yer shoulders an' I don' know where I'd be wi'out ye. An' I'm as pleased for wee Clarey as I woud be if it were one of our own.'

'Ach, it's great to be able to do a good turn. Away down now, like a good man an' tell her. Say, we may leave it a fortnight so I can make sure she'll get her twelve and six. By then The Missus'll be gettin' real worried so there'll be no bother about it atall.'

20

On the last Saturday in September, a glorious autumn morning, the sun melting the rime of frost on the long grass by the roadside, Clare cycled halfway into Armagh and parked her bicycle against the low wall where Andrew Richardson had once found it with subsiding tyres.

Her pause was only momentary. She opened the gates, wheeled her bicycle through, closed them behind her and pedalled slowly up the steep gravel drive that wove its way around the side of the smoothly contoured hill that all but concealed the house itself from those who passed by on the road beyond.

Both June and John had made sure she knew exactly where to turn off the driveway and on to the narrow path that led to the back of the house, where to leave her bicycle out of sight and where to find the stone steps leading down to the biggest of the basement rooms from which June Wiley now ran the entire establishment.

She passed tall, dusty windows protected by thick iron bars and found the heavy wooden door to the basement. She closed it behind her and stepped cautiously down the stone steps that dropped steeply into a long, empty corridor. The sunlight threw bands of heavy shadow down the peeling, whitewashed walls and across the bare, echoing wooden floor which ran past all the basement rooms.

Clare felt like an intruder. She was grateful that her flat school shoes made no sound in the echoing space, her silent step penetrating the defences of a different world and moving her apprehensively towards an unknown objective.

'Good girl yerself,' said June, as Clare came into the big kitchen and took off her coat. 'Yer in good time,' she added, glancing up at the enormous clock which hung on the discoloured walls. 'I'll show you roun' down here. If we're lucky an' they're out this afternoon I can show you the big rooms. You'll have to go up to do the beds, but use the back stairs an' don't stop to look roun' ye,' she warned. 'At all costs don't let anyone see you. I don't understan' the woman at all, but she'd like to pretend this house ran by itself. She can't stan' seein' "staff" as she calls them, especially if it's young ones. She can just about say a civil word to me because she knows she has to,' she added, as she handed Clare a well-starched white apron, thin with age, and a cap that reminded her of Miss Muffet in a long-gone picture book.

The day passed slowly, though Clare was neither bored nor troubled by the tasks to be done. She remembered other first days in her life and wondered if the strange extension in time was because everything was so new. Perhaps it made you more aware of each separate experience, the first time you changed the sheets on the huge four-poster bed in the south guest room, the first time you carpet swept the threadbare rugs in the upstairs corridor, the first time you cleaned windows with June's own strange-smelling mixture of water, methylated spirit and vinegar.

John had told her how lovely the gardens had been before the war. She studied the dim outlines of paths and walkways as she polished the old window glass, so thickened in places it distorted the pattern of trees and shrubs which lay beyond, creating an impressionistic picture of colour and shape. There'd been a rose garden and a white garden and beyond both a pleasure garden with a little fountain and a pergola covered in scented honeysuckle. The flowers had gone during the war, replaced at first by plantings of potatoes and vegetables. After the war, as labour got even scarcer, the plots were grassed over or left to the buttercups and foxgloves. Some rose beds at the front of the house did survive. 'For the benefit of visitors,' said John wryly.

287

Clare wondered if Mr Richardson still kept up his interest in new varieties of garden plants or whether that too had gone with the economies the last years had brought. As she worked her way round to the windows on the south front, she found her answer. Looking down through the cracked and green-stained panes of an ancient conservatory, she could see a prolific vine clinging to the walls of the house. Opposite, on a wooden work bench, where tools and bowls of compost sat ready to use, there was a blaze of bright colour from rows of plants arranged in order of height against the outer glass wall.

'Clare's Delight,' she whispered to herself, as she began to dust.

She smiled as she thought of her window boxes, just beginning to show the sad effects of the chilly nights. But they were still in bloom, amongst them the fuchsias propagated from the one precious cutting she always referred to as 'John Wiley's ill-gotten gains'. With the seedlings of lobelia and alyssum Granny Hamilton had given her and cuttings from a pink geranium of Uncle Jack's, the window boxes had been a delight all summer. It was such a pity the perennials would soon have to be repotted and go back to the windowsills for the winter. She imagined Mr Richardson walking into his conservatory and seeing his precious plants in bloom even when there was snow on the ground outside.

She paused, intrigued by the vase of fine china flowers she'd picked up as she dusted her way along the mantelpiece. The house was so full of objects. Every possible surface was covered with them, so she couldn't dust or carpet sweep without moving something.

There were souvenirs from foreign travels, pieces of decorated brass and copper with swirling patterns and Arabic inscriptions, polished wood trays inlayed with mother of pearl and collections of exotic seashells. Other souvenirs came from nearer home. A collection of individual cups and saucers, all different, very prettily patterned and decorated in gold, small plates and vases in Belleek ware, china mugs with 'A present from Dublin' or 'A present from Galway'. Then there were things made from wood, a Dutch windmill with sails that turned, a lacquered Saint Bernard dog complete with brandy barrel, a miniature cuckoo clock on a stand, a bowl of carved flowers painted in bright colours, an icon with Christ's figure outlined in gold.

Just getting to the windows to clean them meant moving small writing tables, chairs with ladder backs, rotating book-cases and stools with worn tapestry seats, all beautiful pieces of furniture, the wood smooth, its colour mellowed by time. After dusting and polishing them, she'd felt quite upset to find modern magazine racks with shiny, black wooden legs and round, red plastic feet in some of the bedrooms.

'This is Andrew's real home,' she said, wondering which one of the many bedrooms he might have occupied as a little boy, before that ill-fated journey taking him to prep-school in England. Did he still have a room of his own, she asked herself, or was he given whichever one was currently available, when he visited?

How ironic that she should now be spending a whole day each week in the place where he so longed to be. But it would have to remain her secret. She'd tell him all the news of Drumsollen that was likely to come her way via John Wiley, just as she had done over the last year, but she'd not mention her job. It would be too unkind if he were feeling particularly homesick. Besides, it might be really painful for him to know she could see and touch the objects that had meaning for him when he himself was so far away.

She felt sad when she thought about Andrew and his love of Drumsollen. It was bad enough to have lost one's parents, but it must be even harder to feel there was nowhere you belonged, nowhere you felt free to be yourself and do what you wanted to do. She had never forgotten those awful weeks in Belfast with no place of her own, no bedroom to run to when the tears wouldn't stop, no orchard to hide in when everything went wrong, no kitchen to clean when action would ease the tension of anxiety, or the weariness of waiting upon events.

She wondered if there was anywhere Andrew could be himself. Cambridge, probably. But he hardly ever wrote about his studies. From what he had said his great-aunt in Norfolk sounded like a very sympathetic lady. But his Ulster family was more problematic. He was clearly fond of his grandfather and he wrote cheerfully of his cousins, Virginia and Edward, in Caledon, but when he had to visit his aunts in Fermanagh and Cavan he was clearly uneasy. His postcard from Dublin gave away the real distress of coping with his grandmother's sister, a woman who seemed even more unbending in her approach to him than his grandmother herself.

'Moved around like a parcel,' she said aloud, as she moved a stack of boys' annuals from in front of a bookcase, so she could run the Ewbank across the threadbare carpet and pick up the fluff that had fallen from it when she'd dusted.

'You look real tired, Clarey,' said June kindly, when Clare came back into the kitchen in the late afternoon.

'More stairs than at the Grange,' she replied, laughing. 'I feel as if I've walked miles.'

She collapsed gratefully at the enormous scrubbed table where once half a dozen maids sat to prepare vegetables, or pastry, when the Richardsons had a shooting party or weekend guests.

'Here, have a cup of tea.'

June poured her a cup and passed her the milk.

'You can clean the silver when you've had a break. That'll give you a sit-down while I start this casserole for tomorrow.'

Clare shivered and sipped her tea gratefully. Despite having worked so hard, she'd got thoroughly cold in the unheated rooms. The warmth of the kitchen was so comforting. She was so tired, she could just lay her head down on the table and go to sleep on the spot.

'When did you first come here, June?' she asked, as much to help her keep awake as out of curiosity.

'Ah, now yer askin',' June laughed, as she began to count on her fingers. 'I'm forty this year and I came straight here from school as a house maid at fourteen. That woud be 1928, woudn't it?'

Clare nodded and waited.

'Oh, those were the great days,' June began, a smile touching her lips. 'Parties and outings and visits from all the big people, the Brookeboroughs and the O'Neills and the Donegalls. Senator Richardson knew them all. Aye and some of the folk from across the water. They useta like comin' here. They said it was a whole differen' world from London an' the Home Counties, as they called them. Though they did laugh for they coulden understan' some of the sayin's the people here had. William and Edward were still both at home, till Edward married in '29. Great times,' she said wistfully.

'It wasn't quite the same after they married. Edward bought his own place at Caledon but when William married in '31 he brought his wife here. William was in Parliament by then and back an' forth to Westminster as well as to Stormont, so William an' his father ran the place between them. Or that was the idea. But Adeline loved the place as much as they did an' she got that she'd take over if neither of them was about. It was amazin' to everyone how a girl like her, brought up in London, coud take to farmin' an' have such a good idea of it. Mind you, she loved animals an' thought nothin' of sittin' up half the night with the cow man if there was some poor beast in labour. After her wee boy was born, she said she'd be happy to end her days here. She told me once she never missed London at all, except for seein' her parents. Of course, they liked nothin' better but to come over an' see her and wee Andrew so she was very happy here.'

'Why did they send Andrew to school in England?'

'Ach, why indeed? Sure Adeline wanted him to go to school here. An' if he had, sure they might all be alive yet, an' this place the way it useta be,' she said sadly, as she looked round the kitchen whose walls had not seen paint for many a year. 'It was The Missus that insisted. She said if Andrew went to school here, he'd end up talkin' like a local. All the Richardsons had been sent away to school. Did they want the child to be a social outcast? That was what she said, for Adeline told me. Aye, she used to sit at that table just like you're sittin' now, drinkin' tea an' talkin' to me. She was from a very good family herself, but she'd no time for all this business about accent. She just wanted wee Andrew to learn manners and to have a good education an' she diden' see why he needed to go out of Ireland for that. There were plenty of good schools here, she said.'

'But The Missus got her way?'

'She usually did,' said June bitterly. 'An' she still does. More's the pity,' she added, as she took their teacups to the sink and collected the silver polish and the cleaning cloths from the cupboard nearby.

The week that followed Clare's first Saturday at Drumsollen House was a busy one. Apart from fitting in the jobs she'd usually done on a Saturday morning before she went to Margaret's, she had to get ahead with her homework so that Charlie could take them out. He'd insisted that a meal in a hotel was the only proper way to celebrate her seventeenth birthday.

Robert was very uneasy about the whole idea. He hadn't been in a hotel for years and when Charlie proposed The Beresford in Armagh, he immediately dismissed it as being too posh.

'Ach, not at all man,' Charlie retorted. 'Sure can't ye go where ye like these days if ye have the money. An' it's not out of the way expensive. My cousin's wife works in the kitchen, she says the food's great. Ach, come on, Robert. It's Clarey's birthday.'

In the end, Charlie persuaded Robert to go and Clare persuaded him not to wear his stiff collar. They consumed a very good mixed grill followed by ice cream with chocolate sauce and Robert got as far as a wee joke about the amount of cutlery provided. Afterwards, in the Residents' Lounge, Charlie ordered Guinness for Robert and himself and suggested Clare had coffee. When it came and she tasted it, she wasn't entirely sure she liked it, but she appreciated his thoughtfulness. It pleased her to have something she had never had before to mark the occasion.

'We can't quite run to champagne for the lady yet, Robert, but we can treat her to a coffee,' said Charlie, as he handed over a small box which turned out to contain a very superior, new fountain pen.

Clare was altogether delighted with her birthday and the lovely surprises it had brought. Auntie Polly sent another dress, Granny Hamilton remembered this time and bought her a new pair of shoes, Ronnie sent a long letter and enclosed a ten dollar bill. Jessie gave her one of her own sketches, beautifully framed by Harry, and Aunt Sarah sent a blue and gold copy of *Pride and Prejudice*, one of Clare's favourite novels. There were a few cards as well, one from Robert with a short but touching message in his shaky hand, one from Uncle Harry, who had retired with his wife to Newcastle, and one from Uncle Jack who'd got a new job in Belfast after the Richhill jam factory closed down. Most amazing of all, there was a card from Andrew. She was quite certain she'd never mentioned the date of her birthday in his hearing.

The excitements and surprises of her birthday left Clare quite unprepared for a surprise of a quite different kind only a few weeks after her first visit to Drumsollen House.

When she got home from school on the Friday, Robert passed on a message from John Wiley. Could Clarey help June out by going up to the house an hour earlier in the morning? There must be something on, but as John had Senator Richardson in the car when he ran up to the forge and was in a great hurry to be somewhere or other by three o'clock, he wasn't able to give any details.

Clare set Robert's alarm clock for herself, had a quick breakfast and left him still in bed. She arrived at Drumsollen by seven thirty and found the kitchen warm and June already baking.

'What's up, June?' she asked as she took off her coat.

'Oh, bad news, Clarey. Edward's died of a heart attack an'

293

the funeral's at two thirty at Grange Church. We've got forty for tea around four o'clock and there'll be some staying overnight. The Missus hasn't told me about that yet. She gave me a list of the scones and cakes she wanted last night that she might well have given me yesterday mornin'.'

'But why isn't Edward being buried in Caledon?'

'Family vault,' replied June shortly, as Clare donned her apron and cap. 'Are you any good at making sandwiches?' she asked anxiously.

'Not bad,' Clare replied honestly. 'I have an aunt in the championship class. She's taught me a thing or two.'

'Thank God for that. I hate making them,' June admitted unsmiling, as she began to grease baking trays. 'Could you go and dust and tidy the drawing room and dining room now, before The Missus is up. You can dust the guest bedrooms while I give them their breakfast an' find out which ones she wants. After that, it'll take the pair of us all our time to get the food done and the rooms set up for four o'clock.'

June had forgotten she hadn't taken her to see the 'big rooms', as she called them, the previous Saturday, but one look at her face told Clare she was just about coping. With only herself to help, it was hardly surprising she was anxious about the amount to be done.

She collected up her cleaning equipment and made her way cautiously up the nearby wooden stairs, past the maids' pantry and the estate office and on into the front hall.

'My goodness,' she whispered to herself, as she looked around in amazement. Lit by two tall windows and a fanlight over the massive front door, the hall was as large as the bigger classrooms in Beresford Row, rooms that had once been the sitting rooms of the gentry.

From the walls, previous generations of Richardsons in heavy gilt frames looked down on a Pembroke table covered with glossy magazines and decorated with a massive table centre of cut glass positioned exactly below a chandelier of the same design.

All the doors leading out of the hall lay open, revealing yet more ancestors filling up the wall space in the heavily furnished drawing room and dining room. A smaller room, only a little larger than the big kitchen at the Grange, its walls completely clothed in bookcases full of leather-backed volumes of all shapes and sizes, had a smoking fire in the grate and a table already laid for breakfast overlooking the garden.

Clare turned away and got to work on the huge, empty drawing room. At least there was space to move around and there was somewhere to put the statuettes in plaster and bronze, the silver dishes and ewers, the bizarre carvings in very dark wood, the cases of coins, and the displays of medals while she did her dusting. Unlike the cluttered guest bedrooms, not every inch of dust-laden surface was covered with the acquisitions of former centuries.

With a sideways glance at a full length portrait of Archbishop Ussher of Armagh, who appeared to be watching her, Clare gathered up the remnants of dead flowers that had shed their wrinkled leaves all across the floor and scattered pollen and sticky residues on the tables where they'd stood. She turned to the hearth. The ash had already been removed but the fire had not yet been laid. She swept up a fall of damp soot and passed on. Her hands numb with cold already, she worked her way round the massive pieces of furniture just as the smell of bacon and eggs wafted up from the kitchen below.

'Poor old June,' she said softly, figuring out how much work June must have done before she'd even arrived.

She listened carefully at the drawing room door. She didn't much care for being an unseen and unknown creature referred to as 'staff', but she wasn't going to let June down. Not a sound. She walked briskly into the dining room, shutting the door behind her.

'If I'm required to be invisible, then invisible I shall be,' she said firmly, to a hard-faced woman with sausage-shaped ringlets and a powder blue gown, who loured down at her from the wall over the yards-long sideboard.

The morning sun was just beginning to slant through the tall windows overlooking the garden. To her surprise, there was still real warmth in its rays and she paused for a few moments in a patch of light, grateful to escape the deep chill of the unheated room. It was then that she heard voices, a man, soft-spoken and indistinct, and a woman whom it would have been impossible not to hear, her tone so high and clear.

'Thank you, Mrs Wiley. Mr Richardson will serve for us. I've made a list of those who have to stay overnight. I'm afraid my daughter-in-law is not coping at all, despite the generous domestic help she has, so we'll have to rally round instead. I hope that girl of yours is doing her stuff. There are five couples and perhaps . . .'

The voice was cut off as they went into the morning room and shut the door.

'Doing my stuff,' Clare repeated, mimicking the high tone, as she wiped the tiles of the fireplace and brushed up the sawdust that had fallen from the enormous wicker log basket.

After what she'd heard, she could have made up her own mind about The Missus even without June's sharp comments. All she can think about is her daughter-in-law's failure to run her Caledon home as a hotel for the weekend. How dare she say she *wasn't coping* when the poor woman's second husband had just dropped dead, in his early fifties. Her own son, too.

She finished the room, made sure all was quiet outside in the hall and retreated at speed to the kitchen. June was nowhere to be seen, but there was a stack of mixing bowls and dishes by the sink and a mouth-watering smell of baking scones from the oven. She got stuck in to the washing up and had just finished when June reappeared.

She dropped down into a chair, sniffed the air and jumped to her feet again.

'That was close, Clarey. Another few minutes and they'd have burnt,' she said, as she unhooked the cooling racks from the wall.

'No they wouldn't, June. If you hadn't come when you did I

was going to look at them. But don't they drop if you open the oven door too soon?'

'They do indeed. Good girl yerself for thinking of that. You always think about things, don't you?'

'I try,' said Clare, honestly. 'I think The Missus is asking too much of you, June, but if you want to do this tea party I'm sure we can manage between us.'

June nodded and began transferring the fresh scones to the wire cooler. Clare watched for a moment, then took up a tray and followed suit.

'It's not The Missus I'm doin' it for,' June began. 'It's poor Mrs Edward. That woman's had nothing but bad luck in her life an' she's a good sort. An' sure Edward was a good-hearted man hi'self. He'd never a cross word for me when I was only a house maid and made my mistakes as we all do. No, it's not for The Missus, Clarey. To tell you the truth, if it wasn't for the Senator I'd look for an easier billet with decent hours. I'm not fussy. I'd go to the apple peeling up at Gillis if I could be sure they'd have enough work the year round.'

'I wouldn't blame you. You're doing about three people's work here.'

June nodded and smiled for the first time that morning. She was about to say something else when she dropped a scone.

'It's an ill-wind,' she laughed, gathering up the warm fragments on to a clean plate. 'Here, love, put a bit of butter and jam on that one and eat it up before you do the bedrooms. It woud freeze you up there.'

Despite the news that forty guests had become fifty, the preparations for tea went well. June produced tray after tray of scones, fairy cakes and rock cakes. She creamed and iced a couple of sponge cakes and buttered batches of fruit tea bread while Clare set up a sandwich production unit that would have done credit to her aunt.

A little before three thirty, John Wiley, in his best suit, put his head round the kitchen door and said that the Richardsons were back and he was away to collect some other mourners who had come to the service in hired cars.

'But it's not near four o'clock. They told me four,' June cried, as John disappeared.

She turned hastily to the kitchen table, reached out for the next silver salver of sandwiches to take upstairs and let out a howl of pain.

'June, what's wrong,' cried Clare in alarm, as June fell against the table and slid to the floor.

'I'm all right,' she gasped, tears of pain springing to her eyes, as Clare fell to her knees beside her. 'My own fault entirely,' she went on, 'I've twisted my ankle on that damned bad bit of floor. It's been like that for years, as if I didn't know. My own fault, my own fault,' she muttered, as tears streamed down her face.

Clare helped her to sit up with her back to the leg of the table. Then she ran cold water on a clean tea towel.

'Here, try that, while I make an icepack.'

As Clare knocked ice cubes from the tray, she heard June use the chair to struggle to her feet. She turned round and saw her standing on one foot, holding on to the table.

'Is there a bag I can put these in, June?' she asked.

'Aye. Muslin one,' she said, with an effort. 'With the jam-making stuff. Bottom right,' she said, lowering herself on to the chair, her leg stuck out in front of her.

She winced as Clare put the bag of ice against her ankle. She leaned her head in her hands despairingly.

'What in the name o' goodness will we do now? I can't put it t' the groun', it's that sore.'

'Nothing for it, June. I'll have to take the rest of the stuff up and pour the tea, unless some of the women offer to do it. It's not your fault. It was an accident. Could you manage to finish buttering the scones if I take up the sandwiches?'

June nodded weakly and let Clare help her turn back to the table.

'I don't know what she'll say if she sees you,' she said anxiously, as Clare picked up the silver salver.

Clare managed to carry three more trays of food upstairs without being noticed, though dark figures were now standing in the hall watching as a stream of cars drew up to the front door. They unloaded men in morning dress and women in black suits and furs, before driving off to park in the stable yard.

The dining room table with the urn and teapots had been set up hours ago, the teacups inverted in their saucers, lined up like an army about to go into battle. The plates and salvers of food had been placed on other tables in both drawing room and dining room.

It was as she slipped into the drawing room with the last large salver of sandwiches that Clare found herself face to face with a dark figure who stared at her in amazement.

'Clare, what are *you* doing here?'

It was just as obvious from Clare's apron and cap, as it was from Andrew's black suit and pale face, what they were both doing, but before either of them had recovered their wits enough to speak, a familiar high voice cut across the room, which was now beginning to fill.

'Andrew, *qu'est ce que vous dites à la domestique?*' it demanded. '*Viens ici, immediatement,*' it ordered. '*Dites à la bonne de retourner à la cuisine à cette instant et envoyer Wiley à moi.*'

Clare could hardly believe her ears. Speaking French in front of the servants in this day and age, referring to June as Wiley, never mind herself as a domestic. She took one glancé at Andrew. He was rooted to the spot, his face flushed scarlet with embarrassment. She handed him the sandwiches and walked across to face The Missus, who stood fiercely upright in front of the marble fireplace.

'*Madame,*' she began, speaking rapidly in French, 'I regret that my presence displeases you, but there are some things I must say to you. Not all those who engage in domestic service are to be classed as "*domestique*". And even where this label might seem to apply there is still the question of courtesy to which even mere servants are entitled,' she went on, her voice

299

heavy with emotion. 'Mrs Wiley has been working under pressure since very early this morning and has now sprained her ankle. If you will promise to apologise to her for your unfair behaviour towards her, then I will do all I can to ensure that your guests are looked after. If not, then I shall be happy to leave your service this very instant,' she concluded, snatching the Miss Muffet cap from her dark curls and holding it out to the startled lady.

As Clare stood before her and met her hostile stare without flinching, she thought The Missus might take it and slap her across the face with it. But she did not. For what seemed an age, she stood quite still and then sat down abruptly on a high-backed chair.

'Have you studied in Paris?' she asked, reverting to English.

'No, not yet.'

The Missus held out the cap.

'I apologise to you and I shall apologise to Mrs Wiley when tea is over. Do what you can.'

Clare replaced her cap and nodded.

'I shall need some help from your grandson and perhaps some younger members of your family. You won't object, will you?'

The movement of the older woman's head was imperceptible, but the hostility in her eyes had disappeared. For a few seconds, Clare caught a glimpse of a sad woman who had just lost her second son. She felt her own anger cool and became aware of Andrew standing close behind her. He was still clutching the salver of sandwiches.

'Andrew, is there anyone who would pour tea if I make it?'

'Mrs Clarke from Caledon, Auntie's housekeeper. Her daughter, Olive, is here too.'

'You go and ask them. I'll start brewing up. Your grand-mother badly needs a cup of tea,' she said, as she slipped through the solid groups of dark suits and made her way to the dining room.

Before the first pots were brewed, Doreen Clarke and her

daughter appeared at Clare's elbow. She almost smiled to herself at the practised way they set about the job. From the moment they started reversing the teacups, she knew that all would be well.

'I'm Virginia, can I help?'

A tall, striking girl with chestnut hair stood in front of her, a boy, younger and dark, followed a few steps behind.

'Yes, please. Could you take a tray of tea into the drawing room to some of the older people by the fireplace. It will save them having to come for it,' she said, producing some breakfast trays from under the damask-draped table and loading them with cups ready for Doreen and Olive to pour.

'How are you doing? Can I carry something too?' said Andrew as he arrived, just behind his cousins.

'I think we're going to need more hot water. Can you go down for it and tell June all's well. She'll be worrying herself silly.'

'What's happened to June. You said she'd had an accident.'

'Sprained ankle, I told you,' she said hastily, as she filled another large teapot from the boiling urn.

'Yes, but my French wasn't up to that bit. Not at your speed. You sounded like a native.'

'Of France, I hope,' she said sharply, as she handed him an empty teapot. 'Can you rinse this one out in very hot water, please, while you're down there, and bring it back when you bring the kettle.'

'Oh yes, of France all right,' he said, shaking his head, as he reversed carefully from the dining table and wove his way through the dark figures now silently munching their way through the sandwiches and cake.

It was after six before Clare was free to go out to the stable, fetch her bicycle and head for home. Andrew had introduced her properly to Virginia and Edward and together the young people had done all the dishes, while Doreen and Olive set the dining room to rights and put everything away in the kitchen under June's instructions.

The ankle was still very painful, but it was clear nothing was broken. What it needed was a well-earned rest.

Just before six o'clock, the overnight guests ensconced in the drawing room with Senator Richardson and his daughter-in-law, Mrs Richardson excused herself and went down to the kitchen. She arrived just as John Wiley appeared to take June home in the Senator's car and Clare was hanging the wet drying-up cloths on the airer.

'Will you both excuse me a minute or two, please, I'd like a word with Mrs Wiley before she goes,' she said quietly.

Clare and John took themselves off to the far end of the servants' corridor, perched themselves in a window sill and looked at each other.

'I niver thought I'd see the day when that wuman would say "please",' began John, 'let alone apologise to anyone.'

'She hasn't done it yet, John. But she might.'

'What in the world did ye say to her? I heer ye said it in French. Were it too rude to say in English?' he asked, with a wink.

Clare shook her head vigorously.

'I wasn't rude at all. I was very polite. Icily polite. But, honestly I can't remember what I said now. I do know I told her I was going to leave there and then if she didn't apologise to June.'

'Well, somethin's goin' on in there. We'll jus' hafta see whether she's seen the light or whether what she does is just handiness. Ye must be tired out, Clarey, wi' all the excitement an' you here since all hours this mornin'. Woud ye not let me drop you off in the car an' I'll bring your bike down sometime tomorrow?'

'Thanks, John. I'd love a ride in the car, but Jessie an' I are for church in the morning. I don't want to spoil your nice lie-in.'

'Ah, maybe yer right,' he said, standing up, as the kitchen door closed and The Missus appeared at the end of the corridor.

The figure who walked towards them and addressed herself to John did seem less formidable than Clare remembered.

'I've told Mrs Wiley she's to have a proper rest. At least a week, John. And you're to let me know how she is,' she said, her tone modified, her nod of dismissal the product of long years.

'I must congratulate you on your initiative, Clare. And on your command of French,' she began quietly. 'I wish my grandson had so fortunate an accent,' she added wryly. 'I gather he wants to speak to you before you go. After the way you coped today, it would be quite unreasonable of me to object. I hope you will overlook my bad behaviour. I've had a certain amount of provocation, but that is no excuse. I hope I shall see you next week, as usual.'

Clare nodded and watched the tall, unbending figure as she began to climb the stairs. She was shocked to see how slowly she negotiated them, having to use both hands on the banister to pull herself up their shallow rises.

Suddenly very tired, Clare turned back to the now empty kitchen, put away her cap and apron, took her coat from behind the door and picked up the greaseproof parcel of cake June had left for her. She nearly ran into Andrew in the doorway.

'Sorry,' she said, as she collected herself.

'My fault,' he replied, 'I was afraid I might miss you. But I had to wait till Grandmother reappeared before I could come down,' he explained.

'Clare, will you come out for a ride with me tomorrow afternoon?'

'I'm sorry, Andrew, I'd love to, but I haven't got a horse.'

He threw back his head and laughed.

'Neither have I, Clare. Only an old bike that everybody uses when I'm not here. Will that do?'

'Oh yes, that will do fine.'

'At the forge. Two thirty. All right?'

'All right.'

He disappeared back upstairs at speed and she let herself out into the yard, fetched her bicycle and set off down the back lane. The sun had already set, the air was chill. As she freewheeled gently down the slope, a slight mist was rising from the fields by the stream where she and Jessie used to sit and talk secrets. So long ago now, it seemed already like another life. She pedalled slowly, wearily, the short journey home such a great effort.

She turned into the lane and saw that the lamp was already lit in the kitchen though it was still light enough to see outdoors. She parked her bicycle and stood for a moment listening to the deep silence of the countryside.

She looked up and saw the tiniest sliver of a new moon.

'I wonder what happened to the chestnut mare,' she said quietly, before she opened the kitchen door.

21

I t was frosty on Sunday when Jessie and Clare rode into Armagh, but by the time they'd sat through one more sermon on sin, collected newspapers from the shop in Railway Street and cycled back to the pump opposite Charlie Running's cottage, only a dusting of white lay among the tangled grasses in the north-facing hollows. The sun was high in a clear, blue sky, the air completely still. It promised to be a warm, autumn afternoon.

'Where'll ye go?' asked Jessie, who'd talked of nothing but Clare's meeting with Andrew all morning.

'Oh, just for a ride. He didn't mention anywhere in particular,' replied Clare awkwardly.

'Somewhere quiet,' suggested Jessie. 'A fair bit away, or yer sure to bump inta someone ye know.'

Clare looked puzzled, caught her look of long-suffering patience and did her best to look nonchalant.

'Sure you'll want a bit of a snog,' said Jessie, wearily. 'What's the point of goin' out with a fella if ye don't get a bit friendly? Ye don't want half the Grange watchin' over the hedge, now do ye?'

'No, you're right there,' replied Clare hurriedly.

Waking early, the light bright through her window, with no sound of movement from the big kitchen, she'd thought back to the afternoon at Scrabo Tower. Andrew had kissed her so unexpectedly, but she hadn't minded at all. Now she wasn't sure how she felt about it. The kiss hadn't really lasted long enough for her to do much thinking at the time. But a kiss was a kiss. You couldn't argue it away. It meant something. But what? Yes, some boys would kiss any girl who happened to be within reach. But she was sure Andrew Richardson wasn't one of them, any more than Ronnie was. Ronnie certainly cared for her and not just because she was his cousin. But she knew that, even if he hadn't kissed her. Andrew was quite a different matter.

'Dark and fair,' she said to herself. 'Chalk and cheese.' It seemed extraordinary two young men could be so very different, yet she should like each of them so much. She'd known Ronnie for as long as she could remember. Andrew simply stepped into her life. She'd seen very little of him, yet she'd thought about him more than she'd ever admit to Jessie. There were his postcards in the dressing chest. Each one had delighted her. He made her laugh. And yet she never thought he was trying to be funny. She couldn't stand people who tried to be funny.

'Where do you and Harry go?' she asked quickly, hoping to divert Jessie from more intimate questions.

'Maghery,' was the prompt reply. 'They never fish from there on a Sunday, an' ye can get the car right down the wee path to where the boats push off. There's never anyone about. If ye park well over on the right ye can see right across the lake to a wee island. Coney Island, it's called. It's quite romantic,' she added, rather less briskly.

'We're not going by car, you know, Jessie.'

'What? Ye said ye were goin' for a ride,' replied Jessie, her tone bordering on outrage. 'Ye mean t' say he can't even get the aul' man's car to take ye out?'

'No. He said he'd an old bicycle everyone uses when he's not there.'

Jessie raised her eyes heavenward and looked at her new watch, a recent birthday present from Harry.

'I hafta be goin', Clare. John's bringin' Aunt Sarah out fer her lunch an' they'll be expectin' me. For goodness sake, mind yerself. I'm not sure ye ought to be let out. A ride on a bicycle,' she repeated, raising her eyebrows. 'An' him a Richardson from Drumsollen, even if they have lost their cash,' she added, as she wheeled her bicycle back on to the road. 'I'll see ye in a fortnight an' don't let me down for the Ritz on the Saturday. Just go easy at Drumsollen an' don't wear yerself out,' she advised, as she pressed the pedal and swung herself into the saddle.

Clare smiled as she too set off. What would Jessie say if she let on she'd thought Andrew meant a ride on a horse?

'See ye enjoy yerself now,' said Robert, as he undid his boots and pushed them off after their meal. 'It's a great day t' be out. What time did ye say yer young man was comin' at?'

'Half two,' she replied, looking from the clock on the mantelpiece to the wag o' the wall and back. One ran fast and the other ran slow, but it was still only about two.

'Is he at Drumsollen fer long?'

'No, I think he's only here for the funeral. He's at Cambridge and term has started. I'm sure he's got to go back right away.'

'So he's at the books like yerself?' he said, nodding to himself. 'His father was a powerful clever man, so they say. But it niver affected him one bit. He'd talk away t' ye as if he'd been to the school room wi' the rest of us. He useta bring the Drumsollen horses over before the war. I suppose there's none left now,' he said matter-of-factly, as he leaned back in his chair, out of breath from the effort of bending over.

'I don't think so,' she said slowly. 'There was that chestnut mare last year.'

'Aye. I mind that well. Sure the day he first came lookin' after ye I thought I was seein' things he was that like the father, though when he spoke it was the mother I heerd. Many's a time she'd come with a horse on a leading rein if all the men was away. She'd sit down on that aul' bench in her good clothes an' niver give it a thought. Other times she rode a wee black mare with a flash on its brow "Star" she called it. That horse woud a done anythin' fer her. Niver had a bit o' bother shoeing it. She'd stan' by the bridle an' talk to it.'

307

Clare saw a smile play across his lips as he settled himself more comfortably. It was a sign he was ready to tell a story. She'd learnt to watch for it since the days when she first tried to get him to tell her about the people that were in the big photograph of the Sunday School outing in 'the room'. He was such a silent man, it was seldom he talked at any length, but that little smile was always a good omen.

' "Now then, Star," ' she'd say,' he began, speaking very precisely, ' "lift up your foot for Mr Scott," he said, with a little laugh. 'An' ye know that wee mare woud do it. I niver once had to pull her by the fetlocks or say, "Hup there." She woud tell it what to do an' it did it. I niver seen the like of it.'

He stood up abruptly, the smile gone, a look of such sadness passing over his features Clare was quite taken aback.

'Sure the luck went out o' Drumsollen when they took the wee lad to school in England an' none 'o them came back,' he said, sadly. 'June Colvin wept sore over the wee lad. She tole me once she didn't get over him goin' away t'school till she met John an' they had wee Helen,' he added, as he stood up.

He tramped halfway across the kitchen and then turned back on his step, the sadness replaced by a slight twinkle in the eyes.

'Sure maybe we'll be seein' more of young Andrew now, horse or no horse,' he said, as he disappeared into 'the room'.

Although she was five minutes early herself, Clare found Andrew sitting on the low bank at the foot of the lane waiting for her, a decrepit-looking bicycle drawn up on the grass verge by the road.

'Where shall we go?' he said, as he jumped up and came to meet her. ''Fraid I've got to be back by five, John Wiley's taking me to the boat, so we're having an early meal.'

'What about Cannon Hill?'

Clare was amazed at the way the name popped out before she'd even thought about it. The minute she said it, she regretted it. What on earth would she do if William and some of his friends took a notion to go up there or they ran into a collection of aunts and cousins out for a Sunday afternoon walk and she had to introduce them?

'Sounds good. Where is it? Is there a cannon?' he asked enthusiastically, when she told him it had a clear view for miles around.

'I haven't been there since I was a little girl,' she confessed, as they whizzed down the hill towards Scott's Corner and turned right towards Ballybrannan.

'I haven't been on this road for years,' said Andrew suddenly. 'Whose is the big farm opposite the school?'

He plied her with questions all the way and was still talking as they reached the five-barred gate at the foot of the steep slope.

'Oh dear,' said Clare, looking round as she parked her bicycle. 'That wasn't here last time I came.'

A notice had been tied to the gate. In crooked letters on a piece of plywood it said: 'Trespassers will be prosecuted. By order.'

Andrew shook his head and took her hand to help her over.

'No standing whatever in law,' he said firmly. 'You can only prosecute if damage has been caused and as this field is not even being seriously grazed, we'd be hard put to damage anything but an unlucky buttercup. Come on.'

Clare climbed over the gate and waited for him to follow.

'Down in Fermanagh, they don't prosecute, they persecute,' he said, as he dropped lightly on both feet. 'I've never been able to decide whether it's intentional ferocity or inadequate spelling.'

She laughed, her unease resolved. He'd talked so continuously and asked so many questions as they rode along, she hadn't known what to think. Now she could see his face and the set of his body it was perfectly clear. Andrew was happy.

Swinging their clasped hands and avoiding the odd patch of thistle, they made their way towards the tall finger of stone at the summit.

'I know it was Sir Capel Molyneux had it built, but I've forgotten why,' she confessed, as they drew nearer.

'Oh, Sir Capel, was it? Mad as a hatter was Sir Capel, but nice with it, so I've heard. Set up a bird sanctuary in Castledillon. The Molyneux's are our next-door neighbours in the vault of Grange Church. Very quiet neighbours,' he said cheerfully. 'How little were you when you came here last?'

'Nine, I think. Yes. It was August '46. I came to stay with Granda Scott for a holiday,' she explained, 'but it was really to see if he could cope. I wanted to come back to Armagh, but Auntie Polly thought it might be a bit much for him. She said Granda never was any good with children.'

'But it worked?'

'Yes, it did,' she said, as they reached the top of the hill and flopped down, breathless, among the tall stems of buttercup, bright with green seed heads.

'Did he bring you here?'

'No,' she said, shaking her head. 'Poor dear Granda couldn't take me anywhere because of his bad leg. But my other grandparents live just down the road. The curve of the hill hides their farm, but it's not far. My Uncle Jack took Granda and I over to tea one Sunday and I came up here with a collection of aunts and uncles. I couldn't work out who was who that day. There were ten in my father's family.'

'And your mother's?'

'Six. Aunt Mary doesn't keep in touch. She's in Michigan. Florence is in London, Bob's in Antrim, Johnny's in Fermanagh and Auntie Polly's in Toronto now.'

They stood up and began to view the wide expanse of countryside laid out before them.

'I envy you, Clare,' he said suddenly, throwing his head back and staring up at the bright, white clouds streaming across the blue sky from the west. 'You have your whole world spread out around you.'

He waved a hand at the western horizon where the tower and spires of Armagh's two cathedrals rose above the roofs and trees of the city. Then he turned round and gazed over the low hills to the east, their slopes dotted with apple orchards and farms, their small fields a patchwork of ploughed earth, tramped stubble and vivid, green pasture.

'But Andrew, look at all you've done, all you've seen,' she protested. 'My world is like a teacup compared with yours. You've travelled abroad, you've lived in France, you've been all over England. You've been to Scotland. I've never been further from home than Belfast. I've never been in any counties other than Armagh and Down, while you've been to Dublin, stayed in Cavan and goodness knows how many other places in Ireland.'

He smiled sheepishly as they sat down again in a patch of sunshine. They watched in silence as the bright, white clouds cast their shadows across the patterned landscape. Clare looked at him cautiously. A hint of a smile still lingered on his lips, but his eyes were travelling hungrily round the small farms at the foot of the hill as if he were searching for something.

'Don't you want to go back?' she asked.

To her great surprise, he turned towards her, leaned forward and kissed her. She made no effort to move away.

'I'd rather stay here with you,' he admitted. He put his arms round her and kissed her again. And again. As she responded, something said to her that whatever this was, it wasn't snogging.

They sat very close together in the sunshine, their arms around each other. He told her he'd always loved Drumsollen and the countryside around it. All through his time at prepschool he longed to go home, but his visits were always cut short. He'd hardly arrived when he'd be sent on to someone else. Some years, there was no visit at all, though his grandfather always wrote to him and was welcoming.

'I've never really been able to understand why my grandmother so dislikes me, but I know she can't stand the sight of me. If it weren't for Grandfather I'd never set eyes on the place,' he said sadly.

For a moment, he fell silent, such a desolate look on his face she almost gasped.

'Clare, you will you go on writing, won't you?' he burst out, a note almost of desperation in his voice.

She pressed herself gently against him and squeezed his hand.

'Yes, of course I'll write, Andrew. Of course, I will,' she said quietly. 'On one condition, though.'

He looked so crestfallen as she said it she put her hand to his cheek and kissed him gently.

'Don't look so alarmed. It's not so difficult. I only want to know why you don't like writing letters.'

Clare looked at him as she waited for him to reply. The sunlight dappled his pale skin and pulled out hints of red in his fair hair. He was wearing a white shirt, open at the neck and a pair of grey flannels, just like any of the senior boarders from the Royal School who walked out the Portadown Road on a Sunday afternoon. Yet he seemed older by far than the two years separating him from the few boys she'd met through Debating Society. More poised, more relaxed.

'Maybe I haven't a problem anymore,' he said slowly. 'I did manage a page last time. And it was blue,' he said, solemnly.

He looked so bleak she couldn't bear to ask him why the colour of the paper was so important.

'I arrived at prep-school on a Thursday,' he continued, with a rush. 'My parents were killed that night. I spent Friday in the San. with Matron. She was nice, played tiddlywinks with me. But she wasn't there on Saturday and Sunday, so I had to go back to school routine, sport and prep and that sort of thing,' he said flatly. 'On the Sunday we went to the prep hall after lunch and they handed out these sheets of blue paper, so we could write to our parents. I just sat and looked at the paper. I couldn't speak. I suppose I was afraid I might cry. Not done you know. I nearly got a detention when the master on duty wanted to know why I wasn't getting on with it. And then some boy said: "Sir, Richardson's mater and pater were killed in an air-raid in London."'

He turned to her and smiled unexpectedly. 'Isn't it silly, after all this time?'

'No, it isn't. It was a terrible thing to happen. That master should have been sacked. Or someone should. It was unforgivable if he knew, and if he didn't, it was unforgivable for no one to have told him,' she said angrily. 'And you were only seven.'

Suddenly she remembered the school in Belfast. All those rowdy, unknown children, the young man who waved his arms around and scolded them, the echoing yard full of the noise of traffic and her own tears over which she had no control whatever.

'I was luckier,' she said quickly. 'I had Auntie Polly and Uncle Jimmy. But I ended up bottom of my class at school later that year, because I hadn't my mother to help me learn my spellings.'

He drew her even closer and she laid her head on his shoulder.

'I hate to tell you, Andrew, but it's time you were getting back.'

'Oh Lord, so it is,' he said, drawing her to her feet.

'Why don't you try writing to me on sheets of exercise book,' she said as they hurried back down the slope. 'Or wrapping paper,' she added as she climbed over the chained-up gate.

'Or toilet paper?' he suggested.

'Bit thin,' she said. They both laughed.

There was no one about in the narrow lane, so he took her in his arms again. She drew away reluctantly, suddenly aware of time passing. Kissing Andrew was the easiest thing in the world.

'I'll get back next summer, somehow or other, Clare. Don't go marrying anyone in the meantime, will you?' he said awkwardly, as they pulled in at the foot of her lane.

'I'll be far too busy,' she said, laughing. 'I'm going to try for a scholarship.'

'Good,' he said, looking relieved. 'You'll get it. I know you will. We'll celebrate together when I come,' he said firmly.

He looked around hastily. There wasn't a soul anywhere to be seen. He leaned over and kissed her.

'I'll write to you as soon as I get back,' he promised, as he pushed off and freewheeled down the hill, one arm raised high in the air, waving to her until he knew he was out of sight.

Andrew was as good as his word. He wrote regularly and at length through the months that followed. She'd draw out brightly coloured paper decorated with smiling faces or stick figures, laugh, and think longingly back to that one happy afternoon on Cannon Hill. At other times, she was just so glad to hear from him she hardly noticed the paper or decorations.

To her surprise, the months seemed to move at twice the speed she'd expected. With little to look forward to other than the routine of school work and housework, Saturdays at Drumsollen and occasional visits to the Ritz with Jessie, she could hardly believe Christmas was long past and February's mock exams already on top of her.

She confessed to Andrew that she was afraid she'd never find time for all the work she felt she had to do. Writing back, he did his best to reassure her she'd probably done far more already than she realised. He even tried to warn her of the danger of overdoing it, but only the mock results made much difference. They left her little doubt that all would be well. Only then did she realise how anxious she'd been.

One March evening Robert and Charlie went over to Loughgall. She managed to finish her homework early and sat down and wrote him a long letter.

> I really have been a pain, Andrew, as Jessie would say. I know I've talked about nothing but my own concerns in my letters for weeks now. I *am* sorry. The trouble is, the more I do, the more there seems to be and once I make up my mind about something I can be awfully stubborn. Or you could say determined, if you wanted to be more charitable.

314

I know now you were right. I *was* overdoing it. Even Granda, who's all for me getting a scholarship, has been hinting I should maybe have a night out. He keeps asking me when Jessie will be home. Once or twice he's even asked about 'the young man on the chestnut mare'.

However, I promise I shall now try to be more entertaining. But I do have a problem. I lead such a quiet life in my 'teacup' that often I think I've nothing to write about. 'One of Charlie Running's goats got out and chewed the straw jacket on the pump that keeps it from freezing. A fox got away with two of Margaret's chickens. The daffodils at the back of the house are up, but not down.' What stirring stuff compared with your adventures, visiting your great-aunt in Norfolk or going with your uncle to the Merediths' shooting party.

She paused, tapping the end of her fountain pen against her cheek, thinking of the enormous difference between their worlds. A few weeks ago he'd used notepaper from a top London hotel she'd often read about. He said he thought it would make a change from lined A4, so he'd asked his cousin to pinch some for him. She'd been there with his aunt looking the place over to see if she'd like it for her 'coming out' dance!

Clare stared at the window on the orchard side of the house. It reflected back her own image in the lamplight as she sat imagining Caroline's debut. Andrew would go, of course, and dance with all the beautifully dressed girls who had just been presented at court and were also 'coming out'. He would tell her about it, no doubt. He always told her what he was doing, where he'd been and how much he'd like to have her there. And she knew he meant every word of it. It was very strange, very strange indeed.

Only one thing was missing from his letters. In none of them did he say anything about his own work. When she asked him directly he admitted that he found Law studies boring, but he saw no immediate alternative. He'd do what was necessary, however, and get the relevant piece of paper. It would be his

315

passport to a job in Belfast. He hoped his grandfather would use his contacts to find him a place to do his articles.

What he said made perfectly good sense to Clare. She couldn't have spent her favourite month of the year shut up in the boys' room for these last three years without having grasped that, often, you have to do what you don't want to do, for the sake of the future.

She sat for a long time looking at what she had written, thinking of him, remembering the comfort of his arms and the touch of his lips. Jessie always referred to him as 'yer man, Andrew' never as 'your boyfriend'. That was strange too, given how anxious Jessie was to 'get her fixed up'. Yet she knew it was no accident. Jessie was shrewd, and 'boyfriend' was definitely not the right word. She wasn't sure she wanted 'a boyfriend', but she certainly wanted Andrew. She wanted his warm affection and his openness, his way of encouraging her and keeping her spirits up. 'Boyfriends' were passing features of the landscape. Andrew was something quite different.

'How do I see him?' she asked herself, in the quiet of the empty room, where only the tick of two clocks and the hiss of the Tilley lamp broke the quiet of the evening.

'No,' she said firmly, aware of the ambiguity of her question. 'I really mustn't think about seeing him at all. It will be ages yet. He can't possibly come before the middle of August and that's on the other side of the examinations. And the results. An eternity away.'

The results came out the first week in August and she cycled in to collect them. As she stood staring at the thin strip of paper in the spacious entrance hall of the new school building, tears streamed down her face. She'd done even better than she'd dared hope, her average marks far higher than the figure which would give her a County Scholarship.

Hastily, she made her way to the cloakroom, shut herself in one of the lavatories and sat there sobbing till the tears finally stopped.

'What a way to celebrate,' she said to herself, as she washed her face in one of the spotless new hand basins and dried it on an immaculate roller towel.

She stepped out into the echoing corridor and walked slowly back to the entrance hall. All was quiet. Light poured down on to the wide, shallow stairs from the tall, staircase window. Through the wired glass doors of the assembly hall she saw the sunshine spill across the polished floor, obliterating the line markings for netball and badminton. Apart from the school secretary in her office upstairs, she hadn't seen a soul. The handful of other girls who'd done A-level with her were away on holiday. Or had a phone to ring the secretary.

She lingered for a moment longer, so aware that when next she stood in this place, she would be collecting her prizes, one of the very few girls not wearing uniform to walk across the platform. She would be eighteen, a student, her school days over.

Feeling strangely sad and lonely, she collected her bicycle from the back of the building and was just about to ride down the driveway when she saw a tall, blue-clad figure waving to her. It was the school caretaker, the man who had once come looking for Alison Hamilton in her primary school, half her lifetime ago.

'Hello, Mr Stinson, how are you?' she asked, stopping beside him as he hurried over from his house to meet her.

'Gran'. It's very quiet wi'out all you wee lassies in the holidays.'

'Less hard work I should think,' she said, smiling at him.

'Been up to see Elizabeth?' he asked cautiously.

'Good news,' she said. 'I'm for Queens.'

'Ach, good girl yerself. I said to the wife this mornin' ye'd be in till see how ye did. Ah, she'll be that pleased when I tell her. Congratulations. Ye've done well. Lass time I saw yer Granda in town he was full of it. Is he well?'

'Yes, he's in great form. He loves the warm weather.'

'Aye, we don't get a lot of it, but it's been nice so far this summer. Tell him I was askin' for him. I'll look out fer ye on Speech Day,' he said, raising a hand, as she set off down the avenue between the newly planted rose beds.

'Did ye get it, Clare. Did ye get it?'

As she got off her bicycle at the foot of the lane, the eldest of the Robinson children bore down on her.

'Yes, Charlie, I did.'

Without another word, the little boy turned and raced back up the lane.

'She got it,' he shouted, without pausing, as he passed the door of the forge and flew round its far gable on the well-tramped grass path to the farm.

The hammering stopped. Before she'd parked her bicycle against the wall, Charlie Running had rushed out and grabbed her hand.

'Congratulations, Clare, this is just great.'

'Thanks, Charlie,' she said, as she looked up and saw Robert, his hammer still in his hand.

'Diden' I tell ye ye'd get it?' he said, quietly. 'Yer mother an' father woud be proud o' you. An' so am I,' he said, nodding vigorously. 'Come on, Charlie, come up t' the house. As you woud say, we've no champagne so we may make do wi' a drop o' tea.'

He turned quickly, letting the hammer drop on the bench by the door, before he limped off. She was sure there were tears in his eyes.

But a moment later, they were all smiling again. As they reached the front door, a small figure shot up the shortcut from the farm, a plate gripped firmly in his two hands.

'Here y'are,' he said, thrusting the plate with its freshly iced cake into Clare's hands. 'Ma says, "Well done, ye deserve it." Coud I have a wee piece o' cake too?'

The weeks that followed Clare's good news were among the happiest she'd ever spent. The weather stayed dry and warm, Robert was in excellent spirits, and the postman brought nothing but gifts and congratulations. Auntie Polly sent a dress, a skirt and some warm slacks, to help Clare get ready for going up to Belfast. Ronnie wrote a long enthusiastic letter, hinting he might manage a visit the following year. As well as his full time job on a Toronto newspaper he now wrote a regular column in a newspaper for Ulster-Scots exiles. He'd used her accounts of the forge and the events in the community as the basis of some of his weekly articles. 'Much better paid than the beauty hints,' he explained, knowing that otherwise she'd protest at the number of dollars he'd enclosed.

Even Sarah and Sadie wrote in reply to her letters. Sarah said that the Lord had looked kindly upon her and she must not stop going to church now she was a student. Sadie said there was nothing like a good education to help a girl get on in the world.

But the letter that brought greatest joy was from Andrew. As he'd expected, he'd be spending a few days at Drumsollen at the end of August. His good news was that Aunt Helen had invited him to Caledon and she'd said she'd be happy for Clare to come and stay. If that wasn't possible, she hoped she'd come over every day. She knew Ginny and Edward were looking forward to seeing her, as she was herself.

Clare was touched by the warmth of the invitation and overjoyed at the prospect of spending so much time with Andrew. She didn't feel she could leave Robert to go and stay at Caledon but Andrew assured her they'd collect her every day and stop in Armagh for any shopping she had to do.

Each morning, he arrived promptly at the forge with Edward, or Virginia, or both of them. Sometimes he drove Aunt Helen's small car, other times Virginia used the ancient Land Rover she'd bought to help with her job at the riding school where she started as a trainer in a few weeks' time. When all else failed, it was Edward who acted as chauffeur. Then they had to squash into the ancient, blue car he'd borrowed from the handyman who worked full-time on the elegant but crumbling gentleman's residence that was their home.

Clare loved the Caledon house, a long, low pavilion-style

residence with tall windows looking out over the lawns to trees and meadows beyond. It was full of fine furniture, silver and family portraits, but had none of the clutter and neglect she had found at Drumsollen, for it was a much loved home, the rooms full of flowers and plants, books and painting materials.

Aunt Helen had always painted, but had had no heart for it after the death of her husband. Coaxed by Virginia in the last few months, she'd begun again. She made sketches of the four of them and as the days passed it seemed that having four young people instead of two, did wonders for her spirits.

'Such good practice,' she would say, as she took out a pad and scribbled away, producing the head of one of them, a detail of a hand, the outline of the little group as they sat, or lay, resting after some activity.

'I think I should practise on you, Clare,' said Virginia, one afternoon as they relaxed after a vigorous three sets in the shade beside the tennis court. 'Are you game?'

'Depends what you want to practise, Ginny,' Clare laughed, as she propped herself up on one elbow and looked across at her. 'Not First Aid, please.'

'She needs to practise her backhand,' said Edward wearily. 'That's why you and Andrew always beat us.'

Andrew grinned and settled himself more comfortably.

'I'd say myself that you were just outclassed by superior players.'

Virginia poked him with her toe.

'You are a silly. I meant I ought to teach Clare to ride. Practise my teaching technique. Besides, poor old Conker isn't getting nearly enough exercise with all our jaunts and outings.'

'Conker?'

Clare shaded her eyes from the dazzle of the sun and looked quizzically at Ginny who'd rolled over on her stomach and was now resting on her elbows.

'My horse,' she explained. 'Her posh name is Tara Princess but I can't exactly call her that when I'm trying to get her over a fence. She's a chestnut, you see.'

Clare turned out to be an able pupil. She had no fear of either the chestnut mare nor the distance between her saddle and the ground. Ginny insisted on her practising every morning as soon as she arrived. Andrew and Edward observed her critically from the paddock gate. She sat straight-backed yet relaxed, as if she'd been doing it all her life.

'You're a natural,' said Ginny, after ten days, as Clare slid from the saddle and came round to stroke Conker's nose.

'And you're a very good teacher,' replied Clare, 'I'm sure you'll end up with your own riding stables one day.'

To her great surprise, she saw Ginny blush with pleasure and stride off towards the house.

'Come on, Clare. The boys will be waiting. Edward's been working on a yet more ghastly form of his obstacle golf. We'll have to show willing.'

The days passed quickly. Each one of the four young people grew increasingly aware that this holiday was a boundary, the end of one part of their life and the beginning of something quite new. Ginny was excited about the new job but apprehensive and needed to be reassured by the others. Edward was going back to school to do his A-levels, but as yet he had no idea what he wanted to do after. Meantime, he refused to think about it. Apart from cooking omelettes, packing picnic baskets and doing his share of the chores, he devoted himself entirely to devising bizarre games of skill which he usually won.

For Andrew, there'd been success and disappointment. He passed his exams creditably and acquired his 'piece of paper' but his uncle insisted he join the family firm in Winchester to do his articles. As he'd paid for most of his education, there was little Andrew could do but agree.

'Couldn't your grandfather find you something in Belfast?' asked Ginny, on one of the rare, wet afternoons. They were playing Monopoly on the big scrubbed table in the kitchen.

'Yes, I expect so,' Andrew replied sadly, 'but that's not the point. Beggars can't be choosers, as they say.'

'Hmm,' said Edward sharply, as he decided to buy property

on the Old Kent Road. 'Perhaps I'll take economics, become a property developer, make a fortune and *then* decide what I want to do.'

'What would *you* do Ginny, if you had a fortune?' asked Clare, fairly sure she could guess what her new friend would say.

'Oh, you know, Clare. I'd breed horses and train up show jumpers. But it costs a fortune to do it properly.'

'I'm sure Edward wouldn't mind making a fortune for you,' Clare said laughingly, as she saw Edward hold out his hand to Andrew for yet one more rent.

'What about you, Andrew' she asked, as he handed it over. 'If you had Edward's stacks of money?' She waved at his increasing pile of notes. 'What would you do?'

'Buy some cows.'

They all laughed, as Andrew threw a pair of sixes and began to protest.

'Yes, I would. I'd rent some of your spare acres, Edward. Buy a cottage in the village and start a dairy herd. Once I'd got it going, I'd look for a place of my own and see what arable I could have. I don't believe in monoculture, it's bad for the land,' he said calmly, as he moved round the board and once again landed on a piece of Edward's property.

'But what about you, Clare?' asked Ginny, as she lined up a new hotel on Bond Street.

'Travel, I think. Far away places with strange sounding names. But Europe first, France and Germany, all the places I know so well from my reading but have never actually seen.'

'But you wouldn't go and live abroad, would you, Clare?' asked Ginny, with a sideways look at Andrew.

Clare shook her head firmly.

'Oh good,' said Ginny with a sigh. 'I shall need you for my bridesmaid when I find a nice millionaire. I think that would be quicker than waiting for Edward to get rich,' she added, smiling with delight, as Edward landed on her most expensive piece of property.

Although they talked so much and spent so much time together, Clare and Andrew had very little time to be alone. Only in the evening, when he took her back to the forge, would they stop in some quiet field-entrance before they arrived to say a proper goodnight. But one evening at the end of their second week Virginia and Edward went off to a birthday party for a woman who looked after them when they were small, leaving them to their own devices. They'd walked down from the house and turned along the narrow path beside the stream that bounded the estate.

'Only two more days, Clare. How am I ever going to be able to part with you?' he said, taking her in his arms as soon as they were out of sight of the house.

'Perhaps your grandfather will come to our rescue, now he knows how you feel. When you told him about your uncle's plan, you said he hadn't realised how much you wanted to come home.'

'Mmm. He thought I'd be happy to be within reach of London and the bright lights. He said that's what he wanted at my age.'

They moved slowly along the bank of the stream, the evening sunlight spilling through the leaves, catching the shallow ripples and turning them to gold. Clouds of midges rose and fell in the cool, dark shadows beneath the heavy foliage on the far bank. Somewhere a blackbird sang.

'I suppose you do want different things at different ages,' Clare said, wondering if she could ever feel happier than she'd felt in these last weeks.

'I know what I shall always want,' he said firmly, stopping on the narrow path and taking both her hands. 'I want us to be together. However long it takes, that's what I want.'

The next evening, they left Caledon early, so that Clare could bring him to meet Robert properly. Charlie was there when they arrived, but the moment they stepped through the kitchen door, he remembered he'd another call he simply had to make. She'd never seen him disappear so fast in all the time she'd known him.

323

To her surprise, Robert was not at all put out by Andrew's presence on the settle by the stove. By the time she'd made tea, he and Robert were talking about horses as if she wasn't even there.

'He's a right fella,' said Robert, when she came back from seeing him off. 'Many's a young fella looks fine on a well-turned mare, but he's rightly on the ground forby.'

He lit two candles and prepared to put out the lamp before bed.

'You'll not go far astray there.'

22

T he large minute hand of the dusty clock above the blackboard jerked into a vertical position. Despite the scrape of
chairs on the bare wooden floor and latecomers dropping their
books and files on the worn and battered desks, Clare heard its
mechanical click quite distinctly. Lively greetings were thrown
back and forth across the room as long, undergraduate scarves
were unwound and draped over the backs of chairs. Ten o'clock
precisely.

She smiled to herself, glanced across at the empty table below
the noisy clock and went back to her study of the trees in
University Square. The chalk-smeared table would remain
untenanted for at least the next ten minutes. The professor
would arrive, apologise most courteously in French or in
English, or even in his own inimitable mixture of both, and
launch directly into an impassioned reading of French poetry
which defied you to deny it was the most inspired poetry ever
written.

Clare liked Henri Lavalle, enjoyed his lectures and sym-
pathised with his difficulty in arriving on time. This very able
scholar had never managed to figure out that his colleagues in the
department had learnt to lie in wait for him whenever he had a
lecture. All his students knew that there was always someone on
the landing who would want 'a quick word', a signature on a
document, a decision on some piece of departmental business. As
Henri Lavalle was far too courteous to reject their requests, they
saved themselves the effort of a proper visit to his study and he
ended up forever late for his lectures.

The trees in the square were an absolute picture. Even as Clare watched, a few golden fingers of chestnut floated slowly down through the spreading branches. Although there were rustling drifts of leaves on the pavements outside the handsome dwelling which now housed the French and German Department, the trees themselves were by no means bare as yet. Silhouetted against the blue of the sky, or the warm, red brick of the Library, the remaining leaves glowed in the calm, frosty air, their rich colour further enhanced by the slanting beams of sunlight.

Clare thought of Robert limping down to the forge on just such a bright morning, the frost still silvering its black roof where the sun had not yet caught it, beads of moisture hanging on a pair of gates, the long grass still crisp in the shadow of the hedge. She always thought of him in the mornings, particularly when she woke up in the big room in Elmwood Avenue that had once been Ronnie's. For three weeks now, as she'd made her breakfast in the tiny shared kitchen, she'd thought of him lighting the stove, boiling up the kettle and frying his own soda bread on the griddle. Then, as she walked along the leaf-strewn pavements to her lecture rooms her mind filled with a growing sense of excitement, which seemed to expand, day by day, as the horizons of her world spread ever wider.

Despite the many real pleasures of being made welcome and making new friends, Clare's first week in Belfast had not been easy or happy. The more she focused on her new life, the more she worried about Robert. By the time she stood on the Lisburn Road that first Friday evening waiting for Uncle Jack to pick her up on his way from work, she'd almost convinced herself the whole idea of being at university was impossible. She arrived back at the Grange, tense, anxious and uneasy, only to find Robert in the best of spirits, looking forward to seeing her.

'Shure amn't I as right as rain?' he declared, as she sat herself down after their tea and asked him about his week. 'Jamsey brings my dinner in a box of straw, as hot as it would be from the oven, aye an' maybe hotter if the wind was in the wrong direction,' he added, wryly. 'I have more papers than iver I had with all these new ones Charlie brings me, an' that wee lassie of June Wiley's is great. Comes in and redds up the place in no time an' tells me all the news forby.'

'Don't you mind being on your own at night?' she asked tentatively.

'I might think long if I were t' be awake,' he admitted, 'but sure I sleep the best at all.'

She had to admit all the arrangements she'd made with such care were working out really well. Margaret had said it'd be no effort at all to send over hot meals during the week and Clare knew she'd be able to pay for them once she had her first grant cheque. Charlie was only too happy to take Robert to do his shopping when he did his, and Helen Wiley who'd taken over Clare's old job, looking after Margaret's children on Saturday afternoons, was very ready to increase her earnings by coming in for an hour after school.

So Clare's first weekend had gone better than she could have ever imagined. She'd whizzed through the washing and ironing normally done in bits during the week, caught up on the local news, read to Robert from the papers, as she always had, and even managed to get through some work of her own while he was having his rests. When Uncle Jack arrived to take her back to Belfast on Sunday evening, Robert greeted him warmly and said he was expecting Charlie to appear any minute.

'Sure Sunday used to be a long old day, Jack,' he added, as Clare came back into the kitchen with her suitcase. 'But sure I niver know the time goin' these days what with one thing an' another.'

After that first visit, Clare awoke each morning with a rising sense of excitement. Each day held out such promise. There were hundreds of books in the library, friendly people to meet and new places to go. Sometimes she felt so like the little girl let loose in the sweetie shop, hardly knowing where to begin.

In the middle of her second week, Jessie took her to lunch in the Cotter's Kitchen. They sat in the warm, comfortable base-ment restaurant on a bitterly cold day and tried not to giggle as they read their way down the lengthy and mouth-watering menu.

'Bit of a change from Caffollas an' Fortes, an' our ninepence worth of chips after the pictures, isn't it?' said Jessie, raising her perfectly plucked eyebrows as she studied every item.

'Something smells wonderful,' replied Clare smiling, as she took in the decor, the check gingham tablecloths, the old bits of kitchen equipment hung on the walls, the spinning wheel perched on top of the canopy over the hearth. 'I think it must be the roast chicken.'

'D'ye fancy that with chips? Ye can have what ye like, it's my treat. I've had a pay rise.'

'Another one?'

'Mmm. Sold a couple of pictures last week. Expensive ones. Mr Burrows says the other staff get commission when they sell pictures, but because I'm in the office such a lot it's fairer to give me a pay rise. He's very decent like that.'

'How expensive?'

'Couple o' hundred pounds,' she said shyly. 'Hunting scenes. I pointed out how good the horses were and the detail in the shadows. The woman wouldn't have known one end of a horse from another, but the man caught on quick. He was out with the cheque book in no time.'

She winked at Clare as she waved to the waitress.

'Have ye heard from yer man Andrew then?' Jessie asked, as soon as she'd ordered.

'Yes, I had a letter on Monday.'

'A letter? D'ye mean he's learnt to write at last?'

Clare laughed and nodded. She wondered whether it was worth reminding Jessie that Andrew had been writing real letters for nearly a year now. Dear Jessie, she'd never under-stand why Andrew had a such a problem writing letters. It wasn't that she was unsympathetic, she just couldn't imagine a difficulty someone else might have if she hadn't got it herself.

'Woud'ye just look at that,' said Jessie, as the waitress put their meal in front of them. 'Ye'll be anybody's full cousin if ye finish that lot.'

The food was tasty and cooked to a turn and both girls were hungry. In the devoted silence that followed, Jessie forgot all about Andrew's letter-writing capacity. When Clare looked across at her to say how marvellous the chicken was, she found to her surprise that Jessie was totally wrapped up in her own thoughts.

'What about apple pie and ice cream?' Jessie asked suddenly, as the waitress collected their empty plates.

'Not sure I have room,' admitted Clare honestly, as she returned to the present.

Her own thoughts had moved far away and at the very moment Jessie spoke she was remembering the warm summer days she had spent with Andrew, Ginny and Edward.

'Ach, never mind having room, sure this is a celebration,' insisted Jessie firmly.

'Is it?'

Suddenly, Clare felt very uneasy. She felt sure something was about to happen that would bring change to her life. Whatever it was, however good it might be, she didn't want it to happen. Too much was happening already. But she knew you could never say things like that to Jessie.

'I'd love some apple pie,' she said brightly. 'Now tell me the good news.'

To her surprise, Jessie blushed. It was so unlike her, for a moment Clare was completely taken aback.

'We're goin' out tomorra to choose the ring,' she said abruptly.

'Oh Jessie, how marvellous. I'm so pleased,' she said as positively as she could manage, aware that tears were threatening to spill down her cheeks.

She was angry with herself. There was no reason why such happy news should make her feel so ridiculously apprehensive.

'Are you having a party?' she asked quickly.

329

'Yes. One here and one in Tullyard. Ye'd better be free for both or there'll be trouble. Tullyard on Saturday week. Ye'll be home, won't ye?'

'Yes, of course, I will. What would you and Harry like for your engagement present?'

'Ach, away wi' ye. Ye need all the money ye've got.'

Clare smiled. What Jessie lacked in perception she more than made up in kindness. As Robert had once said of her, 'Sure Jessie's that good-natured she'd give you the bite goin' inta her mouth.'

'You won't believe this, Jessie,' she said, as she sampled her apple pie, 'But I'm better off than I've ever been. I can't understand all this business about penniless students. I can pay for Granda's dinners and Helen Wiley to do a bit of tidying and my food, and rent, and the odd coffee in the Union and still have money left over.'

'That's only because ye can make it go twice as far as anyone I know,' said Jessie promptly. 'I don't know how ye manage it. Ye ought to be working in a bank. You'd make their fortune.'

Clare laughed easily, so grateful the dark shadow had passed. How silly one could be sometimes. Jessie and Harry were getting engaged and she would be there at their party in Tullyard, with Mrs Rowentree and Aunt Sarah and all Jessie's friends and neighbours, nearly all of whom she knew herself. She was looking forward to it already.

'*Mam'selles, Messieurs, je regrette beaucoup . . .*'

The familiar voice cut through Clare's thoughts just as she'd begun to consider what she should wear to Jessie's party the following evening.

She rose to her feet as the Professor swept in, the sleeves of his gown flapping like an agitated hen trying to collect her chicks.

'*Asseyez vous,*' he said, hastily, his eyes running round the familiar faces.

Suddenly Clare felt chill, though the room was now warm from the ancient radiators and the heat of young bodies.

'*Mademoiselle Hamilton*,' he began . . .

Although he continued in French and referred to one of the College porters as a 'custodian' his message was clear. A gentleman had arrived by car looking for her. The custodian was waiting for her downstairs. He sincerely hoped it was not '*mauvaises nouvelles*', but the look on his face suggested it was. She stumbled from the room and found the porter at the foot of the stairs. When she saw his face, she felt '*mauvaises nouvelles*' was the very phrase for it.

'There's a Mr Jack Hamilton, miss, at the main entrance. I'm afeerd it's bad news but he wouldn't say what,' he explained as he fell into step beside her. He reached out a hand for her books which she was in danger of dropping.

'Is there anyone in the family poorly?'

'Well, all my grandparents are elderly, but my brother lives with Uncle Jack's parents. He can be a bit wild. He's broken his arm once and he had to have stitches in his leg when he fell off his bicycle. He will go racing around the place,' she said breathlessly, as they rounded the library at speed and made for the main entrance.

She could see Uncle Jack's car parked in the space normally used only by important visitors.

'Mr Hamilton.'

At the sound of his name, Uncle Jack jumped up from his seat by the fire in the Porter's Lodge and came towards her in two great strides. The minute she looked at him, she knew it wasn't Granny or Granda Hamilton or William.

'It's Granda Scott, isn't it?'

He nodded sadly.

'Aye, it is. Jamsey found him in the forge about an hour ago. He'd slipped down beside the anvil. It must've been very quick.'

Clare didn't even notice the chair that suddenly appeared behind her nor the 'custodian's' sad shake of the head.

'Would ye drink a cup of tea, miss? It wouldn't take a minute.'

'That's very kind of you,' Clare said, amazed that her voice

331

was perfectly normal. 'But I shall need to be getting home right away.'

As she walked to Uncle Jack's car, all she could think of was that she had to get out Robert's best shirt and a starched collar. He always got so anxious if someone died and he couldn't find what he needed.

By the time Clare had visited Elmwood Avenue to collect clothes, tell Mrs McGregor what had happened, leave a message for Jessie at the gallery and phone Uncle Bob to ask him to contact the rest of the family, the sun was high in the sky and the promising morning had turned into the loveliest of autumn days.

As they drove out of the city only the merest wisps of cloud remained in the clear blue sky. Beyond the houses and the trees that lined the main road, the steep slopes of the Antrim Hills rose clear of all human habitation, only fields and bushes breaking the sweep as they reached higher, and higher, until at last their crests were free of any sign men could put upon them and the rock faces stood sharp against the sky, shaped only by the frost, by the wind, and by the sun.

Clare looked up at them dry-eyed and silent, leaving Uncle Jack free to concentrate on the road, busy enough at this midday hour.

'I to the hills will lift mine eyes, From whence doth come mine aid, My safety cometh from the Lord, Who heaven and earth hath made,' she repeated quietly, unaware that she had spoken out loud.

Jack glanced across at her, startled by the sound of her voice.

'What do you think, Uncle Jack?' she asked, her tone low, but steady. 'Is there someone up there to help us? Granda never went to church, but he always insisted I went. I'm not sure what he believed. He never talked about things like that.'

'No, Clare, he didn't. None of that generation did,' Jack replied, regretfully. 'If you want to know what Robert believed, you have to look at how he lived. He was a good man.'

She nodded and tears trickled down her cheeks.

'I suppose I'm just worrying about what we have to do.'

'D'you mean, arranging the funeral and suchlike?'

She rummaged in her jacket pockets for a handkerchief, blew her nose, and admitted she didn't know where to start.

'That'll be the least of your problems, love. There'll be plenty to see to what has to be done. Myself for one, your Uncle Bob for another. That's not your problem.'

'What *is* my problem, Uncle Jack?'

She thought he hadn't heard her, but her voice had gone again, so she couldn't repeat the question. Instead, she took a last look at the hills as the road swung away into the gently undulating lowlands beyond Lurgan, where, through a gap in the hawthorn hedge, you might just catch a glimpse of Lough Neagh, shimmering beyond the water meadows.

'You've loved and cared for Robert for half your life, Clare. Your problem is he'll leave a hole in your heart.'

She hadn't expected such directness nor such accuracy. She didn't bother to wipe away the tears, they were flowing far too fast. She just nodded and stared out at the distorted images of trees as Jack turned off the main road and took the road that would bring them home through Loughgall. Already they were in home territory. She and Jessie had cycled, walked, visited and delivered messages over every square mile of it. She knew every house, every tree, every patch of wildflowers. If her world really was a teacup, it was a very full one.

Though the journey from Belfast had taken a long, long hour, the last minutes moved so quickly she couldn't keep up with them. Loughgall was far behind. Now they were passing Scott's Corner, coming up the hill, pausing, turning across the road and bumping into the foot of the lane below the forge. They stopped behind another car already parked there.

It was Charlie Running's.

She got out, took her suitcase from the back seat, stood looking at the silent forge, the door open as usual. Pale smoke was rising from the chimney of the cottage. It was all so ordinary, so normal, it was just as if Robert had stopped off

333

to have a mug of tea with Charlie. But he wasn't. There'd be no Robert to greet her, as he'd greeted her last Friday. There'd be no Robert to greet her, ever again.

She walked quickly on up the path, her legs shaking, to the front door, which stood open as it always did.

'William Perrott of Ballyhenry was fined ten shillings at Armagh Crown Court on Thursday last for driving his horse and cart near Keady without a light . . .'

She heard Charlie's voice as she went through into the kitchen. He was sitting beside a coffin which stood on trestles across the fireplace in the sitting room, reading from Thursday's *Armagh Guardian*.

'Ach, there ye'are, Clare,' he said, jumping to his feet. 'We were waitin' for you. Just finishin' off the paper we were readin' last night.'

He threw his arms round her and she held him tight as he began to sob. Over his shaking shoulders, she saw Robert's face, the marble skin drawn tight over his sharp bones. He was wearing his best black suit with a white shirt and a stiff collar. She had never before seen his face look so clean.

'Robert asked me to see to things for him a long time ago, Clare, after yer Granny died,' Charlie began, collecting himself and wiping his face on his sleeve. 'He reminded me a couple o' weeks ago, just before ye went away. Yer not annoyed wi' me, are ye?'

'No,' she said honestly. 'I'm very grateful. I wouldn't have known what to do,' she said quite steadily. And then her voice gave way again. 'Charlie, what'll we do without him?'

Standing by the coffin, looking down at the details of a face never before seen in repose, Clare felt as if time had stopped. There was no moment beyond this moment. The clocks in the house had all been silenced at the hour of his death. She could not imagine them ever striking again. She stared at the satin and lace that overlapped his dark suit, the one she had brushed for every Twelfth, every funeral, for the last nine years. So clean.

Pristine. After all his years of toil and sweat in the soot and grime, he was so clean he would laugh if he could see himself.

'God bless all here.'

She turned and saw Jamsey lay a large dish wrapped in a clean cloth on the kitchen table. He nodded at Jack who was standing over the kettle, waiting to make a cup of tea, and came to stand beside them.

For a moment, he looked at Robert's face. Silent tears grew in the corners of his eyes. He held out his hand to Clare.

'Ellie, I'm sorry for yer trouble. He was a good father to you.'

'Yes, Jamsey, he was,' she said, shaking his hand and ignoring her own tears.

She wondered if she dare ask him why he'd gone looking for Robert this morning when normally he would have left the water in its usual place, if there was no one around.

'He was gettin' very frail, Robert was,' began Jamsey abruptly. 'I coud hardly hear the hammer when he did a wee bit of work. An' I couden' hear a bit of it this mornin'. His hammerin' days is over, Clarey, an' he's in a better place. Will we sing Robert a hymn before I go?'

Clare nodded.

When the new minister from the parish church on the hill arrived a little later to make arrangements for the funeral service, he was surprised to find three men and a young girl standing by an old man's coffin singing. It was not the singing that puzzled him, for psalms were sung often enough and prayers said, by grieving families. But he had never before heard 'Once in Royal David's City' sung over a coffin.

As Clare struggled with the hours of that tear-stained Friday, Aunt Sarah's words of long ago came back to her. 'All things pass,' she said to herself again and again. What worried her most was what would happen later in the day and on the following day. Scores of visitors would come, for the forge had been a fixed point in the universe for so long, for so many. She wanted to be able to make them all welcome, but however was she to manage?

She was standing down by the forge, saying goodbye to Jack who had to go over to Liskeyborough, when a grocer's van turned into the lane and made its way gingerly towards her. After saying how sorry he was for her trouble, the driver began to unpack and carry into the house enough food to have kept Robert and Clare going for months. Johnny had not forgotten the needs of a wake. As soon as Bob told him of their father's death, he'd rung the grocer in Armagh with whom he'd served his time thirty years earlier and put through an order.

While Johnny was summoning food, Bob was on the phone to the Railway Bar, placing an order which Eddie Robinson went and collected later that afternoon. When Eddie arrived to stack the boxes in Robert's empty bedroom, Margaret came with him, bringing all her better china and glass, so they'd not run short.

Bob and Johnny themselves turned up early the next morning with Sarah and Sadie and made it clear to Clare that whatever she wanted done would be done. To Clare's surprise even Sarah and Sadie made themselves useful without any of their customary awkwardness.

Confused as Clare was by the turbulence of her own feelings, and unsure how she could cope with the days to come, she was soon deeply heartened by those who came to pay their respects. She found herself surrounded by people who would not allow anything to mar the proper and seemly departure of a man whom the whole community had known and respected.

As the hours passed, people came and went. They stood by the coffin in clean clothes and spoke the expected, well-used phrases. Whether they knew her personally or not, all who came offered her their love and support, because they knew Robert had loved her. It seemed as if they spoke to him by comforting her. She knew every soul who had crossed the threshold since she came home, would have done anything she asked of them and been honoured in the asking.

Late on Saturday afternoon, with all the preparations made for a busy evening and her aunts drinking tea by the stove,

Clare slipped out of the house and made her way into the orchard. She went to find some berries or leaves to put in the green glass jar that always sat on the table, something everyday, to complement the florist's wreaths, the heavy creations of massed blooms which filled the whole house with the scent of autumn.

The light was fading, the lank grass already damp with dew, as she made her way along her own, familiar path. At every season, the orchard gave her flowers for the table. The celandines and wood anemones in early spring, the primroses and violets in April and May. After them came the turn of the trees in the hedgerow, blackthorn, wild cherry, crab. In May the whole orchard was a cloud of pink and white, the apple blossom itself. Later, after the damson and pear had shed their short-lived blossoms, there were buttercups and honeysuckle to pick. Then came the fruits of autumn, blackberry clusters with tinted leaves, dark sloes with tiny, dark green leaves and murderous thorns, and hawthorn, crooked twigs hung with passionate red berries and a few surviving bright yellow leaves.

Only in the deepest winter months was she at a loss to find something for the table. Then she would look hopefully at the geraniums stored in the boys' room hoping for a late flower and a few spicy smelling leaves, or remember to ask Jessie for twigs of winter jasmine from her mother's garden. The old green glass jar she found in the rubbish dump had never gone empty. It must not be empty now.

The air was already cool, the sun's rays slanted at shallow angles, picking up the windfalls, pale globes in the tangled grass, well marked by the boring of insects and the determined peckings of the blackbirds.

She ran her eye over the rough barks of the apple trees and made for the hedgerow, spotted some rosehips well out of reach and the feathery fronds of Old Man's Beard, which flew away if only you touched it.

Disappointed, she made for the old well in search of the small sharp-toothed ferns that made their home just above the water level. But there were none. The well was low after a dry autumn, what remained of the ferns were dry and shrivelled.

'There's always the spindleberry,' she said aloud, as she sat herself down where she could contemplate the bars of evening cloud reflected in the clear water.

So many people, so many words spoken. Only when she thought of the spindleberry, a bush which grew right opposite the front door, did it dawn on her it was solitude, not the flowers, that she needed most. Perhaps it'd always been so. Since she'd been a little girl, she'd tramped the lanes and hedgerows 'looking for flowers'. Often she found them, for she had discovered many quiet corners over the year. She knew what bloomed and when it bloomed, unthought of and unseen. In those walks and searches, she'd put together her thoughts as much as the posies she brought home for Robert.

'Just one more posy for Robert,' she whispered.

Tomorrow, somewhere after three, the polished oak coffin would be lowered into the reopened family plot. According to the gravestone, three generations of Scotts had been buried there. But gravestones were recent things and costly. He always said himself he was the fifth blacksmith in the line. Then he'd laugh and say his son Robert was a bank manager and he didn't blame him one bit.

She could smile now. Last night she'd even found herself laughing as Charlie told stories about the mischief the village boys got up to and how Robert would try to get them out of the trouble they'd landed themselves in. So many who'd sat in the big kitchen in the course of the long evening had similar stories to tell about Robert's kindness and shrewdness.

The sun came out below a smoky band of evening cloud and turned to liquid gold the pool of water where she sat. Suddenly, she was sitting by a stream with Andrew, throwing pebbles into the shallow water, delighting in their tiny splash, the way the ripples spread in the dappled shade where the trees overhung the riverbank.

'How long ago was that?' she whispered, as she tossed a

fragment of twig into the sunlit pool and watched the ripples rush towards her.

'How I wish you were here, Andrew,' she said, as she got up, suddenly aware the aunts would wonder where she was.

Deep shadows filled the hedgerows and lay beneath the old trees. She shivered in the chill, misty air and glanced towards the cottage as she made her way back. Through one of the small windows she saw a bent and shadowy figure lean forward to trim a lamp.

For one moment her heart stood still. No, it couldn't be Robert. Robert's days of hammering and lighting lamps were over. He was gone. And she was quite alone.

23

Robert Scott's funeral at Grange churchyard was one of the largest anyone could remember. For so many who stood in the pale, autumn sunshine Robert's passing was not only an immediate personal loss, but one of those events which they recognised as a critical point in their own history and the history of their community.

The crowds of mourners flowed from the churchyard and spread out over the broad, roughly surfaced space opposite the church gates. As they made their way slowly towards the ponies and traps tethered across the road, or the handful of cars parked under the wall of the churchyard itself, they greeted each other with nods and handshakes. A phrase as familiar as the time-honoured 'I'm sorry for your trouble', spoken so often at the wake or at the graveside, echoed back and forth: 'Ah, 'tis the end of an era, the end of an era.'

There were men who had sat on the hard wooden benches of the Orange Hall with Robert when they were just lads of seventeen and he had already served his time. Women who were infants in the schoolroom, when he was a big boy carrying turf for the fire. Their grown sons and daughters, who'd brought work to the forge since they were youngsters. All looked around bleakly as they turned their backs on his grave and called to mind friends and relatives already at rest on the hill top behind them.

Their own youth and prime was now long past, but harder still to bear was the disappearance of the world in which they had grown up, day by day. They knew they could no more halt the changes they saw at every turn than wind back the clock, regain their own lost vigour, or bring Robert back to his rightful place in the forge.

'Ach, the place will be desperate quiet without him,' said Harry Todd, as he shook hands with his cousin John Williamson.

Robert's hammer had echoed like a heartbeat throughout Harry's lifetime, its silences punctuating the weeks as clearly as the church bell.

'An' where will we go for the news?' asked John, a well-off farmer, who didn't appear to recognise either his telephone, or his new television set, as any substitute for the worn and grimy bench inside the half-door.

A sudden chill breeze stirred the dust and blew yellowed leaves against the stone wall below the old schoolroom. Once, long ago now, both men had sat in that large, bare room with Master Ebbitt and young Miss Rowentree, chanting their multiplication tables, the names of the continents, of the Kings and Queens of England and of the counties of Ireland. The building was boarded up now, the roof rapidly deteriorating. It was beginning to look like the cottages where they themselves had been born, storehouses now, a short distance away from the newly built bungalows with running water, electricity and wide, picture windows.

'It's hard on the wee lassie, an' her lost her parents not that long back,' said John, with a slight backward glance to where the family still stood by the graveside, studying the cards on the wreaths laid out on the trampled grass, while the gravedigger and his helper shovelled back and tamped down the dry brown earth.

'Aye. Clever girl she is too. He was that proud o' her whin she got the scholarship. Ah niver heard Robert talk so much about anythin' in all the years I knew him, as he did about that scholarship. What'll happen to her now, I wonder?'

'Sure only time will tell, man. But I'd say she'd make her way. She has a head on her shoulders forby being clever, though

341

she's heartsore at losin' him. Did ye see her drop in the wee posy of flowers after Bob and Johnny threw down the earth? Fuschies, they were. I wondered to meself when I saw them where she had them growin', to have them flower so late. But then, that house always was kinda sheltered.'

They paused and turned to watch June Wiley hurry past with her eldest daughter, Helen. They nodded knowingly as mother and daughter disappeared into the lane that ran from the top of Church Hill down past Robinson's orchard, along by their horse trough and across the front of their potato house and machine shed to come out beside the forge.

'She's doin' the tea for the relatives,' said John, who was June's uncle. 'Bob and Johnny have a fair way to go the night, though I heerd Clarey is for Rowentree's with her friend Jessie afore she goes back t' Belfast.'

'Is that so?' Tom enquired, as he unhitched his pony and trap from the gate into his brother-in-law's field and hoisted himself awkwardly into the driving seat. 'Have ye yer car?'

'Aye, but I parked it beyond by Colvin's to be outa the way o' the hearse,' John replied, turning on his heel.

'Ye'll be down one night soon?' Tom said quickly, to his cousin's departing figure.

John raised a hand in acknowledgement, but didn't pause. His bad leg had started to ache with all the standing. Once it started, it didn't know when to stop.

'Ye'll be welcome,' Tom called, raising his voice. 'There's not many folk call these days. It bees lonely of an evenin'.'

He gathered up his reins and called to the mare. With a last look at the Scotts, arranging wreaths on the closed up grave, he turned the trap back the way he'd come, to his own empty house at Ballynick.

After the crowds of people who had packed the house since Friday evening, Clare found it strange to walk into the big kitchen with her Scott uncles and aunts. Uncle Jack had said he thought he ought to stay with Granny and Granda Hamilton

342

when he took them back to Liskeyborough. Jessie said she'd be down when she'd seen Harry off. But Clare knew no one else would call today, not even dear Charlie. In the unwritten rules of the community, only 'family', or those especially invited by the family, might visit between the laying to rest of a loved one and the necessary taking up again of life on the following day.

'There ye are, love, it's all ready. There's a second pot just brewing,' said June Wiley as she greeted them at the door. 'Now be sure ye eat somethin', for I'm sure ye had no lunch.'

'June, I don't know what I'd have done without you. You've been so good,' said Clare, as she walked outside with her. 'And you too, Helen,' smiling at the tall, fair-haired girl who'd so brightened the days for Robert, these last three weeks.

'Aye, well, Clare, you've done your share t' help yer friends. It's a small thing to help you now. Come up if there's anythin' you want or if you feel lonely. You know yer way.'

She turned back into the house. Sarah and Sadie were handing round sandwiches. Bob and Johnny had brought extra chairs from the sitting room, but Sarah and Sadie seated themselves on the settle when they finished pouring tea. They looked as awkward as ever.

No one sat in Robert's chair. The clocks were silent still but the kettle singing on the stove raised her spirits, a small continuing thing in a world that seemed otherwise to have stopped. She drew it aside before it boiled up and started rattling its lid and pouring out steam.

'Desperate big crowd,' said Johnny, when the silence grew too much for him.

'And such a lovely lot of wreaths,' added Sarah.

Clare listened as they repeated all the comments they'd already made at the graveside while they'd read the labels on the wreaths. That had been her own worst time. Even worse than seeing the coffin lowered into the dry earth. Her eyes were so misted with tears, she couldn't read the words out loud, which they expected her to do. All she could think of were the cards once written for Ellie and Sam.

It was Jessie, dear Jessie who had stepped forward and read out the tributes for her in a voice Clare hardly recognised.

'Clare dear, I don't want to upset you on a day like today, but I think I ought to ask you about my father's will,' began Bob, tentatively, as he put his empty teacup back on the table.

Clare smiled at him and shook her head.

'I don't think he had one. He never mentioned it.'

Bob nodded. It was no more than he expected.

'Would there be anywhere he kept papers or money? I think we should just make sure.'

They left Sarah and Sadie to search the Bible and the huge Bible commentaries, between the pages of which Robert sometimes kept a spare pound or two for emergencies and went into his bedroom. It was already dim and shadowy for as the afternoon drew on towards dusk the heavy furniture absorbed what little light filtered in through the tiny orchard window.

'I think there's an Ulster Bank book in one of those tiny drawers,' Clare said, pointing at the dressing table. 'If there was a will, he'd have put it there.'

'Have you the key?'

Clare shook her head and pulled open both drawers. One contained his pension book and the freewill offering envelopes from the Presbyterian Church, the other held a battered bank book and a yellowed policy document. Provincial Friendly Society Burial Fund, it said. It was dated 1904, the year Robert was married, and was fully paid up in 1929.

'As far as Johnny and I are concerned, Clare, anything father left is yours,' he said quietly, as he picked up the bank book and opened it.

He smiled wryly and handed it to her.

The account had been closed a month earlier with a withdrawal of twenty-one pounds, two shillings and elevenpence.

'Ye'll need to be buying books and suchlike,' Robert said, as she opened the envelope he'd handed her the night before she left for Belfast.

When she drew out the four papery fivers and protested that

344

it was too much and too good of him, he'd laughed and said what he'd always said whenever he'd given her money, even as a very little girl: 'Ah, sure there's corn in Egypt yet.'

She stood leafing through the bank book, aware that Bob was watching her. The entries were almost all in the same hand, a flowing copperplate in black ink that had faded only slightly. The book began in 1931 with a Brought Forward entry of forty-seven pounds, two and tenpence. Over the next fifteen years, Robert's savings had grown to three hundred pounds. In 1946, there were a cluster of withdrawals taking the account right back to fifty pounds. Then there was a deposit of two hundred and sixty. That would be the money for Granny's funeral. She would have had a Burial Fund policy too. The next withdrawal was in August 1947. She knew from the amount that it was for her school uniform. From then on, Robert had made regular small withdrawals. Perhaps some of those payments for gates which Robert had said would cover the rent for weeks hadn't actually turned up after all.

'I'm sorry, Clare, I could have done more. I didn't realise things were so bad,' said Bob, leaning against the chest of drawers by the door.

'You've always been kind and very generous,' she protested. 'He was always saying how good you were, particularly at Christmas.'

For a moment, Clare thought Bob was going to cry himself.

'He was very independent, in his own way,' she went on quickly. 'He wasn't ungracious, just quietly determined. I think maybe I'm a bit like him.'

Bob smiled warmly.

'Clare, will you let me pay the rent for you till you're through university? You won't want to give up the house will you?'

'Oh no, I couldn't do that,' she burst out, horrified at the thought of it. 'It's my home. It's all I have now,' she added more quietly. 'But I can manage the rent. My grant is far more than I imagined it would be.'

'That's because it's a full grant,' he said, knowledgeably. 'The

345

grants are means tested and my father had no means. No means at all,' he added, 'and him worked that hard all his life.'

Suddenly and quite unexpectedly, Bob did burst into tears and Clare put her arms round him.

'Oh yes, he had, Bob,' she insisted. 'He had all the means he needed. When he said, "We'll get what'll do us," he meant it. I don't think he's ever wanted anything he couldn't have. At least, not while I've known him.'

Bob mopped himself up on a large white handkerchief and nodded.

'I think you're right, Clare. It may not always have been like that, but I've felt he was content these last years. There's not many end their life in as good heart as Robert. That's worth more than a fat bank book,' he ended as he put the tattered book back in the drawer. 'What about this?' he asked, picking up the policy.

'I think he asked Charlie to see to that.'

'And what about his clothes? Would you like us to take them all away with us, so you won't have to go through them?'

Clare shook her head.

'That's very thoughtful of you, but Charlie knows an old man in Ballybrannan who's badly in need of them. He says he won't mind all the darns and mends, he'll be only too glad to get them.'

'So that's everything then?'

Clare smiled weakly.

'No, you've forgotten one thing,' she said, as she pulled out the wide central drawer in Robert's washstand and handed Bob his silver fob watch.

He turned it over in his hand and read the inscription on the back: 'Robert Scott 1902, From CR, who will never forget.'

'CR?' he asked, surprised. 'I thought my mother gave him that as a wedding present.'

'So did I,' she admitted honestly, as she surveyed the other items in the drawer, hoping to find a keepsake for Johnny. 'What about these for Uncle Johnny?' she asked, producing a

velvet-lined box with matching tiepin and cufflinks. 'Auntie
Polly sent them from Canada and he was very proud of them.'

Back in the kitchen, Sadie and Sarah were brushing dust and
fluff from their black suits. The Bibles and Bible commentaries
were piled high on the table with the remains of the sandwiches
and cake. Sitting beside them was a single pound note, streaked
and grimy from the pocket of his working trousers.

'It really is time we were going, Bob,' said Sadie sharply, as
they came back into the kitchen.

Johnny was jingling his car keys when Clare offered him the
box with the tiepin and cuff links. He looked at Sarah dubiously
but thrust them into his coat pocket with a hurried word of
thanks as his wife walked past him into the hall to use the
mirror and the last of the daylight to put on her hat.

'Ring me, Clare, if there's anything either of us can do,' Bob
said, as he kissed her goodbye.

'Yer a great girl, Clare,' Johnny said, hugging her awkwardly.

'I hope your studies go well, Clare,' said Sadie, tottering
slightly in her very high heels, as she followed after Bob into the
gathering dusk. 'There's nothing like a good education to help
you get on in life,' she added as Clare walked down the lane
with them to where the cars were parked below the forge.

Of the four black-suited figures she might not see again for
many a day, only Bob seemed sad as he waved to her before he
reversed down to the empty main road.

But the last word was Sarah's. As soon as she'd arranged her
skirt carefully beneath her bottom so that it wouldn't crease,
she wound down the car window and leaned out.

'Make sure you read your Bible every day, Clare,' she said, as
Johnny started the engine. 'You can keep on re-using the notes
I gave you last Christmas. There is just so much to be gained by
rereading the same passages at regular intervals.'

And then Johnny, too, reversed down to the empty main
road and set off on the long journey back to Fermanagh.

There was still light outdoors as the dusk faded and the hush
of evening deepened over the quiet land. Clare stood under the

rose trellis at the front of the house for a long time, listening to the blackbirds as they called and scuffled before settling to roost. When she glimpsed the first star she stepped back into the kitchen and found it so dark she couldn't have picked her way between the abandoned chairs but for the glow of the stove, which cast their tall shadows against the distempered walls.

She carried the chairs back to their place in the sitting room, ignored the scattered remains of tea and dropped down on the settle. It was the first time she had been able to sit quietly by herself since the moments by the well in the orchard the previous day.

She'd always loved the kitchen when it was lit only by the radiance from the stove. Often, when Robert rose to light the lamp, she felt sad as the kindly shadows were driven away. In the flickering firelight, one was not aware of the soot-blackened ceiling or the scuffed, varnished paper that covered the lower half of the walls. The dirt and grime she struggled to keep at bay simply disappeared and she could enjoy the gleam of well-loved objects, the wag of the wall with its brass weights, the shiny black noses of the china dogs on the mantelpiece, the well-polished surface of the mahogany drop-leaf table that saw service only at Christmas, the wink of the glass panes in the corner cupboard.

She looked across at the empty chair and for a moment imagined she saw the faint haze of smoke from his pipe. She smiled to herself. She was sure the smell of his tobacco would always linger in her mind. Judging by the pained look on Sarah's face when she'd come back with Uncle Bob from Granda's room, the Bibles and Bible commentaries were thoroughly pickled in his favourite 'Mick McQuaid' tobacco.

On the mahogany table, an old stone jar held a bunch of gold and bronze chrysanthemums. They were not the impressive blooms the local florists had used for the wreaths, they were spray chrysanthemums, garden grown, smaller and more homely, with a wonderful spicy smell. They had been waiting

348

for her when she came back from the orchard and found John Wiley lighting the Tilley lamp under the watchful eyes of Sadie and Sarah.

'The Senator and The Missus sent these for you, Clare,' he said, drawing her over to the scrubbed table where he'd laid the blooms in their brown-paper wrapping. 'An' I've a wee somethin' here from Andrew forby,' he added quietly, as she bent down to see if there was any rainwater left in the galvanised bucket in the big cupboard.

'Does Andrew know about Granda?' she asked, straightening up immediately.

'Aye. He phones his Granda fairly regular,' he explained, 'but the Richardsons were up at Caledon on Friday, so he got June, an' of course she toll' him. So he rang again later, an' asked the Senator for these.'

John took from the deep pocket of his coat an old tin box. Inside, half a dozen small sprays of fuchsia with the pendant blooms of Clare's Delight were carefully packed in damp moss. She had burst into tears and clutched John as if she would never let him go.

'Ach, there now, Clarey,' he said, putting his arms round her. 'Sure Robert was a good age. You'd not want to 'ave seen him poorly, now woud you?'

She shook her head vigorously and mopped up her tears as quickly as she could. What had made her cry this time was the thought of the Senator, a man she had come to know and like, an exact contemporary of Robert himself, going to his greenhouse and cutting his precious blooms, surely the last blooms of the season, to send to her, because Andrew had asked him if he could spare them.

The fire was dropping low and the room growing chill. Remembering that Jessie would be arriving soon, she stirred herself, made up the stove and lit the lamp. The soft, yellowy light grew as she turned up the wick and the familiar gentle hiss broke the silence of the room. How many times had she watched Robert light the lamp? Now, she would have to go

349

on lighting it until the electric came. According to the newspaper, it wouldn't be long now.

She shook her head and paused, staring up at the soot-blackened boards of the ceiling where tiny flecks of distemper had fallen off, leaving white marks on the dark surfaces. She stood, a large, empty teapot in her hands and knew, suddenly and quite clearly, that she would never look up at the blackened ceiling and see a light bulb hanging there. For a moment, she was completely taken aback.

'And why should I?' she said aloud, recovering herself.

She could imagine how unforgiving the electric light would be, illuminating all the dark corners. It would cast harsh shadows and show up the sad shabbiness of this well-loved room. Yes, of course, 'the electric' made life easier. Granny and Granda Hamilton and their immediate neighbours had all had it put in this year. They all said how much work it saved and how much less cleaning there was. But no one ever spoke of what had been lost when it came.

'Hello, Clare, how're ye doin?'

'Oh, Jessie, how good to see you,' she said, as her friend walked in, the fur collar of her coat beaded with tiny specks of rain. 'You shouldn't have come down for me, you know. I'd have come up later and you could've had longer with Harry.'

'Ach, not atall. He'll be late enough by the time he gets back to Belfast,' she said dismissively, her back to Clare as she slipped off her coat and parked it over a chair. 'Did ye get yer aunties off all right?'

Clare grinned.

'Sarah told me to make sure I read my Bible every day.'

As Jessie raised her hands in a familiar gesture of despair, Clare caught the glint of diamonds.

'Come on, Jessie, let's see it. You kept your gloves on this afternoon,' she said cheerfully.

She saw Jessie's face crumple. She seemed so awkward and uncomfortable and not like her usual self at all. She'd been pale when she'd arrived, but Clare thought it was just the cold of the night air. Now she was beginning to think something was wrong.

'I'd have called the party off, Clare, if it hadn't been for the message ye left me on Friday,' she said, uneasily.

'Of course you would, I know that,' Clare said reassuringly. 'Do you really think Robert would have been very pleased if I'd let you? "Ach, a lot o' nonsense. Shure life goes on. Isn't it grate news about Jessie." That's what he'd have said, Jessie, isn't it?'

Jessie nodded. Robert had no time for sentimentality. But she was still ill-at-ease as she held out her hand for Clare's benefit. The tiny circle of diamonds winked again.

'Oh it's lovely, Jessie,' said Clare warmly. 'Is that a sapphire in the middle?'

'Yes. Harry said it was to match my eyes,' she said flatly. 'He's always saying daft things like that.'

'It's not daft. You have lovely blue eyes and you look gorgeous in that coat. You really can wear posh clothes,' Clare said enthusiastically.

To her great surprise, she saw tears wink in the corner of Jessie's eyes and her lips begin to tremble.

'Oh Jessie, love, what's wrong? What is it? Have I said something?'

For one awful moment Clare wondered if Jessie might be pregnant. Something awful must have happened to upset her so. She hadn't seen her cry like this since the night she'd found her in the barn after her father shot himself.

'Ach, it's nothin' you said. It's just everythin',' she sobbed. 'I have Harry, an' we're engaged an' everythin' in the garden's rosy an' you've lost Robert an' Andrew is away over in England an' . . .'

Jessie voice failed her and she broke down into floods of tears.

'And what, Jessie?' Clare repeated. Whatever Jessie wasn't telling her was going to be very bad news indeed. Suddenly, she felt sick with tension and she couldn't bear to wait a moment longer.

Jessie struggled with a minute scrap of lace and muttered incoherently.

'Please, Jessie,' Clare pleaded. 'Just tell me. Tell me *now*.'

But Jessie was so distraught it took some time before she was able to say anything coherent. When finally Clare grasped what Jessie was saying she felt the blood run from her cheeks and her hands go stone cold.

On the way home from Robert's funeral, Mrs Rowentree had stopped to give a lift to a local girl who'd gone to the same secretarial college in Belfast as Jessie. Maisie Armstrong had got a job in a solicitor's office in Armagh and had come back to live at home. She'd asked Mrs Rowentree how Jessie was and if she and Clare were sharing a flat in Belfast. Mrs Rowentree said no, they weren't, and wondered what had put that idea into the girl's head. When she enquiried further Maisie grew so embarrassed and awkward Mrs Rowentree had pressed her to explain. Finally, she'd blurted out she thought Clare must be going to live permanently in Belfast now because on Friday she'd had to type up all the papers for terminating the tenancy.

Clare sat stunned, unable to grasp how something so awful could happen so quickly and just when it was least expected. It had never occurred to her she might lose her home. Despite all the encouraging things Jessie went on to say she knew suddenly and quite clearly that nothing was going to change matters. Jessie was quite right to be upset. For the second time in ten years she knew she was not only bereft, she would be homeless as well. She wept silently while Jessie made tea.

'Maybe she's talkin' through her hat,' said Jessie, desperately, as she poured for them. 'I shouldn't a' mentioned it till at least we were sure, till we had these damn papers,' she went on, totally distraught at Clare's distress. 'Surely he can't do that,' she declared, 'just put you out when the rent's paid regular and the Scotts have been here since pussy was a kitten.'

'I think he can probably do what he likes,' Clare replied flatly. 'He doubled the rent the minute he got his hands on old Albert's land.'

'Did he?'

Clare nodded wearily.

'That's why I got the job at Drumsollen,' she explained. 'We couldn't have paid the new rent if I hadn't.'

'You never told me that,' Jessie said, accusingly.

'Some secrets are not very exciting. I've always told you all my nice secrets?'

'Clare, is there any whiskey left?'

'There might be,' she replied vaguely, nodding at the glass-fronted cupboard.

Jessie put down her teacup, threw open the glass doors and inspected the remnants in the surviving bottles.

Clare sat quite still, looking up at the blackened ceiling. Some part of her had known. Whenever she lost one thing, she lost everything. Well, not quite everything. She had some friends and she had a room of her own. But the thought of never coming home, of there being nowhere to go on a Friday evening, no place beyond where she lived and worked through the week . . .

'Here, drink that,' said Jessie, taking away her teacup.

She handed her a glass of whiskey to which she'd added a generous splash of spring water.

Clare drank obediently and sat silently looking into the fire. She didn't even notice Jessie refill her glass.

'Jessie dear, I know I said I'd come home with you tonight and we'd spend tomorrow together. Please don't be annoyed with me, but I have to stay here tonight.'

'Aye. I thought you might. Will I stay with you?'

Clare shook her head.

'And have your mother worry herself silly?' she said patiently, as she wiped her damp face.

As time passed and they sat talking together, she began to feel that perhaps things weren't so bad after all. She was tired and rather thirsty, but the heat of the fire was so comforting and Jessie seemed to be in better spirits now.

'Don't worry, it might never happen,' she said reassuringly, as she got up and went outside for a pee.

353

An hour later, Jessie left her to cycle back to Tullyard. Before she went, she insisted Clare get ready for bed and put out the Tilley lamp in the kitchen. She lit a candle for her and made her promise to lock the door and put out the candle the moment she'd gone.

Once outside, Jessie stood in the darkness, listening intently. She heard Clare put the bar on the front door. Then she watched for the tiny wavering light to appear as Clare went into her room and set it down on the washstand by her bed.

'Whoof,' went Clare, after she'd drawn back the bedclothes. The flame flickered and recovered.

'Whoof,' she went, as she tried again.

Outside the bedroom window, Jessie watched and waited. First a giggle, then another whoof and finally the creak of ancient bedsprings. Jessie said a silent thank you. As long as she'd managed to blow the candle out and bar the door she'd be all right. She'd sleep. Jessie had no doubt she'd sleep. After four glasses of Bushmills, she'd never known anyone not.

The papers came next morning, a huge fat packet of them. Clare carried the big envelope back into the house with a handful of other letters and cards, her legs shaking, her heart beating faster, as she sat down at the table and tore it open. She scanned the covering letter hastily. It confirmed all her fears. Their client, Mr Hutchinson, wished to convey his sincere condolences to Miss Hamilton on the death of her grandfather, a much-respected member of the community. Further he wished to assure her he had no intention of insisting on her vacating the property at the customary week's notice. Now that she was resident in Belfast, he appreciated she would need at least *two* weeks to make the necessary arrangements for handing it over. In consideration of her position, no rent would be charged for this two week period, but her attention was drawn to the inventory enclosed and the necessity of leaving the property in a clean condition, ready for immediate occupation by his farm manager, Mr Hanson and his wife and family. He wished her every success with her future career.

With shaking fingers, she unfolded the sheets of an old, handwritten document enclosed with various typewritten sheets. It was a copy of the original lease. She couldn't quite focus on the long sentences, but here and there the words jumped up at her. 'Made this eighth day of October, in the year of our Lord eighteen hundred and thirty between [undecipherable] and Robert Thomas Scott, formerly of Drumsollen, one house and forge with [blank] . . . and three perches of land and rights of commonage as shown.'

She burst into tears. One hundred and twenty-four years exactly before the day she was born, her great-great grandfather had signed his name on both the lease and on this copy made by the same hand. It was there, perfectly clear to see, at the bottom of the beautifully written document.

'Ah, Clarey dear, I'm sorry. Is it from the solicitors?'

She looked up and saw Charlie peering round the door.

'Come and look, Charlie,' she sniffed, knowing he'd have heard what Maisie had told Mrs Rowentree.

'The bugger,' he exclaimed, as he took up the letter and scanned it quickly.

'There's nothing I can do, is there, Charlie? He knows I can't fight back. Even if I could afford a solicitor, he's probably sure he's in the right.'

Charlie nodded his head sadly.

'He's been clever forby. He's waived the rent. He's behaved as if he's being reasonable. An' he's puttin' in a family,' he said, his lips tightening.

'What's clever about that?' asked Clare, looking puzzled.

'Ach, Clare, there'll be desperate bad feelin' at what he's doin' and he knows it, but he'll be able to say, "What does a wee lassie want wi' a house an' her away in Belfast. Aren't there families cryin' out wi' the shortage?" Oh, the same man has no flies on him, he's up to every trick in the book. You can be sure he knows his ground.'

'And there really is *nothing* I can do?' she said, sadly.

He shook his head and pressed his lips together tightly.

'When I heerd about it last night I away in to Armagh and knocked up young Emerson of Munro and Anderson,' he began. 'I used to have a lot of business with him when I was on the Council. He said there's dozens of these old leases still around with a week's notice either way. Even if they seem way out of date to us, they are still perfectly legal. I'm afraid, Clare, till such time as you're so well off you can buy out yer man an' keep the wee place for yer holidays, you'll have to put up with it.'

To her own surprise, she smiled.

'I used to dream what I'd do if I had a lot of money,' she began. 'I'd have the whole place painted inside and out, a new floor in the sitting room where there's a bit of dry rot, new windows at the back, the same style and shape, of course, but a bit bigger to give more light . . .'

She broke off as she saw the desolate look on Charlie's face.

'Ach, ye remind me of Kate. She was the one for makin' things nice, but like you, she loved the old bits and pieces, the brass lamps and the china dogs and the baskets made of glass with that pink twisted edging round them, that ye put yer cake in fer Sunday tea.'

He paused, shuffling the papers of the inventory through his large, worn fingers.

'Well, they're together now, Kate and Robert. An' maybe that's the way it should've been, but Kate said I'd niver be any good by myself. If I hadn't her to keep me straight I'd have got myself shot or finished up on the end of a rope. That's what she used to say.'

'But what on earth did she mean?'

'Ach, the Scotts an' the Runnings were a rebelly lot,' he said, smiling. 'Sure yer man Thomas there made pikes for the United Irishmen,' he said, running his finger under Robert Thomas's name on the lease. 'An' his landlord, Sir Arthur Richardson, put a pile o' money inta the cause, though he kept his name out

356

of it an' no one split on him when it all failed. Some of us has kept up hope. There's been men to follow Tone and Emmett. Myself one of them.'

'But not Granda, surely?'

'No, not Robert, more's the pity, for a more reliable man you'd never find. I reasoned long and hard with him, but he said he could never bring himself to kill a man no matter what the cause might be. But he did say he'd never turn his back on a friend in trouble, whatever he'd done, an' I'd cause enough to be grateful for that.'

Charlie laid out the papers on the table as if he were dealing a hand of cards, his eyes moving restlessly across the lines of text.

'He an' Kate took an awful risk when I'd made a couple o' bad mistakes an' was informed on. The pair of them saved my life. That's when I met Kate first an' fell for her. Aye, an' she for me, tho' she fought it hard, for she loved Robert right enough. She said there was different kinds of love and a man wouldn't understan'. I don't know. Was she right?'

Clare didn't know either. She was just so aware Charlie had now lost them both. She wasn't the only one who was bereft.

24

'Mine yerself, Dan. Drop yer side a bit. Watch the jamb.'
The house clearance men took all the good furniture from Robert's room, the corner cupboard and the best chairs from the sitting room and the mahogany table from the kitchen. They'd risked the odd nail and bit of sharp metal and driven their van right up to the house. Parked outside the kitchen window, it blocked out what light there was on the dim and misty afternoon.

Clare and Jack stood leaning against the table by the window, unable to get on while the bulky furniture was being manoeuvred through the low doorways. The boss man tramped back into the kitchen.

'That's it, miss. I'll be in touch with Mr Scott when we hear from the sale room.'

Clare cast her eyes hurriedly round the kitchen and peered into the sitting room beyond.

'But what about the rest?' she asked, anxiously.

It was getting late in the day for them to come back and collect a second load but she couldn't begin to clear up until all the furniture was gone. She dreaded to think how much would need doing.

'Ah no, miss. The rest's not worth our liftin'. It's only fit for a bonfire,' he said, shortly. 'Except maybe that oul' chair,' he added, casting a practised eye over Robert's well-worn wooden armchair.

He strode across the kitchen, tipped the battered cushion on to the floor and turned it over one-handed, shaking it vigorously. The legs were steady as a rock.

'I'll take this'un outa yer way,' he said, tucking it under his arm.

'No, thank you,' said Clare, with a firmness that surprised her. 'I'm keeping that chair.'

'Oh aye,' he said, indifferently, as he put it down. 'Well then, we'll be off. Good day t' ye.'

He turned on his heel without a backward glance and left. They heard the van start. The exhaust smoke poured through the open door as it shunted back and forth, turning itself round in the confined space before the cottage, so as not to have to back all the way down to the road. Uncle Jack put his arm round her.

'Ach, don't let them upset you, Clare. It's only a job to them, sticks of furniture that maybe have a price tag and maybe not. Will we have a drop of tea?'

She shook her head.

'There's so much to do, Uncle Jack. I've got to finish by Sunday night and they've not taken half the stuff I expected. I know how dirty it's bound to be when we take out the beds.'

She looked around the kitchen and shook her head.

'I doubt if the settle or that corner cupboard has been moved in years.'

He nodded, tightened his lips and looked her straight in the eye.

'I'm afraid the man's right. It'll have to be a bonfire.'

On the space beyond the house, to the left of the shortcut, where the sodden remains of summer-cut nettles made a damp slime, they piled up the kitchen chairs, the salt box, the old hanging bookcase and some tattered curtains. Jack brought a metal teapot full of paraffin from its place in the forge and sprinkled it liberally around, lit the end of a newspaper, poked it between the legs of a chair and moved back hastily.

Flames roared into the chill air, a shower of sparks rose high, dispersing like a spent firework before they reached the branches of the pear tree, as the wood, tinder dry, flared and glowed and collapsed into hot embers.

359

Clare stood rooted to the spot, hypnotised by the flames that leapt up and fell again so quickly. Uncle Jack had to call her twice before she heard him.

'Come on, love, we must keep it going.'

They carried out what they could, broke up what was too big or to awkward to manage between them, kept the hungry flames going all afternoon. Clare thought of Viking funeral pyres, fed with the dead man's possessions, but all she could think off was poor Uncle Bob, in tears over Robert's lack of means.

These few poor sticks of furniture were all a lifetime's work had left behind. The cheap and nasty three-piece suite, whose rexine covers split with time, so that its stuffing leaked blobs of fluff on to the cracked lino of the sitting room floor since ever she'd known it. The carved hallstand full of woodworm where she'd set her jars of lilac and branches of blossom. That's what it amounted to. Hardly a Viking's hoard. Her tears dried on her face in the fierce heat of the flames as they consumed each new offering.

Whether it was pure chance or Uncle Jack's practicality in leaving them somewhere to sit when they took a rest, she never knew, but the very last item to go from the kitchen was the settle. Six feet long, with wooden arms at each end and a high back, it had always seemed so solid she'd assumed it would be too heavy for them to move in one piece. Jack would have to use the axe to break off one end and then lever away the well-scrubbed boards that made the seat. But when they tried it, it wasn't heavy at all. Not for two. They drew it out into the empty room and lined it up, so they could carry it out into the dark night where the bonfire still glowed orange and blue.

'Hold on a minute, Clare,' said Jack.

She lowered her end to the floor and watched Jack bring the Tilley lamp from the deep embrasure of the back window and set it down carefully by the fender.

From the accumulation of dust and fluff underneath the settle, he handed her the broken stem of a clay pipe, a bent spoon and a blunt knife. She came and joined him, kneeling on the dirty floor and watched him pick out from the dust and dirt which lay directly below where the gap between the two planks of the wooden seat had been, a florin, a penny whistle, a folded leaflet advertising De Witts Little Liver Pills, a garter and a dip pen with a rusty nib. They had all fallen through as the gap widened with years of warm fires and the vigorous scrubbing of the Scott women.

'Goodness, Jack, what's this?' she said, startled.

From a pile of undisturbed dust and fluff, she picked up a loose end of fine cord. Attached to it were two gold rings, the smaller one narrow, the larger one broad. They had been tied together, one within the other, fitting so well they'd not separated as she caught them up and blew away the dust. They lay in the palm of her hand now, gleaming in the light of the lamp, as if they'd never lain anywhere except in their own velvet-lined jeweller's box.

'Wedding rings, I suppose,' said Jack, peering at them closely.

'A man's and a woman's,' she said slowly, her eyes drawn by the gleam of gold, by the perfect fit of one ring inside the other.

The image that came to her was irresistible, a pair of lovers, the woman enfolded by the man, their love holding them together over the years.

'They look fairly old to me,' said Jack, matter-of-factly. 'Maybe they'll have an inscription. But we'll hardly see it in this light. Have you a pocket or will I put them in my wallet for you?'

'I've a pocket, thanks,' said Clare, hastily, grateful there were no holes in the pockets of her oldest trousers, the very first pair Auntie Polly had sent her from Canada.

'We mustn't let that fire down too far,' he warned her, as he cast his eyes over the piles of dust and dirt and satisfied himself there was nothing more to be found.

'Right,' said Clare firmly, as she got to her feet and took up the arm of the settle, worn so smooth over the years by the

361

sleeves of those who had sat enjoying the warmth of the fire, the company and the crack.

Jack manoeuvred his end till it pointed through the kitchen door, then together they carried it out into the darkness where the fire glowed, a bright orange circle still with eager blue tongues of flame at its heart.

The next morning, Sunday, was fine and dry. The pale sunlight cast long fingers of shadow from the hedgerows across the silent fields as she and Jack drove back to the house by the forge after an early breakfast at Liskeyborough.

'My very last day,' she heard herself say, as Jack unloaded cardboard boxes, a basket with a bottle of milk for their tea, sandwiches she'd cut while Jack made their breakfast, and an extra stiff brush from the farmyard, so he could help her sweep out the empty rooms before she started to clean.

As she lit the fire, topped up the water tank and filled the kettles, she heard the swish of his brush echoing from Robert's bedroom where they'd dislodged wreaths of cobweb from the walls behind the pieces of furniture the clearance men had been willing to take.

'Are you sure there's no more I can do?' he asked, some hours later, as he perched in the back window of the kitchen, a mug of tea in his hands, so that Clare could sit in the one remaining chair.

'No, you've been great, Uncle Jack,' she said warmly. 'But the rest is my job. I need a few hours yet, but I'll be ready by dark if that's all right with you.'

'Aye that suits me fine. About five, we'll say. Will that be in time for your tea in Belfast?'

'Oh don't worry about that. Mrs McGregor will have gone to church so she'll leave something on a tray. It'll be there whatever time I get back.'

'Ye haven't forgotten the dogs, have ye?' he asked, nodding up at the mantelpiece as he drained his mug.

'Oh no,' she said, smiling. 'They'll be keeping an eye on me

362

till we're ready to go. That's why I asked you for a couple of cardboard boxes. I'll be taking them with me. And Granda's chair. Do you think we can get it into the car all right?' she asked, suddenly anxious.

'We'll manage,' he reassured her. 'I think it'll go across the back seat. But I'll have to leave your big photograph till another time. The glass might get broken with the legs of the chair. I'll keep it in my bedroom for you till you're next up.'

He looked around the empty room as if there was something else he was trying to remember and then, finding there wasn't, he straightened up and put his mug down on the windowsill behind him.

'I'd better be off or I'll have them late for meeting.'

She walked to the door with him, waved as he got into his car and watched as he reversed cautiously on to the road. There were more cars about these days and sometimes on a Sunday a neighbour would go into Armagh for the papers. But no car appeared. As she stood looking down the path to the forge, not a sound disturbed the quiet of the morning. She put her hand out to touch the arch over the door and made no move to start her work.

Suddenly the church bell rang out from the hill. It startled her, reminded her time was passing. She hurried inside and got to work. Jack had not wanted to leave her in the empty house, but she'd insisted. She was so grateful for his help, but she knew she needed to be by herself. However painful it might be, there was a goodbye to be said and she could only say it if she were alone, free to move among all the memories of the years she had spent here.

She worked steadily, methodically, as she had taught herself to do long ago. However hard the work, it left her mind free to plan the weekly essay or to have practice conversations with herself in French or German. Today, however, she wasn't very clear what was going on in her mind. At times, she thought that getting the job done was taking her total attention. When she finally paused at two o'clock to make tea and eat her

363

sandwich, her back and arms ached, yet there was still so much left to do.

She sat by the stove in Robert's chair and looked up at the china dogs in their solitary splendour on what had once been a crowded mantelpiece. In his honour, she had christened them with both the Scott names, the ones she had found on the lease that went back to 1830.

'Well then, Robert and Thomas,' she began. 'How do I do it? How do I say goodbye?'

Her tears caught her unexpectedly, a mug of tea in one hand, a corned beef sandwich in the other. She parked her tea on the stove and fumbled for her handkerchief. As her fingers closed round it, she touched the solid shape of the two rings she'd kept with her, because she'd found that morning she could not bear to be parted from them.

'I'd say those were a brave age, wouldn't you, Jack?' Granda Hamilton had commented the previous evening when she'd brought them out to show to him. Sitting by the fire, both William and her grandmother already in bed, he looked at them with great interest. He fetched a magnifying glass from his workshop and held them up to the new electric light.

'There's somethin' there, Clare, but I can't make it out. Look yerself,' he said, showing her how to angle the glass. 'Your eyes are far sharper than mine.'

'Initials,' she said. 'I think it's E.C.B. on the small ring.'

'What about the broader one?' asked Jack. 'That might be easier to read.'

Clare undid the fine twine but when it fell away she found they were still tied together.

'I'll tell you what that is, Clare,' said her grandfather, as she looked up at him, puzzled by what she'd found. 'It's human hair. It was often used for binding in the old days. It's very strong if you use a fair sized piece and lap it well.'

She was reluctant to unbind the hair, but she so wanted to see what the broader ring might reveal. She released it with a light touch of a sharp razor blade and patiently unwound it, a single long, pale hair with just a hint of red in it. The rings slipped apart and she took up her glass again.

'It's the same, I think,' she said, quickly. 'E.C.B.'

'So they belonged to the same person,' said Jack thoughtfully.

But Clare said nothing. She was still quite sure the rings had belonged to a man and a woman, that one of them had tied them together so that they would stay together. She had no idea what happened after that, whether they'd been lost, or hidden, but before she got into bed that night she replaced the hair and tied it in place before covering it up again with the fine twine, exactly as it had been when she'd first found them.

She finished her sandwich, drained her mug of tea and was about to refill her bucket with fresh water when a thought struck her.

'There was something under Granda's chair yesterday,' she muttered to herself, remembering the way the clearance man had turned it up to slide off the cushion.

She stood up and tilted the chair.

'Yes, there is,' she said, excitedly, as she carried it out into the daylight. 'R.T.S.,' she read, 'Robert Thomas Scott'.

Pleased as she was that the chair had been marked, or made, by her great-grandfather, it was what was carved below the first set of initials that truly delighted her.

'It wasn't a C, it was a G,' she breathed, as she traced out the letters of the second set with her fingers. 'E.G.B., ' she said out loud. 'The letters on the rings.'

'Thank you, Robert, thank you, Thomas,' she said, grinning up at the two guardians of the hearth.

She could not think of a better gift to have been given on this saddest of days. For the rest of her life she would have a reminder of all that was best, of her own past, and of the long past, of all the evenings when Charlie poked his head round the door and roared out his greeting.

'It has to be, it just has to be,' she announced to the empty room. '*ERIN GO BRAGH* – Ireland for ever.'

25

C lare didn't expect the weeks that followed Robert's death to be easy, but she was quite unprepared for the anxiety and the pervasive sense of loss that overwhelmed her as she tried to take up her life again.

Every time the phone rang in the dim, echoing hall below her room, she went rigid, fearful lest some new disaster might come upon her. She would open her door and listen intently as Mrs McGregor came out of her sitting room and picked up the receiver.

'Jean dear, it's your mither. Hurry up now, she's in a call box.'

She'd breathe a sigh of relief, go back to whatever piece of work she'd been struggling with, and give herself a severe talking to. She was letting things get on top of her, she'd say. Going to lectures had become an effort, writing essays an interminable chore. All she felt up to was sitting in her room, staring into the orange glow of the gas fire or watching the laden clouds move steadily past above the bare branches of the rain-soaked trees.

Evening after evening she would sit by the fire, comforted by its warmth and its friendly roar, absorbed in her own thoughts. The loss of Robert was a shock and a blow but, even in her worst moments, she knew she would not wish him back to face another winter, however bad a time it gave her.

'His hammering days are over.'

She wept every time she thought of Jamsey going to look for him in the forge, because he couldn't hear him hammering.

366

'Ye'd not wish to see him poorly.'

She would weep each time she remembered John Wiley taking an old tin box from his pocket, and showing her the fuchsias packed in moss Senator Richardson had sent her.

But her tears brought real relief from the pain of her loss. She grieved for Robert as she had grieved for her parents, sensing the hurt would heal as the wisest of her friends said it would. But there was another hurt that the tears did little for. Once again, with the death of someone dear to her, she had lost the home she loved.

The only person who seemed to understand how she felt about that was Andrew. He wrote often and phoned at an agreed time every two weeks. She knew how truly concerned about her he was and his efforts to cheer her touched her, but he seemed so far away, so remote, a part of a world full of warmth and sunshine as completely lost to her as the summer itself, now long gone.

Friday nights were the worst times, she decided, as she walked back from the last lecture of the week, the rain mizzling down, the street lamps reflecting in the wet road.

'All trying to get home early,' she said to herself, as she glanced at the line of tail lights disappearing up the Malone Road, before she tramped over the pedestrian crossing and turned into Elmwood Avenue.

She had a roof over her head, yes, but she had no home. No lane, no forge, no orchard, no smoking stove, no floor to scrub. She turned her key in the front door and ran upstairs, knowing she couldn't cope with any friendly greeting.

As week followed week, it got so she could hardly bear to leave her room. She forced herself to go to lectures, but shook her head and said no to all the offers of outings, or parties. When Jessie and Harry insisted she go out for a meal with them she told them she had an essay to write. The very thought of the restaurant, brightly lit and decorated for Christmas, was more than she could manage.

The only time she felt any ease at all was when she was

surrounded by her precious possessions, her own books, those she had inherited from Ronnie, the few objects she'd brought from the home she had lost.

Whenever she did try to work, she sat in Robert's chair, the green glass jar she'd used for posies beside her on her table in the window, the sitting room clock and the two white dogs with black shiny noses on her mantelpiece.

Yet people had been so kind to her. She'd been touched by the way Henri Lavalle assured her of his help at any time. Mrs McGregor told her to come down whenever she felt lonely. If her grandparents weren't able to have her to stay over Christmas, she said, she'd be more than welcome to join her small family.

The last week of term arrived, but the first solitary days of the vacation brought no change. Indeed without the pressure of work to keep her going, they were even worse.

'Clare dear, it's your Uncle Jack.'

She raced down stairs, a towel round her wet hair. She hadn't even heard the phone ring as she lay in front of the gas fire combing it through to help it dry.

'Hallo, hallo, Uncle Jack? Is something wrong?'

'Nothing to worry about, love,' he said reassuringly. 'Granny asked me to give you a wee ring. She needs a bit of help and she thought maybe you'd go up for a few days. Sure we haven't laid eyes on you for weeks you've been that busy.'

Clare felt ashamed. Uncle Jack had rung several times to see if he could collect her for the weekend, but she'd made excuses. The farm had only three bedrooms. If Auntie Dolly went off to visit friends, then it wasn't too bad, for she'd have Dolly's room, but if Dolly was at home and Jack went fishing, she had to share a room with William. If Jack was at home as well, then it was a folding bed in Dolly's room and having to listen to her talk about her boyfriends far into the night.

William just about tolerated Jack sleeping in 'his' room at weekends, but having to share with his sister was a different matter. From the moment a visit was even mentioned, he began to grumble and complain.

'Is Dolly away, then?' she asked, surprised, for today was only Wednesday.

'No, Dolly's at home till Friday, but she's off to see Emily and the children at the weekend. We've had a wee bit of bother with William, but you're not to worry yourself. He's all right, but he won't be home for about a week.'

Clare knew he was doing his best to reassure her, but she insisted on having the full story. Given William's characteristic behaviour, it was a familiar enough tale. The previous day Uncle Billy had come over from Richhill to visit Granny. He'd left his motorbike parked in the yard with the key in the ignition. William had seen his chance, slipped out and rode off, managing the powerful machine fairly well till he'd met a tractor coming the other way and filling the narrow lane. He'd ended up in the hedge, cut and bruised, with a broken leg. He was now in the Infirmary in Armagh, his leg in traction, but otherwise unharmed.

Clare sighed. Poor Granny and Granda. And poor Uncle Billy. His motorbike was his pride and joy and no doubt it had suffered damage as much as William. She did her best, but she found it hard to be sorry for her brother William when his behaviour caused so much distress and concern to everyone.

'I can bring you back on Sunday night, Clare,' Jack went on, 'an' we can bring your big photograph. I have it well wrapped up for you.' Could you manage to go up on the bus tomorrow? Granny thinks she ought to go inta Armagh and see him, an' she's walkin' very badly. I think she'd like ye for a bit o' company. She's always talkin' about ye,' he ended quietly.

'Yes, yes, of course, I'll go,' she replied immediately. It did not occur to her that it was the first 'yes' she had said in months.

It was foggy next morning. As she drew back the heavy curtains on the bay window, Clare shivered and wondered what was the warmest thing she could wear.

'Trousers,' she said to herself, as she went to the wardrobe. As she stretched out her hand for the pair Auntie Polly had sent her in August, her hand brushed against the old ones she'd last worn when she'd scrubbed out the house by the forge, to leave it 'in a clean condition as per the lease.'

She gasped, horrified, as she remembered the rings. She searched the pockets frantically, but all she found was a grubby handkerchief and the old penknife Robert used to carve tobacco from his plug of Mick McQuaid.

'What on earth have I done with them?' she cried, totally distraught. 'How can I have lost them?'

Still shivering in her nightie and dressing gown, she began to search the room, throwing open drawers and rifling through the contents. There weren't all that many drawers to search. In a few moments, she stopped, defeated, and flopped down on the unmade bed. Then she remembered.

'Please, please, be there,' she whispered to herself, as she went to her dressing table. From the top drawer, she drew out a small leather box and opened it. Clipped into the red velvet lining were the gold earrings Jessie and Harry had given her for her eighteenth birthday. Beside them, quite safe, the two gold rings bound together exactly as she had found them.

The fog was patchy, but not enough to prevent the almost empty bus from getting on with it. Soon they were out of the city. In the stream bottoms the mist lay thick, the trees and bushes ghostly shapes, but nearer the road the hedgerows were clear and the bare trees stood out, their branches grey etchings over a pale wash. On the smooth curve of a little hill, sheltered by trees, a farmhouse made a perfect composition, the mist softening the harsh detail of rusty roof and ill-placed dung hill. She looked up and saw the sun, a bright disk alternately gleaming and disappearing in the soft, blanketing vapour, as it rose higher in the sky.

She had never found mist beautiful before, but perhaps cycling through it with the moisture clinging to your face and hair was not the best way to appreciate it.

'Single, please, to Loney's Corner,' she said to the conductor, when he came to collect her fare. 'Could you drop me a bit this side of it to save me a walk?'

'Aye, surely. Are ye for the station?'

'More or less,' she agreed, smiling.

'Ach, we nearly always have someone goin' doun that road. Sure a wee extra stop only takes a minit.'

By the time the bus stopped opposite the road that led down to Liskeyborough, the sun was glinting on the whitewash of the south-facing cottages and the mist was dissolving before her eyes.

'Thanks very much,' she shouted, over the roar of the engine, as the conductor handed her down her small suitcase.

She crossed the main road, the throbbing still in her ears, and heard her name called.

'Not speakin' to anyone this mornin'?'

'Sam!' she cried in surprise, finding her cousin perched on a shiny, new tractor that sat vibrating by the roadside.

'I'll give ye a lift if ye can houl' on t' yer case,' he offered as she came alongside.

She scrambled up behind him and settled herself securely on the sack of straw behind his driving seat, one arm holding on firmly.

'Are you for the farm?' she shouted, as he set off.

'No, I'm over the Retreat way. We've sheep on the ten acre, but I'll drop you at Granny and Granda's. How'ye doin'. D'ye like Belfast?'

'Miss the country, Sam. How about you?'

'I'm great. Da and me's started on pigs. It's goin' powerful well.'

They bumped along past familiar fields. It almost looked as if the same cattle were in the same place as the last time she'd come this way. She found it strangely comforting.

'Sam!'

'Aye.'

'Can you drop me up on the hill? I want to look round me.

371

Granny doesn't know when I'm coming, so she won't be looking out yet a while.'

'Sure. I'll hafta t'go on a bit past the gate, it's a bit steep to stop.'

'I need the walk,' she said, laughing. 'You forget how to walk in the big city.'

The noise of the tractor died away as she walked back down the steep slope of the lane to the five-barred gate. The notice was still there, but it hung lopsidedly, one piece of binder twine having given way.

'Trespassers will be prosecuted,' she read, as she climbed over, and parked her case in the hedgerow.

'Or persecuted, if you live in Fermanagh,' she added, as she set out up towards the tall, stone finger.

The grass was beaded with moisture and the slope as steep as she remembered. She was quite out of breath when she got to the top and had to lean a moment against the worn stone of the base of the obelisk. Recovering her breath, she went and propped herself against the low concrete post that carried the observation point for Armagh Observatory.

Wisps of mist still lingered in the wet valley bottoms, but the hillsides were now bathed in sunshine. Even as she watched, the mist dissolved as the sun rose higher. Beyond the orchards and fields to the north-east she caught a sudden sparkle from the broad expanse of Lough Neagh.

'My teacup,' she whispered to herself, as she turned and walked over to look out from the other side of the hill.

It was still there. Of course, it was.

She laughed at herself as she ran her eye over the familiar landmarks, the tall chimney of an old cotton mill, the tower and spires of the cathedrals, the domes of the Observatory poking above the trees that concealed the sharp outlines of her primary school.

The tiny breeze that had helped to disperse the last of the mist fell away. It was now perfectly still. She could feel the warmth of the sun on her face as she looked up at the clear, blue sky.

'I envy you, Clare,' Andrew had said, as they stood side-by-side, looking out over the same countryside, a little over a year ago.

She remembered how his eyes ran hungrily over the farms and fields on the slopes away to the east, as if searching for something. Perhaps she knew now what it was he wanted.

'I'd buy cows.'

They'd all laughed at him, that wet afternoon in Caledon when Ginny amassed a fortune in Monopoly money. Ginny said she wanted to train horses. She herself had admitted how much she wanted to travel. Edward insisted he had no ideas yet. And dear Andrew wanted to farm his cousin's land.

She stood for a long time, her mind filling with images from the past. She thought of her friends over at the Grange, people who would make her welcome anytime, the Robinsons, the Wileys, Jessie's mother and Aunt Sarah, Charlie Running.

Down below the hill, her Hamilton grandparents would make her welcome too, their home always a focal point for all the family, the proliferating relatives she'd had such trouble sorting out when she was a little girl.

'It was there all the time,' she said to herself. 'I thought I'd lost my home. And in one way I had. The bricks and mortar have gone. But that's not the half of it, as Robert would say. There's all the rest, all this. Andrew was right, I have my whole world spread out around me. It *is* mine and no one can take it away from me. Only I can let it go. If I have all this, somewhere I can make a home again. Later, in another place, perhaps.'

She put her hand into her trouser pocket and took out the rings. They caught the sunlight and winked at her. Bonded together with a single long, fair hair with a hint of red they were marked with initials that spoke of a passion for the land of Ireland.

Her thoughts went back to Andrew. She went over all they had shared when they'd been together, the long letters they'd written week after week, when they'd been so far apart. He'd been so tender towards her distress, so eager to help and comfort her. Yes, they too were bound together, by their love for each other and their love of this land spread out all around her.

She took it all in once more and smiled suddenly. Her desolation had gone. Dispersed like the morning mist in the warmth of the sun. She was herself again, the future open before her. But where that future would lead, she could not see, even on such a clear day.